Praise for *The Racketeer*

"Grisham at his best: tilting at injustice." —*The Washington Post*

"The maestro of legal potboilers goes for devilish, *Revenge*-style thrills. . . . [A] tautly plotted new thriller."
—*Entertainment Weekly*

"Devious fun . . . almost impossible to keep up with."
—New York *Daily News*

"Precisely plotted . . . Grisham is back in top form."
—*Publishers Weekly*

"[A] complex tale of cat and mouse . . . Evenly paced, smart legal thriller—trademark Grisham, in other words." —*Kirkus Reviews*

BY JOHN GRISHAM

THE THEODORE BOONE BOOKS

JOHN
GRISHAM

THE
RACKETEER

A Novel

BANTAM BOOKS TRADE PAPERBACKS

New York

2018 Bantam Books Trade Paperback Edition

Copyright © 2012 by Belfry Holdings, Inc.

Published in the United States by Bantam Books, an imprint of Random House, a division of Penguin Random House LLC, New York.

BANTAM BOOKS and the HOUSE colophon are registered trademarks of Penguin Random House LLC.

Originally published in hardcover in the United States by Doubleday, an imprint of The Knopf Doubleday Publishing Group, a division of Penguin Random House LLC., in 2012.

LIBRARY OF CONGRESS CATALOGING-IN-PUBLICATION DATA
Grisham, John
The racketeer : a novel / John Grisham.
p. cm.
ISBN 978-1-9848-1901-7
ebook ISBN 978-0-385-53688-2
1. Prisoners—Fiction. 2. Judges—
Crimes against—Fiction. I. Title.
PS3557.R5355 R33 2012
813'.54—dc23   2012460008

Printed in the United States of America on acid-free paper

randomhousebooks.com

2 4 6 8 10 9 7 5 3 1

Book design by Maria Carella

THE RACKETEER

rack-e-teer   one who obtains money illegally, as by fraud, extortion, etc.

CHAPTER 1

I am a lawyer, and I am in prison. It's a long story.

I'm forty-three years old and halfway through a ten-year sentence handed down by a weak and sanctimonious federal judge in Washington, D.C. All of my appeals have run their course, and there is no procedure, mechanism, obscure statute, technicality, loophole, or Hail Mary left in my thoroughly depleted arsenal. I have nothing. Because I know the law, I could do what some inmates do and clog up the courts with stacks of worthless motions and writs and other junk filings, but none of this would help my cause. Nothing will help my cause. The reality is that I have no hope of getting out for five more years, save for a few lousy weeks chopped off at the end for good behavior, and my behavior has been exemplary.

I shouldn't call myself a lawyer, because technically I am not. The Virginia State Bar swept in and yanked my license shortly after I was convicted. The language is right there in black and white—a felony conviction equals disbarment. I was stripped of my license, and my disciplinary troubles were duly reported in the *Virginia Lawyer Register*. Three of us were disbarred that month, which is about average.

However, in my little world, I am known as a jailhouse lawyer and as such spend several hours each day helping my fellow inmates with their legal problems. I study their appeals and file motions. I prepare simple wills and an occasional land deed. I review contracts for some of the white-collar guys. I have sued the government for legitimate complaints but never for ones I consider frivolous. And there are a lot of divorces.

Eight months and six days after I began my time, I received a thick envelope. Prisoners crave mail, but this was one package I could have done without. It was from a law firm in Fairfax, Virginia, one that represented my wife, who, surprisingly, wanted a divorce. In a matter of weeks, Dionne had gone from being a supportive wife, dug in for the long haul, to a fleeing victim who desperately wanted out. I couldn't believe it. I read the papers in absolute shock, my knees rubbery and my eyes wet, and when I was afraid I might start crying, I hustled back to my cell for some privacy. There are a lot of tears in prison, but they are always hidden.

When I left home, Bo was six years old. He was our only child, but we were planning more. The math is easy, and I've done it a million times. He'll be sixteen when I get out, a fully grown teenager, and I will have missed ten of the most precious years a father and son can have. Until they are about twelve years old, little boys worship their fathers and believe they can do no wrong. I coached Bo in T-ball and youth soccer, and he followed me around like a puppy. We fished and camped, and he sometimes went to my office with me on Saturday mornings, after a boys-only breakfast. He was my world, and trying to explain to him that I was going away for a long time broke both our hearts. Once behind bars, I refused to allow him to visit me. As much as I wanted to squeeze him, I could not stand the thought of that little boy seeing his father incarcerated.

It is virtually impossible to fight a divorce when you're in prison and not getting out soon. Our assets, never much to begin with, were depleted after an eighteen-month pounding by the federal government. We had lost everything but our child and our commitment to each other. The child was a rock; the commitment bit the dust. Dionne made some beautiful promises about persevering and toughing it out, but once I was gone, reality set in. She felt lonely and isolated in our small town. "People see me and they whisper," she wrote in one of her first letters. "I'm so lonely," she whined in another. It wasn't long before the letters became noticeably shorter and further apart. As did the visits.

Dionne grew up in Philadelphia and never warmed to life in the country. When an uncle offered her a job, she was suddenly in a hurry to go home. She remarried two years ago, and Bo, now eleven, is being coached by another father. My last twenty letters to my son went unanswered. I'm sure he never saw them.

I often wonder if I will see him again. I think I will make the effort, though I vacillate on this. How do you confront a child you love so much it hurts but who will not recognize you? We are never going to live together again as a typical father and son. Would it be fair to Bo to have his long-lost father reappear and insist on becoming part of his life?

I have far too much time to think about this.

I am inmate number 44861-127 at the Federal Prison Camp near Frostburg, Maryland. A "camp" is a low-security facility for those of us who are deemed nonviolent and sentenced to ten years or less. For reasons that were never made clear, my first twenty-two months were spent at a medium-security joint near Louisville, Kentucky. In the endless alphabet muck of bureau-speak, it is known as an FCI—Federal Correctional Institution—and it was a far different place than my camp at Frostburg. An FCI is for violent men sentenced to more than ten years. Life there is much tougher, though I survived without being physically assaulted. Being a former Marine helped immensely.

As far as prisons go, a camp is a resort. There are no walls, fences, razor wire, or lookout towers and only a few guards with guns. Frostburg is relatively new, and its facilities are nicer than most public high schools. And why not? In the United States we spend $40,000 a year to incarcerate each prison inmate and $8,000 to educate each elementary school student. Here we have counselors, managers, caseworkers, nurses, secretaries, assistants of many varieties, and dozens of administrators who would be hard-pressed to truthfully explain how they fill their eight hours each day. It is, after all, the federal government. The employee parking lot near the front entrance is packed with nice cars and trucks.

There are six hundred inmates here at Frostburg, and, with a few exceptions, we are a well-behaved group of men. Those with violent pasts have learned their lessons and appreciate their civilized surroundings. Those who've spent their lives in prison have finally found the best home. Many of these career boys do not want to leave. They are thoroughly institutionalized and cannot function on the outside. A warm bed, three meals a day, health care—how could they possibly top this out there on the streets?

I'm not implying this is a pleasant place. It is not. There are many men like me who never dreamed they would one day fall so hard. Men with professions, careers, businesses; men with assets and nice families and country-club memberships. In my White Gang there is Carl, an optometrist who tinkered too much with his Medicare billings; and Kermit, a land speculator who double and triple pledged the same properties to various banks; and Wesley, a former Pennsylvania state senator who took a bribe; and Mark, a small-town mortgage lender who cut some corners.

Carl, Kermit, Wesley, and Mark. All white, average age of fifty-one. All admit their guilt.

Then there's me. Malcolm Bannister, black, aged forty-three, convicted of a crime I had no knowledge of committing.

At this moment, at Frostburg, I happen to be the only black guy serving time for a white-collar crime. Some distinction.

In my Black Gang, the membership is not so clearly defined. Most are kids from the streets of D.C. and Baltimore who were busted for drug-related crimes, and when they are paroled, they will return to the streets with a 20 percent chance of avoiding another conviction. With no education, no skills, and a criminal record, how are they supposed to succeed?

In reality, there are no gangs in a federal camp and no violence. If you fight or threaten someone, they'll yank you out of here and send you to a place that's far worse. There is a lot of bickering, mainly over the television, but I have yet to see someone throw a punch. Some of these guys have served time in state prisons, and the stories they tell are horrifying. No one wants to trade this place for another joint.

So we behave as we count the days. For the white-collar guys, the punishment is humiliation and the loss of status, standing, a lifestyle. For the black guys, life in a camp is safer than where they came from and where they're going. Their punishment is another notch on their criminal records, another step in becoming career felons.

Because of this, I feel more white than black.

There are two other ex-lawyers here at Frostburg. Ron Napoli was a flamboyant criminal lawyer in Philadelphia for many years, until cocaine ruined him. He specialized in drug law and represented many of the top dealers and traffickers in the mid-Atlantic region, from New Jersey to the Carolinas. He preferred to get paid in cash and coke and eventually lost everything. The IRS nailed him for tax evasion, and he's about halfway through a nine-year sentence. Ron's not doing too well these days. He seems depressed and will not, under any circumstances, exercise and try to take care of himself. He's getting heavier, slower, crankier, and sicker. He used to tell fascinating stories about his clients and their adventures in narco-trafficking, but now he just sits in the yard, eating bag after bag of Fritos and looking lost. Someone is sending him money, and he spends most of it on junk food.

The third ex-lawyer is a Washington shark named Amos Kapp, a longtime insider and shifty operator who spent a career slinking around the edges of every major political scandal. Kapp and I were tried together, convicted together, and sentenced ten years apiece by the same judge. There were eight defendants—seven from Washington and me. Kapp has always been guilty of something, and he was certainly guilty in the eyes of our jurors. Kapp, though, knew then and knows now that I had nothing to do with the conspiracy, but he was too much of a coward and a crook to say anything. Violence is strictly prohibited at Frostburg, but give me five minutes with Amos Kapp and his neck would be broken. He knows this, and I suspect he told the warden a long time ago. They keep him on the west campus, as far away from my pod as possible.

Of the three lawyers, I'm the only one willing to help other inmates with their legal problems. I enjoy the work. It's challenging and keeps me busy. It also keeps my legal skills sharp, though I doubt if I have much of a future as a lawyer. I can apply for reinstatement to the bar when I'm out, but that can be an arduous procedure. The truth is I never made any money as a lawyer. I was a small-town practitioner, black on top of that, and few clients could pay a decent fee. There were dozens of other lawyers packed along Braddock Street scrambling for the same clients; the competition was rough. I'm not sure what I'll do when this is over, but I have serious doubts about resuming a legal career.

I'll be forty-eight, single, and in good health, hopefully.

Five years is an eternity. Every day I take a long walk, alone, on a dirt jogging trail that skirts the edges of the camp and follows the boundary, or the "line," as it is known. Step over the line, and you're considered an escapee. In spite of being the site of a prison, this is beautiful country with spectacular views. As I walk and gaze at the rolling hills in the distance, I fight the urge to just keep walking, to step over the line. There is no fence to stop me, no guard to yell my name. I could disappear into the dense woods, then disappear forever.

I wish there was a wall, one ten feet tall, made of solid brick, with coils of glistening razor wire along its top, one that would keep me from gazing at the hills and dreaming of freedom. This is a prison, damn it! We can't leave. Put up a wall and stop tempting us.

The temptation is always there, and, as much as I fight it, I swear it's getting stronger by the day.

CHAPTER 2

Frostburg is a few miles west of the town of Cumberland, Maryland, in the middle of a sliver of land that is dwarfed by Pennsylvania to the north and West Virginia to the west and south. Looking at a map, it is obvious this exiled part of the state was the result of a bad survey and shouldn't belong to Maryland at all, though it's not clear who should have ownership. I work in the library, and on the wall above my little desk is a large map of America. I spend too much time gazing at it, daydreaming, wondering how I came to be a federal prisoner in a remote part of far-western Maryland.

Sixty miles south of here is the town of Winchester, Virginia, population twenty-five thousand, the place of my birth, childhood, education, career, and, eventually, The Fall. I am told that little has changed there since I left. The law firm of Copeland & Reed is still doing business in the same storefront shop where I once worked. It's on Braddock Street, in the Old Town, next door to a diner. The name, painted in black on the window, was once Copeland, Reed & Bannister, and it was the only all-black law firm within a hundred miles. I'm told that Mr. Copeland and Mr. Reed are doing well, certainly not prospering or getting rich, but generating enough business to pay their two secretaries and the rent. That's about all we did when I was a partner there—just manage to scrape by. At the time of

The Fall, I was having serious second thoughts about surviving in such a small town.

I am told that Mr. Copeland and Mr. Reed refuse to discuss me and my problems. They came within an inch of being indicted too, and their reputations were tarnished. The U.S. Attorney who nailed me was blasting buckshot at anyone remotely connected to his grand conspiracy, and he almost wiped out the entire firm. My crime was picking the wrong client. My two former partners have never committed a crime. On so many levels I regret what has happened, but the slander of their good names still keeps me awake. They are both in their late sixties, and in their younger days as lawyers they struggled not only with the challenge of keeping a small-town general practice afloat but also fought some of the last battles of the Jim Crow era. Judges sometimes ignored them in court and ruled against them for no sound legal reason. Other lawyers were often rude and unprofessional. The county bar association did not invite them to join. Clerks sometimes lost their filings. All-white juries did not believe them. Worst of all, clients did not hire them. Black clients. No white client would hire a black lawyer in the 1970s, in the South anyway, and this still hasn't changed much. But Copeland & Reed nearly went under in its infancy because black folks thought the white lawyers were better. Hard work and a commitment to professionalism changed this, but slowly.

Winchester was not my first choice of places to have a career. I went to law school at George Mason, in the D.C. suburbs of Northern Virginia. The summer after my second year, I got lucky and landed a clerkship with a giant firm on Pennsylvania Avenue, near Capitol Hill. It was one of those firms with a thousand lawyers, offices around the world, former senators on the letterhead, blue-chip clients, and a frenetic pace that I thoroughly enjoyed. The highlight was playing gofer in the trial of a former congressman (our client) who was accused of conspiring with his felonious brother to take kickbacks from a defense contractor. The trial was a circus, and I was thrilled to be so close to the center ring.

Eleven years later, I walked into the same courtroom in the E. Barrett Prettyman U.S. Courthouse, in downtown Washington, and suffered through a trial of my own.

I was one of seventeen clerks that summer. The other sixteen, all from top-ten law schools, received job offers. Since I had put all my eggs in one basket, I spent my third year of law school scrambling around D.C., knocking on doors, finding none that were open. At any given moment, there must be several thousand unemployed lawyers pounding the pavement in D.C., and it's easy to get lost in the desperation. I eventually fanned out through the suburbs where the firms are much smaller and the jobs even scarcer.

Finally, I went home in defeat. My dreams of big-league glory were smashed. Mr. Copeland and Mr. Reed did not have enough business and certainly could not afford a new associate, but they had pity on me and cleared out an old storage room upstairs. I worked as hard as possible, though it was often a challenge to put in long hours with so few clients. We got along smoothly, and after five years they generously added my name to the partnership. My income barely rose.

During my prosecution, it was painful watching their good names get dragged through the mud, and it was so senseless. When I was on the ropes, the lead FBI agent informed me that Mr. Copeland and Mr. Reed were going to be indicted if I didn't plead guilty and cooperate with the U.S. Attorney. I thought it was a bluff, but I had no way of knowing for sure. I told him to go to hell.

Luckily, he was bluffing.

I've written them letters, long weepy letters of apology and all that, but they have not replied. I've asked them to come visit so we can talk face-to-face, but they have not responded. Though my hometown is just sixty miles away, I have only one regular visitor.

***

My father was one of the first black state troopers hired by the Commonwealth of Virginia. For thirty years, Henry patrolled the roads and highways around Winchester, and he loved every minute of his job. He loved the work itself, the sense of authority and history, the power to enforce the law, and the compassion to help those in need. He loved the uniform, the patrol car, everything but the pistol on his belt. He was forced to remove it a few times, but he never fired it. He expected white folks to be resentful and he expected black folks to want leniency, and he was determined to show complete fairness. He was a tough cop who saw no gray areas in the law. If an act wasn't legal, then it was certainly illegal, with no wiggle room and no time for technicalities.

From the moment I was indicted, my father believed I was guilty, of something. Forget the presumption of innocence. Forget my rants about being innocent. As a proud career man, he was thoroughly brainwashed by a lifetime of chasing those who broke the law, and if the Feds, with their resources and great wisdom, deemed me worthy of a one-hundred-page indictment, then they were right and I was wrong. I'm sure he felt sympathy, and I'm sure he prayed I would somehow get out of my mess, but he had a difficult time conveying those feelings to me. He was humiliated, and he let me know it. How could his lawyer son get himself so entangled with such a slimy bunch of crooks?

I have asked myself the same question a thousand times. There is no good answer.

Henry Bannister barely finished high school and, after a few minor scrapes with the law, joined the Marine Corps at the age of nineteen. The Marines quickly turned him into a man, a soldier who craved the discipline and took great pride in the uniform.

He did three tours in Vietnam, where he got shot and burned and briefly captured. His medals are on the wall of his study in the small home where I was raised. He lives there alone. My mother was killed by a drunk driver two years before I was indicted.

Henry travels to Frostburg once a month for a one-hour visit. He is retired with little to do, and he could visit once a week if he wanted. But he does not.

There are so many cruel twists in a long prison term. One is the feeling of being slowly forgotten by the world and by those you love and need. The mail, which arrived in bundles during the early months, gradually trickled down to one or two letters a week. Friends and family members who once seemed eager to visit have not been seen in years. My older brother, Marcus, drops in twice a year to kill an hour updating me on his latest problems. He has three teenagers, all at various stages of juvenile delinquency, plus a wife who's crazy. I guess I have no problems after all. In spite of his chaotic life, I enjoy the visits. Marcus has been mimicking Richard Pryor his entire life, and every word he utters is funny. We usually laugh the entire hour as he rails against his children. My younger sister, Ruby, lives on the West Coast, and I see her once a year. She dutifully writes me a letter every week, and I treasure these. I have a distant cousin who served seven years for armed robbery—I was his lawyer—and he comes to see me twice a year because I visited him when he was in prison.

After three years here, I often go months without a visitor, except for my father. The Bureau of Prisons tries to place its inmates within five hundred miles of home. I'm lucky in that Winchester is so close, but it might as well be a thousand miles away. I have several childhood friends who've never made the drive and a few others whom I haven't heard from in two years.

Most of my former lawyer friends are too busy. My running buddy in law school writes once every other month but can't quite squeeze in a visit. He lives in Washington, a hundred fifty miles to the east, where he claims to work seven days a week in a big law firm. My best pal from the Marine Corps lives in Pittsburgh, two hours away, and he's been to Frostburg exactly once.

I suppose I should be thankful that my father makes the effort.

As always, he's sitting alone in the small visiting room with a brown paper sack on the table in front of him. It's either cookies or brownies from my Aunt Racine, his sister. We shake hands but do not embrace—Henry Bannister has never hugged another man in his life. He looks me over to make sure I have not gained weight and, as always, quizzes me about my daily routine. He has not gained a pound in forty years and can still fit into his Marine uniform. He's convinced that eating less means living longer, and Henry's afraid of dying young. His father and grandfather dropped dead in their late fifties. He walks five miles a day and thinks I should do the same. I have accepted the fact that he will never stop telling me how to live my life, incarcerated or not.

He taps the brown bag and says, "Racine sent these."

"Please tell her I said thanks," I say. If he's so worried about my waistline, why does he bring me a bag of fatty desserts every time he visits? I'll eat two or three and give the rest away.

"You talked to Marcus lately?" he asks.

"No, not in the past month. Why?"

"Big trouble. Delmon's got a girl pregnant. He's fifteen, she's fourteen." He shakes his head and frowns. Delmon was an outlaw by the age of ten, and the family has always expected him to pursue a life of crime.

"Your first great-grandchild," I say, trying to be funny.

"Ain't I proud? A fourteen-year-old white girl knocked up by a fifteen-year-old idiot who happens to be named Bannister."

We both dwell on this for some time. Our visits are often defined not by what is said but by what is kept deep inside. My father is now sixty-nine, and instead of savoring his golden years, he spends most of his time licking his wounds and feeling sorry for himself. Not that I blame him. His dear wife of forty-two years was taken away in a split second. While he was lost in his grief, we found out the FBI had an interest in me, and its investigation soon snowballed. My trial lasted for three weeks and my father was in the courtroom every day. Watching me stand before a judge and get sentenced to ten years in prison was heartbreaking. Then Bo was taken away, from both of us. Now Marcus's children are old enough to inflict serious pain on their parents and extended family.

Our family is due some good luck, but that doesn't appear likely.

"I talked to Ruby last night," he says. "She's doing well, says hello, says your last letter was quite funny."

"Please tell her the letters mean so much. She has not missed a week in five years." Ruby is such a bright spot in our crumbling family. She's a marriage counselor, and her husband is a pediatrician. They have three perfect kids who are kept away from their infamous Uncle Mal.

After a long pause, I say, "Thanks for the check, as always."

He shrugs and says, "Happy to help."

He sends $100 every month, and it is much appreciated. It goes into my account and allows me to buy such necessities as pens, writing tablets, paperbacks, and decent food. Most of those in my White Gang get checks from home and virtually no one in my Black Gang gets a penny. In prison, you always know who's getting money.

"You're almost halfway through," he says.

"I'm two weeks shy of five years," I say.

"I guess it flies by."

"Maybe on the outside. I can assure you the clocks run much slower on this side of the wall."

"Still, it's hard to believe you've been in for five years."

It is indeed. How do you survive for years in prison? You don't think about years, or months, or weeks. You think about today—how to get through it, how to survive it. When you wake up tomorrow, another day is behind you. The days add up; the weeks run together; the months become years. You realize how tough you are, how you can function and survive because you have no choice.

"Any idea what you'll do?" he asks. I get this same question every month now, as if my release were just around the corner. Patience, I remind myself. He's my father. And he's here! That counts for a lot.

"Not really. It's too far away."

"I'd start thinking about it if I were you," he says, certain that he would know exactly what to do if he were in my shoes.

"I just finished the third level of Spanish," I say with some pride. In my Brown Gang there is a good friend, Marco, who is an excellent language teacher. Drugs.

"Looks like we'll all be speaking Spanish before long. They're taking over."

Henry has little patience with immigrants, anybody with an accent, people from New York and New Jersey, anyone on welfare, anyone unemployed, and he thinks the homeless should be rounded up and placed in camps that would resemble, in his view, something worse than Guantánamo.

We had harsh words a few years ago, and he threatened to stop the visits. Bickering is a waste of time. I'm not going to change him. He's kind enough to drive over, the least I can do is behave. I am the convicted felon; he is not. He's the winner; I'm the loser. This seems important to Henry, though I don't know why. Maybe it's because I had college and law school, something he never dreamed of.

"I'll probably leave the country," I say. "Go somewhere where I can use the Spanish, somewhere like Panama or Costa Rica.

Warm weather, beaches, people with darker skin. They don't care about criminal records or who's been to prison."

"The grass is always greener, huh?"

"Yes, Dad, when you're in prison, every place has greener grass. What am I supposed to do? Go back home, maybe become an unlicensed paralegal doing research for some tiny firm that can't afford me? Maybe become a bail bondsman? How about a private detective? There are not a lot of options."

He's nodding along. We've had this conversation at least a dozen times. "And you hate the government," he says.

"Oh yes. I hate the federal government, the FBI, the U.S. Attorneys, the federal judges, the fools who run the prisons. There is so much of it I hate. I'm sitting here doing ten years for a noncrime because a hotshot U.S. Attorney needed to jack up his kill quota. And if the government can nail my ass for ten years with no evidence, just think of all the possibilities now that I have the words 'Convicted Felon' tattooed on my forehead. I'm outta here, Pop, just as soon as I can make the break."

He's nodding and smiling. Sure, Mal.

CHAPTER 3

Given the importance of what they do, and the controversies that often surround them, and the violent people they sometimes confront, it is remarkable that in the history of this country only four active federal judges have been murdered.

The Honorable Raymond Fawcett has just become number five.

His body was found in the small basement of a lakeside cabin he had built and frequently used on weekends. When he did not show up for a trial on Monday morning, his law clerks panicked and called the FBI. In due course the agents found the crime scene. The cabin was in a heavily wooded part of southwest Virginia, on the side of a mountain, at the edge of a small, pristine body of water known locally as Lake Higgins. The lake is not found on most road maps.

There appeared to be no forced entry, no fight or struggle, nothing but two dead bodies, bullet holes in both heads, and an empty metal safe in the basement. Judge Fawcett was found near the safe, shot twice in the back of the head, definitely an execution, and there was a large pool of dried blood on the floor around him. The first expert on the scene guessed that the judge had been dead for at least two days. He had left the office around three on Friday afternoon, according to one of his law clerks, with plans to drive straight to the cabin and spend the weekend hard at work there.

The other body was that of Naomi Clary, a thirty-four-year-old divorced mother of two who had recently been hired by Judge Fawcett as a secretary. The judge, who was sixty-six and had five adult children, was not divorced. He and Mrs. Fawcett had been living apart for several years, though they were still seen together around Roanoke when the occasion called for it. It was common knowledge they had separated, and because he was such a prominent man in town, their living arrangements created some gossip. Both had confided in their children and in their friends that they simply did not have the stomach for a divorce. Mrs. Fawcett had the money. Judge Fawcett had the status. Both seemed relatively content, and both had promised no outside affairs. The handshake deal provided they would proceed with the divorce if and when one of them met someone else.

Evidently, the judge had found someone to his liking. Almost immediately after Ms. Clary was added to the payroll, the rumors rippled through the courthouse that the judge was fooling around, again. A few on his staff knew that he had never been able to keep his pants on.

Naomi's body was found on a sofa near the spot where the judge was murdered. She was naked, with both ankles bound tightly together with silver duct tape. She was lying on her back with both wrists taped together behind her. She had been shot twice in the forehead. Her body was covered with small burn marks. After a few hours of debate and analysis, the chief investigators agreed that she had likely been tortured as a means of forcing Fawcett to open the safe. Apparently, it had worked. The safe was empty, its door left open, not a shred of anything left behind. The thief had cleaned it out, then executed his victims.

Judge Fawcett's father had been a framing contractor, and as a kid he tagged along, always with a hammer. He never stopped building things—a new back porch, a deck, a storage shed. When his children were small and his marriage was happy, he had gutted and completely renovated a stately old home in central Roanoke, acting as the general contractor and spending every weekend on a ladder. Years later he renovated a loft apartment that became his love nest, then his home. To him, the hammering, sawing, and sweating were therapy, a mental and physical escape from a job filled with stress. He had designed the A-frame lake cabin and, over a four-year period, had built most of it himself. In the basement where he died, there was a wall covered with fine cedar shelves, all crammed with thick law books. In the center, though, was a hidden door. A set of shelves swung open, and there, perfectly hidden, was the safe. At the crime scene, the safe had been rolled forward some three feet out of the wall and then cleaned out.

The safe was a metal and lead vault mounted on four five-inch wheels. It had been manufactured by the Vulcan Safe Company of Kenosha, Wisconsin, and sold online to Judge Fawcett. According to its specs, it was forty-six inches in height, thirty-six inches in width, forty inches in depth; offered nine cubic feet of storage; weighed 510 pounds; retailed at $2,100; and, when properly sealed, was fireproof, waterproof, and, ostensibly, burglarproof. A keypad on the door required a six-digit code for entry.

Why a federal judge who earned $174,000 a year needed such a secured and hidden container for his valuables was an immediate mystery to the FBI. At the time of his death, Judge Fawcett had $15,000 in a personal checking account, $60,000 in a certificate of deposit earning less than 1 percent a year, $31,000 in a bond fund, and $47,000 in a mutual fund that had underperformed the market for almost a decade. He also had a 401(k) and the standard array of benefits for top federal officials. With almost no debt, his balance sheet was blandly impressive. His real security was in his job. Since the Constitution allowed him to serve until he died, the salary would never stop.

Mrs. Fawcett's family owned a trainload of bank stock, but the judge had never been able to get near it. Now, with the separation, it was even further off-limits. Bottom line: the judge was quite comfortable but far from rich, and not the type who needed a hidden safe to protect his goodies.

What was in the safe? Or, bluntly, what got him killed? Interviews with family and friends would later reveal he had no expensive habits, did not collect gold coins or rare diamonds or anything that needed such protection. Other than an impressive baseball card collection from his youth, there was no evidence the judge had an interest in collecting anything.

The A-frame was tucked away so deeply in the hills that it was nearly impossible to find. A porch wrapped around the cabin, and from any vantage point not another person, vehicle, cabin, home, shack, or boat could be seen. Total isolation. The judge stored a kayak and a canoe in the basement, and he was known to spend hours on the lake, fishing, thinking, and smoking cigars. He was a quiet man, not lonely and not shy, but cerebral and serious.

It was painfully obvious to the FBI there would be no witnesses because there were no other human beings within miles. The cabin was the perfect spot to kill someone and be far away before the crime was discovered. From the moment they first arrived, the investigators knew they were way behind on this one. And, for them, things got worse. There was not a single fingerprint, footprint, piece of fiber, stray hair follicle, or tire mark to help with the clues. The cabin had no alarm system and certainly no surveillance cameras. And why bother? The nearest policeman was half an hour away, and, assuming he could even find the place, what was he supposed to do when he got there? Any braindead burglar would be long gone.

For three days the investigators inspected every inch of the cabin and four acres around it, and they found nothing. The fact that the murderer was so careful and methodic did not help the mood of the team. They were dealing with some real talent here, a gifted killer who left no clues. Where were they supposed to start?

There was already pressure from Justice in Washington. The Director of the FBI was putting together a task force, sort of a special ops unit to descend upon Roanoke and solve the crime.

———

As expected, the brutal murders of an adulterous judge and his young girlfriend were splendid gifts to the media and the tabloids. When Naomi Clary was buried three days after her body was found, the Roanoke police used barricades to keep reporters and the curious away from the cemetery. When Raymond Fawcett was memorialized the following day, at a packed Episcopal church, a helicopter hovered above the building and drowned out the music. The police chief, an old friend of the judge's, was forced to send up his helicopter and shoo away the other one. Mrs. Fawcett was steadfast in the front row among her children and grandchildren, refusing to shed a tear or look at his coffin. Many kind words were spoken about the judge, but some people, especially the men, were thinking, How did this old boy get such a young girlfriend?

When both were good and buried, the attention quickly returned to the investigation. The FBI would not say a word in public, primarily because it had nothing to say at all. A week after the bodies were found, the only evidence on the table was the ballistics reports. Four bullets, hollow points, fired from a .38-caliber handgun, one of a million on the streets and now probably at the bottom of a large lake somewhere in the mountains of West Virginia.

Other motives were being analyzed. In 1979 Judge John Wood was gunned down outside his home in San Antonio. His killer was a contract hit man hired by a powerful drug dealer who was about to be sentenced by Judge Wood, who hated the drug trade and those who worked it. With a nickname like Maximum John the motive was fairly obvious. In Roanoke, the FBI teams looked at every case, criminal and civil, on Judge Fawcett's docket and made a short list of potential suspects, virtually all of whom were involved in the narcotics trade.

In 1988 Judge Richard Daronco was shot and killed while doing yard work around his home in Pelham, New York. The killer was the angry father of a woman who had just lost a case in the judge's courtroom. The father shot the judge, then committed suicide. In Roanoke, the FBI team scoured Judge Fawcett's files and interviewed his clerks. There are always a few whack jobs filing crap in federal court and making outrageous demands, and a list slowly came together. Names but no real suspects.

In 1989 Judge Robert Smith Vance was killed in his home in Mountain Brook, Alabama, when he opened a package that contained a bomb. They found his killer and eventually sent him to death row, but his motive was never clear. The prosecutors speculated he was angry over a recent decision by Judge Vance. In Roanoke the FBI interviewed hundreds of lawyers with cases presently before Judge Fawcett, or in the recent past. Every lawyer has clients who are either crazy or mean enough to seek revenge, and a few of these had passed through Judge Fawcett's courtroom. They were tracked down, interviewed, and eliminated.

In January 2011, a month before the Fawcett murder, Judge John Roll was gunned down near Tucson in the same mass killing that wounded Congresswoman Gabrielle Giffords. Judge Roll was in the wrong place at the wrong time and not the target. His death was of no help to the FBI in Roanoke.

With each passing day, the trail grew colder. With no witnesses, no real crime scene evidence, no mistake by the killer, only a handful of useless tips, and very few suspects from the judge's dockets, the investigation hit dead ends at every turn.

The big announcement of a $100,000 reward did little to spark activity on the FBI hotlines.

CHAPTER 4

Because Frostburg is a camp and light on security, we have more contact with the outside world than most prisoners. Our mail is always subject to being opened and read, but this is rare. We have limited access to e-mail but not the Internet. There are dozens of phones and plenty of rules that govern their use, but we can generally make all the collect calls we want. Cell phones are strictly prohibited. We are allowed to buy subscriptions to dozens of magazines on an approved list. Several newspapers arrive promptly each morning, and they are always available in a corner of the chow hall known as the coffee room.

It is there, early one morning, that I see the headline in the *Washington Post*: **FEDERAL JUDGE MURDERED NEAR ROANOKE.**

I cannot hide a smile. This is the moment.

For the past three years, I have been obsessed with Raymond Fawcett. I never met him, never entered his courtroom, never filed a lawsuit in his domain—the Southern District of Virginia. Virtually all of my practice was in state court. I rarely ventured into the federal arena, and when I did, it was always in the Northern District of Virginia, which includes everything from Richmond north. The Southern District covers Roanoke, Lynchburg, and the massive sprawl of the Virginia Beach–Norfolk metro area. Before Fawcett's passing, there were twelve federal judges working in the Southern District, and thirteen in the Northern.

I have met several inmates here at Frostburg who were sentenced by Fawcett, and without seeming too curious, I quizzed them about him. I did this under the guise of actually knowing the judge, of having tried lawsuits in his court. Without exception, these inmates loathed the man and felt as though he had gone overboard with their sentences. He seemed to especially enjoy lecturing the white-collar guys as he passed judgment and sent them away. Their sentencing hearings generally attracted more press, and Fawcett had a massive ego.

He went to Duke as an undergrad and Columbia for law school, then worked at a Wall Street firm for a few years. His wife and her money were from Roanoke, and they settled there when he was in his early thirties. He joined the biggest law firm in town and quickly clawed his way to the top. His father-in-law was a longtime benefactor to Democratic politics, and in 1993 President Clinton appointed Fawcett to a lifetime position on the U. S. District Court for the Southern District of Virginia.

In the world of American law, such an appointment carries tremendous prestige but not a lot of money. At the time, his new salary was $125,000 a year, about a $300,000 cut in pay from what he was earning as a hardworking partner in a thriving law firm. At forty-eight, he became one of the youngest federal judges in the country and, with five kids, one of the most cash-strapped. His father-in-law soon began supplementing his income, and the pressure eased.

He once described his early years on the bench in a long interview in one of those legal periodicals that few people read. I found it by chance in the prison library, in a stack of magazines about to be discarded. There are not too many books and magazines that escape my curious eyes. Often, I'll read five or six hours a day. The computers here are desktops, a few years out-of-date, and because of demand they take a beating. However, since I am the librarian and the computers are under my control, I have plenty of access. We have subscriptions to two digital legal research sites,

and I have used these to read every opinion published by the late
Honorable Raymond Fawcett.

Something happened to him around the turn of the century,
the year 2000. During his first seven years on the bench, he was
a left-leaning protector of individual rights, compassionate with
the poor and troubled, quick to slap the hands of law enforcement, skeptical of big business, and seemingly eager to chastise
a wayward litigant with an extremely sharp pen. Within a year,
though, something was changing. His opinions were shorter, not
as well reasoned, even nasty at times, and he was definitely moving to the right.

In 2000 he was nominated by President Clinton to fill a
vacancy on the Fourth Circuit Court of Appeals in Richmond.
Such a move is the logical promotion for a talented district court
judge, or one with the right connections. On the Fourth Circuit,
he would have been one of fifteen judges who considered nothing but cases on appeal. The only rung higher than that is the
U.S. Supreme Court, and it is not clear if Fawcett had that ambition. Most federal judges do, at one time or another. Bill Clinton, though, was leaving office, and under something of a cloud.
His nominations were stalled in the Senate, and when George
W. Bush was elected, Fawcett's future remained in Roanoke.

He was fifty-five. His children were already adults or in the
process of leaving home. Perhaps he succumbed to a midlife crisis
of sorts. Maybe his marriage was on the rocks. His father-in-law
had died and left him out of his will. His former partners were
getting rich while he toiled away at workers' wages, relatively
speaking. Whatever the reason, Judge Fawcett became a different man on the bench. In criminal cases, his sentencing became
erratic and far less compassionate. In civil cases, he showed much
less sympathy for the little guy and sided time and again with
powerful interests. Judges often change as they mature, but few
turn as abruptly as Raymond Fawcett.

The biggest case of his career was a war over uranium mining that began in 2003. I was still a lawyer then, and I knew the issues and basic details. You couldn't avoid it; there was a story in the newspapers virtually every day.

A rich vein of uranium ore runs through central and southern Virginia. Because the mining of uranium is an environmental nightmare, the state passed a law forbidding it. Naturally, the landowners, leaseholders, and mining companies that control the deposits have long wanted to start digging, and they spent millions lobbying lawmakers to lift the ban. But, the Virginia General Assembly resisted. In 2003, a Canadian company called Armanna Mines filed a lawsuit in the Southern District of Virginia attacking the ban as unconstitutional. It was a frontal assault with no holds barred, heavily financed, and led by some of the most expensive legal talent money could buy.

As we soon learned, Armanna Mines was a consortium of mining companies from the U.S., Australia, and Russia, as well as Canada. An estimate of the potential value of the deposits in Virginia alone ranged from $15 to $20 billion.

Under the random selection process in effect at the time, the case was assigned to a Judge McKay of Lynchburg, who was eighty-four years old and suffering from dementia. Citing health reasons, he passed. Next in line was Raymond Fawcett, who had no valid reason to recuse himself. The defendant was the Commonwealth of Virginia, but many others soon joined in. These included cities, towns, and counties situated on top of the deposits, as well as a few landowners who wanted no part of the destruction. The lawsuit became one huge, sprawling mess of litigation with over a hundred lawyers involved. Judge Fawcett denied the initial motions to dismiss and ordered extensive discovery. Before long, he was devoting 90 percent of his time to the lawsuit.

In 2004 the FBI entered my life, and I lost interest in the mining case. I suddenly had other, more pressing matters to deal with. My trial started in October 2005 in D.C. By then, the Armanna Mines trial had been under way for a month in a crowded courtroom in Roanoke. At that point, I could not have cared less what happened to the uranium.

After a three-week trial, I was convicted and given ten years. After a ten-week trial, Judge Fawcett ruled in favor of Armanna Mines. There was no possible connection between the two trials, or so I thought as I went away to prison.

Soon, though, I met the man who would eventually kill Judge Fawcett. I know the identity of the murderer, and I know his motive.

Motive is a baffling question for the FBI. In the weeks after the murder, the task force settles on the Armanna Mines litigation and interviews dozens of people connected to the trial. A couple of radical environmental groups had sprung up and operated around the fringes of the litigation. These had been closely monitored by the FBI at the time. Fawcett had received death threats, and during the trial he had moved around with protection. The threats were thoroughly investigated and found not to be credible, but the bodyguards remained close by.

Intimidation is an unlikely motive. Fawcett has made his decision, and though his name is poison among the environmentalists, he has done his damage. His ruling was confirmed in 2009 by the Fourth Circuit, and the case is now headed for the U.S. Supreme Court. Pending the appeals, the uranium has not been touched.

Revenge is a motive, though the FBI says nothing about it. The words "contract killing" are being used by some reporters, who apparently have nothing to base this on except for the professionalism of the killings.

Given the crime scene and the empty safe that was so carefully hidden, robbery seems the likelier motive.

I have a plan, one I have been plotting for years now. It is my only way out.

CHAPTER 5

Every able-bodied federal inmate is required to have a job, and the Bureau of Prisons controls the pay scale. For the past two years, I have been the librarian, and for my labors I get thirty cents an hour. About half of this money, along with the checks from my father, is subject to the Inmate Financial Responsibility Program. The Bureau of Prisons takes the money and applies it to felony assessments, fines, and restitution. Along with my ten-year sentence, I was ordered to pay about $120,000 in various penalties. At thirty cents an hour, it will take the rest of this century and then some.

Other jobs around here include cook, dishwasher, table wiper, floor scrubber, plumber, electrician, carpenter, clerk, orderly, laundry worker, painter, gardener, and teacher. I consider myself lucky. My job is one of the best and does not reduce me to cleaning up after people. I occasionally teach a course in history for inmates pursuing their high school equivalency diplomas. Teaching pays thirty-five cents an hour, but I am not tempted by the higher wages. I find it quite depressing because of the low levels of literacy among the prison populations. Blacks, whites, browns—it doesn't matter. So many of these guys can barely read and write, it makes you wonder what's happening in our educational system.

But I'm not here to fix the educational system, nor the legal, judicial, or prison systems. I'm here to survive one day at a time, and in doing so maintain as much self-respect and dignity as possible. We are scum, nobodies, common criminals locked away from society, and reminders of this are never far away. A prison guard is called a correction officer, or simply a CO. Never refer to one as a guard. No sir. Being a CO is far superior; it's more of a title. Most COs are former cops or deputies or military types who didn't do too well in those jobs and now work in prison. There are a few good ones, but most are losers who are too stupid to realize they are losers. And who are we to tell them? They are vastly superior to us, regardless of their stupidity, and they enjoy reminding us of this.

They rotate COs to avoid one getting too close to an inmate. I suppose this happens, but one of the cardinal rules of inmate survival is to avoid your CO as much as possible. Treat him with respect; do exactly what he says; cause him no trouble; but, above all, try to avoid him.

My current CO is not one of the better ones. He is Darrel Marvin, a thick-chested, potbellied white boy of no more than thirty who tries to swagger but has too much tonnage on his hips. Darrel is an ignorant racist who does not like me because I am black and I have two college degrees, which is two more than he has. A fierce, internal battle rages every time I'm forced to suck up to this thug, but I have no choice. Right now, I need him.

"Good morning, Officer Marvin," I say with a fake smile as I stop him outside the chow hall.

"What is it, Bannister?" he growls.

I hand over a sheet of paper, an official request form. He takes it and makes a pretense of reading it. I'm tempted to help him with the longer words but bite my tongue. "I need to see the warden," I say politely.

"Why do you want to see the warden?" he asks, still trying to read the rather simple request.

My business with the warden is of no concern to the CO, or anyone else, but to remind Darrel of this would only cause trouble. "My grandmother is almost dead, and I would like to go to her funeral. It's only sixty miles away."

"When do you think she might die?" he asks, such a clever smart-ass.

"Soon. Please, Officer Marvin, I have not seen her in years."

"The warden does not approve crap like this, Bannister. You should know this by now."

"I know, but the warden owes me a favor. I gave him some legal advice a few months ago. Please, just pass it along."

He folds the sheet of paper and stuffs it into a pocket. "All right, but it's a waste of time."

"Thanks."

Both of my grandmothers died years ago.

Nothing in prison is designed for the convenience of the prisoner. The granting or denying of a simple request should take a few hours, but that would be too easy. Four days pass before Darrel informs me that I am to report to the warden's office at 10:00 a.m. tomorrow, February 18. Another fake smile, and I say, "Thanks."

The warden is the king of this little empire, with the expected ego of one who rules by edict or thinks he should. These guys come and go and it's impossible to understand the purpose of all the transfers. Again, it's not my job to reform our prison system, so I don't worry about what happens in the administration building.

The current one is Mr. Robert Earl Wade, a career corrections man who's all business. He's fresh off his second divorce, and I did indeed explain to him some of the basics regarding Maryland alimony law. I enter his office; he does not stand or offer a hand or extend any courtesy that might indicate respect. He says, "Hello, Bannister," as he waves at an empty chair.

"Hello, Warden Wade. How have you been?" I ease into the chair.

"I'm a free man, Bannister. Number two is history and I'll never marry again."

"Nice to hear and glad to help."

With the warm-up quickly over, he shoves a notepad and says, "I can't let you guys go home for every funeral, Bannister, you gotta understand this."

"This is not about a funeral," I say. "I have no grandmother."

"What the hell?"

"Are you keeping up with the murder investigation of Judge Fawcett, down in Roanoke?" He frowns and jerks his head back as if he's been insulted. I'm here under false pretenses, and somewhere deep in one of the countless federal manuals there must be a violation for this. As he tries to react, he shakes his head and repeats himself. "What the hell?"

"The murder of the federal judge. It's all over the press." It's hard to believe he could have missed the story of the murder, but it's also entirely possible. Just because I read several newspapers a day doesn't mean everyone does.

"The federal judge?" he asks.

"That's him. They found him with his girlfriend in a lake cabin in southwest Virginia, both shot—"

"Sure, sure. I've seen the stories. What's this got to do with you?" He's ticked off because I've lied to him, and he's trying to think of the appropriate punishment. A supreme and mighty man like a warden cannot get himself used by an inmate. Robert Earl's eyes are darting around as he decides how to react to my trickery.

I need to sound as dramatic as possible because Wade will probably laugh when I answer his question. Inmates have far too much spare time to develop intricate claims of their innocence, or to cook up conspiracy theories involving unsolved crimes, or to gather secrets that might be swapped for a sudden parole. In short, inmates are always scheming ways to get out, and I'm sure Robert Earl has seen and heard it all.

"I know who killed the judge," I say as seriously as possible.

Much to my relief, he does not crack a smile. He rocks back in his chair, pulls at his chin, and begins to nod. "And how did you come across this information?" he asks.

"I met the killer."

"In here or on the outside?"

"I can't say, Warden. But I'm not bullshitting you. Based on what I'm reading in the press, the FBI investigation isn't going anywhere. And it won't."

My disciplinary record is without blemish. I have never uttered a wrong word to a prison official. I have never complained. There is no contraband in my cell, not even an extra packet of sugar from the chow hall. I do not gamble or borrow money. I have helped dozens of fellow inmates, as well as a few civilians, including the warden, with their legal problems. My library is kept in meticulous order. The point being—for an inmate, I have credibility.

He leans forward on his elbows and exposes his yellow teeth. He has dark circles under his eyes, which are always moist. The eyes of a drinker. "And let me guess, Bannister, you would like to share this information with the FBI, cut a deal, and get out of prison. Right?"

"Absolutely, sir. That's my plan."

Finally, the laugh. A long high-pitched cackle that in itself would be the source of much humor. When he winds down, he says, "When is your release?"

"Five years."

"Oh, so this is a helluva deal, right? Just give them a name, and trot right out of here five years ahead of schedule?"

"Nothing is that simple."

"What do you want me to do, Bannister?" he snarls, the laughter long gone. "Call the FBI and tell 'em I gotta guy who knows the killer and is ready to cut a deal? They're probably getting a hundred calls a day, most from fruitcakes sniffing around for the reward money. Why would I risk my credibility playing that game?"

"Because I know the truth, and you know I'm not a fruitcake, nor a bullshitter."

"Why don't you just write them a letter, keep me out of it?"

"I will, if that's what you want. But you'll be involved at some point because I swear I'm going to convince the FBI. We'll cut our deal, and I'll say good-bye. You'll be here for the logistics."

He slumps back in his chair as if overwhelmed by the pressure of his office. He picks his nose with a thumb. "You know, Bannister, as of this morning I have 602 men here at Frostburg, and you are the last one I would expect to sneak in my office with such a screwball idea. The very last."

"Thank you."

"Don't mention it."

I lean forward and stare him in the eyes. "Look, Warden, I know what I'm talking about. I know you can't trust an inmate, but just hear me out. I have some extremely valuable information, and the FBI will be desperate to have it. Please call them."

"I don't know, Bannister. We'll both look like fools."

"Please."

"I might think about it. Now shove off, and tell Officer Marvin that I denied your request to go to the funeral."

"Yes sir, and thanks."

My hunch is that the warden will not be able to resist a little excitement. Running a no-security camp filled with well-behaved inmates is a dull job. Why not get involved in the most notorious murder investigation in the country?

I leave the administration building and head across the quad, the central area of our camp. On the west side are two dormitories that house 150 men each, and these are matched by identical buildings on the east side of the quad. East campus and west campus, as though one were strolling through a pleasant little college.

The COs have a break room near the chow hall, and here I find dear Officer Marvin. If I set foot inside the break room I would probably be shot or hanged. The metal door is open, though, and I can see inside. Marvin is sprawled in a folding chair, cup of coffee in one hand and a thick pastry in the other. He's laughing along with two other COs. If hooked by the necks and weighed together on meat scales, the three would push a thousand pounds.

"What do you want, Bannister?" Darrel growls when he sees me.

"Just wanted to say thanks, Officer. The warden said no, but thanks anyway."

"You got it, Bannister. Sorry about your grandmother."

And with that, one of the guards kicks the door closed. It slams hard in my face, the metal crashes and vibrates, and for a split second it shakes me to the core. I have heard that sound before.

———

My arrest. The Downtown Civic Club met for lunch each Wednesday at the historic George Washington Hotel, a five-minute walk from my office. There were about seventy-five members, and all but three were white. On that day, I happened to be the only black guy in attendance, not that this was of any significance. I was sitting at a long table, choking down the usual rubber chicken and cold peas and shooting the bull with the mayor and a State Farm agent. We had covered the usual topics—

the weather and football—and we had touched lightly on politics, but this was always done with great care. It was a typical Civic Club lunch—thirty minutes for the food, followed by thirty minutes from a speaker who was usually not too exciting. However, on this memorable day I would not be allowed to hear the speech.

There was a commotion at the door of the banquet hall, then, suddenly, a squad of heavily armed federal agents swarmed the room as if they were about to kill all of us. A SWAT team, in complete ninja attire—black uniforms, thick vests, serious firearms, and those German combat helmets made famous by Hitler's troops. One of them yelled, "Malcolm Bannister!" I instinctively stood and mumbled, "What the hell?" At least five automatic rifles were instantly aimed at me. "Hands up," the fearless leader yelled, and I raised my hands. In a matter of seconds my hands were yanked down, slapped together behind me, and for the first time in my life I felt the indescribable pinch of thick cuffs on my wrists. It is a horrible feeling, and unforgettable. I was shoved down the narrow aisle between the dining tables and hustled out of the room. The last thing I heard was the mayor shouting, "This is an outrage!"

Needless to say, the dramatic invasion put a damper on the rest of the Civic Club meeting.

With these paramilitary goons swarming around me, I was taken through the lobby of the hotel and out the front door. Someone had graciously tipped off the local television station, and a camera crew filmed away as I was shoved into the rear seat of a black Chevrolet Tahoe, a goon on each side. As we headed for the city jail, I said, "Is all of this really necessary?"

The leader, riding front-seat shotgun, said, "Just shut up," without turning around.

"Well, I really don't have to shut up," I said. "You can arrest me, but you can't make me shut up. Do you realize this?"

"Just shut up."

The goon on my right placed the barrel of his rifle on my knee.

"Please move that gun, would you?" I said, but the gun did not move.

We drove on. I said, "Are you guys getting your rocks off on this? Must be terribly exciting to dash about like real tough guys, roughing up innocent people, sort of like the Gestapo."

"I said shut up."

"And I said I'm not shutting up. You got a warrant for my arrest?"

"I do."

"Let me see it."

"I'll show it to you at the jail. For now, just shut up."

"Why don't *you* shut up, okay?"

I could see a portion of his neck just under his German combat helmet, and it was turning red as he fumed. I took a deep breath and told myself to be cool.

The helmet. I had worn the same type during my four years in the Marines, four years of active duty that included live combat in the first Gulf War. Second Regiment, Eighth Battalion, Second Division, U.S. Marine Corps. We had been the first U.S. troops to engage the Iraqis in Kuwait. It wasn't much of a fight, but I saw enough dead and wounded on both sides.

Now I was surrounded by a bunch of toy soldiers who'd never heard a shot fired in anger and couldn't run a mile without collapsing. And they were the good guys.

When we arrived at the jail, there was a photographer from the local newspaper. My goons walked me slowly inside, making sure I would be well photographed. Their version of the perp walk.

I would soon learn that another team of government thugs had raided the offices of Copeland, Reed & Bannister at about the same time I was sitting down for lunch with my fellow Civic Club members. With brilliant forethought and meticulous planning, the joint strike force waited until the noon hour when the only person in the office was poor Mrs. Henderson. She reported that they stormed through the front door with guns drawn, yelling, cursing, threatening. They tossed a search warrant on her desk, made her sit in a chair by the window, promised to arrest her if she did little more than breathe, then proceeded to ransack our modest suite of offices. They hauled away all of the computers, printers, and several dozen boxes of files. At some point, Mr. Copeland returned from lunch. When he protested, a gun was aimed at him, and he took a seat beside a weeping Mrs. Henderson.

My arrest was certainly a surprise. I had been dealing with the FBI for over a year. I had hired a lawyer and we had done everything possible to cooperate. I had passed two polygraph examinations administered by the FBI's own experts. We had turned over all of the paperwork that I, as a lawyer, could ethically show anyone. I had kept a lot of this from Dionne, but she knew I was worried sick. I battled insomnia. I struggled to eat when I had no appetite. Finally, after almost twelve months of my living in fear and dreading the knock on the door, the FBI informed my lawyer that the government no longer had any interest in me.

The government lied, and not for the first or last time.

Inside the jail, a place I visited at least twice a week, there was yet another squad of agents. They wore navy parkas with "FBI" stamped in bold yellow lettering across the backs, and they buzzed around with great purpose, though I could not tell exactly what they were doing. The local cops, many of whom I knew well, backed away and looked at me with confusion and pity.

Was it really necessary to send two dozen federal agents to arrest me and confiscate my files? I had just walked from my office to the George Washington Hotel. Any half-assed cop on his lunch break could have stopped me and made the arrest. But that would take the joy out of what these vastly important people did for a living.

They led me to a small room, sat me at a table, removed the handcuffs, and told me to wait. A few minutes later, a man in a dark suit entered the room and said, "I'm Special Agent Don Connor, FBI."

"A real pleasure," I said.

He dropped some papers on the table in front of me and said, "This is the warrant for your arrest." Then he dropped a thick bunch of stapled papers. "And this is the indictment. I'll give you a few minutes to read it."

With that, he turned and left the room, slamming the door behind him as hard as possible. It was a thick metal door, and it crashed and vibrated and the sound rattled around the room for a few seconds.

A sound I will never forget.

CHAPTER 6

Three days after my first meeting with Warden Wade, I am summoned back to his office. When I walk in, he is alone, on the phone, engaged in an important conversation. I stand awkwardly by the door, waiting. When he finishes his end of the chat, with a rude "That'll do," he gets to his feet and says, "Follow me." We walk through a side door into an adjacent conference room painted in the typical government pale green and equipped with far more metal chairs than could ever be used.

An audit last year revealed that the Bureau of Prisons had purchased, for "administrative use," four thousand chairs at $800 per chair. The same manufacturer sold the same chair at wholesale for $79. I shouldn't care anymore, but working for thirty cents an hour gives one a different perspective when it comes to handling money.

"Have a seat," he says, and I sit in one of the ugly and overpriced chairs. He selects one across the table because there must always be a barrier between us. I glance around and count twenty-two chairs. Let it go.

"I called Washington after you left the other day," he says gravely, as if he checks in with the White House on a regular basis. "The bureau advised me to use my own discretion. I kicked it around for a few hours, then got in touch with the FBI down in Roanoke. They've sent two guys up; they're waiting down the hall."

I maintain a poker face, though I am thrilled to hear this.

He points a finger at me and says, "I'm warning you, Bannister. If this turns out to be a scam, and I get embarrassed, then I'll do whatever I can to make your life miserable."

"It's not a scam, Warden, I swear."

"I don't know why I believe you."

"You won't be sorry."

From his pocket he removes his reading glasses, perches them halfway down his nose, and looks at a slip of paper. "I spoke with Assistant Director Victor Westlake, the guy in charge of the investigation. He's sent two of his men to have a chat with you, Agent Hanski and Agent Erardi. I did not reveal your name, so they know nothing."

"Thank you, Warden."

"Stay here." He gently slaps the table, gets to his feet, and leaves the room. As I wait and listen for approaching footsteps, there is a sharp pain in my stomach. If this doesn't work, I'm here for five more years, plus anything more they can possibly tack on.

Special Agent Chris Hanski is the senior guy, about my age with a lot of gray hair. Agent Alan Erardi is his younger sidekick. A newspaper article said there are now forty FBI agents working on the Fawcett case, and I assume these guys are pretty far down the chain of command. This first meeting will be important, as will all of them, but they've clearly sent a couple of foot soldiers to check me out.

The warden is not in the room. I figure he's back in his office, not far away, with an ear stuck to the door.

They begin without using pens and notepads, a clear sign they are here for a little amusement. Nothing serious. I guess they're not smart enough to realize I've spent hours across the table from FBI agents.

"So you want to make a deal," Hanski says.

"I know who killed Judge Fawcett, and I know why. If this information is of any value to the FBI, then, yes, we might be able to make a deal."

"You're assuming we don't already know," Hanski says.

"I'm sure you don't. If you did, why would you be here?"

"We were told to be here because we're checking every possible lead, and we doubt seriously if this will lead anywhere."

"Try me."

They exchange cocky looks. Fun and games. "So you give us the name, and what do you get in return?"

"I get out of prison, and I get protection."

"That simple?"

"No, it's actually very complicated. This guy is a nasty character and he has friends who are even nastier. Plus, I'm not willing to wait two years until he's convicted. If I give you the name, I get out now. Immediately."

"What if he's not convicted?"

"That's your problem. If you screw up the prosecution, you can't blame me."

At this point, Erardi takes out his notepad, uncaps a cheap pen, and writes something down. I have their attention. They are still working much too hard to appear nonchalant, but these guys are under pressure. Their little task force is scrambling because they have no credible leads, according to the newspapers. Hanski continues, "What if you give us the wrong name? Let's say we go chasing after the wrong suspect; meanwhile, you're a free man."

"I'll never be a free man."

"You'll be out of prison."

"And looking over my shoulder for the rest of my life."

"We've never lost an informant in witness protection. Over eight thousand and counting."

"That's what you advertise. Frankly, I'm not too concerned

with your track record or what didn't happen to the others. I'm worried about my own skin."

There is a pause as Erardi stops writing and decides to speak. "This guy sounds like he's in a gang of some sort, maybe a drug dealer. What else can you tell us?"

"Nothing, and I've told you nothing. You can make all the wild guesses you want."

Hanski smiles at nothing that is humorous. "I doubt if our boss will be too impressed with your scheme to get out of prison. As of today, we've had at least two other inmates contact us and claim to have valuable information. Of course, they want out of prison too. This is not unusual."

I have no way of knowing if this is true, but it sounds believable. The knot in my stomach has not gone away. I shrug, offer a smile, tell myself to stay cool. "You guys can play it any way you want. Obviously, you're in charge. You can keep beating your heads against a wall. You can waste time with these other inmates. It's up to you. But when you want to know the name of the person who killed Judge Fawcett, I can give it to you."

"Someone you met in prison?" Erardi asks.

"Or maybe out of prison. You'll never know until we have a deal."

There is a long pause as they stare at me and I stare right back. Finally, Erardi closes his notepad and sticks his pen back in his pocket. Hanski says, "Okay. We'll go tell our boss."

"You know where to find me."

———————

Several times a week, I meet my White Gang at the track, and we walk in wide circles around a field used for soccer and flag football. Carl, the optometrist, will be out in a few months. Kermit, the land speculator, has two more years. Wesley, the state senator, should get out about the same time I do. Mark is the only one with his case still on appeal. He's been here for eighteen months and says his lawyer is optimistic, though he freely admits he falsified some mortgage documents.

We don't talk much about our crimes, and this is usually true in prison. Who you were or what you did on the outside is not important, and it's also too painful to dwell on.

Wesley's wife has just filed for divorce and he's taking it hard. Since I've been through it, as has Kermit, we offer advice and try to cheer him up. I would love to entertain them with the details of my visit from the FBI, but this must be kept quiet. If my plan works, they will show up one day for a walk and I'll be gone, suddenly transferred to another camp for reasons they will never know.

CHAPTER 7

The FBI's temporary headquarters for its Fawcett task force was a warehouse in an industrial park near the Roanoke Regional Airport. When last occupied, the space had been leased by a company that imported shrimp from Central America and froze it for years. Almost immediately it was tagged "the Freezer." It offered plenty of space, seclusion, and privacy away from the press. Carpenters hurriedly built walls and sectioned off rooms, offices, hallways, and meeting places. Technicians from Washington worked around the clock to install the latest high-tech gear and gadgets for communication, data, and security. Trucks filled with rented furniture and equipment ran nonstop until the CC—command center—was stuffed with more desks and tables than would ever be used. A fleet of rented SUVs filled the parking lot. A catering service was hired to haul in three meals a day for the team, which soon numbered close to seventy—about forty agents plus support staff. There was no budget and no concern for costs. The victim was, after all, a federal judge.

A lease was signed for six months, but after three weeks of little progress there was a general mood among the Feds that they might be there longer. Aside from a short list of randomly picked suspects, all of whom were known to be violent and had appeared before Fawcett in the past eighteen years, there were no real leads. A man named Stacks had written the judge a threatening letter in 2002 from prison. Stacks was found working in a liquor store in Panama City Beach, Florida, and had an alibi for the weekend the judge and Ms. Clary were murdered. Stacks had not set foot in Virginia in at least five years. A narco-trafficker named Ruiz had cursed His Honor in Spanish when given a twenty-year sentence in 1999. Ruiz was still in a medium-security prison, but after a few days digging through his past, the FBI decided his former cadre of coke runners were all either dead or in prison too.

One team methodically sifted through every case Fawcett handled during his eighteen years on the bench. He had been a workhorse, handling 300 cases each year, both civil and criminal, while the average for a federal judge is 225. Judge Fawcett had sentenced approximately thirty-one hundred men and women to prison. Laboring under the admittedly shaky assumption that his killer was one of these, a team burned hundreds of hours adding names to its list of possible suspects and then discarding them. Another team studied the cases, both civil and criminal, pending before the judge when he was murdered. Another team spent all of its time on the Armanna Mines litigation, with particular attention paid to a couple of flaky environmental extremists who didn't like Fawcett.

From the moment it got itself organized, the Freezer was a swarming hive of tension, with urgent meetings, frayed nerves, dead ends by the hour, careers on the line, and someone always barking from Washington. The press called nonstop. The bloggers were feeding the frenzy with creative and blatantly false rumors.

Then an inmate named Malcolm Bannister entered the picture.

The task force was run by Victor Westlake, a thirty-year career agent who had a nice office with a nice view in the Hoover

Building on Pennsylvania Avenue in Washington. However, for almost three weeks now he had been holed up in a freshly painted room with no windows in the center of the CC. It was by no means his first road trip. Westlake had made his name years earlier as a master organizer who could rush to the scene of the crime, line up the troops, handle a thousand details, plan the attack, and solve the crime. He had once spent a year in a motel near Buffalo stalking a genius who got his kicks sending parcel bombs to federal meat inspectors. Turned out to be the wrong genius, but Westlake did not make the mistake of arresting his prey. Two years later he nailed his bomber.

Westlake was in his office, standing as always behind his desk, when Agents Hanski and Erardi entered. Since their boss was standing, they stood too. He believed that it was unhealthy, even deadly, to sit for hours behind a desk.

"Okay, I'm listening," he barked, snapping his fingers.

Hanski quickly said, "Guy's name is Malcolm Bannister, black male, aged forty-three, in for ten for RICO violations, federal court in D.C., former lawyer from Winchester, Virginia. Says he can deliver the name of the killer, along with his motive, but of course he wants out of prison."

Erardi added, "Out immediately, but also protection."

"What a surprise. A con wants out. Is he believable?"

Hanski shrugged. "For a con, I suppose. The warden says the guy is not a bullshitter, record is squeaky-clean, says we should listen to the guy."

"What'd he give you?"

"Absolutely nothing. The guy is pretty smart. He might actually know something, and if he does, then this may be his only chance to walk."

Westlake began to pace behind his desk, across the slick concrete floor, to one wall with fresh sawdust scattered in front of it. He paced back to his desk. "What kind of lawyer was he? Criminal? Drug dealers?"

Hanski replied, "Small town, general practice, some criminal experience, not much trial work, though. A former Marine."

As a former Marine himself, Westlake liked this. "His military record?"

"Four years, honorable discharge, fought in the first Gulf War. His father was a Marine and a Virginia state trooper."

"What took him down?"

"You're not going to believe it. Barry the Backhander."

Westlake frowned and smiled at the same time. "Come on."

"Seriously. He handled some real estate transactions for Barry and got caught up in the storm. As you'll recall, the jury nailed them on RICO and conspiracy charges. I think there were eight of them tried at the same time. Bannister was a small fish who got caught in a wide net."

"Any connection to Fawcett?"

"Not yet. We just got his name three hours ago."

"You got a plan?"

"Sort of," Hanski said. "If we assume Bannister knows the killer, then it's safe to assume they met in prison. Doubtful that he would have met the guy on the quiet streets of Winchester; much more likely that their paths crossed in prison. Bannister has been in for five years, with the first twenty-two months in Louisville, Kentucky, a medium-security prison with a population of two thousand. Since then he's been at Frostburg, a camp with six hundred inmates."

"That's a lot of people; plus, they come and go," Westlake said.

"Right, so let's start at the logical place. Let's get his prison records, the names of his cell mates, maybe dorm mates. We'll go to the two prisons, talk to the wardens, the unit managers, the COs, talk to anyone who might know something about Bannister and his friends. We'll begin collecting names and we'll see how many crossed paths with Fawcett."

Erardi added, "He says the killer has nasty friends, thus the desire for protection. Sounds like a gang of some variety. Once we start adding names, we'll concentrate on those with gang connections."

A pause, then a doubtful Westlake said, "And that's it?"

"It's the best we can do for now."

Westlake clicked his heels together, arched his back, gripped his hands behind his head, and breathed deeply. He stretched, and breathed, and stretched, then said, "Okay. Collect the prison records and get started. How many hands do you need?"

"Can you spare two men?"

"No, but you can have them. Go. Get started."

Barry the Backhander. The client I never met until they dragged us into federal court one gray morning and read the entire indictment aloud.

In a ham-and-egg storefront law office, you learn the basics of many mundane legal tasks, but it's difficult to specialize. I tried to avoid divorce and bankruptcy and I never liked real estate, but to survive I often had to take who and what walked in the door. Oddly, it would be real estate that brought about The Fall.

The referral came from a law school pal who was working for a midsized firm in central D.C. The firm had a client who wished to purchase a hunting lodge in Shenandoah County, in the foothills of the Allegheny Mountains, about an hour southwest of Winchester. The client desired great secrecy and demanded anonymity, which should have been the first warning sign. The purchase price was $4 million, and after some haggling, I negotiated a flat fee of $100,000 for Copeland, Reed & Bannister to handle the transaction. Such a fee had never been seen by me or my partners, and we were excited, initially. I set my other files aside and went to research the land records in Shenandoah County.

The lodge was about twenty years old and had been built by some doctors who enjoyed grouse hunting, but as happens with

many such ventures, the partners had reached a disagreement. A
serious one, involving lawyers and lawsuits, even a bankruptcy
or two. After a couple of weeks, though, I had things sorted out
and delivering a clean title opinion to my still anonymous client
would be no problem. A closing date was set and I prepared all the
necessary contracts and deeds. There was a lot of paperwork, but
then again we were going to earn a rather fat fee.

The closing was delayed a month, and I asked my law school
pal for $50,000, or half of the attorneys' fees. This was not uncom-
mon, and since I had invested a hundred hours at this point, I
wanted to get paid. He called back to say the client would not
agree. No big deal, I thought. In a typical real estate transaction, the attorneys are not paid until the closing takes place. I was
informed that my client, a corporation, had changed its name.
I redrafted the documents and waited. The closing was again
delayed, and the sellers began threatening to walk away.

During this time, I was vaguely aware of the name and reputation of a Beltway operative by the name of Barry Rafko or, more
famously, Barry the Backhander. He was about fifty years old and
for most of his adult life had been rummaging around D.C. looking for a lazy way to make a buck. He had been a consultant, a
strategist, an analyst, a fund-raiser, and a spokesman, and he had
worked at the lower levels of a few election campaigns of congressmen and senators, both Democratic and Republican. Didn't
matter to Barry. If he was getting paid he could strategize and
analyze from either side of the street. He hit his stride, though,
when he and a partner opened a lounge near the Capitol. Barry
hired some young hookers to tend bar in miniskirts, and almost
overnight the place became a favorite meat market for the legions
of staffers who swarm the Hill. Low-ranking congressmen and
mid-ranking bureaucrats discovered the place, and Barry was on
the map. With his pockets full of cash, his next venture was an
upscale steak house two blocks from his lounge. He catered to
lobbyists and offered great steaks and wines at reasonable prices,

and before long senators were getting their preferred tables. Barry loved sports and bought lots of tickets—Redskins, Capitals, Wizards, Georgetown Hoyas—which he gave away to his friends. By this time he had founded his own "governmental relations" firm and it was growing rapidly. He and his partner had a fight, and Barry bought his interest in their holdings. Alone, wealthy, and fueled by ambition, Barry set his sights on the top of his profession. Unrestrained by ethical considerations, he became one of the most aggressive purveyors of influence in Washington. If a rich client wanted a new loophole in the tax code, Barry could hire someone to write it, insert it, convince his friends to support it, and then do a masterful job of covering it up. If a rich client needed to expand a factory back home, Barry could arrange a deal whereby the congressman would secure the earmark, send the money home to the factory, and pocket a sizable check for his reelection efforts. Everyone would be thrilled.

In his first brush with the law, he was accused of slipping cash to a senior adviser to a U.S. senator. The charge didn't stick but the nickname did: Barry the Backhander.

Because he operated on the sleazier side of an often sleazy business, Barry knew the power of money, and sex. His yacht on the Potomac became a notorious love boat, famous for wild parties and plenty of young women. He owned a golf course in South Carolina where he took members of Congress for long weekends, usually without their wives.

For Barry, though, the more powerful he became, the more risks he was willing to take. Old friends drifted away, frightened by troubles that seemed inevitable. His name was mentioned in an ethics investigation in the House. The *Washington Post* picked up his scent, and Barry Rafko, a man who had always craved attention, was getting more than his share.

I had no idea, no real way of knowing, that the hunting lodge was one of his projects.

The corporate name changed again; the paperwork was

redone. Another closing was delayed, then a new proposal: my client wanted to lease the lodge for one year at the rate of $200,000 a month, with all rentals to be applied to the purchase price. This led to a week of intense bickering, but a deal was finally reached. I reworked the contracts again and insisted my firm be paid half of our fee. This was done, and Mr. Copeland and Mr. Reed were somewhat relieved.

When the contracts were finally signed, my client was an off-shore company operating on the tiny island of St. Kitts, and I still had no idea who was behind it. The contracts were signed by an unseen corporate representative down there in the Caribbean and shipped overnight to my office. As per our agreement, my client would wire into our law firm trust account the sum of $450,000 and some change, enough to cover the lease payments for the first two months, plus the remainder of our fee, plus some miscellaneous expenses. I would in turn write a $200,000 check to the sellers for each of the first two months, then my client would replenish the account. After twelve months of this, the lease would be converted to a sale, with our little firm due another sizable fee.

When the wired funds hit our bank, the banker called to inform me that our trust account had just received $4.5 million, as opposed to $450,000. I figured someone got carried away with the zeros; plus, there could be worse things than having far too much money in the bank. But something didn't add up. I tried to contact the shell company that was technically my client on St. Kitts but got the runaround. I contacted the law school pal who had referred the case, and he promised to look into the matter. I distributed the first month's rent and the attorneys' fee to our firm and waited for instructions to wire out the excess. Days passed, then weeks. A month later, the banker called to say that another $3 million had just landed in our trust account.

By this time, Mr. Reed and Mr. Copeland were deeply disturbed. I instructed my banker to get rid of the money—wire it back to the source from whence it came, and do so quickly. He grappled with this for a couple of days, only to find that the account in St. Kitts had been closed. Finally, my law school pal e-mailed me instructions to wire half the money to an account in Grand Cayman and the other half to an account in Panama.

As a small-time lawyer, I had zero experience wiring money to numbered accounts, but a few moments of light Google research revealed that I was walking blindly through some of the most notorious tax havens in the world. I wished I had never agreed to work for the anonymous client, in spite of the money.

The wire to Panama bounced back—some $3.5 million. I yelled at my law school pal and he yelled at someone up the line. The money stayed put for two months, drawing interest, though we could not ethically keep any of it. Ethics also required me to take all steps necessary to protect this unwanted money. It was not mine and I certainly made no claim to it, but, nonetheless, I had to safeguard it.

Innocently, or perhaps stupidly, I had allowed the tainted money of Barry the Backhander to rest under the control of Copeland, Reed & Bannister.

Once he had possession of the hunting lodge, Barry did a quick renovation, spruced it up a little, built a spa, and put in a heliport. He leased a Sikorsky S-76 helicopter, and it took about twenty minutes to haul ten of Barry's best friends from D.C. to the hunting lodge. On a typical Friday afternoon, several shuttles were made and the partying began. By this time in his career he had cast aside most bureaucrats and lobbyists and concentrated primarily on congressmen and their chiefs of staff. At the lodge, everything was available: great food and wine, Cuban cigars, drugs, thirty-year-old scotch, and twenty-year-old women. An occasional grouse hunt got organized, but the guests were usually

more preoccupied with the stunning collection of tall blondes at
their disposal.

The girl was from Ukraine. During the trial—my trial—her
handler said, in thickly accented English, that he had been paid
$100,000 cash for the girl, who was taken to the hunting lodge
and given a room. The cash had been handed over by a thug who
testified, for the prosecution, that he had been one of Barry's
many bagmen.

The girl died. The autopsy revealed she had overdosed after a
long night of partying with Barry and his friends from Washington. There were rumors that she failed to wake up one morning
while in bed with a U.S. congressman, though this could not
be proven. Barry circled the wagons long before the authorities
arrived on the scene. Whom the girl had slept with during her last
night on earth would never be revealed. A media storm erupted
around Barry, his businesses, his friends, his jets, yachts, helicop-
ters, restaurants, resorts, and the width and depth of his sordid
influence. As the press stampeded to Barry, his cronies and clients sprinted away. Outraged members of Congress chased down
reporters and demanded hearings and investigations.

The story turned much worse when the girl's mother was
located in Kiev. She produced a birth certificate showing her late
daughter to be only sixteen years old. A sixteen-year-old sex slave
partying with members of Congress at a hunting lodge in the
Allegheny Mountains, barely a two-hour drive from the U.S.
Capitol.

The original indictment ran on for a hundred pages and
accused fourteen defendants of an astonishing variety of crimes.
I was one of the fourteen, and my alleged crime had been what
is commonly known as money laundering. By allowing one of
Barry Rafko's faceless corporations to park money in my firm's

trust account, I had supposedly helped him take dirty cash he pilfered from clients, scrub it up a bit offshore, then turn it into a valuable asset—the hunting lodge. I was also accused of helping Barry hide money from the FBI, the IRS, and others.

Pretrial maneuvering eliminated some of the defendants; several were allowed to peel off and either cooperate with the government or have their own separate trials. My lawyer and I filed twenty-two motions from the day I was indicted until the day I went to trial, and only one was granted. And it was a useless win.

The Department of Justice, through its FBI and U.S. Attorney's Office in D.C., threw everything it had against Barry Rafko and his confederates, including one congressman and one of his aides. It didn't matter if a couple of us might be innocent, nor did it matter that our version of the truth would be distorted by the government.

There I was, sitting in a crowded courtroom with seven other defendants, including the most nefarious political operative Washington had produced in decades. I was guilty all right. Guilty of stupidity for allowing myself to fall into such a mess.

After the jury was selected, the U.S. Attorney offered me one last deal. Plead to one RICO violation, pay a fine of $10,000, and serve two years.

Once again, I told him to go to hell. I was innocent.

CHAPTER 8

Mr. Victor Westlake
Assistant Director, FBI
Hoover Building   **PLEASE FORWARD**
935 Pennsylvania Avenue
Washington, D.C. 20535

Dear Mr. Westlake:
My name is Malcolm Bannister, and I am an inmate at the
Federal Prison Camp at Frostburg, Maryland. On Monday,
February 21, 2011, I met with two of your agents investigating
the murder of Judge Fawcett—Agents Hanski and Erardi. Nice
guys and all, but I got the feeling they were not too impressed
with me and my story.

According to this morning's reports in the Washington Post,
New York Times, Wall Street Journal, and Roanoke
Times, you and your team are still chasing your tails and don't
have much of a clue. I have no way of knowing if you have a
list of credible suspects, but I can guarantee you the real killer is
not on any list compiled by you and your team.

As I explained to Hanski and Erardi, I know the identity of the
killer, and I know his motive.

*In case Hanski and Erardi screwed up the details, and by the
way their note taking was not too impressive, here is my idea
of a deal: I reveal the killer, and you (the Government) agree
to my release from prison. I will not consider some type of
conditional suspension of my sentence. I will not consider parole.
I walk out, a free man, with a new identity and protection by
the guys on your side.*

*Obviously, such a deal will necessitate the involvement of the
Department of Justice and the U.S. Attorney's offices in both
the Northern and the Southern Districts of Virginia.*

*Also, I want the reward money, to which I will be entitled.
According to the* Roanoke Times *this morning, it has just
been increased to $150,000.*

Please feel free to continue chasing your tails.

As a couple of former Marines, we really should talk.

You know where to find me.
Sincerely, Malcolm Bannister #44861-127

My celly is a nineteen-year-old black kid from Baltimore, in
for eight years for selling crack. Gerard is like a thousand other
guys I've seen in the past five years, a young black from the inner
cities whose mother was a teenager when he was born and whose
father was long gone. He dropped out of school in the tenth grade
and found a job as a dishwasher. When his mother went to prison,
he moved in with his grandmother, who was also raising a horde
of cousins. He started using crack, then selling it. In spite of a life
on the streets, Gerard is a kindly soul with no mean streak. He has

no history of violence and no business wasting his life in prison. He's one of a million young blacks being warehoused by the taxpayers. We're approaching 2.5 million prisoners in this country, by far the highest rate of incarceration in any semicivilized nation.

It's not unusual to get a celly you really don't like. I had one who required little sleep, and he played his iPod throughout the night. He had earphones, which are required after 10:00 p.m., but the volume was so high I could still hear the music. It took me three months to get a transfer. Gerard, though, understands the rules. He told me he once slept in an abandoned car for weeks and almost froze to death. Anything is better than that.

Gerard and I begin each day at 6:00 a.m. when a buzzer wakes us. We dress quickly in our prison work clothes, careful to give each other as much space as our ten-by-twelve cell will allow. We make our bunks. He has the top one, and because of my seniority I have the bottom. At 6:30, we hustle over to the chow hall for breakfast.

The chow hall has invisible barriers that dictate where one sits and eats. There is a section for the blacks, one for the whites, and one for the browns. Intermingling is frowned upon and almost never happens. Even though Frostburg is a camp, it is still a prison, with a lot of stress. One of the most important rules of etiquette is to respect each other's space. Never cut in line. Never reach for anything. If you want the salt and pepper, ask someone to pass them, please. At Louisville, my prior home, fights were not unusual in the chow hall, and they were usually started when some jackass with sharp elbows infringed on someone else's space.

Here, though, we eat slowly and with manners that are surprising for a bunch of convicted criminals. Out of our cramped cells, we enjoy the wider spaces of the chow hall. There is a lot of ribbing, and crude jokes, and talk of women. I've known men who spent time in the hole, or solitary confinement, and the worst part of it is the lack of social interaction. A few handle it well, but most start cracking up after a few days. Even the worst loners, and there are plenty of them in prison, need people around them.

After breakfast, Gerard reports to work as a janitor scrubbing floors. I have an hour of downtime before I report to the library, and this is when I walk over to the coffee room and start reading newspapers.

Again, today, there appears to be little progress in the Fawcett investigation. Interestingly, though, his oldest son complained to a reporter from the *Post* that the FBI is doing a lousy job of keeping the family updated. No response from the FBI.

With each passing day, the pressure mounts.

Yesterday a reporter wrote that the FBI was interested in the former husband of Naomi Clary. Their divorce three years ago had been contentious, with both parties accusing the other of adultery. According to the reporter, his sources were telling him the FBI had interrogated this ex-husband at least twice.

The library is in an annex that also houses a small chapel and nurses' station. It is exactly forty feet long and thirty feet wide, with four cubicles for privacy, five desktop computers, and three long tables where inmates are allowed to read, write, and do research. There are also ten stacked tiers that hold, at any given time, about fifteen hundred books, mostly hardbacks. At Frostburg, we are allowed to keep up to ten paperbacks in our cells, though virtually everyone has more. An inmate may visit the library in his off-hours, and the rules are fairly flexible. Two books per week may be checked out, and I spend half of my time keeping up with past-due books.

I spend a fourth of my time as a jailhouse lawyer, and today I have a new client. Roman comes to me from a small town in North Carolina where he owned a pawnshop that specialized in fencing stolen goods, guns primarily. His suppliers were a couple of gangs of coke-crazed idiots who robbed fine homes in broad daylight. Possessing not the slightest hint of sophistication, the thieves were caught in the act and within minutes were squealing on each other. Roman was soon dragged in and hit with all manner of federal violations. He pleaded ignorance, but it turns out his court-appointed lawyer was without a doubt the dumbest person in the courtroom.

I do not claim to be an expert on criminal law, but any green first-year law student could catalog the mistakes made by Roman's lawyer during the trial. Roman was convicted and sentenced to seven years, and his case is now on appeal. He hauls in his "legal papers," the same pile every inmate is allowed to keep in his cell, and we go through them in my little office, a cubicle littered with my personal stuff and off-limits to every other inmate. Roman will not shut up ranting about how bad his defense lawyer was, and it doesn't take me long to agree. IAC (ineffective assistance of counsel) is a common complaint for those convicted at trial, but it's rarely grounds for an appellate reversal in non–death-penalty cases.

I'm excited by the possibility of attacking the lousy performance of a lawyer who's still out there, still making a living and pretending to be much better than he is. I spend an hour with Roman and we make an appointment for another meeting.

It was one of my early clients who told me about Judge Fawcett. The man was desperate to get out of prison, and he thought I could work miracles. He knew precisely what was in the safe in the basement of that cabin, and he was obsessed with getting his hands on it before it disappeared.

CHAPTER 9

I'm back in the warden's office and something is up. He's wearing a dark suit, starched white shirt, paisley tie, and his pointed-toe cowboy boots are fairly gleaming with fresh wax and polish. He's still smug as ever but somewhat twitchy.

"I don't know what you told them, Bannister," he's saying, "but they like your story. I hate to repeat myself, but if this is your idea of a prank, then you'll pay dearly for it."

"It's not a prank, sir." I suspect the warden was eavesdropping next door and knows exactly what I told them.

"They sent four agents here two days ago, snooped all over the place, wanted to know who you hung out with, who you did legal work for, who you played checkers with, where you worked, who you ate with, who you showered with, who you celled with, and on and on."

"I shower alone."

"I guess they're trying to figure out who your buddies are, is that right?"

"I don't know, sir, but I'm not surprised. I figured as much." I knew the FBI was snooping around Frostburg, though I did not see the agents. Secrets are extremely hard to keep in prison, especially when outsiders appear and start asking questions. In my opinion, and based on some experience, it was a clumsy way to dig into my background.

"Well, they're back," he says. "They'll be here at ten and they said it might take some time."

It is five minutes before 10:00 a.m. The same sharp pain hits my gut again, and I try to breathe deeply without appearing obvious. I shrug, as if it's no big deal. "Who's coming?" I ask.

"Hell if I know."

Seconds later, his phone buzzes, and his secretary relays a message.

We're in the same room adjacent to the warden's office. He, of course, is not present. Agents Hanski and Erardi are back, along with a fierce young man named Dunleavy, an assistant U.S. Attorney from the Southern District of Virginia, Roanoke office.

I'm gathering steam, gaining credibility and curiosity. My little group of interrogators is looking more impressive.

Though Dunleavy is the youngest of the three, he is a federal prosecutor, and the other two are simply federal cops. Therefore, Dunleavy has seniority at this moment and seems rather full of himself, not an unusual posture for a man in such a position. He can't be more than five years out of law school, and I assume he'll do most of the talking.

"Obviously, Mr. Bannister," he begins with an obnoxious condescending tone, "we wouldn't be here if we didn't have some interest in your little story."

Little story. What a prick.

"Can I call you Malcolm?" he asks.

"Let's stick with Mr. Bannister and Mr. Dunleavy, for now anyway," I respond. I'm an inmate, and I haven't been called Mr. Bannister in years. I kind of like the sound of it.

"You got it," he snaps, then quickly reaches into a pocket. He pulls out a slender recording device and places it on the table, halfway between me on one side and the three of them on the other. "I'd like to record our conversation, if that's okay."

And with that, my cause takes a giant leap forward. A week ago, Hanski and Erardi were reluctant to remove their pens and take a few notes. Now the government wants to capture every word. I shrug and say, "I don't care."

He flips a switch and says, "Now, you say you know who killed Judge Fawcett, and you want to swap this information for a ticket out of here. And once out, you want our protection. That the basic structure of the arrangement?"

"You got it," I say, mimicking his own words.

"Why should we believe you?"

"Because I know the truth, and because you guys are nowhere near it."

"How do you know this?"

"I just do. If you had a serious suspect, you wouldn't be here talking to me."

"Are you in contact with the killer?"

"I'm not answering that question."

"You gotta give us something, Mr. Bannister, something that will make us feel better about this little deal of yours."

"I wouldn't characterize it as little."

"Then we'll call it whatever you want. Why don't you explain it. How do you see this big deal happening?"

"Okay. It has to be a secret, highly confidential. We have a written agreement, approved by the U.S. Attorney's offices in both the Northern District, where I was prosecuted and sentenced, and the Southern District, where this investigation is taking place. Judge Slater, who sentenced me, will have to sign off on the agreement. Once we've agreed, then I'll give you the name of the killer. You grab him, investigate him, and when the grand jury indicts him for the murder, I will suddenly be transferred to another prison. Except I will not be serving any more time. I leave here as though I'm being transferred, but instead I go into your witness protection program. My sentence will be commuted, my record expunged, my name changed, and I'll probably want some plastic surgery to alter my appearance. I'll get new papers, new looks, a nice federal job somewhere, and, to boot, I get the reward money."

Three stone faces stare at me. Dunleavy finally says, "Is that all?"

"That's it. And it's not negotiable."

"Wow," Dunleavy mumbles, as if in shock. "I guess you've had plenty of time to think about this."

"Far more than you."

"What if you're wrong? What if we pick up the wrong guy, somehow get an indictment, you walk, then we can't prove a case?"

"That'll be your problem. You screw up the prosecution, then it's your fault."

"Okay, but once we have our man, how much evidence will there be?"

"You have the entire federal government at your disposal. Certainly you guys can find enough evidence once you have the killer. I can't do everything for you."

For drama, Dunleavy stands and stretches and paces to one end of the room, as if tortured and deep in thought. Then he returns, takes his seat, glares at me. "I think we're wasting our time here," he says, a bad bluff delivered lamely by a kid who has no business even being in the room. Hanski, the veteran, lowers his head slightly and blinks his eyes. He can't believe how bad this guy is. Erardi never takes his eyes off me, and I can sense the desperation. I can also feel the tension between the FBI and the U.S. Attorney's Office, which is not at all unusual.

I slowly get to my feet and say, "You're right. We're wasting our time. I'm not meeting with you again until you boys send in someone with more than peach fuzz. I've given you my deal, and the next time we chat I want Mr. Victor Westlake at the table, along with one of your bosses, Mr. Dunleavy. And if you're in the room, then I'll walk out."

With that, I leave. I glance back as I close the door, and Hanski is rubbing his temples.

They'll be back.

⸺

The meeting could have been scheduled to take place at the Hoover Building on Pennsylvania Avenue, in Washington. Victor Westlake would have been happy to return home briefly, see the boss, check on his staff, have a nice dinner with his family, and so on. However, the Director wanted to take a quick road trip. He needed to get away from the building for a few hours, so he loaded his entourage onto a sleek private jet, one of four controlled by the FBI, and took off for Roanoke, a forty-minute flight.

His name was George McTavey, aged sixty-one, a career man and not a political appointee, though his politics currently had him in hot water with the President. According to the relentless gossip inside the Beltway, McTavey was barely hanging on to his job. The President wanted a new Director of the FBI. After fourteen years, McTavey needed to go. Morale was low inside the Hoover Building, so the gossip went. In the past few months, McTavey rarely passed up a chance to leave Washington, if only for a few hours.

And it was almost refreshing to focus on such an old-fashioned crime as murder. He had been fighting terror for ten years now, and there had yet to be even the slightest hint that Fawcett's death was related to al-Qaeda or homegrown cells. Gone were the glory days of fighting organized crime and chasing counterfeiters.

In Roanoke, a black SUV was waiting at the bottom of the

jet's staircase, and McTavey and his team were rushed away as if snipers were watching and waiting. A minute later they rolled to a stop outside the Freezer and hustled inside.

A field visit by the Director had two purposes. The first was to raise the spirits of the task force and let them know that in spite of their lack of progress their work had the highest priority. The second was to ratchet up the pressure. After a quick tour of the makeshift facilities and a round of handshakes that would have impressed a politician, Director McTavey was led to the largest meeting room for the briefing.

He sat next to Victor Westlake, an old friend, and they munched on doughnuts as a senior investigator gave a windy summary of the latest, which wasn't much at all. McTavey didn't need to be briefed in person. Since the murder, he'd been talking to Westlake at least twice a day.

"Let's talk about this Bannister fellow," McTavey said after half an hour of a dull narrative that was going nowhere. Another report was quickly passed around the table. "This is the latest," Westlake said. "We started with high school classmates, then moved on to college and law school, and there are no viable suspects. No record of any friends or close acquaintances, of no one, really, who ever crossed paths with Judge Fawcett. No gang members or drug dealers or serious criminals. Next we tracked down as many of his former clients as possible, though this was difficult because we can't get access to a lot of his old files. Again, no one of interest there. He did the small-town-lawyer gig for about ten years, with two older African-American lawyers, and it was a squeaky-clean operation."

"Did he do business in Judge Fawcett's court?" McTavey asked.

"There's no record of him handling a case there. He didn't do much federal work, and besides he was in the Northern District of Virginia. It's fair to say that Mr. Bannister was not a widely sought-after trial lawyer."

"So you believe that whoever killed Fawcett is someone Mr. Bannister met in prison, assuming, of course, we believe he knows the truth."

"Correct. He served the first twenty-two months of his sentence in Louisville, Kentucky, a medium-security facility with two thousand inmates. He had three different cell mates, and he worked in the laundry and the kitchen. He also developed his skills as a jailhouse lawyer and actually helped at least five inmates get out of prison. We have a list of about fifty men he probably knew fairly well, but frankly it's impossible to know everyone he came into contact with at Louisville. And the same at Frostburg. He's been there for the past three years and has served time with a thousand men."

"How long is your list?" McTavey asked.

"We have about 110 names, give or take, but we don't feel too confident about most of these guys."

"How many were sentenced by Fawcett?"

"Six."

"So there's no clear suspect in Bannister's prison history?"

"Not yet, but we're still digging. Bear in mind, this is our second theory, the one that assumes whoever killed the judge was carrying a grudge because of a bad outcome in his court. Our first theory is that it was an old-fashioned murder-robbery."

"Do you have a third theory?" McTavey asked.

"The jealous ex-husband of the dead secretary," Westlake replied.

"That's not credible, right?"

"Right."

"Do you have a fourth theory?"

"No, not at this time."

Director McTavey sipped his coffee and said, "This is really bad coffee." Two flunkies at the far end of the room bolted to attention and disappeared in search of something better.

"Sorry," Westlake said. It was widely known that the Director was a serious coffee man and to provide a brew that didn't measure up was an embarrassment.

"And Bannister's background again?" he asked.

"Ten years, RICO, got caught up in the Barry Rafko mess a few years back, though he wasn't a big player. He had handled some land deals for Barry and got himself convicted."

"So he was not in bed with sixteen-year-old girls?"

"Oh no, that was just our congressmen. Bannister appears to be a good guy, former Marine and all, just picked the wrong client."

"Well, was he guilty?"

"The jury felt so. As did the judge. You don't get ten years unless you've screwed up somewhere."

Another cup of coffee was placed in front of the Director, who sniffed it, then finally took a sip as everyone stopped breathing. Then another sip, and everyone exhaled.

"Why do we believe Bannister?" McTavey asked.

Westlake quickly passed the buck. "Hanski."

Agent Chris Hanski was sitting on go. He cleared his throat and dove in. "Well, I'm not sure we believe Bannister, but he makes a good impression. I've interviewed him twice, watched him carefully, and I've seen no signs of deception. He's bright, shrewd, and has nothing to gain by lying to us. After five years in prison, it's quite possible he bumped into someone who wanted to knock off Judge Fawcett or to rob him."

"And we really have no idea who this person might be, right?"

Hanski looked at Victor Westlake, who said, "As of today, that's right. But we're still digging."

"I don't like our chances of discovering the identity of the killer based on who Mr. Bannister may have bumped into in prison," McTavey said, sounding perfectly logical. "We could be chasing dead ends for the next ten years. What's the downside of cutting a deal with Bannister? Look, the guy is a white-collar crook who has already served five years for criminal activity that seems rather harmless in the scheme of things. Don't you think so, Vic?"

Vic was nodding gravely.

McTavey pressed on: "So the guy gets out of prison. It's not as though we're releasing a serial killer or a sexual predator. If the guy is right, then this case is solved and we can go home. If the guy is conning us, what's the big deal?"

At that moment, no one around the table could envision a big deal.

"Who will object to it?" McTavey asked.

"The U.S. Attorney's Office is not on board," Westlake said.

"No surprise there," McTavey said. "I'm meeting with the Attorney General tomorrow afternoon. I can neutralize the U.S. Attorney. Any other problems?"

Hanski cleared his throat again. "Well, sir, Mr. Bannister insists he will not give us the name until a federal judge signs an order of commutation. I'm not sure how this will work, but the commuting of his sentence will become automatic when the grand jury indicts our mystery guy."

McTavey brushed him off. "We got lawyers to handle all that. Does Bannister have one?"

"Not that I know of."

"Does he need one?"

"I'll be happy to ask him," Hanski said.

"Let's get this deal done, okay?" McTavey said impatiently. "There's a big upside and a small downside. Based on our progress so far, we're due for a break."

CHAPTER 10

A month has passed since the murders of Judge Fawcett and Naomi Clary. Newspaper reports of the investigation have become shorter and less frequent. The FBI had no comment in the beginning, and after a month of frantic work with nothing to show for it, the task force seems to have vanished now. In the past month, an earthquake in Bolivia, a school-yard shooting in Kansas, the overdose of one rap star and the detoxification of another have all conspired to divert our attention to more important matters.

This is all good news for me. The investigation may appear quiet on the surface, but internally the pressure grows. My worst nightmare is a bold headline announcing the arrest of someone, but that appears less and less likely. The days pass, and I wait patiently.

I see clients by appointment only. I meet them at my cubicle in the library. They haul in their legal papers, a stack of assorted pleadings, orders, motions, and rulings that as inmates we have the right to keep in our cells. The COs cannot touch our legal papers.

For most of my clients, two appointments will suffice to convince them that there is nothing to be done with their cases. During the first appointment, we review the basics, and I go through their papers. Then I'll spend a few hours doing research. During the second appointment, I usually deliver the bad news that they're out of luck. There's no loophole to save them.

In five years, I have helped six inmates gain early release from prison. Needless to say, this adds mightily to my reputation as a masterful jailhouse lawyer, but I caution every new client that the odds are stacked heavily against him.

This is what I explain to young Otis Carter, a twenty-three-year-old father of two who'll spend the next fourteen months here at Frostburg for a crime that should not have been a crime. Otis is a country boy, a Baptist with a deep faith, a happily married electrician who still cannot believe he's in a federal prison. He and his grandfather were indicted and charged with violating the Civil War Battlefield and Artifact Preservation Act of 1979 (as amended in 1983, 1989, 1997, 2002, 2008, and 2010). His grandfather, aged seventy-four and suffering from emphysema, is in a Federal Medical Center in Tennessee, also serving fourteen months. Because of his medical condition, he will cost the taxpayers about $25,000 a month.

The Carters were hunting for artifacts on their two-hundred-acre farm adjacent to the New Market Battlefield State Historical Park, in the Shenandoah Valley, less than an hour from my hometown of Winchester. The farm has been in the family for over a hundred years, and from the time he could walk, Otis accompanied his grandfather as he "went digging" for Civil War relics and souvenirs. Over the decades, his family assembled an impressive collection of minié balls, cannonballs, canteens, brass buttons, pieces of uniforms, a couple of battle flags, and several dozen guns of all varieties. This they had done legally. It is illegal to remove artifacts and relics from a National Historic Landmark, which is federal land, and the Carters were well aware of this law. Their private little museum, in a converted hay barn, was stocked with items they had found on their own property.

However, in 2010, the Civil War Battlefield and Artifact Preservation Act was amended again. In response to efforts by preservationists to restrict development near battlefields, some last-minute language was added to a one-hundred-page amendment. It became illegal to dig for relics "within two miles" of the borders of a National Historic Landmark, regardless of whose land one happened to be digging on. The Carters were not informed of the new rules; indeed, the language was buried so deep in the amendment virtually no one knew about it.

Over the years, the federal agents had harassed Otis's grandfather and accused him of digging on protected land. They periodically stopped by his home and demanded to see his museum. When the law changed, they waited patiently until they caught Otis and his grandfather scouring a wooded area of Carter property with metal detectors. The Carters hired a lawyer who advised them to plead guilty. Criminal intent is no longer required for many federal crimes. Lack of knowledge is no defense.

As the victim of the Racketeer Influenced and Corrupt Organizations Act (RICO), an often misguided and famously flexible federal law, I am keenly interested in the proliferation of the federal criminal code, now at twenty-seven thousand pages and counting. The Constitution names only three federal offenses: treason, piracy, and counterfeiting. Today there are over forty-five hundred federal crimes, and the number continues to grow as Congress gets tougher on crime and federal prosecutors become more creative in finding ways to apply all their new laws.

Otis could possibly attack the constitutionality of the amended law. This would take several years of litigation and would drag on long after he's paroled and back home with his family. As I explain this to him during our second meeting, he seems to lose interest. If he can't get out right now, why bother? But the case intrigues me. We decide to discuss it later.

If my grand scheme falls flat, I might take Otis's case and fight all the way to the Supreme Court. That will keep me busy for the next five years.

———

The Supreme Court has twice refused to consider my case. Though we couldn't prove it, there was a strong feeling that my appeals were hurried through the system because of the government's enthusiasm in putting away Barry Rafko and his confederates, me included.

I was convicted in November 2005 and sentenced two months later to ten years. At my sentencing I was "remanded," which meant I was taken into custody. A few lucky federal felons are allowed to "self-surrender," or remain free until ordered to report to a facility. They have time to prepare, but most are not given this luxury.

My lawyer thought I would get five or six years. Barry the Backhander, the star defendant, the target, the colorful villain everyone enjoyed hating, got twelve years. Surely I deserved less than half the time of that slimeball. Dionne, my beautiful and loving and fiercely supportive wife, was in the courtroom, sitting bravely next to my humiliated father. I was the only one of the eight sentenced that day, and as I stood before Judge Slater, with my lawyer to my right, I had trouble breathing. This cannot be happening, I said to myself, over and over, as I took in the blurred images around me. I don't deserve this. I can explain. I am not guilty. Slater scolded and preached and played for the press, and I felt like a battered heavyweight in the fifteenth round, sagging on the ropes, covering my face, waiting for the next shot to the face. My knees were putty. I was sweating.

When Judge Slater said "ten years," I heard a gasp behind me as Dionne collapsed in tears. As they led me away, I glanced back for the last time. I've seen this a hundred times in movies, TV shows, and in real-life court reporting—the last, frantic farewell look of the condemned. What do you think about as you're leaving the courtroom and you're not going home? The truth is that nothing is clear. There are too many random thoughts, too much fear, anger, and raw emotion to understand what is happening.

Dionne had both hands over her mouth, in shock, crying, tears everywhere. My father had his arm around her, trying to console her. That was the last thing I saw—my beautiful wife distraught and destroyed.

Now she's married to someone else.

Thanks to the federal government.

My jurors came from the District. A few appeared bright and educated, but most were not, shall I say, sophisticated. After three days of deliberations, they announced to the judge that they were making little progress. And who could blame them? By unloading a sizable chunk of the federal code, the prosecutors had adopted the timeworn strategy of throwing as much mud as possible against the wall and hoping something would stick. This overkill had turned what should have been a relatively easy case against Barry Rafko and the congressman into a legal quagmire. I had spent countless hours working on my own defense, and I couldn't understand all of the prosecution's theories. From the beginning, my lawyer had predicted a hung jury.

After four days of deliberations, Judge Slater delivered what is commonly referred to in trial circles as the "dynamite charge." This is basically a demand that the jurors get back there and reach a verdict, at all costs. You're not going home until we have a verdict! Such a charge rarely works, but I wasn't so lucky. An hour later, the exhausted and emotionally spent jurors returned with unanimous verdicts against all defendants, on all counts. It was obvious to me and many others that they did not understand most of the code sections and intricate theories used by the prosecution. One of the jurors was later quoted as saying, "We just assumed they were guilty, or else they wouldn't have been charged in the first place." I used this quote in my appeals, but it apparently went unheard.

I watched the jurors carefully throughout the trial, and they were overwhelmed from the opening statements. And why shouldn't they have been? Nine different lawyers gave their versions of what had happened. The courtroom had to be redesigned and renovated to make room for all of the defendants and all their lawyers.

The trial was a spectacle, a farce, a ridiculous way to search for the truth. But as I learned, the truth was not important. Perhaps in another era, a trial was an exercise in the presentation of facts, the search for truth, and the finding of justice. Now a trial is a contest in which one side will win and the other side will lose. Each side expects the other to bend the rules or to cheat, so neither side plays fair. The truth is lost in the melee.

Two months later I returned to the courtroom for the sentencing. My lawyer had requested that I be allowed to self-surrender, but Judge Slater was not impressed with our request. After he gave me ten years, he ordered me into remanded custody.

It is indeed remarkable that more federal judges are not shot. For weeks afterward, I conceived all manner of schemes to inflict a slow, torturous death upon Slater.

I was taken to the courtroom by the U.S. Marshals and led to a holding cell in the courthouse, then to the D.C. jail, where I was stripped, searched, given an orange jumpsuit, and placed in a crowded cell with six other inmates. There were only four cots. The first night I sat on the concrete floor, just me and my thin blanket with holes in it. The jail was a noisy zoo, overcrowded and understaffed, and sleep was impossible. I was too frightened and too stunned to close my eyes, so I sat in a corner and listened to the yells and screams and threats until dawn. I stayed there a week, eating little, sleeping little, urinating in a filthy open toilet that didn't flush and was within ten feet of my cell mates. At one time, there were ten of us in the cell. I never showered. A bowel movement required an urgent plea to visit the "shit room" down the hall.

The transporting of federal prisoners is done by the U.S. Marshals, and it is a nightmare. Prisoners of all security levels are lumped together, with no regard for our crimes or the risks we might pose. Therefore, we were all treated like savage murderers. With every movement my hands were cuffed, my ankles chained, and I was attached to the inmate in front of me and the one behind. The mood is nasty. The marshals have one job—to move the inmates safely with no escapes. The inmates, many of them rookies like me, are frightened, frustrated, and bewildered.

Fourteen of us left D.C. on a bus, an unmarked rig that had hauled schoolchildren decades earlier, and headed south. The handcuffs and chains were not removed. A marshal with a shotgun sat in the front seat. After four hours, we stopped at a county jail in North Carolina. We were given a wet sandwich and allowed to urinate behind the bus, still chained and bound. The handcuffs and leg irons were never removed. After two hours of waiting, we left with three additional prisoners and headed west. For the next six days, we stopped at county jails in North Carolina, Tennessee, and Alabama, picking up prisoners, occasionally dropping one off, sleeping in a different cell each night.

The county jails were the worst: tiny cramped cells with no heat, air-conditioning, sunlight, or suitable sanitation; food that dogs would ignore; little water; Bubbas for guards; a much higher threat of violence; local inmates who resented the intrusion of "federal prisoners." I could not believe conditions so deplorable existed in this country, but I was naive. As our journey continued and our moods soured, there was a marked increase in the level of bitching on the bus. This ceased when a veteran inmate explained the concept of "diesel therapy." Complain or make trouble, and the marshals will keep you on the bus for weeks and give you a free tour of dozens of county jails.

There was no hurry. The marshals can transport prisoners during daylight hours only; thus the distances tend to be short. They had absolutely no interest in our comfort or privacy.

We eventually made it to a distribution center in Atlanta, a notoriously bad place where I was kept in solitary confinement for twenty-three hours a day while my paperwork inched across someone's desk in Washington. After three weeks of this, I was losing my sanity. Nothing to read, no one to chat with, terrible food, bad guards. Eventually, we were re-shackled and loaded onto another bus and driven to the Atlanta airport where we boarded an unmarked cargo plane. Chained to a hard plastic bench and sitting knee to knee, we flew to Miami, though we had no idea where we were headed. One of the marshals kindly informed us. In Miami we picked up a few more, then flew to New Orleans, where we sat in suffocating humidity for an hour as the marshals loaded on even more.

On the plane, we were allowed to talk, and the chatter was refreshing. Most of us had just endured days of solitary, so we plunged into conversation. This was not the first trip for some of the boys, and they told other stories of being transported in chains, courtesy of the federal government. I began to hear descriptions of prison life.

At dark, we arrived in Oklahoma City, where we were shuffled onto a bus and taken to another distribution center. The place was not quite as bad as Atlanta, but by then I was thinking about suicide. After five days in solitary confinement, we were re-shackled and taken back to the airport. We flew into Texas, world capital of lethal injection, and I daydreamed of seeing the needle stuck into my arm and floating away. Eight tough guys, all Hispanic, boarded "Con Air" in Dallas, and we flew to Little Rock,

then Memphis, then Cincinnati, where my flying days ended. I
spent six nights in a tough city jail before a pair of marshals drove
me to the prison in Louisville, Kentucky.

Louisville is five hundred miles from my hometown of Winchester, Virginia. Had I been allowed to self-surrender, my father
and I would have made the drive in about eight hours. He would
have dropped me off at the front gate and said good-bye.

Forty-four days, twenty-six of them in solitary, too many
stops to remember. There is no logic in this system and no one
cares. No one is watching.

The real tragedy of the federal criminal system is not the
absurdities. It is the ruined and wasted lives. Congress demands
long, harsh sentences, and for the violent thugs these are appropriate. Hardened criminals are locked away in "U.S. Pens," fortresses
where gangs are rampant and murders are routine. But the majority of federal prisoners are nonviolent, and many are convicted of
crimes that involved little, if any, criminal activity.

For the rest of my life I will be regarded as a criminal, and I
refuse to accept this. I will have a life, freed from my past and far
away from the tentacles of the federal government.

CHAPTER 11

Rule 35 of the Federal Rules of Criminal Procedure provides the only mechanism for the commutation of a prison sentence. Its logic is brilliant and fits my situation perfectly. If an inmate can solve another crime, one that the Feds have an interest in, then the inmate's sentence can be reduced. Of course, this takes the cooperation of the investigating authorities—FBI, DEA, CIA, ATF, and so on—and of the court from which the inmate was sentenced.

If all goes as planned, I may soon have the privilege of seeing the Honorable Judge Slater, and it will be on my terms.

The Feds are back.

The warden is much nicer to me these days. He figures he has a prize that some big people desire, and he needs to be in the thick of things. I take a seat at his desk and he asks if I want coffee. This offer is almost too surreal to comprehend—the almighty warden offering coffee to an inmate.

"Sure," I say. "Black."

He punches a button and relays our wishes to a secretary. I notice he's wearing cuff links today, a good sign.

"Got the big boys here today, Mal," he informs me smugly, as if he's coordinating all efforts to find the murderer. Since we are such good pals now, he's using my first name. Until now it's been Bannister this and Bannister that.

"Who?" I ask.

"The director of the task force, Victor Westlake, from Washington, and a bunch of lawyers. I'd say you have their attention."

I cannot keep from smiling, but only for a second.

"This guy who killed Judge Fawcett, was he ever here, at Frostburg?" the warden asks.

"Sorry, Warden, I can't answer that."

"Either here or Louisville, I take it."

"Maybe, or maybe I knew him before prison."

He frowns and rubs his chin. "I see," he mumbles.

The coffee arrives, on a tray, and for the first time in years I drink from a cup not made of plastic or paper. We kill a few minutes talking about nothing. At 11:05, his secretary informs him through the intercom on his desk, "They are in place." I follow him through the door and into the same conference room.

Five men in the same dark suits, same white shirts with button-down collars, same bland ties. If I had seen them in a crowd from half a mile away, I could have said, "Yep, Feds."

We go through the usual stiff introductions and the warden reluctantly excuses himself. I sit on one side of the table and my five new buddies sit on the other. Victor Westlake is in the middle, and to his right are Agent Hanski and a new face, Agent Sasswater. Neither of these two will say a word. To the left of Westlake are the two assistant U.S. Attorneys—Mangrum from the Southern District of Virginia and Craddock from the Northern. The rookie Dunleavy got left behind.

Thunderstorms had rolled through just after midnight, and Westlake begins by saying, "Quite a storm last night, huh?"

I narrow my eyes and stare at him. "Seriously? You want to talk about the weather?"

This really pisses him off, but he's a pro. A smile, a grunt, then,

"No, Mr. Bannister, I'm not here to talk about the weather. My boss thinks we should make a deal with you, so that's why I'm here."

"Great. And, yes, it was quite a storm."

"We'd like to hear your terms."

"I think you know them. We use Rule 35. We sign an agreement, all of us, in which I give you the name of the man who killed Judge Fawcett. You pick him up, investigate him, do your thing, and when a federal grand jury indicts him, I walk. That very day. I transfer out of Frostburg and disappear into witness protection. No more time; no more criminal record; no more Malcolm Bannister. The deal is confidential, locked away, buried, and signed by the Attorney General."

"The AG?"

"Yes sir. I don't trust you or anyone in this room. I don't trust Judge Slater or any other federal judge, prosecutor, assistant prosecutor, FBI agent, or anybody else working for the federal government. The paperwork must be perfect; the deal unbreakable. When the killer is indicted, I walk. Period."

"Will you use an attorney?"

"No sir. I can handle that."

"Fair enough."

Mangrum suddenly produces a file and removes several copies of a document. He slides one across the table, and it comes to a rest in front of me, in perfect position. I glance at it and my heart begins to pound. The heading is the same as all of the motions and orders filed in my case: "In the United States District Court of Washington, D.C.; United States of America versus Malcolm W. Bannister." In the center of the page, in all caps, are the words "RULE 35 MOTION."

"This is a proposed court order," Mangrum says. "It's just a starting point, but we've spent some time on it."

Two days later, I am placed in the rear seat of a Ford SUV and driven away from Frostburg, my first exit from the camp since the day I arrived three years earlier. No leg chains today, but my wrists are cuffed in front of me. My two buddies are U.S. Marshals, names withheld, but they are nice enough. After we get through the weather, one of them asks if I've heard any good jokes. Lock away six hundred men and give them plenty of idle time, and the jokes come in waves.

"Clean or dirty?" I ask, though there are few clean jokes in prison.

"Oh, dirty of course," the driver says.

I tell a couple and get some good laughs as the miles fly by. We're on Interstate 68, zipping through Hagerstown, and the feeling of freedom is exhilarating. In spite of the handcuffs, I can almost taste the life out there. I watch the traffic and dream of owning and driving a car again, of going anywhere. I see fast-food restaurants at the interchanges and I salivate at the thought of a burger and fries. I see a couple walking hand in hand into a store, and I can almost feel the touch of her flesh. A beer sign in the window of a bar makes me thirsty. A billboard advertising Caribbean cruises takes me to another world. I feel as if I've been locked up for a century.

We turn south on Interstate 70 and are soon in the Washington-Baltimore sprawl. Three hours after we leave Frostburg, we arrive in the basement of the federal courthouse in downtown D.C. Inside the building, the handcuffs are removed; I proceed with one marshal in front of me, the other behind.

The meeting takes place in the chambers of Judge Slater, who's as prickly as ever and seems to have aged twenty years in the past five. He considers me a criminal and barely acknowledges my presence. Fine, I don't care. It is evident that a lot of conversations have taken place between his office, the U.S. Attorney's

Office, the FBI, and the Attorney General of the United States. At one point, I count eleven people around the table. The Rule 35 motion, with the attached agreement, has increased in size and runs for twenty-two pages. I have read every word five times. I even demanded some of my own language.

The agreement, in short, gives me everything I want. Freedom, a new identity, government protection, and the reward money of $150,000.

After the usual throat clearing, Judge Slater takes charge. "We will now go on the record," he says, and his court reporter begins her stenography. "Even though this is a confidential matter and the court's order will be sealed, I want a record of this hearing." A pause as he shuffles papers. "This is a motion by the United States for Rule 35 relief. Bannister, have you read this entire motion, agreement, and proposed order?"

"I have, Your Honor."

"And I believe you are an attorney, or, shall I say, were an attorney."

"That's correct, Your Honor."

"Does the motion, agreement, and order meet your approval?"

Damn right it does, old boy. "Yes sir."

He goes around the table and asks the same questions. It's all a formality because everyone has already agreed. And, most important, the Attorney General has signed the agreement.

Slater looks at me and says, "You understand, Mr. Bannister, that if the name you provide does not lead to an indictment, then the agreement is null and void after twelve months, your sentence will not be commuted, and you will serve the remaining time in full?"

"Yes sir."

"And that until there is an indictment you will remain in the custody of the Bureau of Prisons?"

"Yes sir."

After more discussion about the terms of the agreement,

Judge Slater signs the order and the hearing is over. He does not say farewell and I do not curse him the way I'd like to. Again, it's a miracle that more federal judges are not whacked.

I am swarmed by an entourage and led down the stairs to a room where more dark suits are waiting. A video camera has been set up for my benefit, and Mr. Victor Westlake is pacing. I am asked to sit at the end of the table, face the camera, and offered something to drink. It's a very nervous bunch, desperate to hear me utter the name.

CHAPTER 12

His name is Quinn Rucker, black male, aged thirty-eight, from Southwest D.C., convicted two years ago of distributing narcotics and sentenced to seven years. I met him at Frostburg. He walked away about three months ago and has not been seen since. He comes from a large family of drug dealers who've been active and successful for many years. These are not street dealers by any means. They are businessmen with contacts up and down the East Coast. They try to avoid violence but they are not afraid of it. They are disciplined, tough, and resourceful. Several have gone to prison. Several have been killed. To them, that's just part of the overhead."

I pause, take a breath. The room is silent.

At least five of the dark suits are taking notes. One has a laptop and has already pulled up the file on Quinn Rucker, who had made several cuts and was on the FBI's top-fifty list of suspects, primarily because of his time with me at Frostburg and his escape from it.

"As I said, I met Quinn at Frostburg, and we became friends. Like a lot of inmates, he was convinced I could file a magic motion and get him out, but not in his case. He was not doing well in prison because Frostburg was his first gig. This happens to some of the new guys who have not seen other prisons. They don't appreciate the camp atmosphere. Anyway, as his time dragged on he got restless. He couldn't imagine doing five more years. He has a wife, a couple of kids, cash from the family business, and a lot of insecurities. He was convinced some of his cousins were moving in, taking over his role, stealing his share. I listened to a lot of this but didn't swallow all of it. These gang guys are generally full of crap and like to exaggerate their stories, especially when it comes to money and violence. But I liked Quinn. He was probably the best friend I've made yet in prison. We never celled together but we were close."

"Do you know why he walked away?" Victor Westlake asks.

"I think so. Quinn was selling pot and doing well. He was also smoking a lot of it. As you know, the quickest way out of a federal camp is to get caught with drugs or alcohol. Strictly prohibited. Quinn got word through a snitch that the COs knew about his business and they were about to bust him. He's extremely smart and savvy, and he never kept the drugs in his cell. Like most of the guys who sell on the black market, he hid his inventory in common areas. The heat was on, and he knew if he got caught he'd be sent away to a tougher place. So he walked. I'm sure he didn't walk far. Probably had someone waiting close by."

"Do you know where he is now?"

I nod, take my time, say, "He has a cousin, don't know his name, but he owns a couple of strip clubs in Norfolk, Virginia, near the naval base. Find the cousin, and you'll find Quinn."

"Under what name?"

"I don't know, but it's not Quinn Rucker."

"How do you know this?"

"Sorry, but that's none of your business."

At this point, Westlake nods at an agent by the door, and he disappears. The search is on.

"Let's talk about Judge Fawcett," Westlake says.

"Okay," I reply. I cannot count the number of times I have lived for this moment. I have rehearsed this in the darkness of my cell when I couldn't sleep. I have written it in narrative form, then destroyed it. I have said the words out loud while taking long, lonely walks around the edges of Frostburg. It's hard to believe this is finally happening.

"A big part of his gang's business was running cocaine from Miami to the major cities along the East Coast, primarily the southern leg—Atlanta, Charleston, Raleigh, Charlotte, Richmond, and so on. Interstate 95 was the favored route because it is so heavily traveled, but the gang used every state highway and county road on the map. Most of it was mule running. They would pay a driver $5,000 to rent a car and haul a trunkload of coke to a distribution center in—pick a city. The mule would make the drop, then turn around and drive back to south Florida. According to Quinn, 90 percent of the coke snorted in Manhattan gets there in a car rented by a mule in Miami and driven north as if on legitimate business. Detection is virtually impossible. When mules are caught, it's because someone snitched. Anyway, Quinn had a nephew who was working his way up the ladder of the family business. The kid was mule running, and he got caught speeding on Interstate 81 just outside of Roanoke. He was in a rented Avis van and said he was delivering antique furniture to a store in Georgetown. There was indeed furniture in the van, but the real cargo was cocaine with a street value of $5 million. The state trooper was suspicious and called for a backup. The nephew knew the rules and refused to allow a search of the van. The second trooper was a rookie, a real eager beaver, and he began poking around the cargo bay of the van. He had no warrant, no probable cause, and no permission to search. When he found the cocaine, he went ballistic and everything changed."

I pause and take a sip of water. The agent with the laptop is pecking away, no doubt sending directives all over the East Coast.

"What is the nephew's name?" Westlake asks.

"I don't know, but I don't think his last name was Rucker. Within his family, there are several last names and a fair number of aliases."

"And so the nephew's case was assigned to Judge Fawcett?" Westlake asks, prompting me along, though no one seems to be in a hurry. They're hanging on every word and anxious to find Quinn Rucker, but they want the whole story.

"Yes, and Quinn hired a big lawyer in Roanoke, one who assured him the search was blatantly unconstitutional. If the search was thrown out by Fawcett, then so was the evidence. No evidence, no trial, no conviction, nothing. Somewhere in the process, Quinn learned that Judge Fawcett might look more favorably upon the nephew's case if some cash could change hands. Serious cash. According to Quinn, the deal was brokered by their lawyer. And, no, I do not know the name of the lawyer."

"How much cash?" Westlake asks.

"Half a million." This is met with great skepticism, and I am not surprised. "I found it hard to believe too. A federal judge taking a bribe. But then I was also shocked when an FBI agent was caught spying for the Russians. I guess under the right circumstances, a man will do just about anything."

"Let's stay on subject here," Westlake says, irritated.

"Sure. Quinn and the family paid the bribe. Fawcett took the bribe. The case crept along until one day when there was a hearing on the nephew's motion to exclude the evidence that was seized during a bad search. Much to everyone's surprise, the judge ruled against the nephew, in favor of the government, and ordered a trial. With no defense, the jury found the kid guilty, but the lawyer felt good about their chances on appeal. The case is still rattling on appeal. In the meantime, the nephew is serving an eighteen-year sentence in Alabama."

"This is a nice story, Mr. Bannister," Westlake says, "but how do you know Quinn Rucker killed the judge?"

"Because he told me he was going to do it, out of revenge and to retrieve his money. He talked about it often. He knew exactly where the judge lived, worked, and liked to spend his weekends. He suspected the money was hidden somewhere in the cabin, and he firmly believed he wasn't the only one who'd been ripped off by Fawcett. And, because he told me, Mr. Westlake, he will target me as soon as he's arrested. I might walk out of prison, but I'll always look over my shoulder. These people are very smart— look at your own investigation. Nothing. Not a clue. They hold grudges, and they are very patient. Quinn waited almost three years to kill the judge. He'll wait twenty years to get me."

"If he's so smart, why would he tell you all of this?" Westlake asks.

"Simple. Like a lot of inmates, Quinn thought I could file some brilliant motion, find a loophole, and get him out of prison. He said he would pay me; said I would get half of whatever he took off Judge Fawcett. I've heard this before, and since. I looked at Quinn's file and told him there was nothing I could do."

They have to believe I'm telling the truth. If Quinn Rucker is not indicted, then I'll spend the next five years in prison. We're still on opposite sides, me and them, but we're slowly reaching common ground.

CHAPTER 13

Six hours later, two black FBI agents paid the cover charge at the Velvet Club, three blocks away from the Norfolk Naval Base. They were dressed like construction workers and mixed easily with the crowd, which was half white, half black, half sailors, and half civilians. The dancers were also half-and-half, affirmative action all around. Two surveillance vans waited in the parking lot, along with a dozen more agents. Quinn Rucker had been spotted, photographed, and identified entering the club at 5:30. He worked as a bartender, and when he left his post at 8:45 to go to the restroom, he was followed. Inside the restroom, the two agents confronted him. After a brief discussion, they agreed to leave through a rear door. Quinn understood the situation and made no sudden moves. Nor did he seem surprised. As with many escapees, the end of the run was in many ways a relief. The dreams of freedom crumble under the challenges of living normally. Someone is always back there.

He was handcuffed and taken to the FBI office in Norfolk. In an interrogation room, the two black agents served him coffee and began a friendly chat. The crime was nothing more than an escape, and he had no defense. He was dead guilty and headed back to prison.

They asked Quinn if he was willing to answer a few basic questions about his escape some three months earlier. He said sure, why not? He volunteered that he had met an unnamed accomplice not far from the camp at Frostburg and had been driven back to D.C. He hung around there for a few days, but his presence was not well received. Escapees draw attention, and his boys did not appreciate the possibility of the FBI poking around and looking for him. He began muling cocaine from Miami to Atlanta, but the work was slow. He was damaged goods and his "syndicate," as he called it, was wary of him. He saw his wife and kids occasionally, but knew the danger of getting too close to home. He spent time with an old girlfriend in Baltimore, but she, too, was less than excited about his presence. He drifted around, picking up an occasional drug run, then got lucky when his cousin gave him a job tending bar at the Velvet Club.

Next door, in a larger interrogation room, two of the FBI's veteran interrogators were listening to the conversation. Another team was upstairs, waiting and listening. If things went well, it would be a long night for Quinn. Things had to go well for the FBI. With no physical evidence so far, it was imperative that the interrogation produce some proof. The FBI was worried, though, because they were dealing with a man who'd been around the block a few times. It was unlikely their suspect could be intimidated into saying much.

As soon as Quinn was taken out the back door of the Velvet Club, FBI agents cornered his cousin and demanded information. The cousin knew the ropes and had little to say until he was threatened with charges for harboring a fugitive. He had an impressive criminal record, state charges, and another indictment would likely send him back to the pen. He preferred life on the outside and began singing. Quinn was living and working under the assumed name of Jackie Todd, though his wages were being paid in cash and off the books. The cousin led the FBI agents to a run-down trailer park a half mile away and showed them the furnished mobile home Quinn was leasing month to month. Parked next to the trailer was a Hummer H3, 2008 model, with North Carolina license plates. The cousin explained that Quinn preferred to walk to work and hide the Hummer, weather permitting.

Within an hour, the FBI had a search warrant for the trailer and the Hummer, which was towed to a police lot in Norfolk, opened and examined. The main door of the mobile home was locked but flimsy. One good jolt with a bat hammer and the agents were inside. The place was remarkably neat and clean. Working with a purpose, six agents combed the place from side to side, twelve feet, and from end to end, fifty feet. In the only bedroom, between the mattress and the box spring, they found Quinn's wallet, keys, and cell phone. The wallet contained about $500 in cash, a fake North Carolina driver's license, and two prepaid Visa credit cards valued at $1,200 each. The cell phone was of the disposable, prepaid variety, perfect for a man on the run. Under the bed, the agents found a Smith & Wesson short-barrel, .38-caliber handgun, loaded with hollow-point bullets.

Handling it carefully, the agents immediately assumed it was the same handgun used to kill Judge Fawcett and Naomi Clary.

The key chain included a key to a mini–storage unit two miles away. In a drawer in the kitchen, an agent found Quinn's home office—a couple of manila files with scant paperwork. One form, though, was a six-month lease agreement for a unit at Macon's Mini-Storage, signed by Jackie Todd. The lead investigator called Roanoke, where a federal magistrate was on duty, and a search warrant was e-mailed back to Norfolk.

The file also included a North Carolina car title issued to Jackie Todd for the 2008 Hummer H3. No liens were noted; thus it was safe to assume Mr. Todd had paid in full, on the spot, either in cash or by check. No checkbook or bank statements were found in the drawer; none were expected. A bill of sale for the vehicle revealed that it was purchased on February 9, 2011, from a used-car lot in Roanoke. February 9 was two days after the bodies were found.

Fresh search warrant in hand, two agents entered Jackie Todd's tiny unit at Macon's Mini-Storage, under the careful and suspecting gaze of Mr. Macon himself. Concrete floor, unpainted cinder-block walls, a solitary lightbulb stuck in the ceiling. There were five cardboard boxes stacked against one wall. A quick look revealed some old clothes, a pair of muddy combat boots, a 9-millimeter Glock pistol with the registration number filed off, and, finally, a metal box stuffed neatly with cash. The agents took all five cardboard boxes, thanked Mr. Macon for his hospitality, and hurried away.

Simultaneously, the name Jackie R. Todd was being run through the National Crime Information Center computer system. There was a hit, in Roanoke, Virginia.

At midnight, Quinn was moved next door and introduced to Special Agents Pankovits and Delocke. They began by explaining they were used by the FBI to interrogate escapees. This was nothing more than a routine briefing, a little fact-finding probe that they always enjoyed because who wouldn't love to talk to an escapee and get all the details. It was late, and if Quinn wanted to get some sleep in the county jail, they would be happy to start first thing in the morning. He declined and said he would like to get it over with. Sandwiches and soft drinks were brought in. The mood was lighthearted and the agents were extremely cordial. Pankovits was white and Delocke was black, and Quinn seemed to enjoy their company. He nibbled on a ham-and-swiss while they told a story about an inmate who'd spent twenty-one years on the run. The FBI sent them all the way to Thailand to bring him home. What great fun.

They asked about his escape and movements in the days that followed it, questions and answers that had already been covered by his first interrogation. Quinn refused to identify his accomplice and gave them no names of anyone who had helped him along the way. This was fine. They did not press and seemed to have no interest in going after anyone else. After an hour of friendly chitchat, Pankovits remembered that they had not read him his *Miranda* rights. There was no harm in this, they said, because his crime was obvious and he had not implicated himself in anything other than the escape. No big deal, but if he wanted to continue, he would have to waive his rights. This he did by signing a form. By this time he was being called Quinn, and they were Andy, for Pankovits, and Jesse, for Delocke.

They carefully reconstructed his movements over the past three months, and Quinn did a surprisingly thorough job of recalling dates, places, and events. The agents were impressed and commended him on having such a fine memory. They paid particular attention to his earnings; all in cash of course, but how much for each job? "So, on the second run from Miami to Charleston," Pankovits said, smiling at his notes, "the one a week after last New Year's, Quinn, you got how much in cash?"

"I believe it was six thousand."

"Right, right."

Both agents scribbled furiously as if they believed every single word uttered by their subject. Quinn said he'd been living and working in Norfolk since mid-February, about a month. He lived with his cousin and a couple of his girlfriends in a large apartment not far from the Velvet Club. He was being paid in cash, food, drink, sex, and pot.

"So, Quinn," Delocke said as he tallied up a pile of numbers, "looks to me as though you've earned about $46,000 since you left Frostburg, all cash, no taxes. Not bad for three months' work."

"I guess."

"How much of this have you spent?" Pankovits asked.

Quinn shrugged as if it really didn't matter now. "I don't know. Most of it. It takes a lot of money to move around."

"When you were running the drugs from Miami and back, how did you rent cars?" Delocke asked.

"I didn't rent them. Someone else did, gave me the keys. My job was to drive carefully, slowly, and not get stopped by the cops."

Fair enough, and both agents happily concurred. "Did you buy a vehicle?" Pankovits asked without looking up from his note taking.

"No," Quinn said with a smile. Silly question. "You can't buy a car when you're on the run and have no papers."

Of course not.

At the Freezer in Roanoke, Victor Westlake sat before a large screen, frozen at the image of Quinn Rucker. A hidden camera in the interrogation room was sending the video across the commonwealth to a makeshift room outfitted with an astonishing supply of gadgets and technology. Four other agents sat with Westlake, all staring at the eyes and expressions of Mr. Rucker.

"No way," mumbled one of the other four. "This guy's too smart for this. He knows we'll find the trailer, the wallet, the fake ID, the Hummer."

"Maybe not," mumbled another. "Right now, it's just an escape. He's thinking we have no clue about the murder. This is nothing serious."

"I agree," said another. "I think he's betting, playing the odds. He thinks he can survive a few questions, then get hauled back to jail and then to prison. He's thinking he'll call his cousin at some point and tell him to grab everything."

"Wait and see," said Westlake. "Let's see how he reacts when the first bomb hits."

At 2:00 a.m., Quinn said, "Can I use the restroom?"

Delocke stood and escorted him out of the room and down the hall. Another agent loitered about, a show of force. Five minutes later, Quinn was back in his seat.

Pankovits said, "It's rather late, Quinn, you want to check in at the jail and get some sleep? We have plenty of time."

"I'd rather be here than in the jail," he said sadly. "How much more time you think I'll get?" he asked.

Delocke replied, "Don't know, Quinn. That's up to the U.S. Attorney. Bad part is that they won't send you back to a camp. Ever. You're headed for a real prison."

"You know, Jesse, I sorta miss the camp. Wasn't so bad after all."

"Why'd you leave it?"

"Stupid. Why? Because I could. Just walk away and nobody seemed to care."

"We interview twenty-five guys a year who walk away from a federal camp. 'Stupid,' I think, is the best word."

Pankovits shuffled some papers and said, "Now, Quinn, I think we've got a handle on the time line here. Dates, places, movements, cash earnings. All of this will be included in your presentence report. The good part is that you didn't do anything exceptionally bad over the past three months. Some drug running, which of course will not help you, but at least you didn't hurt anyone, right?"

"Right."

"And this is the complete story, right? Nothing left out? You're telling us everything?"

"Yep."

The two agents stiffened somewhat and frowned. Pankovits

said, "What about Roanoke, Quinn? Did you spend any time in Roanoke?"

Quinn looked at the ceiling, gave it a thought, and said, "Maybe I passed through once or twice, but that's all."

"Are you sure about that?"

"Yes, I'm sure."

Delocke opened a file, scanned a sheet of paper, and asked, "Who is Jackie Todd?"

Quinn's eyes closed as his mouth fell open slightly. A soft guttural sound, one from deep inside, came out, as if he'd been struck somewhere below the belt. His shoulders dropped. If he'd been white, he would have turned pale. "Don't know," he finally said. "Never met him."

Delocke continued: "Really? Well, it looks like Mr. Jackie R. Todd was arrested on Tuesday night, February 8, at a bar in Roanoke. Public drunk, assault. The police report says he got in a fight with some other drunks and spent the night in jail. Next morning, he posted a cash bond of $800 and walked out."

"Wasn't me."

"Is that so?" Delocke slid across a sheet of paper, and Quinn slowly picked it up. It was a mug shot, clearly one of himself.

"Not much doubt about it, Quinn, right?"

Quinn laid down the sheet of paper and said, "Okay, okay. So I had an alias. What was I supposed to do? Play hide-and-seek with my real name?"

"Of course not, Quinn," Pankovits said. "But you lied to us, didn't you?"

"You're not the first cops I've lied to."

"Lying to the FBI can get you five years."

"Okay, I fibbed a little."

"No surprise there, but now we can't believe anything. I guess we'll have to start over."

Delocke said, "On February 9, one Jackie Todd walked into a

used-car lot in Roanoke and paid $24,000 cash for a 2008 Hummer H3. This ring a bell, Quinn?"

"No. Wasn't me."

"Didn't think so." Delocke slid across a copy of the bill of sale. "And you've never seen this before, have you?"

Quinn looked at it and said, "No."

Pankovits snapped, "Come on, Quinn. We're not half as stupid as you think we are. You were in Roanoke on February 8, went to the bar, got in a fight, went to jail, bonded out the next morning, went back to your motel room at the Safe Lodge, back to the room you paid cash for, got some more cash and bought yourself a Hummer."

"Where's the crime in paying cash for a vehicle?"

"None whatsoever," Pankovits said. "But you weren't supposed to have that much cash at that point."

"Maybe I was wrong with some of the dates and some of the cash payments. I can't remember everything."

"Do you remember where you bought the guns?" Delocke asked.

"What guns?"

"The Smith & Wesson .38 we found in your trailer and the Glock 9-millimeter we found in your storage unit, about two hours ago."

"Stolen guns," Pankovits added helpfully. "More federal offenses."

Quinn slowly locked his hands behind his head and stared at his knees. A minute passed, then another. Without blinking and without moving a muscle, the two agents stared at Quinn. The room was silent, still, tense. Finally, Pankovits shuffled some papers and raised one. He said, "The preliminary inventory shows a wallet with $512 cash, a fake driver's license from North Carolina, two prepaid Visa cards, a prepaid cell phone, the aforementioned Smith & Wesson .38, a bill of sale and a title for the Hummer, a lease agreement for the mini–storage unit, an insurance certificate for the vehicle, a box of bullets for the .38, and a few other items, all taken from the mobile home you were renting for $400 a month. From the mini–storage unit, we have inventoried some clothing, the Glock 9-millimeter, a pair of combat boots, some other items, and, most important, a metal box with $41,000 in it, cash, all in $100 bills."

Quinn slowly folded his arms across his chest and stared at Delocke, who said, "We have all night, Quinn. How about an explanation?"

"I guess the mule was busier than I remember. There were a lot of trips to Miami and back."

"Why didn't you tell us about all the trips?"

"Like I said, I can't remember everything. When you're on the run like that, you tend to forget things."

"Do you remember using either of the guns for anything, Quinn?" Delocke asked.

"No."

"Did you use the guns, or do you just not remember using the guns?"

"I did not use the guns."

Pankovits found another sheet of paper and studied it gravely. "You sure about that, Quinn? This is a preliminary ballistics report."

Quinn slowly pushed his chair back and got to his feet. He stretched and walked a few steps to a corner. "Maybe I need a lawyer."

CHAPTER 14

There was no ballistics report. The Smith & Wesson .38 was at the FBI crime laboratory at Quantico and would be analyzed as soon as the technicians arrived for work in about five hours. The sheet of paper Pankovits held like a weapon was a copy of some useless memo.

He and Delocke had an entire repertoire of dirty tricks, all approved by the U.S. Supreme Court. Using them would depend on how far Quinn allowed things to go. The immediate problem was the "lawyer" comment. If Quinn had said, clearly and unequivocally, "I want a lawyer!" or "I'm not answering any more questions until I have a lawyer!" or something along those lines, the interrogation would have ended immediately. But he hedged and used the word "maybe."

Timing was crucial here. To divert attention away from the issue of a lawyer, the agents quickly changed the scenery. Delocke stood and said, "I need to take a leak."

Pankovits said, "And I need more coffee. How about you, Quinn?"

"No."

Delocke slammed the door as he left. Pankovits stood and stretched his back. It was almost 3:00 a.m.

Quinn had two brothers and two sisters, ages twenty-seven to forty-two, all at one point or another involved in the family's drug-trafficking syndicate. One sister had eased out of the actual smuggling and selling but was still involved in various laundering operations. The other had left the business, moved away, and tried to avoid the family altogether. The youngest of the siblings was Dee Ray Rucker, a quiet young man who studied finance at Georgetown and knew how to move money around. He had one gun charge but nothing significant. Dee Ray really didn't have the stomach for the fear and violence of the street life and tried to stay away from it. He lived with his girlfriend in a modest condo near Union Station, and it was there that the FBI found him shortly after midnight: in bed, unburdened by outstanding warrants or ongoing criminal investigations, oblivious to what was happening to his dear brother Quinn, carefree, and sleeping soundly. He was taken into custody without resistance but with an enormous amount of bitching. The squad of agents who snatched him offered little explanation. At the FBI building on Pennsylvania Avenue, he was hustled into a room where he was placed in a chair and surrounded by agents, all wearing navy parkas with "FBI" in bright yellow. The scene was photographed from several angles. After an hour of sitting handcuffed and being told nothing, he was removed from the room, walked back to the van, and driven home. He was deposited at the curb without another word.

His girlfriend fetched him some pills and he eventually settled down. He would call his lawyer in the morning and raise hell, but the entire episode would soon be forgotten.

In the drug trade, you don't expect happy endings.

When Delocke returned from the restroom, he held the door open for a moment. A slender, attractive secretary of some variety entered with a tray of drinks and cookies, which she set on the edge of the table. She smiled at Quinn, who was still standing in the corner, too confused to acknowledge her. After she left, Pankovits popped a can of Red Bull and poured it over ice. "You need a Red Bull, Quinn?"

"No." He served them all night at the bar, Red Bull and vodka, but had never cared for the taste. The break in the action gave him a moment to catch his breath and try to organize his thoughts. Should he continue, or should he remain silent and insist on a lawyer? His instincts were for the latter, but he was extremely curious about how much the FBI knew. He was reeling from what they had already discovered, but how far could they go?

Delocke fixed himself a Red Bull too, over ice, and munched on a cookie. "Have a seat, Quinn," he said, waving him back to the table. Quinn took a few steps and sat down. Pankovits was already taking notes. "Your older brother, I believe they call him Tall Man, is he still in the D.C. area?"

"What's he got to do with anything?"

"Just filling in some gaps here, Quinn. That's all. I like to have all the facts, or as many as possible. Have you seen much of Tall Man in the past three months?"

"No comment."

"Okay. Your younger brother, Dee Ray, is he still in the D.C. area?"

"I don't know where Dee Ray is."

"Have you seen much of Dee Ray in the past three months?"

"No comment."

"Did Dee Ray go to Roanoke with you when you got arrested?"

"No comment."

"Was anyone with you when you got arrested in Roanoke?"

"I was alone."

Delocke exhaled in frustration. Pankovits sighed as if this were just another lie and they knew it.

"I swear I was alone," Quinn said.

"What were you doing in Roanoke?" Delocke asked.

"Business."

"Trafficking?"

"That's our business. Roanoke is part of our territory. We had a situation there and I had to take care of it."

"What kind of situation?"

"No comment."

Pankovits took a long pull of his Red Bull and said, "You know, Quinn, the problem we have right now is that we can't believe a word you're saying. You lie. We know you lie. You even admit you lie. We ask a question, you give us a lie."

"We're getting nowhere, Quinn," Delocke chimed in. "What were you doing in Roanoke?"

Quinn reached forward and took an Oreo. He pulled off the top, licked the creme, stared at Delocke, and finally said, "We had a mule down there who we suspected of being an informant. We lost two shipments under strange circumstances, and we figured things out. I went to see the mule."

"To kill him?"

"No, we don't operate that way. I couldn't find him. He apparently got word and took off. I went to a bar, drank too much, got in a fight, had a bad night. The next day, a friend told me about a good deal on a Hummer, so I went to see it."

"Who was the friend?"

"No comment."

"You're lying," Delocke said. "You're lying and we know you're lying. You're not even a good liar, Quinn, you know that?"

"Whatever."

"Why did you title the Hummer in North Carolina?" Pankovits asked.

"Because I was on the run, remember? I was an escapee, trying not to leave a trail. Get it, fellas? Fake ID. Fake address. Fake everything."

"Who is Jakeel Staley?" Delocke asked.

Quinn hesitated for a second, tried to shake it off, and answered nonchalantly, "My nephew."

"And where is he now?"

"Federal pen somewhere. I'm sure you guys know the answer."

"Alabama, serving eighteen years," Pankovits said. "Jakeel got busted near Roanoke with a van full of cocaine, right?"

"I'm sure you have the file."

"Did you try to help Jakeel?"

"When?"

Both agents overreacted with feigned frustration. Both took a sip of Red Bull. Delocke reached for another Oreo. There were a dozen left on the platter, and there was a pot full of coffee. From the looks of things, they planned to be there all night.

Pankovits said, "Come on, Quinn, stop playing games. We've established that Jakeel was busted in Roanoke, lots of coke, lots of years ahead in the pen, and the question is whether or not you tried to help the boy."

"Sure. He's part of the family, part of the business, and he got busted in the course of his employment. The family always steps forward."

"Did you hire the lawyer?"

"I did."

"How much did you pay the lawyer?"

Quinn thought for a moment, then said, "I don't really remember. It was a sackful of cash."

"You paid the lawyer in cash?"

"That's what I just said. Nothing wrong with cash, last time I checked. We don't use bank accounts and credit cards and things the Feds can follow. Just cash."

"Who gave you the cash to hire the lawyer?"

"No comment."

"Did you get the cash from Dee Ray?"

"No comment."

Pankovits slowly reached for a thin file and removed a sheet of paper. "Well, Dee Ray says he gave you all the cash you would need in Roanoke."

Quinn shook his head and offered a nasty smile that said, "Bullshit."

Pankovits slid across an eight-by-ten color enlargement of a photograph of Dee Ray surrounded by FBI agents, with his hands cuffed, his mouth open, and his face angry. Delocke explained, "We picked up Dee Ray in D.C. about an hour after we brought you in. He likes to talk, you know. In fact, he talks a lot more than you do."

Quinn stared at the photo and was speechless.

***

The Freezer. Four in the morning. Victor Westlake stood, again, and walked around the room. Movement was needed to fight off sleep. The other four agents were still awake, their systems pumped with over-the-counter amphetamines, Red Bull, and coffee. "Damn, these guys are slow," one of them said.

"They're methodical," another replied. "They're wearing him down. The fact that he's still talking after seven hours is incredible."

"He doesn't want to go to the county jail."

"Can't blame him there."

"I think he's still curious. Cat and mouse. How much do we really know?"

"They're not going to trick him. He's too smart."

"They know what they're doing," Westlake said. He sat down and poured another cup of coffee.

In Norfolk, Pankovits poured a cup of coffee and asked, "Who drove you to Roanoke?"

"Nobody. I drove myself."

"What kind of car?"

"I don't remember."

"You're lying, Quinn. Someone drove you to Roanoke the week before February 7. There were two of you. We have witnesses."

"Then your witnesses are lying. You're lying. Everybody's lying."

"You bought the Hummer on February 9, paid cash, and there was no trade-in. How did you get to the used-car lot that day when you bought the Hummer? Who took you?"

"I don't remember."

"So you don't remember who took you?"

"I don't remember anything. I was hungover and still about half drunk."

"Come on, Quinn," Delocke said. "These lies are getting ridiculous. What are you hiding? If you're not hiding something, then you wouldn't be lying so much."

"What, exactly, do you want to know?" Quinn asked, hands in the air.

"Where did you get all that cash, Quinn?"

"I'm a drug dealer. I've been a drug dealer most of my life. I've spent time in prison because I'm a drug dealer. We burn cash. We eat cash. Don't you understand this?"

Pankovits was shaking his head. "But, Quinn, according to your story, you were not working much for the family after your escape. They were afraid of you, right? Am I right about this?" he asked, looking at Delocke, who quickly confirmed that, yes, his partner was right about this.

Delocke said, "The family shunned you, so you began making runs down south and back. You say you earned about $46,000, which we now know is a lie, because you spent $24,000 on the Hummer and we found $41,000 in your storage unit."

Pankovits said, "You came across some cash, Quinn. What are you hiding?"

"Nothing."

"Then why are you lying?"

"Everybody's lying. I thought we all agreed on that."

Delocke tapped the table and said, "Let's go back a few years, Quinn. Your nephew Jakeel Staley is in jail, here in Roanoke, waiting on a trial. You paid his lawyer some amount in cash for legal services, right?"

"Right."

"Was there more cash? A little extra to help grease the system? Maybe a bribe so the court would go easy on the kid? Anything like that, Quinn?"

"No."

"Are you sure?"

"Of course I'm sure."

"Come on, Quinn."

"I paid the lawyer in cash. I assumed he kept the money for his fee. That's all I know."

"Who was the judge?"

"I don't remember."

"Does Judge Fawcett ring a bell?"

Quinn shrugged. "Maybe."

"Did you ever go to court with Jakeel?"

"I was there when he was sentenced to eighteen years."

"Were you surprised when he got eighteen years?"

"Yes, matter of fact I was."

"He was supposed to get a lot less, wasn't he?"

"According to his lawyer, yes."

"And you were in court so you could get a good look at Judge Fawcett, right?"

"I was in court for my nephew. That's all."

The tag team paused at the same moment. Delocke took a sip of his Red Bull. Pankovits said, "I need to go to the men's room. You okay, Quinn?"

Quinn was pinching his forehead. "Sure," he replied.

"Get you something to drink?"

"How about a Sprite?"

"You got it."

Pankovits took his time. Quinn sipped his drink. At 4:30, the interrogation was resumed when Delocke asked, "So, Quinn, have you kept up with the news during the past three months? Read any newspapers? Surely you've been curious about your own escape and whether or not it's made the news?"

Quinn said, "Not really."

"Did you hear about Judge Fawcett?"

"Nope. What about him?"

"Murdered, shot twice in the back of the head."

No reaction from Quinn. No surprise. No pity. Nothing.

"You didn't know that, Quinn?" Pankovits asked.

"No."

"Two hollow-point bullets, fired from a .38-caliber handgun identical to the one we found in your trailer. Preliminary ballistics report says there's a 90 percent chance your gun was used to kill the judge."

Quinn began smiling and nodding. "Now I get it, this is all about a dead judge. You boys think I killed Judge Fawcett, right?"

"That's right."

"Great. So we have wasted, what, seven hours with this bullshit. You're wasting my time, your time, Dee Ray's time, everybody's time. I ain't killed nobody."

"Have you ever been to Ripplemead, Virginia, population five hundred, deep in the mountains west of Roanoke?"

"No."

"It's the nearest town to a small lake where the judge was murdered. There are no black people in Ripplemead, and when one shows up, he gets noticed. The day before the judge was murdered, a black man matching your description was in town, according to the owner of a gas station."

"A positive ID, or just a wild guess?"

"Something in between. We'll show him a better photo of you tomorrow."

"I'm sure you will, and I'll bet his memory improves greatly."

"It usually does," Delocke said. "Four miles west of Ripplemead the world comes to an end. The asphalt stops, and a series of gravel roads disappear into the mountains. There's an old country store called Peacock's, and Mr. Peacock sees everything. The day before the murder, he says a black man stopped by asking for directions. Mr. Peacock can't remember the last time he saw a black man in his part of the world. He gave a description. Matches you very well."

Quinn shrugged and said, "I'm not that stupid."

"Really? Then why did you hang on to the Smith & Wesson? When we get the final ballistics report, you're dead, Quinn."

"The gun's stolen, okay? Stolen guns make the rounds. I bought it from a pawnshop in Lynchburg two weeks ago. It's probably changed hands a dozen times in the past year."

A good point, and one they could not argue with, at least not until the ballistics tests were completed. When they had the proof, though, no jury would believe Quinn's story about a stolen gun.

Pankovits said, "We found a pair of combat boots in your mini–storage unit. A cheap pair of fake Army surplus, canvas, camouflage, all that crap. They are fairly new and have not been used that much. Why do you need combat boots, Quinn?"

"I have weak ankles."

"Nice. How often do you wear them?"

"Not often if they're in storage. I tried them, they rubbed a blister, I forgot about them. What's the point?"

"The point is that they match a boot print we took from the soil not far from the cabin where Judge Fawcett was murdered," Pankovits said, lying but doing so effectively. "A match, Quinn. A match that puts you at the scene."

Quinn dropped his chin and rubbed his eyes. They were bloodshot and tired. "What time is it?"

"Four fifty," Delocke replied.

"I need some sleep."

"Well, that might be difficult, Quinn. We checked with the county jail and your cell is quite crowded. Eight men, four bunks. You'll be lucky to get a spot on the floor."

"I don't think I like that jail. Could we try another one?"

"Sorry. Wait till you see death row, Quinn."

"I ain't going to death row because I didn't kill anybody."

Pankovits said, "Here's where we are, Quinn. Two witnesses put you in the vicinity at the time of the murder, and the vicinity is not exactly a busy street corner. You were there and you were noticed and remembered. Ballistics will nail your ass. The boot print is icing on the cake. That's the crime scene. After the crime, it gets even better, or worse, depending on one's perspective. You were in Roanoke the day after the bodies were found, Tuesday, February 8, by your own admission and by way of the city's jail records and court docket. And suddenly you had a satchelful of cash. You posted bond, then paid $24,000 for the Hummer, pissed away plenty more, and when we finally catch you, there's another stash hidden in a mini-storage. Motive? There's plenty of motive. You had a deal with Judge Fawcett to rule in favor of Jakeel Staley. You bribed him, something like $500,000, and after he took the cash, he forgot about the deal. He threw the book at Jakeel, and you vowed revenge. Eventually, you got it. Unfortunately, his secretary got in the way too."

Delocke said, "A death penalty case, Quinn, open and shut. Federal death penalty."

Quinn's eyes closed as his body shrank. He began breathing rapidly as sweat formed above his eyebrows. A minute passed, then another. The tough guy was gone. His replacement said weakly, "You got the wrong guy."

Pankovits laughed, and Delocke, sneering, said, "Is that the best you can do?"

"You got the wrong guy," Quinn repeated, but with even less conviction.

"That sounds pretty lame, Quinn," Delocke said. "And it'll sound even weaker in the courtroom."

Quinn stared at his hands as another minute passed. Finally, he said, "If you boys know so much, what else do you want?"

Pankovits replied, "There are a few gaps. Did you act alone? How did you open the safe? Why did you kill the secretary? What happened to the rest of the money?"

"Can't help you there. I don't know nothing about it."

"You know everything, Quinn, and we're not leaving until you fill in the gaps."

"Then I guess we're going to be here for a long time," Quinn said. He leaned forward, placed his head on the table, and said, "I'm taking a nap."

Both agents stood and picked up their files and notepads. "We'll take a break, Quinn. We'll be back in half an hour."

CHAPTER 15

Though pleased with the progress of the interrogation, Victor Westlake was worried. There were no witnesses, no ballistics report linking Quinn's .38 to the crime scene, no boot print, and no simultaneous interrogation of Dee Ray. There was motive, if they believed Malcolm Bannister's story about the bribe. The strongest evidence so far was the fact that Quinn Rucker was in Roanoke the day after the bodies were found and that he had too much cash. Westlake and his team were exhausted from the all-nighter, and it was still dark outside. They reloaded with coffee and took long walks around the Freezer. They occasionally checked on the screen for images of their suspect. Quinn was lying on the table but not sleeping.

———

At 6:00 a.m., Pankovits and Delocke returned to the interrogation room. Each had a tall glass with a refill of Red Bull and ice. Quinn got off the table and settled himself into his chair for another round.

Pankovits went first. "Just got off the phone with the U.S. Attorney, Quinn. We briefed him on our progress here with you, and he says his grand jury will convene tomorrow and hand down the indictment. Two counts of capital murder."

"Congratulations," Quinn replied. "I guess I'd better find me a lawyer."

"Sure, but it might take more than one. I'm not sure how much you understand about federal racketeering laws, Quinn, but they can be brutal. The U.S. Attorney will take the position that the murders of Judge Fawcett and his secretary were the actions of a gang, a well-known and well-organized gang, with you, of course, as the triggerman. The indictment will include a lot of charges, including capital murder, but also bribery. And, most important, it will name not only you but other nefarious characters such as Tall Man, Dee Ray, one of your sisters, your cousin Antoine Beck, and a couple dozen other relatives."

Delocke added, "You guys can have your own wing on death row. The Rucker-Beck gang, all lined up, cell to cell, just waiting for the needle." Delocke was smiling and Pankovits was amused. A couple of comedians.

Quinn began scratching the side of his head and talking to the floor. "You know, I wonder what my lawyer would say about this, got me locked in this dark room, no windows, all night long, started at, what, 'bout nine last night and here it is six in the morning, nine straight hours of nonstop bullshit from you two, accusing me of bribing a judge, then killing a judge, and now threatening me with death, and not only my ass but my whole family as well. You say you got witnesses out there, all lined up and ready to testify, and ballistics on a stolen gun, and a boot print where some sumbitch stepped in mud, and how am I supposed to know if you're telling the truth or lying your ass off because I wouldn't trust the FBI with anything, never have, never will. Lied to me the first time I got busted and sent away, and I assume you're lying here tonight. Maybe I lied a little, but can you honestly tell me right now that you ain't lied to me tonight? Can you?"

Pankovits and Delocke stared at him. Maybe it was fear, or guilt. Maybe it was delirium. Whatever, Quinn was really talking.

"We are telling the truth," Pankovits managed to say.

"And chalk up another lie. My lawyer will get to the bottom of this. He'll nail your ass in court, expose you, expose all your lies. Show me the boot print analysis. Now, I want to see it."

"We're not authorized to show it to anyone," Pankovits said.

"How convenient." Quinn leaned forward with an elbow on each knee. His forehead almost touched the edge of the table, and he kept talking to the floor. "What about the ballistics report? Can I see that?"

"We're not authorized—"

"What a surprise. My lawyer'll get it, whenever and wherever I get to see my lawyer. I've asked for him all night, and my rights have been violated."

"You have not asked for your lawyer," Delocke said. "You've mentioned a lawyer in vague terms, but you have not requested one. And you've kept talking."

"As if I had a choice. Either sit here and talk or go to the drunk tank with a bunch of winos. I've been there before, you know, and I ain't afraid of it. It's just part of the business, you know? You do the crime, you do the time. You know the rules when you get into the business. You see all your friends and family shipped off, but they come back, you know? You do your time and you get out."

"Or you escape," Delocke said.

"That too. Pretty stupid, I guess, but I had to walk."

"Because you had to settle a score, right, Quinn? For two years in prison you thought about Judge Fawcett every day. He took your money, then he broke the deal. In your business, he had to go down, right?"

"That's right."

Quinn was rubbing his temples, staring at his feet, almost mumbling. The agents took a deep breath and exchanged a quick smile. Finally, the first hint of an admission.

Pankovits rearranged some papers and said, "Now, Quinn,

let's look at where we are. You've just admitted Judge Fawcett had to go down, is that right? Quinn?"

Quinn was still leaning on his elbows, staring at the floor, rocking now as if in a daze. He did not respond.

Delocke read from his legal pad and said, "According to my notes, Quinn, I asked the question, and I quote, 'In your business, he had to go down, right?' and you replied, 'That's right.' Do you deny this, Quinn?"

"You're putting words in my mouth. Stop it."

Pankovits jumped in: "Okay, Quinn, we need to inform you of some recent developments. About two hours ago, Dee Ray finally admitted he gave you the cash to pass along to Judge Fawcett, and that he, Tall Man, and some of the others helped you plan the murder. Dee Ray's come clean, and he's already got a deal—no death penalty, no capital murder. We picked up Tall Man two hours ago, and now we're looking for one of your sisters. This is getting ugly."

"Come on. They don't know nothing."

"Of course they do, and they'll be indicted with you tomorrow."

"You can't do that, man. Come on. It'll kill my mother. Poor woman's seventy years old and got a bad heart. You can't be messing with her like that."

"Then step up, Quinn!" Pankovits said loudly. "Take the heat! You did the crime. As you like to say, now do the time. No sense taking the rest of your family down with you."

"Step up and do what?"

"Cut a deal. Give us the details, and we lean on the U.S. Attorney to lay off your family," Pankovits said.

"And there's something else," Delocke added. "If we do the right deal, there will be no death penalty. Just life, no parole. Seems the Fawcett family does not believe in the death penalty, nor do they want a long, painful trial. They want the case closed, and the U.S. Attorney will respect their wishes. According to him, he will consider a plea agreement, one that will save your life."

"Why should I believe you?"

"You don't have to, Quinn. Just wait a couple of days for the indictments to come down. There could be as many as thirty people named for various charges."

Quinn Rucker stood slowly and stretched his hands as high as possible. He took a few steps in one direction, then another, and began saying, "Bannister, Bannister, Bannister."

"Beg your pardon, Quinn," Pankovits said.

"Bannister, Bannister, Bannister."

"Who's Bannister?" Delocke asked.

"Bannister is a rat," Quinn said bitterly. "Scum, an old friend in Frostburg, a crooked lawyer who claims he's innocent. Nothing but a rat. Don't pretend you don't know him, because you wouldn't be here if he wasn't a rat."

"Never met the man," Pankovits said. Delocke was shaking his head no.

Quinn sat down and thrust both elbows onto the table. He was wide-awake now, his narrow eyes glaring at the two agents, his thick hands rubbing each other. "So what's the deal?" he asked.

"We can't make deals, Quinn, but we can make things happen," Pankovits said. "For starters, we call off the dogs in D.C., and your family and gang are left alone, for now anyway. The U.S. Attorney has been taking heat for five weeks, ever since the murder, and he's desperate for some good news. He assures us, and we can assure you, that there will be no capital murder charge and that it will be a stand-alone indictment. Just you, for the two killings. Plain and simple."

Delocke said, "That's one half, the other half is a video statement from you confessing to the crimes."

Quinn wrapped his hands around his head and closed his eyes. A minute passed as he fought himself. "I really want my lawyer," he finally said through clenched teeth.

Delocke replied, "You can do that, Quinn, of course you can. But Dee Ray and Tall Man are in custody right now, singing like birds, and things are only getting worse. It might be a day or two before your lawyer can get down here. You say the word, and we'll turn your brothers loose and leave them alone."

Quinn suddenly snapped and yelled, "All right!"

"All right what?"

"All right, I'll do it!"

"Not so fast, Quinn," Pankovits said. "We need to go over a few things first. Let's review the facts, put things in order, set the stage, make sure we're all on the same page with the crime scene. We need to make sure that all important details are included."

"Okay, okay. But can I have some breakfast?"

"Sure, Quinn, no problem. We have all day."

CHAPTER 16

One of the few virtues of prison life is the gradual acquisition of patience. Nothing moves at a reasonable pace, and you learn to ignore clocks. Tomorrow will come around soon enough; surviving today is enough of a challenge. After my quick trip to D.C., I roam around Frostburg for a couple of days reminding myself that I have become a very patient person, that the FBI will move quickly, and, regardless, there is nothing more I can do. Much to my surprise, and relief, events unfold rapidly.

I do not expect the FBI to keep me in the loop, so I have no way of knowing they have arrested Quinn Rucker and that he has confessed. This news is delivered by the *Washington Post*, on Saturday, March 19, front page, beneath the fold: SUSPECT ARRESTED IN MURDER OF FEDERAL JUDGE. There is a large black-and-white photo of Quinn, one of his mug shots, and I stare into his eyes as I take a seat in the coffee room just after breakfast. The article is rather light on facts but heavy on suspicion. Obviously, all news is being parceled out by the FBI, so there's not much detail. The arrest, in Norfolk, of an escaped felon, one with a conviction for drug trafficking and a long history of gang involvement in the D.C. area. There is no whiff of a motive, no clue as to how the FBI decided Quinn was their man, and only a passing reference to a ballistics report. Most important, the article states, "After waiving his *Miranda* rights, the suspect voluntarily underwent a lengthy interrogation and provided the FBI with a videotaped confession."

I met Quinn Rucker two years ago, not long after he arrived at Frostburg. After he settled in, he made his way to the library and asked me to review his sentencing order. In prison, you learn to make friends slowly, with great caution, because few people are genuine. Naturally, the place is swarming with crooks, cons, and scam artists, and everyone is looking out for his own skin. With Quinn, though, things were different. He was instantly likeable, and I'm not sure I've met another person with as much charisma and sincerity. Then the mood would swing, and he would withdraw into himself and suffer through his "dark days," as he called them. He could be cranky, rude, and harsh, and the potential for violence was not far from the surface. He would eat alone and speak to no one. Two days later, he would be telling jokes over breakfast and challenging the serious players to a game of poker. He could be loud and cocky, then quiet and vulnerable. As I've said, there is no violence at Frostburg. The nearest thing to a fight I've seen was an episode in which a hillbilly we called Skunk challenged Quinn to a fistfight to settle a gambling dispute. Skunk was at least four inches shorter and thirty pounds lighter than Quinn, but the fight never happened. Quinn backed down and was humiliated. Two days later, he showed me a homemade knife, a "shank," that he'd bought on the black market. He planned to use it to slice Skunk's throat.

I talked him out of the killing, though I wasn't convinced he was serious. I spent a lot of time with Quinn and we became friends. He was convinced I could work some legal magic, spring us both from prison, and we would become partners of some sort. He was tired of the family business and wanted to go straight. There was a pot of gold waiting out there, and Judge Fawcett was sitting on it.

Henry Bannister is waiting in the visitors' room, sitting sadly in a folding chair while a young mother and her three children squabble nearby. The room will fill up as the morning goes on, and Henry prefers to get his visits over with earlier rather than later. The rules allow a family member to sit and chat with an inmate from 7:00 a.m. to 3:00 p.m. each Saturday and Sunday, but one hour is enough for Henry. And for me as well.

If things go as planned, and I have little reason to believe they will, this could be my last visit with my father. I may not see him again for years, if ever, but I can't discuss this. I take the brown bag of cookies from Aunt Racine and nibble on one. We talk about my brother, Marcus, and his rotten children and my sister, Ruby, and her perfect ones.

Winchester averages one murder per year, and the quota was filled last week when a husband arrived home early from work and saw a strange truck parked in his driveway. He sneaked into his house and caught his wife with one of his acquaintances, both enthusiastically violating their marriage vows. The husband had picked up his shotgun, and when the tomcat saw it, he attempted to jump through an unopened bedroom window, naked. He didn't make it, and gunfire followed.

Henry thinks the guy might get off and relishes telling the story. It seems the entire town is split between guilt and justifiable homicide. I can almost hear the relentless gossip in the Old Town coffee shops I once visited. He dwells on this story for a long time, probably because we do not want to cover family issues.

But cover them we must. He changes subjects and says, "Looks like that little white girl is thinking about an abortion. Maybe I won't be a great-grandfather after all."

"Delmon will do it again," I say. We always expect the worst out of the kid.

"We need to get him sterilized. He's too stupid to use condoms."

"Buy him some anyway. You know Marcus is too broke."

"I only see the kid when he wants something. Hell, I'll probably get hit up for the abortion. I think the girl's trash."

While on the topic of money, I can't help but think about the reward in the Fawcett case. A hundred and fifty thousand dollars cash. I've never seen so much money. Before Bo was born, Dionne and I realized one day we had saved $6,000. We put half in a mutual fund and took a cruise with the remainder. Our frugal habits were soon forgotten, and we never again had that kind of cash. Just before I was indicted, we refinanced our house to squeeze out every last drop of equity. The money went for legal fees.

I'll be rich and on the run. I remind myself not to get excited, but it's impossible.

Henry needs a new left knee, and we talk about this for some time. He's always poked fun at old folks who dwell on their ailments, but he's getting just as bad. After an hour, he's bored and ready to go. I walk with him to the door, and we shake hands stiffly. As he leaves, I wonder if I will ever see him again.

Sunday. No word from the FBI, or anyone else. I read four newspapers after breakfast and learn almost nothing new about Quinn Rucker and his arrest. However, there is one significant development. According to the *Post*, the U.S. Attorney for the Southern District of Virginia will present the case to the grand jury tomorrow. Monday. If the grand jury issues an indictment, then, in theory and by agreement, I am supposed to become a free man.

There is a surprising amount of organized religion in prison. As troubled men, we seek solace, peace, comfort, and guidance.

We've been humiliated, humbled, stripped bare of dignity, family, and assets, and we have nothing left. Cast into hell, we look upward for a way out. There are a few Muslims who pray five times a day and stick to themselves. There is a self-appointed Buddhist monk with a few followers. No Jews or Mormons that I know of. Then there are us Christians, and this is where it gets complicated. A Catholic priest comes in twice a month for Mass at eight on Sunday mornings. As soon as the Catholics clear out of the small chapel, a nondenominational service is held for those from mainline churches—Methodist, Baptist, Presbyterian, and so on. This is where I fit in on most Sundays. At 10:00 a.m., the white Pentecostals gather for a rowdy service with loud music and even louder preaching, along with healing and speaking in tongues. This service is supposed to end at 11:00 a.m. but often runs longer as the spirit moves among the worshippers. The black Pentecostals get the chapel at 11:00 a.m. but sometimes must wait while the white ones simmer down. I've heard stories of harsh words between the two groups, but so far no fights have erupted in the chapel. Once they get the pulpit, the black Pentecostals keep it throughout the afternoon.

It would be wrong to get the impression that Frostburg is filled with Bible-thumpers. It is not. It's still a prison, and the majority of my fellow inmates would not be caught dead in a church service.

As I leave the chapel after the nondenominational service, a CO finds me and says, "They're looking for you in the admin building."

CHAPTER 17

Agent Hanski is waiting with a new player in my game—Pat Surhoff, U.S. Marshal. We make our introductions and gather around a small table not far down the hall from the warden's office. He, of course, would never be seen on the premises on a Sunday, and who could blame him?

Hanski whips out a document and slides it across. "Here's the indictment," he says. "Came down late Friday afternoon in Roanoke, still a secret, but it will be released to the press first thing in the morning." I hold it like a brick of gold and have trouble focusing on the words. *United States of America versus Quinn Al Rucker.* It's been stamped in the top right corner, with last Friday's date in blue ink.

"The *Post* said the grand jury meets in the morning," I manage to say, though it's obvious what's already happened.

"We're playing the press," Hanski says smugly. Smug, but a much nicer guy this time around. Our roles have changed dramatically. Once I had been a shifty-eyed con looking for a deal and probably scamming the system. Now, though, I'm the golden boy about to walk out of here and take some cash with me.

I shake my head and say, "I'm at a loss for words, guys. Help me here."

Hanski is ready to pounce. "Here's what we have in mind, Mr. Bannister."

"How about Mal now?" I ask.

"Great. I'm Chris and he's Pat."

"Got it."

"The Bureau of Prisons has just reassigned you to the medium-security joint at Fort Wayne, Indiana. Reason unknown, or not given. Some type of rule violation that pissed off the big guys. No visitors for six months. Solitary confinement. Anyone who's curious can find you online with the Inmate Locator service, but they'll soon hit a brick wall. After a couple of months in Fort Wayne, you'll be reassigned again. The goal is to keep you moving throughout the system and buried in it."

"I'm sure this will be quite easy for the bureau," I say, and they both laugh. Man, have I changed teams or what?

"In a few minutes, we'll do the handcuff and ankle-chain routine, for the last time, and walk you out of here, just like a normal transfer. You'll get in an unmarked van with Pat and another marshal, and they'll drive you west, headed for Fort Wayne. I'll follow. Sixty miles down the road, just this side of Morgantown, we'll stop at a motel where we have some rooms. You'll change clothes, have some lunch, and we'll talk about the future."

"In a few minutes?" I say, shocked.

"That's the plan. Is there anything in your cell that you cannot live without?"

"Yes. I have some personal stuff, paperwork and such."

"Okay. We'll get the prison to box up everything tomorrow and we'll get it to you. It's best if you don't go back there. If someone saw you gathering your things, they might ask questions. We don't want anyone here to know you're leaving until you're gone."

"Got it."

"No farewells and all that crap, okay?"

"Okay." For a second I think about my friends here at Frostburg, but quickly let it go. This day is coming for all of them too, and once you're free, you don't look back. I doubt seriously if friendships made in prison endure on the outside. And in my case, I will never be able to catch up with the old pals and reminisce. I am about to become another person.

"You have $78 in your prison account. We'll forward that to Fort Wayne, and it'll get lost in the system."

"Screwed once more by the federal government," I say, and again they think I'm funny.

"Any questions?" Hanski asks.

"Sure. How did you get him to confess? He's too smart for that."

"We were surprised, frankly. We used a couple of our veteran interrogators, and they have their methods. He mentioned a lawyer a couple of times but backed off. He wanted to talk, and he seemed overwhelmed by the fact that he'd been caught, not for the escape, but for the murder. He wanted to know how much we knew, so we kept talking. For ten hours. Through the night into the early morning. He didn't want to leave and go to jail, so he stayed in the room. Once he became convinced that we knew what we knew, he broke down. When we mentioned the possibility of his family being indicted, along with most of his gang, he wanted to cut a deal. He eventually gave us everything."

"And by everything you mean?"

"His story is basically what you told us. He bribed Judge Fawcett with $500,000 to save his nephew, and the judge screwed him. Kept the money and nailed the kid. In Quinn's world, that's a crime that cannot be forgiven and must be avenged. He stalked Judge Fawcett, trailed him to his cabin, broke in on the judge and his secretary, and got his revenge."

"How much of the money was left?"

"About half of it. Quinn claims he broke into the judge's apartment in Roanoke, went through everything, and couldn't find the money. He suspected it was being kept somewhere else, somewhere safer. That's why he followed Fawcett to the cabin. He overpowered the judge on the front porch and got inside. He wasn't sure the money was there but was determined to find its location. He did some bad things to the secretary and convinced Fawcett to find the money. Thus, the hidden safe. In Quinn's mind, the money belonged to him."

"And I guess he felt he had to kill them?"

"Oh sure. He couldn't leave two witnesses behind. There's no remorse, Mal. The judge had it coming; the secretary just got in the way. Now he's facing two counts of capital murder."

"So it's a death penalty case?"

"Most likely. We've never executed anyone for killing a federal judge, and we'd love to make Quinn Rucker our first example."

"Did he mention my name?" I ask, certain of the answer.

"Indeed he did. He strongly suspects you're our source, and he's probably plotting revenge. That's why we're here now, ready to go."

I want to leave, but not so fast. "Quinn knows about Rule 35; in fact every federal inmate knows a lot about the rule. You solve a crime on the outside, and you get your sentence commuted. Plus, he thinks I'm a brilliant lawyer. He and his family will know that I'm out, not in prison, not in Fort Wayne or any other facility."

"True, but let's keep them guessing. It's also important for your family and friends to believe you're still locked up."

"Are you worried about my family?" I ask.

Pat Surhoff finally speaks. "On some level, yes, and we can provide protection for them if you so choose. Doing so will obviously disrupt their lives."

"They'll never agree to it," I reply. "My father would throw a punch if you mentioned it to him. He's a retired state trooper who's certain he can take care of himself. My son has a new father and a new life." I cannot comprehend the phone call to Dionne to inform her that Bo might be in danger because of something I've done in prison. And there's a part of me that does not believe Quinn Rucker would harm an innocent boy.

"We can discuss it later, if you'd like," Surhoff says.

"Let's do that. I'm having far too many random thoughts right now."

Hanski says, "Freedom awaits you, Mal."

"Let's get out of here." I follow them down a hallway and to another building where three COs and the captain are waiting. I'm handcuffed and shackled at the ankles, then escorted down a sidewalk to a waiting van. An uninformed bystander would think I'm being led to my execution. A marshal named Hitchcock is behind the wheel. Surhoff slides the door shut beside me and climbs into the front passenger seat. Away we go.

I refuse to look back for a parting shot of Frostburg. I have enough images to last for years. I watch the countryside pass by and cannot suppress a smile. A few minutes later, we pull in to the parking lot of a shopping center. Surhoff jumps out, opens the sliding door, reaches over, and unlocks the handcuffs. Then he frees my ankles. "Congratulations," he says warmly, and I decide that I like this guy. I hear the chains rattle for the last time and massage my wrists.

Soon, we accelerate onto Interstate 68 and head west. It's almost springtime, and the rolling hills of far western Maryland are showing signs of life. The first few moments of freedom are almost overwhelming. For five years I have dreamed of this day, and it is exhilarating. There are so many thoughts competing for attention. I can't wait to choose my own clothing, to put on a pair of jeans. I can't wait to buy a car and drive anywhere I want. I long for the feel of a woman's body and for the taste of a steak and a cold beer. I refuse to worry about the safety of my son and father. They will not be harmed.

The marshals want to talk, and so I listen. Pat Surhoff is saying, "Now, Mal, you are no longer in the custody of anyone. If you choose to enter the Witness Security Program, more commonly known as witness protection, we, the U.S. Marshals Service, will take care of you. We provide for your security, safety, and health. We will get you a new identity with authentic documentation. You will receive financial assistance for housing, living expenses, and medical care. We'll find you a job. Once you're up and running, we don't monitor your daily activities, but we're always close by if you need us."

He sounds as though he's reading from a brochure, but the words are music. Hitchcock chimes in, "We've had over eight thousand witnesses in the program, and not a single one has ever been harmed."

I ask the obvious question: "Where will I live?"

"It's a big country, Mal," Hitchcock replies. "We've relocated witnesses a hundred miles from their homes and two thousand miles away. Distance is not that crucial, but, generally speaking, the farther the better. You like warm weather or snow? Mountains and lakes or sun and beaches? Big cities or small cities? Small towns are problematic, and we recommend a place with a population of at least 100,000."

"It's easier to blend in," Surhoff adds.

"And I get to choose?" I ask.

"Within reason, yes," Hitchcock says.

"Let me think about it."

Which I do for the next ten miles or so, and not for the first time. I have a pretty good idea of where I'm going, and for what reasons. I glance over my shoulder and see a familiar vehicle. "I'm assuming that's the FBI right behind us."

"Yes, Agent Hanski and another guy," Surhoff says.

"How long will they follow us?"

"They'll be gone in a few days, I suppose," Surhoff says as he and Hitchcock exchange looks. They don't really know, and I'm not going to press them.

I ask, "Does the FBI routinely keep up with witnesses like me?"

Hitchcock replies, "It depends. Usually, when a witness enters witness protection, he has some unfinished business with the person or persons he snitched on. So the witness may have to go back to court to testify. In that case, the FBI wants to keep up with the witness, but they do it through us. Always through us. Over time, though, as the years go by, the FBI sort of forgets about the witnesses."

Pat changes the subject. "One of the first things you have to do is change your name, legally of course. We use a judge in Fairfax County, Northern Virginia, who keeps the files locked. It's pretty routine, but you need to select a new name. It's best if you keep the same initials, and keep it simple."

"For example?"

"Mike Barnes. Matt Booth. Mark Bridges. Mitch Baldwin."

"Sounds like a bunch of white fraternity brothers."

"Yes, it does. But so does Malcolm Bannister."

"Thanks."

We ponder my new name for a few miles. Surhoff opens a laptop and pecks away. He says, "In this country, what's the most common surname beginning with the letter *B*?"

"Baker," Hitchcock guesses.

"That's number two."

"Bailey," I guess.

"That's number three. Bell is number four. Brooks number five. The winner is Brown, with twice as many customers as Baker in second place."

"One of my favorite African-American writers is James Baldwin," I say. "I'll take it."

"Okay," Surhoff says, tapping keys. "First name?"

"How about Max?"

Hitchcock nods his approval as Surhoff enters the name Max. "I like it," Hitchcock says, as if sniffing a fine wine. Surhoff looks up and says, "There are about twenty-five Max Baldwins in the United States, so it works fine. A good solid name, not too common, not too exotic or weird. I like it. Let's dress it up a bit. Middle name? What works here, Max?"

Nothing works in the middle with Max in front. Then I

think of Mr. Reed and Mr. Copeland, my two former partners, and their tiny shop on Braddock Street in Winchester. Copeland & Reed, Attorneys and Counselors at Law. In their honor, I select Reed.

"Max Reed Baldwin," Surhoff says. "It'll work. Now, a little suffix to bring it to an end, Max? Junior, the Third, the Fourth. Shouldn't get too fancy here."

Hitchcock is shaking his head no. "Leave it alone," he says almost under his breath.

"I agree," I say. "Nothing on the end."

"Great. So we have a name. Max R. Baldwin, right Max?"

"I guess. Let me mull it over for an hour or so. I need to get used to it."

"Of course."

As unsettling as it is, selecting a new name to be used for the rest of my life will be one of my easier decisions. Quite soon I'll be confronted with choices far more difficult—eyes, nose, lips, chin, home, job, family history, and what kind of fictional childhood did I have? Where did I go to college and what did I study? Why am I single and have I been married? Children?

My mind is spinning.

CHAPTER 18

A few miles east of Morgantown, we exit the interstate and find the lot of a Best Western, one of the older-style motels where you can park directly in front of your room. Men are waiting, agents of some variety, FBI, I presume, and as I slide out of the van, wonderfully unshackled, Hanski rushes up and says, "Room 38 here is yours." One of the unnamed agents unlocks the door and hands me the key. Inside, there are two queen-sized beds, and on one there is a selection of clothes. Hanski and Surhoff close the door behind us.

"I got your sizes from the prison," Hanski says, waving an arm at my new wardrobe. "If you don't like it, fine. We can go shopping."

There are two white shirts and one of blue plaid, all with button-down collars; two pairs of khakis and one pair of pre-washed and faded jeans; a brown leather belt; a stack of boxers, neatly folded; two white T-shirts; several pairs of socks still in the wrappers; a pair of brown moccasins that look presentable; and the ugliest pair of black loafers I've ever seen. Overall, not a bad start. "Thanks," I say.

Hanski continues, "Toothbrush, toothpaste, shaving stuff, all in the bathroom. There's a small gym bag over there. Anything else you need, we'll run to the store. You want some lunch?"

"Not now. I just want to be alone."

"No problem, Mal."

"It's now Max, if you don't mind."

"Max Baldwin," Surhoff added.

"That was quick."

They leave and I lock the door. I slowly strip out of the prison garb—olive shirt and pants, white socks, black thick-soled, lace-up shoes, and boxer shorts that are frayed and worn thin. I put on a pair of the new boxers and a T-shirt, then crawl under the covers and stare at the ceiling.

For lunch, we walk next door to a low-budget seafood joint with a drive-through and all the crab legs one can eat for $7.99. It's just Hanski, Surhoff, and I, and we enjoy a long meal of mediocre seafood that is, nonetheless, delicious. With the pressure off, they actually crack jokes and comment on my wardrobe. I return the insults by reminding them that I'm not a white frat boy like them and from now on I'll buy my own clothes.

As the afternoon moves along, they let me know that we have work to do. A lot of decisions must be made. We return to the motel, to the room next to mine, where one of the two beds is covered with files and papers. Hitchcock joins us, so there are four in the room, all supposedly working together, though I'm skeptical. I tell myself over and over that these guys are now on my side, that the government is my protector and friend, but I cannot fully accept this. Perhaps over time they can gain my trust, but I doubt it. The last time I spent hours with government agents I was promised I would not be prosecuted.

By now, the new name has stuck and that decision is final. Hanski says, "Max, we're leaving here in the morning, and we need to decide where we're going. That will be determined by what changes in appearance you have in mind. You've made it clear that you want your face altered, which presents a challenge."

"You mean with my testimony?" I ask.

"Yes. Rucker's trial could be six months from now, or a year."

"Or he may plead guilty and not go to trial," I say.

"Sure. But let's assume he doesn't do that. Let's assume he goes to trial. If you have the surgery now, your new face will be on display when you testify. If you wait until after the trial, you'll be much safer."

"Safer then, but what about now?" I ask. "What about the next six months? The Rucker gang will come after me, we know that. They're already thinking of ways, and the sooner the better for them. If they can get me before the trial, then they rub out a valuable witness. The next six months are the most dangerous, so I want the surgery now. Immediately."

"Okay. What about the trial?"

"Come on, Chris. There are ways to hide me, you know that. I can testify behind a screen or a veil. It's been done. Don't you watch television or movies?"

This gets a chuckle here and there, but the mood is pretty serious. The thought of testifying against Quinn Rucker is terrifying, but there are ways to protect me.

"We did one last year," Hitchcock says. "A big drug trial in New Jersey. The informant looked nothing like his old self, and we put a panel in front of the witness stand so only the judge and jury could see him. We used a voice-altering device, and the defendants had no idea who he was or what he looked like."

"They'll certainly know who I am," I say. "I just don't want them to see me."

"All right," Hanski says. "It's your decision."

"Then consider it final," I say.

Hanski pulls out his cell phone and heads for the door. "Let me make some calls."

When he's out of the room, Surhoff says, "Okay, while he's doing that, can we talk about a destination? Give us some guidance here, Max, so we can get busy finding a place."

I say, "Florida. Except for the Marines, I've lived my entire life in the hills and mountains. I want a change of scenery, beaches and views of the ocean, a warmer climate." I rattle this off as if I've spent hours contemplating it, which in fact I have. "Not south Florida, it's too hot. Maybe Pensacola or Jacksonville, up north where it's a bit milder."

The marshals absorb this, and I can see their minds racing. Surhoff begins hitting keys on his laptop, looking for my new place in the sun. I relax in a chair, my bare feet on the bed, and cannot help but relish where I am. It's almost 4:00 p.m. Sunday afternoons were the worst days at Frostburg. Like most of the inmates, I didn't work on the Sabbath and often grew bored. There were pickup basketball games and long walks on the jogging trail, anything to stay busy. Visitation was over, and those who had seen their families were usually subdued. Another week was beginning, one just like the last one.

Slowly, the prison life is fading. I know it will be impossible to forget, but it's time to start the process of putting it all behind me. Malcolm Bannister is still an inmate, somewhere, but Max Baldwin is a free man with places to go and things to see.

After dark, we drive into Morgantown in search of a steak house. Along the way, we pass a strip club. Nothing is said, but I am sorely tempted. I have not seen a naked woman in five years, though I've certainly dreamed of them. However, I'm not sure gawking at a bunch of strippers will be that fulfilling at this point. We find the restaurant that's been recommended and get a table: just three old pals having a nice dinner. Hanski, Surhoff, and I order the largest fillets on the menu, and I wash mine down with three draft beers. They stick with iced tea, but I can tell they envy my drinks. We turn in before ten, but sleep is impossible. I watch television for an hour, something I did little of at Frostburg.

At midnight, I pick up the copy of the indictment Hanski left behind and read every word. There is no mention of a ballistics report or of any witnesses. There is a lengthy narrative about the crime scene, the bullet wounds, causes of death, the burn marks on Naomi Clary's body, and the empty safe, but no descriptions of physical evidence. So far, Quinn's confession is all they have. That, and the suspicion surrounding the cash in his possession. An indictment can be amended by the prosecution at almost any time, and this one needs some work. It appears to be a rush job intended to turn down the heat.

I am not being critical; it's a gorgeous document.

CHAPTER 19

For Stanley Mumphrey, the U.S. Attorney for the Southern District, the event would be the biggest moment yet in his brief career as a federal prosecutor. On the job for two years now, appointed by the President, he had found it all rather mundane, and though it was a fabulous addition to his résumé, it was somewhat unfulfilling. Until, of course, Judge Fawcett and Ms. Clary were murdered. Instantly, Stanley's career had new meaning. He had the hottest case in the country and, like many U.S. Attorneys, planned to make the most of it.

The gathering was advertised as a press conference, though none of the authorities planned to answer any questions. It was a show, nothing more, nothing less. A carefully orchestrated act intended to (1) feed some egos and (2) let the public, especially the potential jurors, know that the Feds had their man, and his name was Quinn Al Rucker.

By 9:00 a.m., the podium was covered with portable mikes, all advertising the television and radio stations from whence they came. The courtroom was packed with reporters of all stripes. Men with bulky cameras stepped on each other as they jockeyed for position, all under the watchful eyes of courtroom deputies.

In the rule books and decisions that govern the practice and procedure of criminal law, at both the state and the federal levels, nowhere is it written that the "announcement" or "handing down" or "delivering" or "issuance" of an indictment must be publicized. In fact, almost none of them are. They are formally registered with the clerk once the grand jury makes its decision, and eventually served upon the defendant. An indictment is only one side of the case—the prosecution's. Nothing contained within an indictment is evidence; at trial, the jury never sees it. The grand jury that issues an indictment hears only one side of the case, that presented by the government.

Occasionally, though, an indictment is too hot, too important, just too damned much fun, to be allowed to flow benignly through the system. It must be publicized by those who've worked so hard to catch a criminal and who will bring him to justice. Stanley Mumphrey did nothing to apprehend Quinn Rucker, but he was certainly the man who would put him on trial. In the federal pecking order, the U.S. Attorney far outranks a mere FBI agent; therefore, the event belonged to Stanley. As was customary, he would share (reluctantly) the spotlight with the FBI.

At 9:10, a door opened beside the bench, and a platoon of hard-nosed men in black suits flooded the space behind the podium. They jostled for position, all with their hands cupped over their balls. The arrangement here was crucial because the frame was only so wide. Standing at the podium, side by side, were Stanley Mumphrey and Victor Westlake—head prosecutor, head cop. Behind them were FBI agents and assistant prosecutors, inching together, squeezing, trying to find a good view of the cameras so the cameras could hopefully see them. The lucky ones would listen intently to Mr. Mumphrey and Mr. Westlake, and they would frown and act as if they had no clue there was a camera within two miles of the courthouse. It was the same pathetic routine perfected by members of Congress.

"This morning, we have an indictment in the murder case of Judge Raymond Fawcett and Ms. Naomi Clary," Mumphrey said slowly, his voice nervous and at least two octaves higher than normal. He'd been struggling in the courtroom, losing the slam-dunk cases he assigned to himself, and the most common criticism was that he seemed jittery and out of place. Some felt that it was perhaps because he had spent so little time in the courtroom during his unremarkable ten-year career.

Stanley picked up the indictment and held it higher, as if those watching were now expected to read the print. "This indictment is for two counts of murder. The defendant is one Quinn Al Rucker. And, yes, I fully expect to seek the death penalty in this case." This last sentence was supposed to send ripples of drama through the crowd, but Stanley's timing was off. Drama came quickly, though, when an aide flashed a large black-and-white photo of Quinn on a screen. Finally, the world saw the man who killed the judge and his secretary. Guilty!

Reading shakily from his notes, Stanley gave the background on Quinn and managed to convey the impression that Quinn had escaped from prison for the sole purpose of exacting revenge against the judge. At one point, Victor Westlake, standing sentry-like at his shoulder, frowned and glanced down at his notes. But Stanley marched on, almost blubbering about his beloved friend and mentor Raymond Fawcett, how much the judge meant to him, and so on. His voice actually shook a bit when he tried to explain how honored he was to have the awesome responsibility of seeking justice for these "gruesome" murders. It would have taken about two minutes to read the entire indictment, then go home. But no. With a crowd like this, and millions watching, Stanley found it necessary to ramble on and give a speech, one about justice and the war on crime. After several painful digressions, he got back on track near the end when it was time to hand off. He praised Victor Westlake and the entire Federal Bureau of Investigation for its work, work that was "superhuman, tireless, and brilliant."

When he finally shut up, Westlake thanked him, though it was unclear if he was thanking him for shutting up or for passing along so many compliments. Westlake was far more experienced in these productions than young Stanley, and he spoke for five minutes without saying anything. He thanked his men, said he was confident the case had been solved, and wished the prosecution well. When he finished and took a step back, a reporter yelled a question. Westlake snapped, "No comment," and indicated it was time to go. Stanley, though, wasn't ready to leave all those cameras. For a second or two he smiled goofily at the crowd, as if to say, "Here I am." Then Westlake whispered something to him.

"Thank you," Stanley said and backed away. The event was over.

I watch the press conference in my Best Western room. The thought crosses my mind that, with Stanley in charge, Quinn may have a fighting chance after all. If the case goes to trial, though, Stanley will likely step aside and allow one of his seasoned assistants to handle matters. No doubt he'll continue to work the media and begin plotting his run for a higher office, but the serious trial work will be done by the pros. Depending on how long things are delayed, Stanley might even be out of a job. He serves a four-year term, same as the President. When a challenger captures the White House, all U.S. Attorneys are terminated.

When the press conference is over and the CNN talking heads begin babbling, I switch channels but find nothing of interest. Armed with the remote, I have total control over the television. I am adjusting to freedom with remarkable ease. I can sleep until I wake up. I can choose what I wear, though the choices so far are limited. Most important, there is no cell mate, no one else to contend with in a ten-by-twelve cube. I've measured the motel room twice—approximately sixteen feet wide and thirty feet long, including the bathroom. It's a castle.

By mid-morning, we're on the road, going south now, on Interstate 79. Three hours later we arrive at the airport in Charleston, West Virginia, where we say farewell to Agent Chris Hanski. He wishes me well, and I thank him for his courtesies. Pat Surhoff and I board a commuter flight to Charlotte, North Carolina. I have no documentation, but the Marshals Service and the airline speak in code. I just follow Pat, and I have to admit I'm excited as I board the small plane.

The airport in Charlotte is a large, open, modern place, and I stand on a mezzanine for two hours and watch the people come and go. I am one of them, a free man, and I will soon have the ability to walk to the counter and buy a ticket going anywhere.

At 6:10, we board a nonstop flight to Denver. The code pulled off an upgrade, and Pat and I sit side by side in first class, compliments of the taxpayers. I have a beer and he has a ginger ale. Dinner is roasted chicken and gravy, and I suppose most of the passengers eat it for sustenance. For me, it's fine dining. I have a glass of Pinot Noir, my first sip of wine in many years.

―――――

Victor Westlake and his entourage left the press conference and drove four blocks to the downtown law office of Jimmy Lee Arnold. They presented themselves to the receptionist, who was expecting them. Within minutes, she led them down a narrow hall to a large conference room and offered coffee. They thanked her and declined.

Jimmy Lee was a fixture in the Roanoke criminal bar, a twenty-year veteran of the drug and vice wars. He had represented Jakeel Staley, Quinn Rucker's nephew, four years earlier. Like so many of the lone gunmen who labor near the fringes of the underworld, Jimmy Lee was a character. Long gray hair, cowboy boots, rings on his fingers, red-framed reading glasses perched on his nose. Though he was suspicious of the FBI, he welcomed them into his domain. These were not the first agents to visit; there had been many over the years.

"So, you got an indictment," he said as soon as the introductions were over. Victor Westlake gave a bare-bones summary of the case against Quinn Rucker. "You represented his nephew Jakeel Staley a few years back, right?"

"That's right," Jimmy Lee said. "But I never met Quinn Rucker."

"I'm assuming the family, or the gang, hired you to represent the kid."

"Something like that. It was a private contract, not a court appointment."

"Who from the family did you deal with?"

Jimmy Lee's mood changed. He reached into a coat pocket and withdrew a small recorder. "Just to be safe," he said as he pressed a button. "Let's get this on the record. There are three of you, one of me. I wanna make sure there's no misunderstanding of what's said. Any problems with this?"

"No," Westlake replied.

"Good. Now, you asked me who I dealt with from the family when I was hired to represent Jakeel Staley, right?"

"Right."

"Well, I'm not sure I can answer that. Client confidentiality and all. Why don't you tell me why you're interested in this?"

"Sure. Quinn Rucker gave a confession. Said he killed Judge Fawcett because the judge reneged on a bribe; said he, the gang, paid $500,000 cash to Fawcett for a favorable ruling on the motion to suppress the search that yielded a van-load of coke." Westlake paused and watched Jimmy Lee carefully. Jimmy Lee's eyes yielded nothing. He finally shrugged and said, "So?"

"So, did you have any knowledge of this bribe?"

"If I knew about it, then that would be a crime, wouldn't it? You think I'm stupid enough to admit to a crime. I'm offended."

"Oh, don't be offended, Mr. Arnold. I'm not accusing you of anything."

"Did Quinn Rucker implicate me in the bribe?"

"He's been vague so far, said only that a lawyer was the intermediary."

"I'm sure this particular gang of thugs has access to a lot of lawyers."

"Indeed. Were you surprised when Judge Fawcett denied the motion to suppress?"

Jimmy Lee smiled and rolled his eyes. "Nothing surprises me anymore. If you believe in the Constitution, then it was a bad search and the evidence, 150 kilos of pure coke, should have been kicked out. That would take some spine, and you don't see much of that anymore, especially in big drug busts. It takes balls for a judge, state or federal, to exclude such wonderful evidence, regardless of what the cops did to get it. No, I wasn't surprised."

"How long did you practice in Judge Fawcett's courtroom?"

"Since the day he was appointed, twenty years ago. I knew him well."

"Do you believe he would take a bribe?"

"A cash bribe for a favorable ruling?"

"And a lighter sentence."

Jimmy Lee crossed his legs, hanging one ostrich-skin boot on a knee, and locked his hands together just below his gut. He thought for a moment, then said, "I've seen judges make some outrageous decisions, but usually out of stupidity or laziness. But, no, Mr. Westlake, I do not believe Judge Fawcett, or any other state or federal judge within the Commonwealth of Virginia, would take a bribe, cash or otherwise. I said nothing surprises me, but I was wrong. Such a bribe would shock me."

"Would you say Judge Fawcett had a reputation for high integrity?"

"No, I wouldn't say that. He was okay his first few years on the bench, then he changed and became a real hard-ass. My clients have all been charged with crimes, but they're not all criminals. Fawcett didn't see it that way. He was much too happy to send a guy away for twenty years. He always sided with the prosecution and the cops, and to me that's not integrity."

"But he didn't take money?"

"Not to my knowledge."

"Here's our quandary, Mr. Arnold. If Quinn Rucker is telling the truth, then how did he manage to get the money to Fawcett? Here's a tough street kid from D.C. who's never met Fawcett before. There had to be an intermediary somewhere along the line. I'm not saying it's you, and there's no suggestion that you're involved in his story. But you know the system. How did the $500,000 change hands?"

Jimmy Lee was shaking his head. "If the system involves bribery, then I don't know how it works, okay? I resent the implication. You're talking to the wrong man."

"Again, I'm not implicating or accusing you of anything."

"You're getting pretty damned close." Jimmy Lee slowly got to his feet and reached for the recorder. "Let's say this little meeting is over."

"No need for that, Mr. Arnold."

Jimmy Lee picked up the recorder and returned it to a pocket. "It's been a real pleasure," he said as he yanked open the door and disappeared down the hall.

———

Directly across Church Street, Dee Ray Rucker was entering another law office as Victor Westlake and his agents left Jimmy Lee's.

Quinn had been arrested the previous Wednesday night and had spent the first ten hours of his captivity in the interrogation room. After he confessed, on camera, he was finally taken to the Norfolk City Jail, placed in solitary, and slept for twelve straight hours. He was not allowed to use the phone until Saturday morning, and it took most of the day to reach a family member who was willing to talk. Early Saturday evening, Quinn was driven from Norfolk to Roanoke, a four-and-a-half-hour journey.

Once Dee Ray realized his older brother was in jail for killing a federal judge, he scrambled to find a lawyer who would take the case. Several in D.C. and Virginia declined. By late Sunday afternoon, another Roanoke character named Dusty Shiver had agreed to represent Quinn through the initial stages of the prosecution, but he reserved the right to step down if a trial became imminent. For obvious reasons, the local bar was more than a little nervous about representing a man charged with knocking off such an important part of the judiciary.

Dusty Shiver had once practiced law with Jimmy Lee Arnold, and they were cut from the same mold. In law, most partnerships, large and small, blow up, usually over the issue of money. Jimmy Lee got stiffed on a fee, blamed his partners, and moved across the street.

Dusty had managed to spend an hour with Quinn at the jail early Monday morning, before the indictment was announced. He was surprised to learn his client had already confessed. Quinn was adamant that he was coerced, tricked, pressured, threatened, and that the confession was bogus. He was claiming to be innocent. After leaving the jail, Dusty stopped by the U.S. Attorney's office and picked up a copy of the indictment. He was poring over it when his secretary buzzed in with the report that Mr. Dee Ray Rucker had arrived.

Of the two, Dusty, with long gray hair, faded jeans, and a red leather vest, looked more like a drug trafficker, and Dee Ray, in a Zegna suit, looked more like a lawyer. They greeted each other cautiously in Dusty's cluttered office. The first issue was the retainer, and Dee Ray opened his Prada attaché and produced $50,000 in cash, which Dusty counted and stuck in a drawer.

"Do you know he's already confessed?" Dusty asked as he tucked the money away.

"He what?" asked Dee Ray, shocked.

"Yes, he's confessed. He says he signed a written statement admitting to the murders, and supposedly there's also a video. Please tell me he's too smart for that."

"He's too smart for that. We never talk to cops, never. Quinn would not voluntarily confess to anything, even if he was dead guilty. That's not our M.O. If a cop shows up, we start calling lawyers."

"He says the interrogation lasted all night long, he waived his rights, asked for a lawyer several times, but the two FBI agents kept hammering away. They tripped him up, got him confused, and he began hallucinating. He couldn't shut up. They said he was facing two counts of capital murder and that the entire family would be indicted since the killings were a part of gang business. They lied to him and said they could help him if he cooperated, that the family of Judge Fawcett was opposed to the death penalty, and so on. After hours of this, they broke him and he gave them what they wanted. Says he doesn't remember all that happened; he was too fatigued. When he woke up and tried to recall what had happened, it was all a dream, a nightmare. It took several hours before he realized what he had done, but even now he can't remember everything."

Dee Ray listened, too stunned to speak.

Dusty continued, "He does remember the FBI agents telling him that they have a ballistics report that matches one of his guns to the crime scene, and there is supposedly a boot print of some sort. Plus, there are witnesses who place him in the vicinity at the time of the murders. Again, some of this is vague."

"When can you see the confession?"

"I'll meet with the U.S. Attorney as soon as possible, but nothing will happen fast. It might be weeks before I see a written confession and the video, as well as the other evidence they plan to use."

"If he asked for a lawyer, why didn't they stop the interrogation?"

"That's a great question. Usually, though, the cops will swear that the defendant waived his rights and did not ask for a lawyer. His word against theirs. In a case this important, you can bet the FBI agents will swear to hell and back that Quinn never mentioned a lawyer. Just like they'll swear they did not threaten him, or lie to him, or promise him a deal. They got their confession, now they're trying to build a case with physical evidence. If they find nothing, then the confession is all they have."

"Is it enough?"

"Oh yes."

"I don't believe this. Quinn's not stupid. He would never agree to an interrogation."

"Has he ever killed anyone before?"

"Not that I know of. We have other people who do that sort of thing."

"Why did he escape from prison?"

"You ever been to prison?"

"No."

"Neither have I, but I know lots of guys who've served time. Everybody wants out."

"I suppose," Shiver said. "You ever heard of a guy named Malcolm Bannister?"

"No."

"Quinn says they served time together at Frostburg and that he's the guy who's behind these accusations; says he and Bannister were friends and talked at length about Judge Fawcett and his dirty work. He's really bitter at Bannister."

"When can I see my brother?"

"Not until Saturday, regular visitation. I'll go back to the jail this afternoon with a copy of the indictment. I can pass along any messages if you'd like."

"Sure, tell him to keep his mouth shut."

"I'm afraid it's too late for that."

CHAPTER 20

The details are vague and unlikely to become clearer. Pat Surhoff is willing to tell me that the clinic is a part of the U.S. Army hospital at Fort Carson, but that would be hard to deny. He cautiously says that the clinic specializes in RAM—radical appearance modification—and is used by several agencies of the federal government. The plastic surgeons are some of the best and have worked on a lot of faces that might otherwise get blown off if not radically modified. I grill him just to watch him squirm, but he does not divulge much else. After my surgery, I will convalesce here for two months before moving on.

My first appointment is with a therapist of some variety who wants to make sure I'm ready for the jolting experience of changing not only names but faces as well. She's pleasant and thoughtful, and I easily convince her that I'm eager to move on.

The second meeting is with two doctors, both male, and a female nurse. The woman is needed for the feminine perspective of how I will look afterward. It doesn't take me long to realize that these three are very good at what they do. Using sophisticated software, they are able to take my face and make almost any change. The eyes are crucial here, they say more than once. Change the eyes and you change everything. Sharpen the nose a bit. Leave the lips alone. Some Botox in the folds of the cheeks should work. Definitely shave the head and keep it that way. For almost two hours we fiddle and tinker with the new face of Max Baldwin.

In the hands of less experienced surgeons, this might be a gut-wrenching experience. For the past twenty-five years, all of my adult life, I have looked basically the same, my face shaped by genetics, weathered by the years, and, luckily, unblemished by wounds or injuries. It's a nice, solid face that's served me well, and to suddenly ditch it forever is no small step. My new friends say there is no need to change anything, only a few ways to improve. A nip here, a tuck there, a bit of tightening and straightening, and, voilà, a new version that's every bit as handsome and much safer. I assure them I'm much more concerned with safety than vanity, and they readily agree. They've heard this before. I cannot help but wonder how many informants, snitches, and spies they've worked on. Hundreds, judging by their teamwork.

As my new look comes together on the large computer screen, we have serious discussions about accessories, and the three seem genuinely excited when a pair of round tortoiseshell glasses is placed on Max's face. "That's it!" the nurse says excitedly, and I have to admit Max looks a lot smarter and hipper. We spend an entire half hour playing around with various mustache schemes, before tossing the idea altogether. We split 2–2 on the idea of a beard, then decide to just wait and see. I promise not to shave for a week so we'll have a better idea.

Because of the gravity of what we're doing, my little team is in no hurry. We spend the entire morning redesigning Max, and when everyone is happy, they print a high-definition rendering of my new look. I take it with me back to my room and tack it to the wall. A nurse studies it and says she likes it. I like her too, but she's married and does not flirt. If she only knew.

I pass the afternoon reading and walking around the unrestricted areas of the base. It's much like killing time at Frostburg, a place far away in both distance and memory. I keep coming back to my room, to the face on the wall: a slick head, slightly pointed nose, slightly enhanced chin, leaner cheeks, no wrinkles, and the eyes of someone new. The middle-aged puffiness is gone. The eyelids are not quite as large. Most important, Max is staring through a pair of round designer frames, and he looks pretty damned hip.

I'm assuming it's just that easy, that these doctors can deliver a face that looks exactly like Max on the wall. But even if they get close, I'll be pleased. No one will recognize their new creation, and that's all that matters. I'm too close to judge whether I'll look better before or after, but the truth is that I'll look good enough. Safety is indeed far more important than vanity.

At seven the next morning, they prep me and roll me into a small operating room. The anesthesiologist goes through his routine, and I happily float away.

The operation lasts for five hours and is a great success, according to the doctors. They have no way of knowing because my face is wrapped like a mummy's. It will be weeks before the swelling is all gone and the new features take shape.

Four days after he was indicted, Quinn Rucker made his initial appearance in court. For the occasion, he was kept in the same orange jumpsuit he'd been wearing since his arrival at the Roanoke City Jail. He was handcuffed and chained to his waist, and his ankles were bound and chained. A bulletproof vest was strapped over his shoulders and around his midsection, and no fewer than a dozen heavily armed guards, agents, and deputies escorted him out of the jail and into a bulletproof Chevrolet Suburban. No threats had been made on his life and a secret route would be taken to the federal courthouse, but the authorities were taking no chances.

Inside the courtroom, reporters and onlookers filled the seats long before Rucker's scheduled appearance at 10:00 a.m.

His arrest and indictment were big news, with no intervening mass murder or celebrity breakup to steal his thunder. Outside the courtroom, the bindings and armor were removed, and Quinn entered unshackled. As the only participant in an orange jumpsuit, and virtually the only black guy in the courtroom, Quinn certainly looked guilty. He sat at a table with Dusty Shiver and one of his associates. Across the aisle, Stanley Mumphrey and his brigade of assistants pushed files around with great importance, as if preparing to argue before the Supreme Court.

Out of respect to their fallen comrade, the other eleven judges in the Southern District had recused themselves from the case. The initial appearance would be in front of Ken Konover, a U.S. Magistrate, who would look and act very much like a presiding judge. Konover took the bench and called things to order. He rattled off a few preliminaries, then asked if the defendant had read the indictment. "He has," Dusty responded, "and we waive a formal reading."

"Thank you," replied Konover.

Seated in the first row behind the defense table was Dee Ray, fashionably dressed as always, and obviously concerned.

Konover said, "Does the defendant wish to enter a plea at this time?"

On cue, Dusty stood and nodded at his client, who likewise got to his feet, awkwardly, and said, "Yes sir. Not guilty."

"Very well, a plea of not guilty is hereby entered." Dusty and Quinn sat down.

Konover said, "I have here a motion to set bail, Mr. Shiver. Do you want to be heard on this?" His tone left no doubt that nothing Dusty could say would persuade the court to grant a reasonable bail, if any.

Sensing the inevitable, and wishing not to embarrass himself, Dusty said, "No, Your Honor, the motion speaks for itself."

"Mr. Mumphrey?"

Stanley stood and walked to the podium. He cleared his throat and said, "Your Honor, this defendant has been indicted for the murder of a federal judge. The United States feels strongly that he should be held without bail."

"I agree," Konover said quickly. "Anything further, Mr. Mumphrey?"

"No sir, not at this time."

"Mr. Shiver?"

"No, Your Honor."

"The defendant shall be remanded to the custody of the U.S. Marshals Service." Konover tapped his gavel, stood, and left the bench. The initial appearance lasted less than ten minutes.

———————

Dee Ray had been in Roanoke for three days and was tired of the place. He leaned on Dusty Shiver, who leaned on a friend at the jail, and a quick meeting was arranged with the accused. Since visits with the family were on weekends only, this one would take place off the record, in a room used to test drunk drivers for blood alcohol content. No record of it would ever be entered. The brothers did not suspect anyone was listening. The FBI recorded their conversation, a portion of it being:

QUINN: I'm here because of Malcolm Bannister, Dee, you understand what I'm saying?

DEE RAY: I got it, I got it, and we'll deal with it later. Right now you gotta tell me what happened.

QUINN: Nothin' happened. I didn't kill nobody. They tricked me into the confession, like I said. I want something done about Bannister.

DEE RAY: He's in prison, right?

QUINN: Probably not. Knowing Bannister, he probably used Rule 35 to get out.

DEE RAY: Rule 35?

Quinn: Everybody on the inside knows Rule 35. Ain't
important now. He's out and he needs to be found.

A long pause.

Dee Ray: Lot of time, lot of money.
Quinn: Look, little brother, don't tell me about time. The
Fibbies got nothin' on me, I mean nothin'. That don't
mean they can't nail my ass. If this thing goes to trial in
a year or so, Bannister might be their star witness, hear
what I'm sayin'?
Dee Ray: And what's he gonna say?
Quinn: He'll say whatever it takes, he don't care. He's out,
man, he cut the deal. He'll say we talked about Judge
Fawcett back in prison. That's what he'll say.
Dee Ray: Did you?

Another long pause.

Quinn: Yeah, we talked about him all the time. We knew
he kept cash.

A pause.

Quinn: You gotta get Bannister, Dee Ray. Okay?
Dee Ray: Okay. Let me talk to Tall Man.

CHAPTER 21

Three weeks post-surgery and I'm climbing the walls. The bandages are off and the stitches are gone, but the swelling is taking forever. I look in the mirror a hundred times a day, waiting for things to improve, waiting for Max to emerge from the bruising and puffiness. My surgical team stops by constantly to tell me how great I look, but I'm sick of these people. I can't chew, can't eat, can't walk for more than five minutes, and so most of my time is spent rolling around in a wheelchair. Movements must be slow and calculated; otherwise, I could rip out some of the fine artwork that has gone into the face of Max Reed Baldwin. I count the days and often think I'm in prison again. Weeks pass, and the swelling and bruising slowly go away.

Is it possible to be in love with a woman you've never actually touched? I have convinced myself the answer is yes. Her name is Vanessa Young, and I met her at Frostburg, in the visitors' room on a cold wintry Saturday morning. I shouldn't say that I met her, but I saw her for the first time. She was there visiting her brother, a guy I knew and liked. We met later, during another visit, but we couldn't touch. I wrote her letters and she wrote a few back, but it became painfully obvious, at least to me, that my infatuation with Vanessa was not exactly a two-way street.

I cannot begin to contemplate the hours I've invested fantasizing about this woman.

Over the past two years, our lives have changed dramatically, and now I am emboldened to contact her. My new best friend, Pat Surhoff, informed me that I cannot write or receive letters while at Fort Carson, but I write one anyway. I work on it for days, tweaking, editing, killing time. I bare my soul to Vanessa, and practically beg her to see me.

I'll find a way to mail it later.

———————

Surhoff is back to fetch me. We leave Fort Carson in a hurry and drive to Denver, where we board a nonstop flight to Atlanta. I wear a baseball cap and big sunglasses, and I do not catch a single curious glance. I bitch about the seating arrangement; we're sitting side by side in coach, not first class. Pat says Congress is cutting budgets everywhere. After a hearty lunch of raisins and Cokes, we get down to business. He opens a delightful little file with all sorts of goodies: a Virginia court order changing my name to Max Reed Baldwin; a new Social Security card issued to the same guy; a birth certificate proving I was born in Memphis to parents I've never heard of; and a Florida driver's license with a fake photo taken from the computerized rendering my doctors and I concocted before the surgery. It looks so real that not even I can tell it's fake. Pat explains that I'll get another in a month or so when my face finally comes together. Same for a passport. We fill out applications for Visa and American Express cards. At his suggestion, I've been practicing a different handwriting, one that resembles chicken scratch but is not much worse than the old one. Max signs a six-month lease for a one-bedroom condo in Neptune Beach, a few miles east of Jacksonville, and he applies for a checking account at SunCoast Bank. Pat tells me there's a branch office three blocks from the condo. The reward money of $150,000 will be wired into the account as soon as it's up and running, and from there I can do with it what I want. Because I will hit the ground with so much cash, the powers that be feel as though I don't need much from them. I really can't gripe about this. He says the IRS will grant me a waiver from any taxes on the money and provides the name of an accountant who knows both the IRS code and whatever code the marshals use. He hands me an envelope with $3,000 in cash and says this should be enough to get me plugged in. We talk about the ins and outs of leasing a car, as opposed to buying one, and he explains that a lease is easier and will help build a good credit rating.

He hands me a two-page summary of the life of Max Baldwin, and it reads like an obituary. Parents, siblings, education, employment history, and I'm intrigued to know that I've spent most of my life in Seattle and have been divorced twice, no children. I'm relocating to Florida because it's about as far away from wife number two as I can get. It's important for me to memorize this fiction and stick with the script. I have an employment history (all with government agencies) and a credit score.

On the issue of employment, I have two choices. The first is that of a procurement officer at the Mayport Naval Station a few miles north of Neptune Beach, starting salary of $48,000, two months of training required. The second is that of an account manager for the Veterans Administration, also at $48,000 a year. It's best if I remain a federal employee, at least for the first few years. However, Pat stresses for the tenth time, my life now belongs to me, and I can do whatever I want. The only boundaries are those dictated by my past.

Just as I begin to feel somewhat overwhelmed, he reaches into his briefcase and pulls out the toys. The first is an Apple iPad, mine courtesy of the government, and already registered to Max. As the librarian, Malcolm had access to computers (but not the

Internet), and I worked hard to keep my skills as fresh as possible. But this thing blows me away. We spend a full hour in an intense tutorial. When I'm exhausted, he pulls out an iPhone. It's his, not mine because I'll have to select a service provider and buy my own phone, but he walks me through this amazing device. The flight is over before we can finish.

I find a computer store in the Atlanta airport and I kill an hour browsing through the gadgets. Technology will be the key to my survival, and I am determined to know the latest. Before we leave Atlanta, I mail the letter to Vanessa Young. No return address.

We land in Jacksonville at dark, rent a car, and drive thirty minutes to the beaches east of the city. Atlantic Beach, Neptune Beach, Jacksonville Beach, you can't tell where one ends and the other begins. It's a cool area with hundreds of neat cottages, some residential, some rentals, and assorted small hotels and modern condos facing the ocean. The raisins for lunch are long forgotten and we are starving. We find a seafood place on a pedestrian mall a block from the water and devour oysters and shrimp. It's a young crowd at the bar, lots of pretty girls with tanned legs, and I can't help but stare. So far, everyone is white, and I wonder if I'll stand out. The Jacksonville metro area has a million people and 18 percent of them are black, so Pat does not think my ethnicity will be a problem. I attempt to explain what it's like being black in a white world but realize, again, that some things cannot be fully covered over dinner, if ever.

I change the subject and ask questions about the Witness Security Program. Pat is based in Virginia and will soon return home. Another marshal will become my contact, my handler, and this person will not in any way attempt to keep me under surveillance. He, or she, will always be close by in case of problems, or trouble. Typically, my handler will have several other "persons" to monitor. If there is a hint of something gone wrong, I will be moved at once to another location, but, Pat assures me, this rarely happens.

What will it take for the bad guys to find me? Pat says he doesn't know because this has never happened. I press him: "But surely you've had to relocate some people."

"I've never been involved in a relocation, but, yes, it has happened. To my knowledge, and I've been handling informants for ten years, there has not been a serious threat against one. But I've heard of a couple, maybe three, who became convinced they had been discovered. They wanted to move, so we swooped in and they vanished, again."

For obvious reasons, neither the law library nor the general library at Frostburg offered books on witness protection, so my knowledge is limited. But I know the program has not been perfect. "So no problems whatsoever? That's hard to believe."

"I didn't say it was perfect. There's a great story from thirty years ago, a legend in the business. We had a serious Mafia informant who squealed on the family and took down some big bosses, one of the FBI's biggest grand slams ever. This guy had a bull's-eye on him you could hit blindfolded. We took him deep, buried him, and a few years passed. He was a postal inspector in a town of fifty thousand, perfect cover, but he was a crook, right? A thug by birth, and it was impossible for him to stay clean. He opened a used-car lot, then another. He got into the pawnshop business, started fencing stolen goods, and eventually found his way into the marijuana trade. We knew who he was, but the FBI did not. When he got indicted, he called his handler to come bail him out of jail. The handler freaked out, as did everyone along the ladder, all the way up to the Director of the FBI. There was a mad scramble to get him out of jail and off to a new location. Jobs were threatened, deals were cut, judges were pleaded with, and they eventually got his charges dismissed. But it was a close call. So don't start laundering money again."

He thinks his last comment is funny. "I've never laundered money," I say without a smile.

"Sorry."

We finish dessert and head for my new home. It's on the seventh floor of a tower, one of four in a cluster lined up along the beach, with tennis courts and pools scattered below. Pat explains that most of the units are rentals, but a few have permanent residents. I'm here for six months, and then it's up to me. It's a one-bedroom unit, furnished, with a kitchen-den combo, nice sofa and chairs, nothing luxurious but not cheap either. After he's gone, I stand on my small balcony and stare at the moon over the ocean. I breathe the salty air and listen to the waves gently roll ashore.

Freedom is exhilarating, and indescribable.

I forgot to close the curtains, and I wake up to a blinding sun. It is my first true morning as a liberated and unwatched person, and I can't wait to feel sand between my toes. There are a few early birds on the beach, and I hustle down there, my face partially hidden behind a cap and sunglasses. No one notices; no one cares. People who roam aimlessly up and down beaches are lost in their own worlds, and I am quickly getting lost in mine. I have no family, no job, no responsibilities, and no past. Max is starting a brand-new life.

Pat Surhoff retrieves me around noon, and we have a sandwich for lunch. Then he drives me to the Mayport Naval Station, where I have an appointment with a doctor who knows the code. The surgery is progressing nicely, no complications whatsoever. I'll return in two weeks for another exam.

Next, we go to the SunCoast Bank branch near the condo, and as we get close, Pat preps me for what's coming. He will not go inside, because it's important for me to establish the account myself. No one in the bank knows the code; it's strictly aboveboard. For the time being, Max Baldwin is semiretired, not working, and pondering a move to the area. He wants to open a standard checking account, no frills, and so on, and will put down $1,000 cash as the initial deposit. Once the account is opened, Max will return to the bank and get the proper wiring instructions. Inside the bank, I am routed to the lovely Gretchen Hiler, a fortyish bleached blonde who's spent far too much time in the sun. She has a small desk in a tight cubicle and no wedding ring. She has no way of knowing that she is the first woman I've been truly alone with in over five years. Try as I do, I cannot stop a lot of improper thoughts. Or maybe they're just natural. Gretchen is a chatterbox, and at this moment so am I. We go through the paperwork quickly, with me proudly giving a real address. I put down a thousand in cash. She fetches some temporary checks and promises more in the mail later. When all business has ended, we keep talking. She gives me her card and is willing to help in any way. I promise to call when I get a cell phone; the bank needs a phone number. I almost ask her to dinner, primarily because I'm convinced she might say yes, but I wisely let it pass. There will be plenty of time for that later, after I'm more comfortable and my face is easier to look at, hopefully.

I proposed to Dionne when I was twenty-four years old, and from that moment until the day I was sentenced and taken into custody, I was never unfaithful. There was one near miss, with the wife of an acquaintance, but we both realized things would end badly. As a small-town lawyer, I saw a lot of divorces, and I was constantly amazed at the awful ways men could screw up their lives and families simply because they couldn't resist temptation. A quickie, then a casual fling, then something more serious, and before long they were in court getting their eyeballs clawed out and losing their kids, along with their money. The truth was

I adored my wife and I was getting all the sex I wanted at home. The other part of the truth was that I never fancied myself as a ladies' man.

Before Dionne, I had girlfriends and enjoyed my single days, but I never hopped blindly from one bed to another. Now, forty-three and single, I have a hunch there are a lot of women around my age who are looking for companionship. I can feel the urge, but at the same time all movements must be calculated.

As I walk out of the bank, I feel a sense of accomplishment. I just pulled off the first little mission of my secret existence. Pat has been waiting in the car, and when I get in he says, "Well?"

"No problem."

"What took so long?"

"The account manager is a cute girl and she threw herself at me."

"Has this always been a problem?"

"I wouldn't call it a problem, but, yes, women are attracted to me. I've always had to fight them off with a stick."

"Keep fighting. It's been the downfall of many men."

"So you're an expert on women?"

"Not at all. Where are we going now?"

"Shopping. I want some decent clothes."

We find a men's store and I spend $800 upgrading my wardrobe. Once again, Pat waits in the car. We agree that two men, both in their early forties, one white and the other black, shopping together, might raise an eyebrow or two. My goal is to raise as few eyebrows as possible. Next, he drops me off at a Florida Cellular office where I open an account and buy an iPhone. With it in my pocket, I finally feel like a real American, connected.

We spend the next two days running errands and getting Max firmly established. I write my first check to a car-leasing agency and drive away in a used Audi A4 convertible, mine for the next twelve months at $400 a pop and fully insured. Now that I'm mobile, and now that Pat and I are getting on each other's nerves, he starts talking about his exit. I'm ready for the independence and he's ready to go home.

I visit Gretchen again to check on the bank's wiring instructions and explain to her that a substantial sum of money is on the way. Pat clears things with his higher-ups, and the reward money is moved from some buried account to SunCoast. I assume that everybody involved in the wire transfer invokes all the standard precautions.

I have no way of knowing the wire is being watched.

CHAPTER 22

Dusty Shiver's motion to suppress the confession was not at all unexpected. It was lengthy, well written, well reasoned, and backed up by a thirty-page affidavit signed by Quinn Rucker in which he fully recanted his confession. Three days after it was filed, Victor Westlake and two of his agents met with Stanley Mumphrey and two of his assistants. Their goal was to plow through the motion and prepare responses to it. Neither Mumphrey nor anyone else in his office was aware of the interrogation tactics used by Agents Pankovits and Delocke, nor did they know that Westlake and four of his men had watched by closed circuit the ten-hour marathon and had a tape of it. This information would never be revealed to the U.S. Attorney; thus, it would never be known to the defense, the judge, or anyone else.

Stanley had been fully briefed by his lieutenants and took control of the meeting. He began by saying, "The first and most important issue is the allegation that the defendant wanted to talk to a lawyer."

Westlake nodded to an agent who whipped out some papers. Westlake said, "We have here two affidavits from Agents Pankovits and Delocke, our two interrogators, in which they respond to the allegations. As you will see, they say that the defendant mentioned a lawyer on a couple of occasions but never specifically demanded one. He never stopped the interrogation. He wanted to talk."

Stanley and his men scanned the affidavits. After a few minutes, Stanley said, "Okay, point number two. The defendant claims he was repeatedly threatened with the death penalty by both agents. If true, this of course would be highly improper and would probably kill the confession."

Westlake replied as he shook his head. "Look at the bottom of page seven, both affidavits. The agents state, under oath, that they made no threats whatsoever. These are very skilled interrogators, Stan, and they know the rules as well as anybody."

Stanley and his men flipped to page seven and read the text. Perfect. Whatever Quinn claimed in his affidavit, there were two FBI agents willing to tell what really happened. Stanley said, "Looks good. The third point is that the agents promised the defendant he would not be put on trial for capital murder."

"Page nine," Westlake said. "Our agents know they do not have the authority to make deals. Only the U.S. Attorney can do that. Frankly, I find such an allegation ludicrous. Rucker is a career thug. He should know that prosecutors make deals, not cops."

"I agree," Stanley said quickly. "The next allegation is that the FBI agents threatened to prosecute other members of Rucker's family."

"Don't they always say that, Stan? They give a confession, free and voluntarily, then can't wait to tear it up and say they were threatened. You've seen this many times." Of course Stan had, though he really had not. Westlake went on, "Though I must say it wouldn't be a bad idea to round up all the Ruckers and give 'em the needle."

Westlake's men laughed. Stanley's men laughed. A regular party.

"What about the allegation that the interrogators were abusive and pushed the suspect past the point of exhaustion?"

"Here's the truth, Stan," Westlake replied. "The agents repeatedly asked Rucker if he wanted to stop and continue later. He said no because he did not want to spend the night in the county jail.

We checked and the jail was packed, badly overcrowded. They informed Rucker of this, and he didn't want to go there."

This made perfect sense to Stanley. He said, "Okay, the next three items need to be addressed, but I don't think we'll say much about them in our response. There is the allegation that the FBI agents lied about having a ballistics report that linked the murders to the Smith & Wesson handgun confiscated from the defendant. Unfortunately, as we now know, the ballistics excluded this weapon."

"Lying is permissible, especially in a high-level interrogation such as this, Stanley," Westlake said, much like a wise old professor.

"Got that, but just to satisfy my curiosity—did your agents actually lie about this?"

"Of course not. No, definitely not. Page twelve of their affidavits."

"Didn't think so. What about this next allegation—that your agents lied about the existence of a crime scene boot print that matched some boots taken from the defendant?"

"Not true, Stan. The imagination of a desperate lawyer and his guilty client."

"Do you have a boot print?"

Westlake glanced at one of his agents, as though there just might be a boot print that he had somehow forgotten. The agent shook his head. "No," Westlake admitted. "There's no boot print."

"And next we have the allegation that your agents lied about a couple of eyewitnesses. The first supposedly saw the defendant in the town of Ripplemead about the time of the killings. Any truth to this?"

Westlake shifted his weight from one ass cheek to the other and offered a condescending smile. "Stan, look, I'm not sure you appreciate what it takes to break down a guilty suspect. There are tricks, okay, and—"

"I get it."

"And you have to instill fear, to make the suspect think you have a lot more proof than maybe you actually have."

"I've seen no report from such a witness."

"And you will not. He doesn't exist."

"We're on the same side, here, Vic. I just need to know the truth so we can respond to the motion to suppress, understand?"

"I understand."

"And the second witness, the one at the country store near the cabin. He doesn't exist either, right?"

"Right."

"Did the agents use any other tricks that I don't know about?"

"No," Westlake said, but no one in the room believed him.

"So, to summarize our case against Quinn Rucker, we have no eyewitnesses, no ballistics, no boot print, no fingerprints, no physical evidence of any kind, correct?"

Westlake nodded slowly but said nothing.

"We have a defendant who was in the Roanoke area after the murders, but no proof he was here beforehand, right?"

More nodding.

"And our defendant was caught with more cash than one would normally carry around, substantially more, I would say."

Westlake agreed.

"But then Mr. Rucker is a self-confessed drug runner from a family notorious for trafficking, so cash would not be a problem." Stanley shoved his legal pad away and rubbed his temples. "Gentlemen, we have a confession and nothing else. If we lose the confession, then Mr. Rucker walks and there's no trial."

"You can't lose the confession, Stan," Westlake said. "It's unthinkable."

"I have no plans to lose it, but I can see the judge taking a dim view of the interrogation. The length of it bothers me. Ten hours throughout the night. An obviously fatigued suspect who's a seasoned crook and would probably want to see a lawyer. Two veteran interrogators who know all the tricks. This might be a close call."

Westlake listened with a smile and after a long pause said, "Let's not forget our star witness, Stan. Malcolm Bannister will testify that Quinn Rucker talked repeatedly of murdering Judge Fawcett. He wanted revenge, and he wanted his money back."

"True, and his testimony, plus the confession, will get a conviction. But standing alone, his testimony is not enough."

"You don't sound too confident, Stan."

"Quite the contrary. This is the murder of a federal judge. I cannot imagine another federal judge showing any sympathy for Quinn Rucker. We'll have the confession, and we have Malcolm Bannister. We'll get a conviction."

"Now you're talking."

"By the way, what's up with our boy Bannister?"

"Safe and sound, buried deep by the U.S. Marshals."

"Where is he?"

"Sorry, Stan. Some things we cannot talk about. But have no worries. He'll be here when we need him."

CHAPTER 23

Pat Surhoff's replacement is Diana Tyler. I meet them for lunch after a long morning at the hospital, where I was examined and was told to return in a month. Ms. Tyler is a tall, pretty woman of about fifty, with a short haircut, little makeup, a navy blazer, and no wedding band. She's pleasant enough and over salads gives me her spiel. She lives "in the area" and works with a few others who share my situation. She is available 24/7 and would like to have a chat by phone at least once a week. She understands what I'm going through and says it's natural to keep looking over my shoulder. With time, though, those fears will go away, and my life will become quite normal. If I leave town, and they stress this is something I can now do whenever I want, she would like the details of my trip in advance. They want to keep close tabs on me until long after I testify against Quinn Rucker, and they persist in painting the picture of a safe and pleasant future that I will know one day when all of the initial hurdles have been cleared.

They mention the two job interviews, and I throw a curve by explaining I'm not ready for employment. With cash in the bank and unrestrained freedom, I'm just not ready to start a new career. I want to travel some, take long drives, and maybe go to Europe. Traveling is fine, they agree, but the cover works best if I have a real job. We decide to talk about it later. This leads to a conversation about a passport and an updated driver's license. Another week and my face should be ready to be photographed, and Diana promises to arrange the documentation.

Over coffee, I give Pat a letter to my father. The return address is the federal correctional facility in Fort Wayne, Indiana. He will send it to the prison there, and someone will mail it to Henry Bannister in Winchester, Virginia. In the letter I explain to old Henry that I screwed up at Frostburg and have been busted back to a regular prison. I am in solitary confinement and can have no visitors for at least three months. I ask him to notify my sister, Ruby, in California and my brother, Marcus, in D.C. I tell him not to worry; I'm fine and I have a plan to work my way back to Frostburg.

Pat and I say our farewells. I thank him for his courtesies and professionalism, and he wishes me well. He assures me my new life will be rewarding and secure. I'm not sure I believe this, because I'm still looking over my shoulder. I strongly suspect the FBI will monitor me for some time, at least until the day when Quinn Rucker is convicted and sent away.

The truth is I cannot afford to trust anyone, including Pat Surhoff, Diana Tyler, the U.S. Marshals Service, and the FBI. There are a lot of shadows back there, not to mention the bad guys. If the government wants to watch me, there's little I can do. They can obtain court orders to snoop into my bank account, to listen to my phone calls, to monitor my credit card activity, and to watch everything I do online. I anticipate all of the above, and my challenge in the near future is to deceive them without letting them know they are being deceived. Taking one of the two jobs would only allow them another opportunity to spy.

During the afternoon, I open another checking account at Atlantic Trust and move $50,000 from the SunCoast account.

Then I do the same thing at a third bank, Jacksonville Savings. In a day or two, once the checks have cleared, I will begin withdrawing cash.

As I putter around the neighborhood in my little Audi, I spend as much time looking in the mirror as I do watching the road. It's already a habit. When I walk the beach, I check out every face I see. When I walk into a store, I immediately find cover and watch the door I just came through. I never eat in the same restaurant twice, and I always find a table with a view of the parking lot. I use the cell phone only for routine matters, and I assume someone is listening. I pay cash for a laptop, set up three Gmail accounts, and do my browsing in Internet cafés using their servers. I begin experimenting with prepaid credit cards I buy at a Walgreens pharmacy. I install two hidden cameras in my condo, just in case someone drops in while I'm away.

Paranoia is the key here. I convince myself someone is always watching and listening, and as the days pass, I fall deeper into my own little world of deception. I call Diana every other day with the latest news in my increasingly mundane life, and she gives no hint of being suspicious. But then, she would not.

The lawyer's name is Murray Huggins, and his small Yellow Pages ad announces specialties in just about everything. Divorce, real estate, bankruptcy, criminal matters, and so forth, pretty much the same ham-and-egg routine we followed at dear old Copeland, Reed & Bannister. His office is not far from my condo, and one look suggests the laid-back beach practice of a guy who comes in at nine and is on the golf course by three. During our first appointment, Murray tells me his life story. He had great success in a big law firm in Tampa but burned out at the age of fifty and tried retirement. He moved to Atlantic Beach, got a divorce, got bored, and decided to hang out his shingle. He's in his sixties now, happy in his little office, where he puts in a few hours here and there and chooses his clients carefully.

We go through my biography, and I, for the most part, stick to the script. A couple of ex-wives in Seattle and so forth. I add my own new wrinkle of being a fledgling screenwriter who is polishing up my first script. With a lucky break here and there, the script has been optioned by a small production company that does documentaries. For various business reasons, I need to establish a small front in Florida.

For $2,500, Murray can build a few firewalls. He'll set up an LLC—limited liability company—in Florida, with M. R. Baldwin as the sole owner. The LLC will then form a corporation in Delaware with Murray as the sole incorporator and me as the sole owner. The registered address will be his office, and my name will appear in none of the corporate documents. He says, "I do this all the time. Florida attracts a lot of folks who are trying to start over." If you say so, Murray.

I could do this myself online, but it's safer to route it through a lawyer. The confidentiality is important. I can pay Murray to do things the shadows will never suspect and be unable to trace. With his seasoned guidance, Skelter Films comes to life.

Two and a half months after the arrest of Quinn Rucker, and two weeks after I move into my beachfront condo, I am informed over coffee one morning by Diana that the Feds would like to have a meeting. There are several reasons for this, the most important being their desire to update me on their case and talk about the trial. They want to plan my testimony. I am certain they also want to get a good look at Max Baldwin, who, by the way, is an improvement over Malcolm Bannister.

The swelling is gone. The nose and chin are a bit sharper. The eyes look much younger, and the round red tortoiseshell glasses give the look of a pretty cool, cerebral documentary filmmaker. I shave my face once a week so there is always some stubble, with just a touch of gray mixed in. The slick scalp requires a razor every other day. My cheeks are flatter, primarily because I ate little during my recovery and I've lost weight. I plan to keep it off. All in all, I look nothing like my former self, and while this is often unsettling, it is also comforting.

The suggestion is that I return to Roanoke to meet with Stanley Mumphrey and his gang, but I flatly say no. Diana assures me that the FBI and the U.S. Attorney's Office do not know where I'm hiding, and I pretend to believe this. I do not want to meet them in Florida. After some haggling, we agree to meet at a hotel in Charleston, South Carolina. Diana books our tickets, and we fly out of Jacksonville, on the same flight but nowhere close to each other.

From the moment we walk into the lobby of the hotel, I know I'm being watched and probably photographed. The FBI can't wait to see how I look. I catch a couple of quick glances but keep moving. After a sandwich in my room, I meet Diana in the hallway, and we walk to a suite two floors above us. It is well guarded by two thick boys in black suits who appear ready to begin firing away at the slightest provocation. As a marshal, Diana has no role in the prosecution; therefore, she remains outside with the two Dobermans while I enter and meet the gang.

Stanley Mumphrey has brought three of his assistants, and their names are lost in the deluge of introductions. My pal Agent Chris Hanski is back, no doubt to eyeball me for a good before-and-after. He has a sidekick, name instantly forgotten. As we awkwardly take seats around a small conference table, I can't help but notice amid the pile of papers a couple of identical photos. It's Malcolm Bannister, and these guys were looking at him. Now they're gawking at Max. The transformation impresses them.

Since Hanski is the only one who actually met me before the change, he goes first. "I gotta say, Max, you look younger and fitter, not sure you're that much cuter, but all in all not a bad makeover." He's jovial and this is supposed to break the ice.

"That means so much," I say with a fake smile.

Stanley holds the copied photo and says, "Not even close, Max. No one would suspect you and Malcolm are the same. It's pretty remarkable."

We're all on the same team now, so we banter back and forth like old friends. But there's no foundation, so the conversation begins to lag. "Is there a trial date?" I ask, and this changes the mood.

"Yes," Stanley says. "October 10, in Roanoke."

"That's only four months away," I reply. "Seems pretty quick."

"We're pretty efficient in the Southern District," Stanley says smugly. "The average is eight months from indictment to trial. This case has a bit more pressure behind it."

"Who's the judge?"

"Sam Stillwater, on loan from the Northern District. All of Fawcett's colleagues in the Southern recused themselves."

"Tell me about the trial," I say.

Stanley frowns, as does the rest of the gang. "It might be rather brief, Max, not a lot of witnesses, not a lot of proof. We'll establish Rucker was in the vicinity at the time. We'll prove he had a lot of cash when we caught him. We'll go into the prosecution of his nephew, the sentencing by Judge Fawcett, maybe there was a revenge element at work." Stanley pauses here, and I can't resist a jab. "Pretty overwhelming stuff," I say like a smart-ass.

"No doubt. Then we have the confession, which the defense has attacked. We have a hearing next week before Judge Stillwater, and we expect to win and keep the confession. Other than that, Max, the star witness might just be you."

"I've told you everything. You know my testimony."

"Right, right, but we want to cover it again. Now that we've filled in a few gaps, let's nail it down to perfection."

"Sure. How's my buddy Quinn holding up?"

"Quinn's not doing too well these days. He doesn't like solitary confinement, or the food, the guards, the rules. Says he's innocent—what a surprise. I think he misses the good life at the federal country club."

"So do I." This gets a light laugh or two.

"His lawyer convinced the judge that Quinn needed a psychiatric evaluation. The doctor said he can stand trial but needs some antidepressants. He's quite moody and often goes days without speaking to anyone."

"That sounds like the Quinn I knew. Does he mention me?"

"Oh yes. He doesn't like you either. He suspects you're our informant and that you'll testify against him at trial."

"When do you have to submit your list of witnesses?"

"Sixty days before the trial."

"Have you told Quinn's lawyer that I will testify?"

"No. We do not divulge anything until forced to do so."

"That's the way I remember it," I say. These guys forget that I was once on the receiving end of a federal prosecution, with FBI agents sifting through every aspect of my life and a U.S. Attorney's office threatening to incarcerate not only me but my two innocent partners as well. They think we're pals now, one big happy team walking lockstep toward another just verdict. If I could, I would knife them in the back and poison their case.

They—the federal government—took away five years of my life, along with my son, my wife, and my career. How dare they sit here as if we're trusted partners.

We eventually get around to my testimony and spend a couple of hours in review. This ground has been covered before and I find it tedious. Mumphrey's chief assistant has a script, a Q&A, for me to study, and I have to admit it's pretty good. Nothing has been left out.

I try to visualize the surreal setting of my testimony. I will be brought into the courtroom wearing a mask. I will sit behind a panel or a partition of some manner that will prevent the lawyers, the defendant, and the spectators from seeing my face once the mask is removed. I will look at the jurors. The lawyers will pitch questions over the wall, and I will answer, my voice distorted. Quinn and his family and their thugs will be there, straining for any hint of recognition. They'll know it's me, of course, but they'll never see my face.

As certain as it seems, I seriously doubt if it will ever happen.

CHAPTER 24

Diana calls with the news that she has in her possession my new Florida driver's license and my new passport. We meet for coffee at a waffle house and she hands them over. I give her an itinerary with a lot of gaps in it.

"Taking a trip, huh?" she says, gazing at it.

"Yep, I can't wait to try out the new passport. The first three nights are in Miami, South Beach, beginning tonight. I'm leaving and driving down as soon as my coffee cup is empty. From there, I'll fly to Jamaica for a week or so, then to Antigua, and maybe Trinidad. I'll call you at each stop. I'll leave my car at the Miami airport so you can tell the FBI exactly where it is. And while you're at it, ask them to please leave me alone while I bounce around the Caribbean."

"Leave you alone?" she asks, feigning ignorance.

"You heard me. Let's not play games here, Diana. I may not be the most heavily protected witness in the country, but I'm probably in the top three. Somebody's always watching. There's one guy, I call him Crew Cut, who I've seen five times in the past two weeks. He's not very good, so please pass this along to the Fibbies when you make your report. Six feet even, 180 pounds, Ray-Bans, blond goatee, drives a Cooper and sports a crew cut. Really, really sloppy. I'm surprised."

So is she. She keeps her eyes on my itinerary and can think of nothing to say. Busted.

I pay for the coffee and hit the road, Interstate 95 straight south for 350 miles. The weather is hot and muggy, the traffic heavy and slow, and I love every mile of the trip. I stop frequently to refuel, to stretch my legs, and to watch for movements behind me. I expect none. Since the FBI knows where I'm going, they won't bother with a tail. Besides, I assume there is a GPS tracking monitor brilliantly hidden somewhere in my car. Seven hours later, I stop in front of the Blue Moon Hotel, one of the many small, renovated boutique hotels in the heart of the Art Deco District at South Beach. I get my briefcase and small bag from the trunk, hand the keys to the valet, and walk into a scene from *Miami Vice*. Ceiling fans turn slowly as guests in white-wicker chairs gossip and drink.

"Checking in, sir?" the pretty girl asks.

"Yes. Max Baldwin," I reply, and for some reason it is a proud moment. I, Mighty Max, am drowning in more freedom than I can absorb at the moment. Plenty of cash, fresh papers that are legit, a convertible that will take me anywhere—it's almost overwhelming. But I am jolted back to life when a tall, tanned brunette strolls through the lobby. Her top is what's left of a string bikini and covers almost nothing. Her bottom is a sheer skirt that covers even less.

I hand over a Visa card for the charges. I could also use either cash or a prepaid credit card, but since the Fibbies know where I'm staying, there's no need to be deceptive. I'm sure the Miami office has been notified, and there's probably a set of eyes not too far away. If I were really paranoid, I could believe that the FBI has already been in my room and perhaps hidden a bug or two. I get to my room, see no bugs or spooks, take a quick shower, and change into shorts and sandals. I go to the bar to check out the talent. I eat alone in the hotel café and catch the eye of a fortyish woman who is dining with what appears to be a female friend. Later, back in the bar, I see her again and we introduce ourselves.

Eva, from Puerto Rico. We're having a drink when the band starts. Eva wants to dance, and though it's been years, I hit the floor with all the energy I have.

Around midnight, Eva and I make it to my room, where we immediately undress and hop into bed. I almost pray the FBI has the room wired for even the meekest of sounds. If so, Eva and I give them an earful.

I hustle out of the cab at a curb on 8th Avenue, in downtown Miami. It's 9:30 a.m., already hot, and after a few minutes of brisk walking, my shirt is sticking to my back. I don't think I'm being followed, but I duck and dart just the same. The building is a squat five-story box, so ugly you can't believe someone paid an architect to design it. But then I doubt if most of the tenants are cutting-edge companies. One happens to be called Corporate Registry Services, or CRS, a name so bland and innocuous that no one would ever know the company's business. And most people would not want to.

CRS may be perfectly legitimate, but it attracts a lot of clients who are not. It's an address, a drop-off, a front, a phone-answering service that a corporation can hire to buy some measure of authenticity. Since I have not called ahead, I kill an hour waiting for an account representative. Loyd is his name, and he eventually leads me back to a small, stuffy office and offers me a chair across from his landfill of a desk. We chat for a few minutes as he scans the questionnaire I've filled out.

"What is Skelter Films?" he finally asks.

"A documentary film production company."

"Who owns it?"

"Me. Incorporated in Delaware."

"How many films have you made?"

"None. Just getting started."

"What are the chances of Skelter Films being around two years from now?"

"Slim."

He hears this shadiness all the time and it doesn't faze him. "Sounds like a front."

"That's pretty accurate."

"We require an affidavit in which you swear under oath that your company will not be engaged in criminal activities."

"I swear it will not."

He's heard this before too. "Okay, here's how we operate. We provide Skelter with a physical address, here in this building. When we get mail, we forward it to wherever you say. We provide a phone number, and all incoming calls will be handled by a live voice who'll chirp whatever you want. 'Good morning, Skelter Films, how can I direct your call?' Or something else. You got partners?"

"No."

"Any employees, fictional or otherwise?"

"I'll have a few names, all fictional."

"No problem. If the caller asks for one of these ghosts, our girl will say whatever you want. 'Sorry, he's filming on location,' or whatever. You write the fiction, and we'll deliver it. As soon as we get a call, we notify you. What about a Web site?"

I'm not sure about this, so I say, "Not yet. What are the pros?"

Loyd shifts weight and leans on his elbows. "Okay, let's say Skelter is a legitimate company that will make lots of documentaries. If so, it will need a Web site for all the usual reasons— marketing, information, ego. On the other hand, let's pretend Skelter is a real corporation but not a real film company. Maybe it's trying to just give that impression, for whatever reason. A Web site is a great way to bolster the image, to sort of fudge on reality. Nothing illegal, mind you. But we can establish a Web site with stock photos and biographies of your staff, your films, awards, ongoing projects, you name it."

"How much?"

"Ten grand."

I'm not sure I want or need to spend the money, not at this point anyway. "Let me ponder it," I say, and Loyd shrugs. "How much for your basic registry services?"

"Address, phone, fax, and everything related is $500 a month, payable six months in advance."

"You accept cash?"

Loyd smiles and says, "Oh yes. We prefer cash." No surprise there. I pay the money, sign a contract, sign the affidavit form promising to keep my activities legal, and leave his office. CRS boasts of nine hundred satisfied clients, and as I walk through the lobby, I can't help but feel as though I've joined some manner of underworld filled with shell companies, faceless crooks, and foreign tax evaders. What the hell.

After two more nights with Eva, she wants me to go home to Puerto Rico with her. I promise to think about it, then slip away from the Blue Moon and drive to the Miami International Airport, where I park in long-term and shuttle to the terminals. I pull out a credit card and my new passport and buy a one-way ticket to Montego Bay on Air Jamaica. The plane is packed: half dark-skinned native Jamaicans and half pale-white tourists headed for the sun. Before we take off, the lovely attendants are serving rum punch. The flight takes forty-five minutes. On the ground, the Customs agent takes far too long studying my passport, and I'm starting to panic when he finally waves me through. I find the bus to Rum Bay Resort, an all-inclusive, singles-only, fairly notorious stretch of topless beaches. For three days, I sit in the shade by the pool and ponder the meaning of life.

From Jamaica, I fly to Antigua, in the Leeward Islands of the eastern Caribbean. It's a lovely island, a hundred square miles, with mountains and white beaches and dozens of resorts. It's also known as one of the world's friendlier tax havens these days, and this is one reason for my visit. If I wanted nothing more than a good party, I would have stayed in Jamaica. The capital is St. John's, a bustling town of thirty thousand situated on a deep harbor that attracts cruise ships. I check into my room in a small inn on the edge of St. John's, with a beautiful view of the water, boats, and yachts. It's June, the off-season, and for $300 a night I will eat like a king, sleep until noon, and relish the fact that no one knows who I am, where I came from, or anything about my past.

CHAPTER 25

The Freezer had been dismantled a month earlier, and Victor Westlake was settled back into his routine and office on the fourth floor of the Hoover Building in Washington. Though the murders of Judge Fawcett and Naomi Clary were technically solved, many doubts and questions remained. The most pressing issue, of course, was the validity of Quinn Rucker's confession. If the judge suppressed it, the government would be left with little proof with which to go forward. The murders were solved, but the case was not closed, at least in Westlake's opinion. He was still spending two hours each day dealing with it. There was the daily report on the business of Max Baldwin: his movements, meetings, phone calls, Internet activity, et cetera. So far, Max had done nothing to surprise them. Westlake did not like the trip to Jamaica and beyond, but there was nothing he could do about it. They were watching as closely as possible. There was the daily report on Rucker's family. The FBI had obtained court approval to monitor phone conversations of Dee Ray Rucker, Sammy (Tall Man) Rucker, their sister Lucinda, and four relatives involved in the D.C. unit of their trafficking operation.

On Wednesday, June 15, Westlake was in a staff meeting when he was summoned to the phone. It was urgent, and within minutes he was in a conference room with technicians who were working quickly to prepare the audio. One of them said, "The call came to Dee Ray's cell phone last night at 11:19, not sure where it came from, but here it is. The first voice is Dee Ray, the second is Sully. We have not yet identified Sully." Another technician said, "Here it is."

DEE RAY: Yeah.

SULLY: Dee Ray, Sully here.

DEE RAY: What you got?

SULLY: Got the snitch, man. Bannister.

DEE RAY: No shit, man.

SULLY: No shit, Dee Ray.

DEE RAY: Okay, don't tell me how, just tell me where.

SULLY: Well, he's a beach bum now, in Florida. Name is Max Baldwin, lives in a little condo in Neptune Beach, east of Jacksonville. Seems to have some money, taking it easy, you know. The good life.

DEE RAY: What's he look like?

SULLY: A different dude. Lots of surgery. But the same height, down a few pounds. Same walk. Plus we got a fingerprint and a match.

DEE RAY: A fingerprint?

SULLY: Our firm is good. They followed him down the beach and saw him toss a water bottle in the trash. They picked it up, got a print.

DEE RAY: That is good.

SULLY: Like I said. What now?

DEE RAY: Sit tight. Let me sleep on it. He ain't going nowhere, right?

SULLY: No, he's a happy boy.

DEE RAY: Beautiful.

Westlake slowly fell into a chair, slack-jawed and pale, too shaken to speak for a moment. Then, "Get me Twill." A flunky disappeared, and while he waited, Westlake rubbed his eyes and contemplated his next move. Twill, the top assistant, arrived in a rush, and they listened to the tape again. For Westlake, it was even more chilling the second time around.

"How in the . . . ," Twill mumbled.

Westlake was recovering. "Call Bratten at the Marshals Service."

"Bratten had surgery yesterday," Twill said. "Newcombe is in charge."

"Then get Newcombe on the phone. We can't waste time here."

I've joined a gym and I spend an hour there each day around noon, walking uphill on a treadmill and doing reps with light weights. If I plan to spend so much time on the beach, I need to look the part.

After some steam and a long shower, I am dressing when the cell phone starts buzzing in the top of my locker. It's dear Diana, and an odd time for her to be calling. "Hello," I say quietly, though the locker room is not busy.

"We need to talk," she says abruptly, the first-ever hint that something might be out of place.

"About what?"

"Not now. There are two FBI agents in the parking lot in a maroon Jeep Cherokee, parked next to your car. They'll give you a ride."

"And how exactly do you know where I am at this moment, Diana?"

"Let's discuss it later."

I sit in a folding chair. "Talk to me, Diana. What's going on?"

"Max, I'm ten minutes away. Follow orders, get in the Jeep, and I'll tell you everything I know as soon as I see you. Let's not do it over the phone."

"Okay." I finish dressing and try to act as calm as always. I walk through the gym and smile at a yoga instructor I've been smiling at for a week now and make my way to the front door. I glance outside and see the maroon Jeep parked next to my car. At this point it's fairly obvious that something dreadful has happened, so I swallow hard and step into the blinding midday sun. The driver hops out and, without a word, opens a rear door. I ride for seven minutes in complete silence until we park in the driveway of a quaint duplex cottage with a "For Rent" sign in the front yard. It's a block from the ocean. As soon as the engine is turned off, both agents jump out and scan the periphery, as if snipers might be up there, just waiting. The knot in my stomach feels like a bowling ball.

We make it inside without getting shot, and Diana is waiting. "Nice place you have here," I say.

"It's a safe house," she replies.

"Oh, okay. And why are we hiding in a safe house in the middle of a perfectly fine day?"

A gray-haired man enters from the kitchen and thrusts out a hand. "Max, I'm Dan Raynor, U.S. Marshal, supervisor for this area." We shake hands like old friends and he's actually smiling as if we're about to have a long lunch.

"A real pleasure," I say. "What's going on?"

There are four of them—Raynor, Diana, and the two nameless FBI agents—and for a few seconds they're not sure of the protocol here. Whose territory? Who's included? Who stays and who leaves? As I've already learned, these cross-agency turf fights can be confusing.

Raynor does the talking. "Max, I'm afraid there's been a breach. To put it bluntly—your cover has been blown. We have no idea how this happened."

I sit down and wipe my forehead. "Who knows what?" I ask.

Raynor says, "We don't know much, but there are some folks

flying in from Washington right now. They should be here in an hour or so. Evidently, the FBI picked up something last night from a wiretap. There was some chatter among the Rucker family, and the FBI heard it."

"They know where I am?"

"They do. They know exactly where you're living."

"We're very sorry about this, Max," Diana says, and I glare at her and her stupidity as if I could strangle her.

"Gosh, that means so much," I say. "Why don't you just shut up?"

"I'm sorry."

"That's twice you've said that. Please don't say it again, okay? It means nothing. It's totally useless."

She's stung by my harshness, but I really don't care. My only concern right now is my own skin. The four people staring at me, along with their higher-ups and their entire government, are all responsible for the "breach."

"Would you like some coffee?" Diana asks meekly.

"No, I'd like some heroin," I say. They find this funny, but then we could all use a laugh. Coffee is poured and a platter of cookies makes the rounds. We begin the process of waiting. As surreal as it is, I begin thinking about where to go next.

Raynor says they'll get my car after dark. They're waiting on a black male agent from the Orlando office who will be my double for the next day or so. Under no circumstances will I be allowed to return to my condo to live, and we haggle about how to retrieve my sparse belongings. The Marshals Service will take care of the lease and turn off the utilities. Raynor thinks I'll need a different vehicle, but I push back initially.

The FBI agents leave and return with sandwiches. The clock seems to stop as the walls close in. Finally, at 3:30, Mr. Victor Westlake walks in the front door and says, "Max, I'm sorry." I do not stand, nor do I offer a hand to shake. The sofa is all mine. He has three other dark suits with him and they scramble for kitchen chairs and stools. When everyone is introduced and seated, Westlake begins, "This is highly unusual, Max, and I don't know what to say. As of now, we have no idea where the breach occurred, and we may never find out."

"Just tell me what you do know," I say.

Westlake opens a file and pulls out some papers. "Here's the transcript of a phone conversation we caught last night between Dee Ray Rucker and someone named Sully. Both were on cell phones. Dee Ray was in D.C. Sully made the call from somewhere around here."

I read the transcript while the rest of them hold their breath. It takes a few seconds, then I place it on the coffee table. "How'd they do it?" I ask.

"We're still working on it. One theory is that they used a private company to track you down. We monitor a handful of firms that specialize in corporate espionage, surveillance, missing persons, private snooping, and the like. These are ex-military types, ex-spies, and, I'm ashamed to say, a few ex–FBI agents. They're good and they have the technology. For the right fee, they could gather a lot of information."

"From where? From the inside?"

"We don't know yet, Max."

"If you did know, you wouldn't tell me. You would never admit it if the breach was caused by someone within the government—the FBI, the Marshals Service, the U.S. Attorney's Office, the Department of Justice, the Bureau of Prisons. Hell knows who else. How many people are plugged into this little secret, Mr. Westlake? Several dozen, maybe more. Did the Ruckers find me because they picked up my scent, or did they follow the FBI because the FBI was following me?"

"I assure you there was no internal breach."

"But you just said you don't know. Your assurances mean

nothing at this point. The only certainty right now is that everyone involved will cover their ass and point fingers, starting right
now. I don't believe anything you say, Mr. Westlake. You or anybody else."

"You have to trust us, Max. This situation is urgent, perhaps
lethal."

"I trusted you until this morning, and look where I am now.
There's no trust. Zero."

"We have to protect you until the trial, Max. You understand
this. After the trial, we lose interest. But until then, we have to
make sure you're safe. That's why we tapped the phones. We were
monitoring the Ruckers and we got lucky. We're on your side,
Max. Sure, there was a screwup somewhere, and we'll find out
what happened. But you're sitting here in one piece because we
were doing our jobs."

"Congratulations," I say, and go to the bathroom.

The real fight breaks out when I inform them I'm leaving
witness protection. Dan Raynor rants about how dangerous my
life will be if I don't allow them to scoop me up and deposit me a
thousand miles away, under yet another name. Too bad. I'll take
my chances hiding on my own. Westlake begs me to stay with
them. My testimony will be crucial at trial, and without it there
may be no conviction. I remind him repeatedly that they have a
confession, and no federal judge is going to suppress it. I promise
I'll show up for the trial. I argue that my life will be safer when
only I know where I'm hiding. There are simply too many agents
involved in protecting me. Raynor reminds me more than once
that the Marshals Service has never lost an informant within its
protection, over eight thousand and counting, and I repeatedly
remind him someone will be the first casualty. Someone other
than me.

The discussion is often heated, but I'm not backing down.
And all they can do is argue. They have no authority over me. My

sentence was commuted and I'm not on parole. I agreed to testify, and I plan to do so. My agreement with the Marshals Service plainly states that I can leave witness protection anytime I want.

"I'm leaving," I declare and get to my feet. "Will you be so kind as to drive me back to my car?"

No one moves. Raynor asks, "What are your plans?"

"Why would I share my plans with you?"

"What about the condo?"

"I'll leave in a couple of days, then it's all yours."

"So you are leaving the area?" Diana asks.

"I didn't say that. I said I'm leaving the condo." I look at Westlake and say, "And please stop following me. There's a good chance someone is watching you as you watch me. Give me a break here, okay?"

"That's not true, Max."

"You don't know what's true. Just stop following me, okay?"

Of course he does not say yes. His cheeks are red and he's really pissed, but then again this is a man who usually gets his way. I walk to the door, yank it open, and say, "If you won't give me a ride, I'll just walk."

"Take him back," Westlake says.

"Thanks," I say over my shoulder and leave the cottage. The last thing I hear is Raynor calling out, "You're making a big mistake, Max."

I ride in the backseat of the Jeep as the same two agents chauffeur me in silence. In the parking lot outside the gym, I get out and say nothing. They drive away, but I doubt they go far. I get into my little Audi, put the top down and go for a drive along the beach on Highway A1A. I refuse to look in the rearview mirror.

Victor Westlake returned to Washington on a government jet. When he arrived in his office after dark, he was briefed on the news that Judge Sam Stillwater had denied the defense motion to suppress the confession of Quinn Rucker. While no great surprise, it was still a relief. He called Stanley Mumphrey in Roanoke and congratulated him. He did not inform the U.S. Attorney that their star witness was about to leave witness protection and disappear into the night.

CHAPTER 26

I sleep with a gun, a Beretta 9-millimeter, legally purchased by me and duly licensed by the State of Florida. I haven't fired a weapon in twenty years, since my days as a Marine, and I have no desire to start shooting now. It's resting on the cardboard box that passes as a nightstand beside my bed. Another box on the floor is filled with the possessions I need—my laptop, iPad, some books, a shaving kit, a Ziploc bag filled with cash, a couple of files with personal records, and a prepaid cell phone with unlimited minutes and a Miami area code. A cheap suitcase, one that will fit into the Audi's rather small trunk, is packed with my wardrobe and ready to go. Most of these items—the gun, the cell phone, the suitcase—were purchased recently just in case a quick exit became necessary.

Well, said exit is now at hand. Before dawn, I load the car and wait. I sit on my terrace for the last time, sipping coffee and watching the ocean fade into pink, then orange as the sun peeks over the horizon. I've watched this many times and never grow tired of it. On a clear morning, the perfect sphere rises from the water and says hello, good morning, what another fine day it's going to be.

I'm not sure where I'm headed or where I'll end up, but I plan to be near a beach so I can begin each day with such quiet perfection.

At 8:30, I walk out of the condo, leaving behind a refrigerator half filled with food and beverages, a motley assortment of dishes and utensils, a nice coffeepot, some magazines on the sofa, and some bread and crackers in the pantry. For forty-six days I lived here, my first real home after prison, and I'm sad to be leaving it. I thought I would stay longer. I leave the lights on, lock the door behind me, and wonder how many more temporary hiding places await me before I am no longer forced to keep running. I drive away and am soon lost in the heavy commuter traffic going west into Jacksonville. I know they're back there, but maybe not for long.

Two hours later, I enter the sprawl north of Orlando and stop for breakfast at a pancake house. I eat slow, read newspapers, and watch the crowd. Down the street, I check into a cheap motel and pay cash for one night. The clerk asks for some ID with a photo and I explain that I lost my wallet last night in a bar. She doesn't like this, but she likes the idea of cash, so why bother. She gives me a key and I go to my room. Working the Yellow Pages and using my prepaid cell phone, I eventually find a detail shop that can squeeze me in at three that afternoon. For $199, the kid on the other end promises to make my car look like a new one.

Buck's Pro Shine is on the backside of a large assembly-line car wash that's doing a bustling business. My car and I are assigned to a skinny country kid named Denny, and he takes his job seriously. In great detail, he lays out his plan for washing and shining and is surprised when I say that I'll wait. "Could take two hours," he says. "I have nowhere to go," I reply. He shrugs and moves the Audi onto a wash rack. I find a seat on a bench under a canopy and start reading a Walter Mosley paperback. Thirty minutes later, Denny finishes the exterior wash and starts the vacuum. He opens both doors, and I ease over for a chat. I explain I'm leaving town, so the suitcase stays in the backseat and the cardboard box in the trunk is not to be touched. He shrugs again, whatever. Less work for him. I take a step closer and tell Denny that I'm going through a bad divorce and I have reason to believe my wife's law-yers are watching every move I make. I strongly suspect there is a GPS tracking device hidden somewhere in or on the car, and if Denny finds it, I'll slide him an extra $100 bill. At first he is hesitant, but I assure him it's my car and there's nothing illegal about disarming a tracking device. Her slimy lawyers are the ones breaking the law. Finally, there's a twinkle in his eye and he's on board. I pop the hood, and together we start combing the car. As we do so, I explain there are dozens of different devices, all shapes and sizes, but most are attached with a strong magnet. Depending on the model, the battery can last for weeks, or the device can even be hot-wired to the car's electrical system. Some antennas are external, some internal.

"How do you know all this?" he asks, flat on his back, his head under the car, poking around the chassis.

"Because I hid one on my wife's car," I reply, and he finds it funny.

"Why haven't you looked for yourself?" he asks.

"Because I was being watched."

We search for an hour and find nothing. I am beginning to think maybe my car was bug-free after all when Denny removes a small panel behind the right headlight. He's on his back, his shoulder squeezed against the right front tire. He snaps something loose and hands it to me. The waterproof covering is the size of a cell phone and made of hard black plastic. I remove it and say, "Bingo." I've looked at a hundred of these online and have never seen one like this, so I assume it's government issued. No brand name, no markings, numbers, or letters. "Nice work, Denny," I say, and hand him a $100 bill.

"Can I finish detailing now?" he asks.

"Sure." I drift away, leaving him to his labors. Next to the car wash there is a small shopping center with half a dozen low-end stores. I buy a cup of stale decaf and sit in the window of a coffee shop, watching the parking lot. An elderly couple in a Cadillac park, get out, and shuffle into a Chinese buffet. As soon as they're inside, I exit the coffee shop and walk through the lot as if I'm headed to my car. Behind the Cadillac, I quickly bend over and slap the tracking device onto the bottom of the fuel tank. Ontario license plates—perfect.

Denny is washing windows, sweating profusely, lost in his work. I tap him on the shoulder, startle him, and say, "Look, Denny, nice work and all, but something's come up. I need to hit the road." I'm peeling off cash and hand him three $100 bills. He's confused, but I don't care.

"Whatever you say, man," he mumbles, staring at the money.

"Gotta run."

He pulls a towel off the top of the car. "Good luck with the divorce, man."

"Thanks."

West of Orlando, I take Interstate 75 north, through Ocala, then Gainesville, then into Georgia, where I stop in Valdosta for the night.

Over the next five days, my wanderings take me as far south as New Orleans, as far west as Wichita Falls, Texas, and as far north as Kansas City. I use interstate highways, state routes, country roads, and national parkways. All expenses are paid in cash, so, to my knowledge, there is no trail. I double back a dozen times and become convinced there is no one behind me. My journey ends in Lynchburg, Virginia, where I roll in just after midnight and once again pay cash for a motel room. So far, only one place has refused to do business because I claim to have no ID. Then again, I'm not lodging at Marriotts or Hiltons. I'm tired of the road and eager to get down to business.

I sleep late into the next morning, then drive an hour to Roanoke, the last place anyone who knows Max Baldwin would expect to find him. Fortified with that knowledge, and a new face, I am confident I can move around with anonymity in a metro area of 200,000 people. The only troublesome part of my package is the Florida license plates on my car, and I contemplate renting another one. I decide against this because of the paperwork. Plus, the Florida angle will pay off later.

I drive around the city for a while, checking out the landscape, downtown, the old sections, and the inevitable sprawl. Malcolm Bannister visited Roanoke on several occasions, including once as a seventeen-year-old high school football player. Winchester is just three hours north, on Interstate 81. As a young lawyer there, Malcolm drove down twice to take depositions. The town of Salem adjoins Roanoke, and Malcolm spent a weekend there once at a friend's wedding.

That marriage ended in divorce, same as Malcolm's. The friend was never heard from again after Malcolm went to prison.

So I sort of know the area. The first motel I try belongs to a national chain and has rather strict rules about registration. The old lost-wallet ruse fails me, and I am denied a room when I cannot produce an ID. No problem—there is an abundance of inexpensive motels in the area. I drift to the southern edge of Roanoke and find myself in a less than affluent part of Salem where I spot a motel that probably offers rooms by the hour. Cash will be welcomed. I opt for the daily rate of $40 and tell the old woman at the front desk I will be around for a few days. She's not too friendly, and it dawns on me that she might have owned the place back in the good ole days when blacks were turned away. It's ninety degrees, and I ask if the air-conditioning is working. Brand-new units, she says proudly. I park around back, directly in front of my room and far away from the street. The bed linens and floors are clean. The bathroom is spotless. The new window unit hums along nicely, and by the time I unload my car, the temperature is below seventy. I stretch out on the bed and wonder how many illicit hookups have occurred here. I think of Eva from Puerto Rico and how nice it would be to hold her again. And I think of Vanessa Young and what it will be like to finally touch her.

At dark, I walk down the street and eat a salad at a fast-food place. I'm down twenty pounds since I left Frostburg, and I'm determined to keep losing, for now anyway. As I leave the restaurant, I see stadium lights and decide to take in a game. I drive to Memorial Stadium, home of the Salem Red Sox, Boston's Class High-A affiliate. They're playing the Lynchburg Hillcats before a nice crowd. For $6, I get a seat in the bleachers. I buy a beer from a vendor and soak in the sights and sounds of the game.

Nearby is a young father with his two sons, T-ballers, I suspect, no more than six years old and wearing Red Sox jerseys and caps. I think of Bo and all the hours we spent playing catch in the backyard while Dionne sat on the small patio and sipped iced tea. It seems like yesterday that we were all together, a little family with big dreams and a future. Bo was so small and cute, and his father was his hero. I was trying to turn him into a switch-hitter, at the age of five, when the Feds entered my life and wrecked things. What a waste.

And, other than myself, no one really cares anymore. I suppose my father and siblings would like to see my life made whole again, but it's not a priority. They have their own lives to worry about. Once you go to prison, the world assumes you deserve it, and all pity comes to an end. If you polled my former friends and acquaintances in my hometown, I'm sure they would say something like, "Poor Malcolm, he just crawled in bed with the wrong people. Cut some corners. Got a bit greedy. How tragic." Everyone is quick to forget because everyone wants to forget. The war on crime needs casualties; poor Malcolm got himself captured.

So it's just me, Max Reed Baldwin, free but on the run, scheming some way to exact revenge while riding off into the sunset.

CHAPTER 27

For the sixth day in a row, Victor Westlake sipped his early morning coffee while scanning a brief memo on Mr. Max Baldwin. The informant had vanished. The GPS tracker had finally been removed from a Cadillac Seville owned by an elderly Canadian couple as they ate lunch near Savannah, Georgia. They would never know they had been cyber-tracked by the FBI for three hundred miles. Westlake had punished the three field agents assigned to monitor Baldwin's car. They lost him in Orlando and picked up the wrong scent as the Cadillac headed north.

Baldwin wasn't using his iPhone, his credit cards, or his initial Internet service provider. The court-approved snooping on those fronts would expire in a week, and there was almost no chance it would be renewed. He was neither a suspect nor a fugitive, and the court was reluctant to allow such extensive eavesdropping on a law-abiding citizen. His checking account at SunCoast had a balance of $4,500. The reward money had been tracked as it was split and bounced around the state of Florida, but the FBI eventually lost its trail. Baldwin had moved the money so fast the FBI lawyers could not keep pace with their requests for search warrants. There were at least eight withdrawals totaling $65,000 in cash. There was one record of a wire transfer of $40,000 to an account in Panama, and Westlake assumed the rest of the money was offshore. He had grudgingly come to respect Baldwin and his ability to disappear. If the FBI couldn't find him, maybe he was safe after all.

If Baldwin could avoid credit cards, his iPhone, use of his passport, and getting himself arrested, he could remain hidden for a long time. There had been no more chatter from the Rucker clan, and Westlake was still dumbfounded by the fact that a gang of narco-traffickers in D.C. had located Baldwin near Jacksonville. The FBI and the Marshals Service were investigating themselves, but so far not a clue.

Westlake placed the memo in a pile of papers and finished his coffee.

———

I find the office of Beebe Security in a professional office building not far from my motel. The Yellow Pages ad boasted twenty years of experience, a law enforcement background, state-of-the-art technology, and so on. Almost all of the ads in the Private Investigations section used this same language, and I cannot remember, as I park my car, what attracted me to Beebe. Maybe it is the name. If I don't like the outfit, I'll go to the next name on my list.

If I had seen Frank Beebe walk down the street, I could've said, "There goes a private detective." Fifty years old, thick-chested with a gut pressuring his shirt buttons, polyester pants, pointed-toe cowboy boots, full head of gray hair, the obligatory mustache, and the cocky swagger of a man who's armed and unafraid. He closes the door to his cramped office and says, "What can I do for you, Mr. Baldwin?"

"I need to locate someone."

"What type of case?" he asks as he lands hard in his oversized executive chair. The wall behind him is covered with large photos and seminar certificates.

"It's not really a case. I just need to find this guy."

"What will you do after you find him?"

"Talk to him. That's all. There's no cheating husband or delinquent debtor. I'm not looking for money or revenge or anything bad. I just need to meet this guy and find out more about him."

"Fair enough." Frank uncaps his pen and is ready to take notes. "Tell me about him."

"His name is Nathan Cooley. I think he also goes by Nat, too. Thirty years old, single, I think. He's from a small town called Willow Gap."

"I've been through Willow Gap."

"Last I knew, his mother still lives there, but I'm not sure where Cooley is now. A few years back, he got busted in a meth sting—"

"What a surprise."

"And spent a few years in federal prison. His older brother was killed in a shoot-out with the police."

Frank is scribbling away. "And how do you know this guy?"

"Let's just say we go way back."

"Fair enough." He knows when to ask questions and when to let them pass. "What am I supposed to do?"

"Look, Mr. Beebe—"

"It's Frank."

"Okay, Frank, I doubt there are many black folks in and around Willow Gap. That, plus I'm from Miami, and I have Florida tags on my little foreign car. If I show up and start poking around, asking questions, I probably won't get too far."

"You'd probably get shot."

"I'd like to avoid that. So, I figure you can do the job without raising suspicion. I just need his address and phone number if possible. Anything else would be gravy."

"Have you tried the phone book?"

"Yes, and there are quite a few Cooleys around Willow Gap. No Nathan. I wouldn't get too far making a bunch of cold calls."

"Right. Anything else?"

"That's it. Pretty simple."

"Okay, I charge a hundred bucks an hour, plus expenses. I'll drive to Willow Gap this afternoon. It's about an hour from here, way back in the boondocks."

"So I've heard."

The first draft of my letter reads:

Dear Mr. Cooley:

My name is Reed Baldwin and I am a documentary filmmaker in Miami. Along with two partners, I own a production company called Skelter Films. We specialize in documentaries dealing with the abuse of power by the federal government.

My current project deals with a series of cold-blooded murders carried out by agents of the Drug Enforcement Administration. This topic is very close to me because three years ago my seventeen-year-old nephew was gunned down by two agents in Trenton, New Jersey. He was unarmed and had no criminal record. Of course, an internal investigation showed no fault on the part of the DEA. The lawsuit filed by my family was dismissed.

In researching this film, I believe I have uncovered a conspiracy that reaches the highest levels of the DEA. I believe certain agents are encouraged to simply murder drug dealers, or suspected drug dealers. The purpose is twofold: First, such murders obviously stop criminal activity. Second, they avoid lengthy trials and such. The DEA is killing people instead of arresting them.

To date, I have uncovered about a dozen of these suspicious killings. I have interviewed several of the families, and they all feel strongly that their loved ones were murdered. This brings me to you: I know the basic facts regarding the death of your brother, Gene, in 2004. There were at least three DEA agents involved in the shooting, and, as always, they claim they acted in self-defense. I believe you were on the scene at the time of the shooting.

Please allow me the opportunity to meet, buy you lunch, and discuss this project. I am currently in Washington, D.C., but I can drop things here and drive to southwest Virginia at your convenience. My cell phone number is 305-806-1921.

Thank you for your time.

Sincerely,
M. Reed Baldwin

The clock slows considerably as the hours pass. I go for a long drive south down Interstate 81 and check out Blacksburg, home of Virginia Tech, then Christiansburg, Radford, Marion, and Pulaski. It's mountainous terrain and a pretty drive, but I'm not sightseeing. I may need one of these towns in the near future, and so I take notes of truck stops, motels, and fast-food joints near the interstate. The truck traffic is heavy and there are automobiles from dozens of states, so no one notices me. Occasionally, I leave the four-lane and venture deep into the hills, driving through small towns without stopping. I find Ripplemead, population 500, the nearest hamlet to the lakeside cabin where Judge Fawcett and Naomi Clary were murdered. I eventually wander back to Roanoke. The lights are on; the Red Sox are playing again. I buy a ticket and have a hot dog and a beer for dinner.

Frank Beebe calls me at eight the next morning, and an hour later I'm in his office. As he pours coffee, he says, matter-of-factly, "Found him in the town of Radford, a college town of about 16,000. He got out of prison a few months ago, lived with his mother for a while, then moved away. I talked to his mother, a tough old gal, and she said he bought a bar in Radford."

I'm curious, so I ask, "How did you get her to talk?"

Frank laughs and lights another cigarette. "That's the easy part, Reed. When you've been in this business as long as I have, you can always spew some bullshit and get people talking. I figured his mother still has a healthy fear of anyone connected to the prison system, so I told her I was a federal prison agent and needed to chat with her boy."

"Isn't that impersonating an officer?"

"Nope, no such thing as a federal prison agent. She didn't ask for a card, and if she had, then I would've given her one. I keep a bunch of cards. On any given day, I can be one of many different federal agents. You'd be amazed how easy it is to fool people."

"Did you go to the bar?"

"I did, but I didn't go in. I wouldn't fit. It's just off the campus of Radford University, so the crowd is a lot younger than me. It's called Bombay's and it's been around for some time. According to city records, it changed hands on May 10 of this year. The seller was one Arthur Stone, and your boy Nathan Cooley was the buyer."

"Where does he live?"

"Don't know. Nothing in the land records. I suspect he's renting, so there would be no record of that. Hell, he could be sleeping above the bar. It's an old two-story building. You're not going there, are you?"

"No."

"Good. You're too old and you're too black. It's an all-white crowd."

"Thanks. I'll meet him somewhere else."

I pay Frank Beebe $600 in cash, and on the way out I ask, "Say, Frank, if I needed a fake passport, you got any ideas?"

"Sure. There's a guy in Baltimore I've used before, does most anything. But passports are tricky these days, Homeland Security and all that crap. If they catch you, they really get excited."

I smile and say, "It's not for me."

He laughs and says, "Gee, I've never heard that before."

My car is packed and I leave town. Four hours later I'm in McLean, Virginia, looking for a copy center that offers executive services. I find one in an upscale shopping center, pay a hookup fee, and plug in my laptop to a printer. After ten minutes of fiddling and haggling, I get the damned thing to work and print the letter to Nathan Cooley. It's on Skelter Films stationery, complete with an address on 8th Avenue in Miami and a full selection of phone and fax numbers. On the envelope, I write: "Mr. Nathan Cooley, c/o Bombay's Bar & Grill, 914 East Main Street, Radford, Virginia 24141." To the left of the address, I write in bold letters: "Personal and Confidential."

When it's perfect, I cross the Potomac and drive through central D.C., looking for a post office drop box.

CHAPTER 28

Quinn Rucker turned his back to the bars, stuck his hands through, and touched his wrists behind him. The deputy slapped on the handcuffs as another one opened the cell door. They escorted Quinn to a cramped holding area where three FBI agents were waiting. From there, they walked him through a side door and into a black SUV with dark windows and more armed guards. Ten minutes later, he arrived with full escort at the rear door of the federal building, where he was whisked inside and up two flights of stairs.

Neither Victor Westlake, nor Stanley Mumphrey, nor any other lawyer in the room had ever taken part in such a meeting. The defendant was never brought in for a chat. If the police needed to talk to the accused, they did so at the jail. If his appearance was needed in court, the judge or magistrate called a hearing.

Quinn was led into the small conference room, and the handcuffs were removed. He shook hands with his lawyer, Dusty Shiver, who, of course, had to be present but was uncertain about the meeting. He had cautioned the Feds that his client would say nothing until he, Dusty, allowed him to speak.

Quinn had been in jail for four months and was not doing well. For reasons known only to his keepers, he was locked down in solitary confinement. Contact with his guards was minimal.

The food was dreadful and he was losing weight. He was also taking antidepressants and sleeping fifteen hours a day. Often, he refused to meet with anyone from his family, or with Dusty. One week he demanded the right to plead guilty in exchange for life in prison; the next week he wanted a trial. He had fired Dusty twice, only to rehire him days later. He occasionally admitted killing Judge Fawcett and his girlfriend but always recanted and accused the government of doping his food. He had threatened the guards with promises of death and the deaths of their children, only to offer tearful apologies when his mood changed.

Victor Westlake was in charge of the meeting and began by saying, "Let's get to the point, Mr. Rucker. We have it on good intelligence that you and some of your fellow conspirators desire to knock off one of our witnesses."

Dusty touched Quinn's arm and said, "Not a word. Do not speak until I say so." Quinn smiled at Westlake as if killing a government witness would be a delight.

Westlake kept going: "The purpose of this little get-together is to warn you, Mr. Rucker, that if any of our witnesses are harmed, then you will face additional charges, and not just you. We'll go after every member of your family."

Quinn was grinning, and he blurted, "So, Bannister is on the run, huh?"

"Shut up, Quinn," Dusty said.

"I don't have to shut up," Quinn said. "I hear Bannister has left the warm sun of Florida."

"Shut up, Quinn!" Dusty snarled again.

"Got him a new face, probably a new name, the works," Quinn continued.

Stanley Mumphrey said, "We'll indict Dee Ray, Tall Man, several of your cousins, anybody and everybody we can throw the book at, Quinn, if you harm any of our witnesses."

"You don't have any witnesses," Quinn shot across the table. "Only Bannister."

Dusty threw his hands up and slumped in his chair. "I advise you to shut up, Quinn."

"I hear you," Quinn said. "I hear you."

Westlake managed to maintain a scowl as he stared at the defendant, but he was stunned. The meeting was supposed to intimidate Quinn, not frighten the government. How on earth were they able to find Bannister in Florida and now know he had fled? It was a chilling moment for Westlake and his assistants. If they could find their informant, they would certainly bring him in.

"Your entire family could face capital murder charges," Stanley plowed on in a feeble attempt to sound tough.

Quinn just smiled. He stopped talking and folded his arms across his chest.

I have to see Vanessa Young. A meeting has an element of risk; to be seen together by the wrong people would create questions I'm not ready to answer. But a meeting is inevitable and has been for several years.

I saw her at Frostburg, on a snowy day when many visitors didn't make the drive. While I was talking to my father, Henry, she walked in and sat at the next table. She was there to visit her brother. She was gorgeous, early forties, soft brown skin, beautiful sad eyes, long legs, and tight jeans. The whole package. I could not keep my eyes off her, and Henry finally said, "You want me to leave?" Of course not, because if he left, then my visiting time was over. The longer he stayed, the longer I could look at Vanessa. Before long, she was looking back, and we were soon making serious eye contact. The attraction was mutual, at first.

But there were a couple of sticking points. First, my incarceration and, second, her marriage, which, as it turned out, was a mess. I leaned on her brother for information, but he wanted to stay out of it. We swapped a few letters, but she was afraid of getting caught by her husband. She tried to visit more often, to see both her brother and me, but she had two teenagers who were complicating her life. After her divorce was final, she dated other men, but nothing worked. I begged Vanessa to wait for me, but seven years is a long time when you're forty-one. When her kids left home, she moved to Richmond, Virginia, and our long-distance romance cooled off. Vanessa's background is such that she is extremely cautious and keeps one eye on the rearview mirror. I guess we have that much in common. Using encrypted e-mails, we manage to arrange a time and place. I warn her that I look nothing like the Malcolm Bannister she met in prison. She says she'll take that chance. She can't wait to see the new-and-improved version.

As I park outside the restaurant, in a suburb of Richmond, I have a bad case of the butterflies. I'm a wreck because I am about to finally touch the woman I have dreamed about for almost three years. I know she wants to touch me too, but the guy she was so physically attracted to back then looks entirely different now. What if she doesn't approve? What if she prefers Malcolm to Max? It's also unnerving to realize I'm about to spend time with the only person, outside the Feds, who knows both men.

I wipe perspiration from my forehead and consider leaving. Then I get out and slam the door.

She's at the table, and as I almost stutter-step over, she smiles. She approves. I kiss her gently on the cheek and sit down, and for a long time we just look at each other. Finally, I say, "Well, what do you think?"

Vanessa shakes her head and says, "Pretty astonishing. I would have never known. Got any ID?" We both laugh and I say, "Sure, but it's all bogus. It says I'm Max now, not Malcolm."

"You look thin, Max."

"Thanks, and you too." I caught a glimpse of her legs under the table. Short skirt. Funky high heels. She's dressed for action.

"Which do you prefer?" I ask.

"Well, I suppose I don't have a choice now, do I? I think you're cute, Max. I like the new you, the whole ensemble. Whose idea was the designer eyeglasses?"

"My consultant, same guy who suggested the slick head and four days of stubble."

"The more I see, the more I like."

"Thank God. I'm a nervous wreck."

"Relax, baby. We're in for a long night."

The waiter takes our drink orders—a martini for me, diet soda for her. There are a lot of things I don't want to discuss, namely my sudden exit from prison and witness protection. The brother she visited in prison got out but is already back behind bars, so we leave him out of the conversation. I ask about her kids, a daughter who's twenty and in college and a son who's eighteen and drifting.

At one point, as I'm talking, she stops me and says, "You even sound different."

"Good. It's a new speech pattern I've been practicing for months now. A much slower delivery and a deeper voice. Does it seem genuine?"

"I think so. Yes, it's working."

She asks where I'm living, and I explain I've yet to find a home. I'm moving around, trying to avoid getting trailed by the FBI and others, lots of cheap motels. I'm not a fugitive, but I'm not exactly in the clear. Our dinner arrives, but we hardly notice.

She says, "You look a lot younger. Maybe I should see your plastic surgeon."

"Please, don't change a thing." I talk about the changes— primarily the eyes, nose, and chin. I amuse her by describing the meetings with my surgical team and our efforts to design a new face. I'm also twenty pounds lighter and she thinks I need to put on a few pounds. As our nerves settle we relax and talk like a couple of old friends. The waiter asks if our food is okay, since we've hardly touched it. We hit a number of topics, but in the back of our minds we're both thinking the same thing. I finally say, "Let's get outta here."

The words are barely spoken and she's reaching for her purse. I pay cash for the meal and we're in the parking lot. I don't like the idea of her apartment and she agrees. It's rather small and bare, she explains. We check into a hotel I spotted down the street and order a bottle of champagne. Two kids on their wedding night could not possibly exert more energy than Vanessa and I. There was so much ground to cover, so much catching up to do.

CHAPTER 29

While Vanessa is at work, I run a few errands around Richmond. At one store, I spend $70 on a cheap prepaid cell phone with one hundred minutes of call time, and at another I buy the identical phone and plan for $68. I'll give one phone to Vanessa and keep the other. At a pharmacy, I load up on prepaid credit cards. I have an appointment with a man who owns a camera shop and calls himself a videographer, but his fee is too high. If I'm lucky and get an interview, I'll need two people—a cameraman and a gofer. This guy says he works with a full crew or doesn't work at all.

Vanessa and I have a sandwich for lunch in a deli not far from her office. For dinner, we go to a bistro in the Carytown section of Richmond. Our after-dinner routine is remarkably, and wonderfully, similar to the night before, and in the same hotel room. This could be habit forming. Our plans for the third night, though, are derailed when her son calls. He's passing through town and needs a place to stay. She figures he'll need some money too.

We're finishing dinner when the cell phone in my pocket vibrates. The caller ID says "Unknown," but then all calls to this phone are unknown. Expecting big news, I say to Vanessa, "Excuse me," and step away from the table. In the foyer of the restaurant, I answer the phone.

A vaguely familiar voice says, "Mr. Reed Baldwin, this is Nathan Cooley. I got your letter."

I tell myself to speak slowly and deeply. "Yes, Mr. Cooley, thanks for the call." Of course he got my letter—how else would he have my phone number?

"When do you want to talk?" he asks.

"Anytime. I'm in Washington right now and we finished filming today. I have some downtime, so right now is perfect. What about you?"

"I'm not going anywhere. How did you find me?"

"The Internet. It's hard to hide these days."

"I guess so. I usually sleep late, then work at the bar from about two until midnight."

"How about lunch tomorrow?" I say, a bit too eagerly. "Just the two of us, no cameras or recorders or stuff like that. I'm buying."

A pause, and I hold my breath. "Okay, I guess. Where?"

"It's your neck of the woods, Mr. Cooley. You pick the time and place. I'll be there."

"Okay, at the Radford exit off Interstate 81 there is a place called Spanky's. I'll meet you there at noon tomorrow."

"I'll be there."

"How will I recognize you?" he asks, and I almost drop my phone. Recognition is a far greater issue than he'll ever realize. I have subjected myself to surgery that radically altered my face. I shave my head every other day and my beard once a week. I have starved off twenty pounds. I wear fake tortoiseshell glasses with round red frames, along with black T-shirts, fake Armani sport coats, and canvas sandals one would find only in Miami or L.A. I have a different name. I have a different voice and delivery.

And this entire charade has been carefully put together not to mislead the people who want to follow me or kill me but to conceal my real identity from you, Mr. Nathan Cooley.

I say, "I'm six feet tall, black, thin, a slick head, and I'll be wearing a white straw hat, Panama style."

"You're black?" he blurts.

"Yep. Is that a problem?"

"No. See you tomorrow."

I return to the table where Vanessa is waiting anxiously. I say softly, "It's Cooley. We're meeting tomorrow."

She smiles and says, "Go for it." We finish dinner and reluctantly say good-bye. We kiss outside the restaurant and act like a couple of teenagers. I think about her all the way to Roanoke.

I arrive fifteen minutes early and park so that I can watch the vehicles as they turn in to the Spanky's lot. The first thing I'll see is his car, or truck, and this will reveal a lot. Six months ago he was in prison, where he had served a little over five years. He has no father, an alcoholic mother, and no education past the tenth grade, so his choice of vehicle will be interesting. As we talk, my plans are to make a mental note of everything I can possibly see—clothing, jewelry, watch, cell phone.

The traffic picks up as the lunch crowd rolls in. At 12:03, a sparkling-new silver Chevrolet Silverado half-ton pickup arrives, and I suspect it's Nathan Cooley. It is, and he parks on the other side of the lot. He glances around nervously as he walks to the front entrance.

It's been four years since I've seen him, and he appears to have changed little. Same weight, same blond shaggy hair, though he once shaved his head in prison. He looks twice at the Florida tags on my car, then goes inside. I take a deep breath, put the Panama hat on my head, and walk to the door. Be cool, you idiot, I mumble to myself as my bowels flip. This will take a steady hand and nerves of steel.

We meet inside the front foyer and exchange pleasantries. I remove the hat as we follow the hostess to a booth in the rear. Across the table, we face each other and talk about the weather. For a moment, I'm almost overwhelmed by my ruse. Nathan is talking to a stranger, while I'm talking to a kid I once knew quite well. He doesn't seem at all suspicious: no staring at my eyes or nose; no squinting, or raised eyebrows, or distant glances as he listens to my voice. And, thankfully, no "You kinda remind me of a guy I once knew." Nothing, so far.

I tell the waitress I really want a beer, a tall draft, and Nathan hesitates before saying, "The same." The success of this long-shot mission could well depend on alcohol. Nathan was raised in a culture of hard drinking and meth addiction. Then he spent five years in prison, clean and sober. I'm assuming he's back to his old habits now that he's out. The fact that he owns his own bar is a good indication.

For a hillbilly who was never taught how to dress, he looks okay. Washed jeans, a Coors Light golf shirt some salesman left at the bar, and combat boots. There is no jewelry and no watch, but he does have an incredibly ugly prison tattoo inside his left forearm. In short, Nathan is not flashing around money with his appearance.

The beer arrives and we tap glasses. "Tell me about this film," he says.

Out of habit, I nod, pause, tell myself to speak slowly, clearly, and as deeply as possible. "I've been making documentaries for ten years now, and this is the most exciting project I've seen."

"Look, Mr. Baldwin, what is a documentary film exactly? I watch some movies and all, but I don't think I've seen too many documentaries."

"Sure. They're typically small, independently produced films that you don't see in the big movie houses. They're not commercial. They're about real people, real problems, real issues, no big movie stars and all that. Really good stuff. The best win awards at film festivals and get some attention, but they're never going to make a lot of money. My company specializes in films that deal with the abuse of power, primarily by the federal government, but also by big corporations." I take a sip, tell myself to go slow. "Most are about an hour long. This one might run for ninety minutes, but we'll decide that later."

The waitress is back. I order a chicken sandwich, and Nathan wants a basket of wings.

"How'd you get into the bar business?" I ask.

He takes a gulp, smiles, says, "A friend. The guy who owned the bar was going under, not from the bar, but from other properties. Recession got him, I think. So he was trying to unload Bombay's. He was looking for some fool to take the deed and assume the debts, and I said what the hell. I'm only thirty, no job, no prospects, why not take a chance? So far, though, I'm making money. It's kinda fun. Lots of college girls hanging around."

"You're not married?"

"No. Don't know how much you know about me, Mr. Baldwin, but I just finished a five-year prison sentence. Thanks to the federal government, I ain't had too many dates recently; just now getting back in the game. Know what I mean?"

"Sure. The prison time arose out of the same incident in which your brother was killed, right?"

"You got it. I pled guilty and went away for five. My cousin is still in prison, Big Sandy over in Kentucky, a bad place. Most of my cousins are either locked up or dead. That's one reason I moved to Radford, Mr. Baldwin, to get away from the drug business."

"I see. Please call me Reed. My father is Mr. Baldwin."

"Okay. And I'm Nathan, or Nate." We tap glasses again as if we're suddenly much closer. In prison we called him Nattie.

"Tell me about your film company," he says. I anticipated this, but it is still shaky ground.

I take a gulp and swallow slowly. "Skelter is a new company

based in Miami, just me and two partners, plus a staff. For years I worked for a bigger production company in L.A., an outfit called Cove Creek Films, you may have heard of it." He has not. He just glanced at the rear end of a shapely young waitress. "Anyway, Cove Creek has won a ton of awards and made decent money in this business, but last year it blew up. Big fight over creative control and which projects to do next. We're still in the middle of some nasty litigation that looks like it will drag on for years. There's an injunction in federal court in L.A. that prohibits me from even talking about Cove Creek or the lawsuit, pretty crazy, huh?" To my relief, Nathan is rapidly losing interest in my film company and its problems.

"Why are you based in Miami?"

"I went there a few years ago working on a film about bogus government defense contractors and fell in love with the place. I live on South Beach. Ever been there?"

"No." Except for the trips arranged by the U.S. Marshals Service, Nathan has never ventured more than two hundred miles from Willow Gap.

"It's a happening place. Beautiful beaches, gorgeous girls, wild nightlife. I got a divorce four years ago and I'm enjoying the single life again. I spend about half the year there. The other half, I'm on the road filming."

"How do you film a documentary?" he asks, then knocks back some beer.

"It's far different from a feature film. It's usually just me and a cameraman, maybe a technician or two. The story is the important part, not the scenery or the actor's face."

"And you want to film me?"

"Absolutely. You, maybe your mother, maybe other members of the family. I want to go to the place where your brother was killed. What I'm after here, Nathan, is the truth. I'm onto something, something that could really be big. If I can prove the DEA systematically knocks off drug dealers, that they murder them in cold blood, then we might be able to bust these sumbitches. My nephew was breaking bad, getting deeper into the crack trade, but he was not a hard-core dealer. Stupid, yes, but not dangerous. He was seventeen and unarmed, and he was shot three times from point-blank range. A stolen pistol was left at the scene, and the DEA claims it belonged to him. They're a bunch of liars."

Nathan's face slowly contorts into anger and he looks as if he wants to spit.

I press on: "The film will be the story of three, maybe four of these murders. I'm not sure if my nephew's will be included because I'm the filmmaker. Maybe I'm too close to his death. I've already filmed the story of Jose Alvarez in Amarillo, Texas, a nineteen-year-old undocumented worker who was shot fourteen times by DEA agents. Problem is, no one in his family speaks English and there's not much sympathy for illegal immigrants. I've filmed the story of Tyler Marshak, a college boy in California who was peddling marijuana. The DEA broke into his dorm room like a bunch of Gestapo goons and shot him dead in his bed. You may have read about it." He has not. The Nathan Cooley I knew played video games hours a day and never looked at a newspaper or magazine. Nor does he have the innate curiosity to check out either Skelter Films or Cove Creek.

"Anyway, I have some great footage of the dorm room, the autopsy, and statements from his family, but they're currently tied up in a lawsuit against the DEA. I may not be able to use this."

Lunch arrives and we order more beer. Nathan rips chicken off the bone and wipes his mouth with a napkin. "Why are you so interested in my brother's case?"

"Let's say I'm curious. I don't know all the facts yet. I would like to hear your version of what happened and walk through the drug bust at the scene. My lawyers have filed Freedom of Information applications to get the DEA records and also the court file. We'll plow through the paperwork, but there's a good chance the DEA has covered up everything. That's what they typically do.

We will slowly piece things together, and at the same time we'll see how you and your family look on camera. The camera doesn't like everyone, Nathan."

He says, "I doubt if the camera likes my mother."

"We'll see."

"Not so sure about that. She probably won't do it. You mention anything about Gene's death and she falls all to pieces." He licks his fingers and selects another wing.

"Perfect. That's what I want to capture on film."

"What's the time frame here? What are we looking at?"

I take a bite of my sandwich and chew for a while as I ponder. "Maybe a year. I'd like to finish all the filming within the next six months, then have that much time to cut, splice, edit, maybe reshoot some stuff. You can tinker with these things forever and it's hard to let go. As far as you're concerned, I would like to shoot some initial footage, maybe three or four hours, and send that to my producers and editors in Miami. Let them see you, hear you, get a feel for the story and your ability to tell it. If we all agree, then we'll keep shooting."

"What's in it for me?"

"Nothing, other than the truth and exposing the men who killed your brother. Think about it, Nathan. Wouldn't you love to see these bastards charged with murder and put on trial?"

"Damned right I would."

I lean in fiercely, my eyes on fire. "Then do it, Nathan. Tell me his story. You have nothing to lose and a lot to gain. Tell me about the drug trade, how it wrecked your family, how Gene got caught up in it, how it was simply a way of life in these parts, there were no other jobs. You don't have to name names—I don't want to get anyone in trouble." I take a sip and finish off my second beer. "Where was Gene the last time you saw him?"

"Lying on the ground, hands behind his back, getting handcuffed. Not a single shot had been fired by anyone. The deal was gone, the bust was over. I was handcuffed and led away, then I heard gunshots. They said Gene tripped an agent and sprinted into the woods. Bullshit. They killed him in cold blood."

"You gotta tell me this story, Nathan. You gotta take me back to the scene and reenact it. The world needs to know what the federal government is doing in its war on drugs. It's taking no prisoners."

He takes a deep breath to let the moment pass. I'm talking too much, and too fast, so I spend a few minutes with my sandwich. The waitress asks if we want another round. "Yes, please, for me," I say, and Nathan quickly follows. He finishes off a wing, licks his fingers, and says, "My family is causing problems right now. That's why I moved away and came to Radford."

I shrug as if this is his problem, not mine, but I'm not surprised. I ask, "If you cooperate, and the rest of your family does not, will that cause more trouble?"

He laughs and says, "Trouble is the norm with the Cooleys. We are notorious for feuding."

"Let's do this. Let's sign a one-page agreement, already prepared by my lawyers and in English so plain you don't need to hire your own lawyers unless you enjoy pissing away money, and the agreement will state that you, Nathan Cooley, will cooperate fully in the making of this documentary film. In return, you'll be paid a fee of $8,000, which is the minimum required of actors in these projects. From time to time, or whenever you want, you can review the film in progress, and—and this is crucial—if you don't like what you see, you can walk and I cannot use any of your footage. That's a pretty fair deal, Nathan."

He nods as he searches for loopholes, but Nathan is not the type to analyze things quickly. Plus, the alcohol is urging him on. I suspect he's drooling over the word "actor."

"Eight thousand dollars?" he repeats.

"Yes, as I said, these are low-budget films. Nobody will make a lot of money."

The interesting point here is that I mentioned money before

he did. I sweeten the deal by adding, "Plus, you'll get a small piece of the back end."

A piece of the back end. Nathan is probably thinking of something else.

"That means that you'll get a few bucks if the movie sells some tickets, but don't expect it," I say. "You're not doing this for the money, Nathan. You're doing it for your brother."

The plate in front of him is littered with bones. The waitress brings our third round and removes the scraps. It's important to keep him talking because I don't want him thinking.

"What kind of guy was Gene?" I ask.

He shakes his head and looks as if he might cry. "My big brother, you know. Our dad disappeared when we were small. Just me and Gene." He narrates a few stories about their childhood, funny stories about two kids trying to survive. We finish our third beers, order another round, but vow to stop after that.

At ten the following morning, Nathan and I meet at a coffee shop in Radford. He looks over the contract, asks a few questions, and signs it. I sign as the vice president of Skelter Films and hand over a check for $8,000 drawn on a company bank account in Miami.

"When do we start?" he asks.

"Well, Nathan, I'm here and I'm not leaving. The sooner, the better. What about tomorrow morning?"

"Sure. Where?"

"I've been thinking about that. We're in southwest Virginia, where mountains are important. In fact, the land here has a lot to do with the story. The remoteness of the mountains and so on. I think I'd like to be outdoors, at first anyway. We can always move around. Do you live in town or in the country?"

"I'm renting a place just outside town. From the backyard, there's a nice view of some hills."

"Let's take a look. I'll be there at ten in the morning with a small crew and we'll check out the lighting."

"Okay. I talked to my mother and she says no way."

"Can I talk to her?"

"You can try, but she's pretty tough. She doesn't like the idea of you or anybody else making a movie about Gene and our family. She thinks you'll make us look like a bunch of ignorant mountain folk."

"Did you explain that you have the right to monitor the film as it progresses?"

"I tried to. She was drinking."

"Sorry."

"I'll see you in the morning."

CHAPTER 30

Nathan is living in a small, redbrick house on a narrow road a few miles west of the Radford city limits. His nearest neighbor lives in a double-wide trailer half a mile closer to the state highway. His front lawn is neatly mowed and there are a few shrubs lining the narrow front porch. He's outside playing with his yellow Lab as we arrive and park in the drive behind his shiny new truck.

My ace crew consists of my new assistant, Vanessa, who will be called Gwen on this project, and two freelancers from Roanoke—Slade, the videographer, and his assistant, Cody. Slade bills himself as a filmmaker and works out of his garage. He owns the cameras and equipment, and he looks the part—long hair in a ponytail, jeans with holes in the knees, a couple of gold chains around his neck. Cody is younger and sufficiently grungy. Their fee is $1,000 a day plus expenses, and part of the deal is that they do what they're supposed to do and stay as quiet as possible. I have promised to pay them in cash and I've made no reference to Skelter Films or anything else. It might be a documentary film, or it might be something else. Just do as I say and offer no details to Nathan Cooley.

Vanessa arrived in Radford last night, and we bunked together in a nice hotel where we registered in her name and used a pre-paid credit card. She told her boss she had the flu and, under doctor's orders, can't leave the house for several days. She knows nothing about filmmaking, but then neither do I.

After a round of awkward introductions in the driveway, we check out the surroundings. Nathan's backyard is a large open area that slopes up the side of a hill. A herd of whitetail deer scamper over a fence when they see us. I ask Nathan how long it takes to cut his grass, and he says three hours. He points to a tractor shed where a fancy John Deere riding mower is parked. It looks new. He says he's a country boy who prefers the outdoors, likes to hunt and fish and pee off the back porch. Plus, he still thinks of prison and life there with a thousand men surviving in close quarters. No sir, he loves the open spaces. While we walk and talk, Slade and Cody wander aimlessly about, mumbling to each other as they look at the sun and rub their chins.

"I like it here," I say, pointing, taking charge. "I want those hills in the frame."

Slade seems to disagree, but he and Cody nonetheless start hauling gear from their van. The setup takes forever, and to show my artistic temperament, I start barking about the time. Gwen has brought along a small makeup kit, and Nathan reluctantly agrees to a touch-up with powder and a bit of blush. I'm sure it's his first, but he needs to feel like an actor. Gwen is wearing a short skirt and a blouse that's hardly buttoned, and part of her act is to see how easily the boy can be teased. I pretend to look over my notes, but I watch Nathan as he watches Gwen. He loves the attention and teasing.

When the camera, lights, monitor, and sound are almost ready, I take Nathan aside, just the two of us, director and star, to contemplate my vision.

"Okay, Nathan, I want you to be very serious. Think about Gene, his murder at the hands of the federal government. I want you to be somber, no smiles, no fun here, okay?"

"Got it."

"Speak slowly, almost painfully. I'll ask the questions, you look at the camera and just talk. Act naturally. You're a nice-looking guy and I think the camera will like you, but it's important to just be yourself."

"I'll try," he says, and it's obvious Nathan is really looking forward to this.

"One last thing, and I should have mentioned it yesterday. If this film does what we hope, and blows the cover off the DEA, then there could be some retribution, some payback. I don't trust the DEA for one second—a bunch of rogue thugs—and they might do anything. That's why it's important for you to be, shall we say, out of the business."

"I'm clean, man," he says.

"You're not dealing in any way?"

"Hell no. I'm not going back to prison, Reed. That's one reason I moved over here, away from my family. They're still cooking meth and selling it, not me."

"Okay. Just think of Gene."

Cody puts the mike on him and we get situated. We're on a set, in folding chairs with lights and wiring all around us. The camera is over my shoulder, and for a moment I feel like a real kick-ass investigative journalist. I look at Gwen and say, "Did you forget the still shots? Come on, Gwen!"

She jumps as I bark and grabs a camera. I say, "Just a couple of stills, Nathan, so we'll have a clear record of the lighting." He frowns at first, then smiles at Gwen as she snaps away. Finally, after we've been here for an hour, we start filming. I hold a pen with my left hand and scribble on a legal pad.

Malcolm Bannister was right-handed, just in case Nathan might be suspicious, which he does not seem to be.

To loosen him up, I start with all the basics: name, age, employment, education, prison, criminal record, children, no marriages, and so on. A couple of times I tell him to relax, repeat something, we're just having a conversation. His childhood—different homes, schools, life with his big brother, Gene, no father, a rocky relationship with his mother. At this point, he says, "Look, Reed, I'm not going to say bad things about my mother, okay?"

"Of course not, Nathan. That's not at all what I intended." And I quickly change the subject. We get around to the meth culture of his youth. With some hesitation, he finally opens up and paints a depressing picture of a rough adolescence filled with drugs, booze, sex, and violence. By the time he was fifteen, he knew how to cook meth. Two of his cousins were burned alive when a lab blew up in a mobile home. He was sixteen when he first saw the inside of a jail cell. He dropped out of school and life got crazier. At least four of his cousins have served time for drug distribution; two are still locked away. As bad as prison was, it did get him away from the drugs and alcohol. He was sober for the five years he was incarcerated and is now determined to stay away from the meth. Beer is another matter.

We break at noon. The sun is overhead, and Slade is concerned about the brightness of the conditions. He and Cody stroll around, looking for another spot. "How long can you go today, Nathan?" I ask.

"I'm the boss," he says smugly. "I can go in whenever I want."

"Great. So a couple more hours?"

"Why not? How am I doing?"

"Terrific. It took you a few minutes to settle down, but now you're very smooth, very sincere."

Gwen adds, "You're a natural storyteller, Nathan." He likes this. She's back with the makeup routine, wiping perspiration from his forehead, brushing, touching, flirting, revealing. He craves the attention.

We brought sandwiches and soft drinks and eat under the shade of an oak tree next to the toolshed. Slade likes this spot and we decide to move the set. Gwen whispers to Nathan about using the restroom. This makes him uncomfortable, but by now he can hardly keep his eyes off her legs. I walk away and pretend to be on the cell phone, talking to important people in Los Angeles.

Gwen disappears into the back door of the house. She will later report that the house has two bedrooms but only one with furniture, nothing in the den but a sofa, a chair, and a huge HD television, one bathroom in need of a good scrubbing, a kitchen with a sink full of dirty dishes and a refrigerator filled with beer and cold cuts. There is an attic with a fold-down staircase. The floors are covered with cheap carpeting. There are three doors— front, back, and garage—and all three are secured with thick dead bolts that have obviously been added recently. There appears to be no alarm system—no keypads or sensors over the windows and doors. In his bedroom closet, there are two rifles and two shotguns. In the closet in the spare bedroom, there is nothing but a pair of muddy hunting boots.

While she is inside, I continue my fake phone chat while I watch Nathan from behind large sunglasses. He keeps his eyes on the back of his house, nervous that she is inside, alone. Slade and Cody are getting the set rewired. When she returns, Nathan relaxes and apologizes for his sloppy housekeeping. She coos and works on his hair. When everything is in place, we plunge into the afternoon session.

He mentions a motorcycle accident when he was fourteen, and I dissect this for half an hour. We delve into his sketchy employment history—bosses, co-workers, duties, wages, dismissals. Back to the drug trade with details about how to cook meth, who taught him, key ingredients, and so on. Romances, girl-friends? He claims to have impregnated a young cousin when he was twenty, but has no idea what happened to the mother or child. He had a serious girl before he went to prison, but she forgot about him. Judging by the way he looks at Gwen, it's obvious this boy is wired.

He's thirty years old, and other than the death of his brother and a prison sentence his life has been unremarkable. After three hours of prodding and poking, I extract anything and everything of interest. He says he needs to get to work.

"We have to visit the place where Gene was killed," I say as Slade turns off the camera and everybody relaxes.

"It's outside of Bluefield, about an hour from here," he says.

"Bluefield, West Virginia?"

"That's right."

"And why were you there?"

"We were making a delivery, but the buyer was an informant."

"I have to see this, Nathan, to walk through it all, to recapture the scene, the violence, the moment, the place where Gene was shot and killed. It was at night, right?"

"Yeah, long after midnight." Gwen is tapping his face with a cloth, removing the makeup. "You're really good on camera," she says softly, and he smiles.

"When can we go there?" I ask.

He shrugs and says, "Whenever. Tomorrow if you want."

Perfect. We agree to meet at his house at 9:00 a.m. and caravan through the mountains into West Virginia, to the remote, abandoned mine site where the Cooley brothers walked into a trap.

———

We've had a good day with Nathan. He and I got on well as filmmaker and actor, and at times he and Gwen seemed ready to strip and have a go. Late in the afternoon, she and I find our way to Bombay's on Main Street in Radford, next to the college campus, and take a table by the dartboard. It's far too early for the college crowd, though a few rowdies are at the bar enjoying happy-hour discounts. I ask the waitress to inform Nathan Cooley that we are having a drink, and within seconds he appears with a big smile. We invite him to have a seat, which he does, and we start downing beers. Gwen drinks little and manages to sip on a glass of wine while Nathan and I knock back a few pints.

Coeds straggle in and the place gets louder. I ask about specials, and there's an oyster po'boy on the chalkboard. We order two and Nathan disappears to yell at the cook. We have dinner and stay until after dark. Not only are we the only blacks in the bar, but we are also the only patrons over the age of twenty-two. Nathan stops by occasionally to check on us, but he's a busy man.

CHAPTER 31

At nine the following morning we return to Nathan's house, and once again he's in the front yard playing with his dog, waiting. I am assuming he meets us outside because he doesn't want us inside. I explain that my little Audi is in bad need of service, and it might be best if we could ride over in his pickup. An hour each way will give us two hours alone with Nathan and no distractions. He shrugs and says okay, whatever, and away we go, with Slade and Cody following in their van. I'm in the front seat; Gwen is folded into the backseat of the club cab. She's wearing jeans today because Nathan couldn't keep his eyes off her legs yesterday. She will be a bit more aloof, just to keep him guessing.

As we head west toward the mountains, I admire the interior of the truck and explain that I've never spent much time in such vehicles. The seats are leather, there is an advanced GPS system, and so on. Nathan is really proud of the truck and chatters on about it.

To change the subject, I bring up his mother and claim to really want to meet her. Nathan says, "Look, Reed, you're welcome to try, but she doesn't like what we're doing. I talked to her last night again, and I explained the whole project, and how important it is, and how much you need her, but I got nowhere."

"Can't we at least talk, say hello, you know?" I almost turn and smile at Gwen now that we know Nathan deems the project "important."

"I doubt it. She's a tough woman, Reed. Drinks a lot, nasty temper. We're not on good terms right now."

Being the pushy investigative journalist, I decide to plow into sensitive matters. "Is it because you've gotten away from the family business, that you're making money with your bar?"

"That's kind of personal, isn't it?" Gwen scolds from the rear.

Nathan takes a deep breath and glances out the side window. He grips the wheel with both hands and says, "It's a long story, but Mom has always blamed me for Gene's death, which is crazy. He was the big brother, the leader of the gang, the head chef in the meth lab, plus he was an addict. I was not. I used the stuff occasionally, but I never got hooked. Gene, he was out of control. This place we're going to was a run Gene made once a week. Occasionally, I tagged along. I shouldn't have been there the night we got busted. We had a guy, I won't use any names, but he was running meth for us on the west side of Bluefield. We didn't know it, but he got busted, flipped, told the DEA when and where. We walked into a trap, and I swear I could do nothing to help Gene. As I've told you, we surrendered and they were taking us in. I heard gunshots, and Gene was dead. I've explained this to my mother a hundred times, but she won't hear it. Gene was her favorite and his death is all my fault."

"Terrible," I mumble.

"Did she visit you in prison?" Gwen asks sweetly from behind.

Another long pause. "Twice." Nothing is said for at least three miles. We're on the interstate now, headed southwest, listening to Kenny Chesney. Nathan clears his throat and says, "To tell you the truth, I'm trying to get away from my family. My mom, my cousins, a bunch of deadbeat nephews. Word's out that I own a nice bar and I'm doing okay, so it won't be long before these clowns start begging for money. I need to get farther away."

"Where would you go?" I ask with great sympathy.

"Not far. I love the mountains, the hiking and fishing. I'm a hillbilly, Reed, and that'll never change. Boone, North Carolina, is a nice place. Somewhere like that. Someplace where there are no Cooleys in the phone book." He laughs at this, a sad little chuckle.

A few minutes later he rocks us with: "You know, I had a buddy in prison kinda reminds me of you. Malcolm Bannister was his name, great guy, black dude from Winchester, Virginia. A lawyer who always said the Feds got him for no reason."

I listen and nod along as if this is of no consequence whatsoever. I can almost feel Gwen seize up in the rear seat. "What happened to him?" I manage to ask. My mouth has never been drier.

"I think Mal's still in prison. Couple more years, maybe. I've lost track. It's something, something in the voice, maybe the mannerisms, something, can't quite put my finger on it, but you remind me of Mal."

"It's a big world, Nathan," I say, in a deeper voice, thoroughly unconcerned. "And remember, to white folks we all look the same."

He laughs and Gwen manages an awkward laugh too.

While I was mending at Fort Carson, I worked with an expert who videoed me for hours and made a list of habits and mannerisms I had to change. I practiced for hours, but once I landed in Florida, I stopped practicing. Natural moves and habits are hard to break. My mind is frozen and I can't think of anything to say.

Gwen comes through with: "Nathan, you mentioned some nephews a few minutes ago. How long will this go on, do you think? I mean, it looks like the meth business is becoming generational for a lot of families."

Nathan frowns and considers this. "I'd say it's pretty hopeless. There are no jobs except for coal, and so many young men just don't want to work in the mines anymore. Plus, they start getting high when they're fifteen, hooked at sixteen. The girls are pregnant at sixteen, kids having kids, babies nobody wants. Once you start screwing, you don't stop. I don't see much future around here, not for people like me."

I'm listening but not hearing; my head is spinning as I wonder how much Nathan knows. How suspicious is he? What have I done to tip him off? I'm still undercover—I'm sure of it—but what's he thinking?

———

Bluefield, West Virginia, is a town of eleven thousand located on the extreme southern tip of the state, not far from the Virginia line. We skirt around it on Highway 52 and are soon on winding roads that fall and rise dramatically. Nathan knows the area well, though it's been years since he was here. We turn onto a county road and fall deeper into a valley. The asphalt ends and we zigzag along gravel and dirt roads until we stop at the edge of a creek. Old willow oaks hang overhead and block the sun. The weeds are knee-high. "Here we are," he says as he turns off the ignition.

We get out and I tell Slade and Cody to get their gear. We will not be using lighting and I want the smaller, handheld camera. They scramble around, grabbing equipment.

Nathan walks to the edge of the creek and smiles at the bubbling water. "How often did you come here?" I ask.

"Not much. We had several drop points around Bluefield, but this was the main one. Gene had been making runs here for ten years, but not me. The truth was I didn't work in the business as much as he wanted me to. I could see trouble. I tried to find other jobs, you know. I wanted out. Gene wanted me to get more involved."

"Where were you parked?"

He turns and points, and I decide to move his truck and Slade's van to keep them out of the frame. Relying on my vast directorial skills, I want to shoot an action piece with Nathan approaching the scene on foot and the camera right behind him. We practice this for a few minutes, then begin rolling. Nathan is doing the narrative.

"Louder, Nathan. You gotta be louder," I bark from the side.

Nathan is walking toward the scene and talking: "It was about two in the morning when we arrived here, me and Gene. We were in his truck, I was driving. As we pulled up, right about here, we could see the other vehicle over there, backed into those trees, where it should have been." He keeps walking and pointing. "Everything appeared normal. We parked near the other vehicle, and our man, let's call him Joe, so Joe gets out and says hello. We say hello and walk to the back of Gene's truck. In a locked toolbox, there are about ten pounds of meth, good stuff, most of it cooked by Gene himself, and under a sheet of plywood there is a small cooler, also with about ten pounds. Total drop was roughly twenty pounds, with a wholesale value close to $200,000. We got the stuff out of the truck and moved it into the trunk of Joe's car, and as soon as he slammed the trunk, all hell broke loose. There must've been a dozen DEA agents all over us. I don't know where they all came from, but they were quick. Joe disappeared, never to be seen again. They dragged Gene over by his truck. He was cussing Joe and making all sorts of threats. Me, I was just so damned scared I could hardly breathe. They had us, dead guilty, and I knew I was headed to prison. They handcuffed me, went through my wallet, my pockets, and then led me down the trail over there. As I was walking away, I looked over my shoulder and I could barely see Gene on the ground, with both hands behind his back. He was angry and still cussing. A few seconds later, I heard gunshots, and then I heard Gene scream when he got hit."

Loudly, I say, "Cut," and walk around in circles for a moment. "Let's do it again," I say, and we go back to the starting point. After the third take, I'm satisfied and seize upon the next idea. I ask Nathan to stand on the spot where Gene was lying the last time he saw him. We place a folding chair there and Nathan sits down. When the camera is rolling, I ask, "Now, Nathan, what was your initial reaction when you heard gunfire?"

"I couldn't believe it. They threw Gene down, on the ground, and there were at least four DEA agents standing above him. His hands were already behind his back, not yet handcuffed. He had no weapon. There was a shotgun and two 9-millimeters in the truck, but we had not removed them. I don't care what the DEA said later, Gene was unarmed."

"But when you heard the gunshots?"

"I stopped in my tracks and yelled something like, 'What is that? What's happening?' I yelled for Gene, but the agents shoved me forward, down the trail. I couldn't look back—I was too far away. At one point, I said, 'I wanna see my brother,' but they just laughed and kept pushing me into the darkness. We finally got to a van and they shoved me inside. They drove me to the jail in Bluefield, and the whole time I'm asking about my brother. 'What happened to my brother? Where is Gene? What have you done with Gene?'"

"Let's cut for a minute," I say to Slade. I look at Nathan. "It's okay to show some emotion here, Nathan. Think of the people watching this film. What do you want them to feel as they listen to this awful story? Anger? Bitterness? Sadness? It's up to you to convey these feelings, so let's try it again, but this time with some emotion. Can you do it?"

"I'll try."

"Roll it, Slade. Now, Nathan, how did you first learn that your brother was dead?"

"The next morning at the jail, a deputy came in with some paperwork. I asked him about Gene, and he said, 'Your brother's dead. Tried to run from the DEA, and they shot him down.' Just like that. No sympathy, no concern, nothing." Nathan pauses and swallows hard. His lips begin to quiver and his eyes are moist. Behind the camera, I give him a thumbs-up. He continues: "I didn't know what to say. I was in shock. Gene didn't try to run. Gene was murdered." He wipes a tear with the back of his hand. "I'm sorry," he says softly, and the kid is really in pain. There's no acting here, just real emotion.

"Cut," I say, and we take a break. Gwen rushes in with a brush and some tissue. "Beautiful, just beautiful," she says. Nathan stands and walks to the creek, lost in his thoughts. I tell Slade to start rolling again.

We spend three hours at the site, shooting and reshooting scenes that I create on the fly, and by 1:00 p.m. we're hungry and tired. We find a fast-food place in Bluefield and choke down burgers and fries. Riding back to Radford, the three of us are silent until I tell Gwen to call Tad Carsloff, one of my partners in Miami. Carsloff's name was mentioned by the CRS secretary when Nathan called our home office number two days earlier.

Feigning a real conversation, Gwen says, "Hello, Tad, it's Gwen. Great. You? Yeah, well, we're riding back to Radford with Nathan. We spent the morning at the site where his brother was murdered, pretty powerful stuff. Nathan did a fantastic job of narration. He doesn't need the script, it just comes natural." I sneak a look at Nathan behind the wheel. He cannot suppress a smug little smile.

Gwen continues with her one-way dialogue. "His mother?" A pause. "She hasn't budged yet. Nathan says she wants no part of the film and doesn't approve. Reed wants to try again tomorrow." A pause. "He's thinking of going to their hometown, to film the grave site, talk to old friends, maybe some guys he worked with, you know, that sort of thing." A pause as she listens intently to nothing. "Yes, things couldn't be better here. Reed is thrilled with the first two days and Nathan is just wonderful to work with. Really powerful stuff. Reed says he'll call later this afternoon. Ciao."

We ride in silence for a mile or two as Nathan soaks up the praise. Finally, he says, "So we're going to Willow Gap tomorrow?"

"Yes, but you don't have to go if you don't want to," I say. "I figure after two days you've had enough of this."

"So you're finished with me?" he asks sadly.

"Oh no. After tomorrow, I'm going home to Miami and I'll spend a few days looking at footage. We'll begin the editing, trying to whittle things down. Then, in a couple of weeks, whenever you can work us in, we'll be back for another round of shooting."

"Have you told Nathan about Tad's idea?" Gwen says from the backseat.

"No, not yet."

"I think it's brilliant," she says.

"What is it?" Nathan asks.

"Tad is the best editor in the company, and we collaborate on everything. Because this film involves three or four different families, different murders, he has suggested we bring you guys together, same place, same time, and just let the cameras run. Put you all in a room, in a very comfortable setting, and let the conversation begin. No script, no direction, just the facts, as brutal as they are. As I've told you, we have researched half a dozen cases, and they are all remarkably similar. We'll pick the best three or four—"

"Yours is definitely the best," Gwen interjects.

"And let you, the victims, compare stories. Tad thinks this could be beyond powerful."

"He's right," Gwen chirps. "I would love to see it."

"I tend to agree," I say.

"Where would we meet?" Nathan says, practically on board.

"We're not that far along, but probably Miami."

"Have you been to South Beach, Nathan?" Gwen asks.

"No."

"Oh, boy. For a single guy, thirty years old, you will not want to leave. The partying is nonstop and the girls are . . . How would you describe them, Reed?"

"Haven't noticed," I say, on script.

"Right. Let's just say they are beautiful and hot."

"This is not about partying," I say, scolding my assistant. "We could also do it in the D.C. area, which would probably be more convenient to the families."

Nathan says nothing, but I know he's voting for South Beach.

Vanessa and I spend the afternoon in a hotel room in Pulaski, Virginia, a half hour southwest of Radford. We go over my notes from Fort Carson and try anxiously to figure out what made Nathan suspicious. To hear him utter the name Malcolm Bannister was chilling enough; now we need to understand why. Malcolm pinched his nose when he was thinking. He tapped his fingers together when he listened. He cocked his head slightly to the right when he was amused. He dipped his chin when he was skeptical. He stuck his right index finger into his right temple when he was bored with a conversation.

"Just keep your hands still and away from your face," Vanessa advises. "And speak lower."

"Was my voice too high?"

"It tends to go back to normal when you're talking a lot. Stay quieter. Not as many words."

We argue about the seriousness of his suspicion. Vanessa is convinced Nathan is fully on board and looking forward to a trip to Miami. She is certain no one from my past could recognize me now. I tend to agree, but I'm still stunned by the reality that Nathan uttered my old name. I can almost believe he had a twinkle in his eye when he did so, as if to say, "I know who you are, and I know why you're here."

CHAPTER 32

Nathan insists on going with us to his hometown of Willow Gap, so for the second morning we work our way through the mountains as he drives and Gwen gushes about the reactions in Miami. She says to Nathan that Tad Carsloff and other important people down there in the home office watched all of our footage last night and are beyond thrilled. They simply love Nathan on camera and are convinced he is the turning point in the production of our documentary. More important, one of our major investors is visiting Miami and happened to watch the tape from Virginia. The guy is so impressed with Nathan and the entire film so far that he is willing to double down on his money. The guy's worth a bundle and thinks the movie should run at least ninety minutes. It could lead to indictments within the DEA. It could explode into a scandal like Washington has never seen.

As I listen to this chatter, I am on the phone, presumably speaking with the home office, but there's no one on the other end. I grunt occasionally and say something profound, but mainly I'm just listening and brooding and acting as though the creative process can be burdensome. Sometimes I glance at Nathan. The boy is all in.

Over breakfast, Gwen stressed again that I should say as little as possible, speak deeply and slowly, and keep my hands away from my face. I'm happy to let her do the talking, something she's quite good at.

Gene Cooley is buried behind an abandoned country church in a small, weedy cemetery with about a hundred graves. I tell Slade and Cody I want several shots of the grave and its surroundings, then I step away for another important phone call. Nathan, now quite the actor and full of himself, suggests that he kneel beside the grave while the camera rolls, and Gwen loves the idea. I nod from a distance with the cell phone stuck to my jaw, whispering to no one. Nathan even manages to work up a few more tears, and Slade zooms in for a close-up.

For the record, Willow Gap has five hundred people, but you'll never find them. Downtown proper is an overgrown alley with four crumbling buildings and a country store with a post office attached to it. A few folks are moving about, and Nathan becomes nervous. He knows these people, and he does not want to be seen with a camera crew. He explains that most of the residents, including his family and friends, live out from town, off the narrow country lanes and deep in the valleys. They are suspicious people by nature, and I now understand why he wanted to accompany us.

There is no school he and Gene attended; the kids from Willow Gap are bused an hour away. "Made it easy to quit," Nathan says, almost to himself. He reluctantly shows us a tiny, empty four-room cottage where he and Gene lived once, for about a year. "It was the last place I remember living with my father," he says. "I was about six, I guess, so Gene was about ten." I cajole him into sitting on the broken front steps and talking, to the camera, about all the places he and Gene lived. For the moment, he forgets about the glamour of acting and becomes sullen. I ask him about his father, but he wants no part of that conversation. He gets angry and barks at me, and suddenly he's acting again. A few minutes later, Gwen, very much on his side now and wary of me, tells him he's superb.

As we loiter around the front of the shack, I pace as if lost in a deep creative funk. I finally ask where his mother is living now. He points and says, "About ten minutes down that road, but we are not going there, okay?"

I reluctantly agree and step away to chat on the phone again.

After two hours in and around Willow Gap, we've seen enough. I make it known I'm not too pleased with what we've shot, and I become irritable. Gwen whispers to Nathan, "He'll get over it."

"Where was Gene's meth lab?" I ask.

"It's gone," he answers. "Blew up not long after he died."

"That's just great," I mumble.

We finally load up everything and leave the area. For the second day in a row, lunch is a burger and fries just off an interstate exit. When we're on the road again, I finish another imaginary phone call and stick the phone in my pocket. I turn so I can see Gwen, and it's obvious I have big news. "Okay, here's where we are. Tad has been talking nonstop to the Alvarez family in Texas and the Marshak family in California. I mentioned these two cases to you, Nathan, if you'll recall. The Alvarez boy was shot fourteen times by DEA agents. The Marshak kid was asleep in his college dorm room when they broke in and shot him before he woke up. Remember?"

Nathan is nodding as he drives.

"They've found a cousin in the Alvarez family with good English and he's willing to talk. Mr. Marshak has sued the DEA and his lawyers have told him to keep quiet, but he's really pissed and wants to go public. Both can be in Miami this weekend, at our expense, of course. Both have jobs, though, so the filming has to be done on a Saturday. Two questions, Nathan: First, do you want to go and do this? And second, can you go on such short notice?"

"Have you told him about the DEA files?" Gwen asks before he can answer.

"Not yet. I just found out this morning."

"What is it?" Nathan asks.

"I think I told you our lawyers have filed the necessary paperwork to obtain copies of the DEA files on certain cases, including Gene's. Yesterday, a federal judge in Washington ruled in our favor, sort of. We can see the files, but we cannot actually have possession of them. So the DEA in D.C. is sending the files to the DEA office in Miami, and we will have access to the materials."

"When?" Gwen asks.

"As early as Monday."

"Do you want to see Gene's file, Nathan?" Gwen asks cautiously, protectively.

He doesn't answer quickly, so I chime in: "We won't be shown everything, but there will be a lot of photos—crime scene stuff and statements from all of the agents, probably a statement from the informant who set you guys up. There will be ballistics reports, the autopsy, photos of that. It could be fascinating."

Nathan clenches his jaws and says, "I'd like to see it."

"So you're in?" I ask.

"What's the downside?" he asks, and this question gets a lot of consideration for the next few minutes. Finally, I reply, "Downside? If you are still dealing, then the DEA would come after you with a vengeance. We've had this discussion."

"I'm not dealing. I told you that."

"Then there's no downside. You're doing it for Gene and for all of the DEA's murder victims. You're doing it for justice."

"And you're gonna love South Beach," Gwen adds.

I close the deal by saying, "We can leave tomorrow afternoon out of Roanoke, fly straight to Miami, do the shoot on Saturday, play on Sunday, see the DEA file on Monday morning, and you're home that night."

Gwen says, "I thought Nicky had the jet in Vancouver."

I reply, "He does, but it'll be here tomorrow afternoon."

"You have a jet?" Nathan asks, and he looks at me in pure amazement.

This is amusing to Gwen and me. I laugh and say, "Not mine, personally, but our company leases one. We travel an awful lot and sometimes it's the only way to get things done."

"I can't leave tomorrow," Gwen says, looking at her schedule on her iPhone. "I'll be in D.C., but I'll just fly down Saturday. I'm not gonna miss the three families in the same room at the same time. Incredible."

"What about your bar?" I ask Nathan.

"I own the place," he says smugly. "And I got a pretty good manager. Plus, I'd like to get outta town for a few days. The bar is ten, twelve hours a day, six days a week."

"And your parole officer?"

"I'm free to travel. I just have to notify him, that's all."

"This is exciting," Gwen says, almost squealing with delight. Nathan is smiling like a kid at Christmas. Me, I'm all business as usual. "Look, Nathan, I need to nail this down right now. If we're going, then say so. I have to call Nicky and line up the jet, and I have to call Tad so he can arrange flights for the other families. Yes or no?"

Without hesitation, Nathan says, "Yep. Let's go."

"Great."

Gwen asks, "Which hotel would Nathan like, Reed?"

"I don't know. They're all good. Your call." I tap keys on my phone and begin another unilateral conversation.

"You want to be right on the beach, Nathan, or one block off?"

"Where are the girls?" he asks and laughs at his own incredible humor.

"Okay, on the beach it is."

By the time we return to Radford, Nathan Cooley thinks he's booked into one of the coolest hotels in the world, on one of the hippest beaches, and he'll arrive there by private jet, which will only be fitting for such a serious actor.

Vanessa leaves in a mad dash for Reston, Virginia, D.C. suburbs, some four hours away. Her first destination is a nameless organization renting space in a run-down strip mall. It's the workshop of a group of talented forgers who can create virtually any document on the spot. They specialize in fake passports, but for the right price they can produce college diplomas, birth certificates, marriage licenses, court orders, car titles, eviction notices, driver's licenses, credit histories—there's no limit to their mischief. Some of what they do is illegal and some is not. They brazenly advertise on the Internet, along with an astonishing number of competitors, but claim to be careful about whom they work for.

I found them several weeks ago after an exhaustive search, and to validate their reliability, I sent a $500 check drawn on Skelter Films for a fake passport. It arrived in Florida a week later, and I was floored at its seeming authenticity. According to the guy on the phone, a real expert, there was an eighty-twenty chance the fake passport would clear Customs in the event I tried to leave the country. There was a 90 percent chance I would be able to enter any country in the Caribbean. Problems will arise, though, if I try to reenter the United States. I explained that this will not happen, not with my new fake passport. He explained that nowadays, in the age of terror, the U.S. Customs Service is much more concerned with who's on the No Fly List than who's fudging with phony papers.

Because it's a rush job, Vanessa forks over $1,000 in cash, and they get down to business. Her forger is a nervous geek with an odd name that he reluctantly divulged. Like his colleagues, he works in a cramped, fortified cubicle with no one else in sight.

The atmosphere is suspicious, as though everyone there is violating some law and half expecting a SWAT team any minute. They don't like drop-ins. They prefer the shield of the Internet so no one sees their shady business.

Vanessa hands over the memory card from her camera, and on a twenty-inch screen they look at the shots of a smiling Nathan Cooley. They select one for the passport and driver's license, and go through his data—address, date of birth, and so on. Vanessa says she wants the new documents in the name of Nathaniel Coley, not Cooley. Whatever, the geek says. He could not care less. He is soon lost in a flurry of high-speed imaging. It takes him an hour to produce an American passport and a Virginia driver's license that would fool anyone. The passport's blue vinyl binding is sufficiently worn, and our boy Nathan, who's never traveled far, has now seen all of Europe and most of Asia.

Vanessa hustles into D.C., where she picks up two first-aid kits, a pistol, and some pills. At 8:30, she turns around and heads south for Roanoke.

CHAPTER 33

The airplane is a Challenger 604, one of the finer private jets available for charter. Its cabin seats eight comfortably and allows those under six feet two to move around without scraping the ceiling. A new one costs something like $30 million, according to the data and specs online, but I'm not in the market. I only need a quick rental, at $5,000 an hour. The charter service is out of Raleigh, and it has been paid in full with a Skelter Films check drawn on the bank in Miami. We're set for a 5:00 p.m. Friday departure out of Roanoke, just two passengers—Nathan and me. I spend most of Friday morning trying to convince the charter service that I will e-mail copies of our passports as soon as I can locate mine. My story is that I have temporarily misplaced it and I'm turning my apartment upside down.

For trips outside the country, a private charter service must submit its passengers' names and copies of their passports several hours before departure. The U.S. Customs Service checks this information against its No Fly List. I know that neither Malcolm Bannister nor Max Reed Baldwin is on the list, but I don't know what might happen when Customs receives a copy of Nathaniel Coley's fake passport. So I stall, hoping and believing that the less time Customs has with both passports, the luckier I might get. Finally, I inform the charter service that I've found mine, and I kill another hour before e-mailing it and Nathaniel's to the office in Raleigh. I have no idea what Customs will do when it receives the copy of my passport. Quite possibly, my name will trigger an alert and the FBI will be notified. If this happens, it will be, to my knowledge, the first trace of me since I left Florida sixteen days ago. I tell myself this is no big deal because I'm neither a suspect nor a fugitive. I'm a free man who can travel anywhere without restrictions, right?

But why does this scenario bother me? Because I don't trust the FBI.

I drive Vanessa to the Roanoke Regional Airport, where she catches a flight to Miami, through Atlanta. After I drop her off, I drive around until I find the small terminal for private aircraft. I have hours to kill, so I find a parking place and hide my little Audi between two pickup trucks. I call Nathan at his bar and deliver the bad news that our flight has been delayed. According to "our pilots," there is a bug in a warning light. No big deal, but "our technicians" are hard at work and we should take off around 7:00 p.m.

The charter service e-mailed me a copy of our itinerary, and the Challenger is scheduled to be "repositioned" in Roanoke at 3:00 p.m. On the dot, it lands and taxis to the terminal. The adventure at hand makes me both nervous and excited. I wait half an hour before calling the charter service in Raleigh to explain that I will be delayed, until approximately 7:00 p.m.

The hours pass and I fight boredom. At 6:00 p.m., I stroll into the terminal, ask around, and meet one of the pilots, Devin. I turn on the charm and chat up Devin as if we're old pals. I explain that my co-passenger, Nathan, is the subject of one of my films and we're headed off for a few days of beach fun. I don't know the kid that well. Devin asks for my passport, and I hand it over. Without being obvious, he checks my face with my photo, and all is well. I ask to take a look at the airplane.

Will, the other pilot, is in the cockpit reading a newspaper as I step onto a private jet for the first time in my life. I shake his hand like a politician and comment on the stunning display of screens, switches, instruments, dials, meters, and so on. Devin shows me around. Behind the cockpit is the small kitchen, or galley, complete with microwave, a sink with hot and cold water, full bar, drawers filled with china and flatware, and a large ice bin where the beer is just waiting. I specifically asked for two brands, one with alcohol and one without. Behind one door is a collection of snacks in case we get hungry. Dinner will not be served, because I do not want a flight attendant on board. The people at the charter service insisted that the aircraft's owner required the use of a flight attendant, at which time I threatened to cancel. They backed down, so it will be just Nathan and me on the trip south.

The cabin is furnished with six large leather chairs and a small sofa. The decor is soft earth tones and very tasteful. The carpet is plush and spotless. There are at least three screens for movies and, as Devin goes on proudly, a surround sound system. We move from the cabin to the restroom, then the cargo hold. I'm traveling light and Devin takes my carry-on bag. I hesitate as if I've forgotten something. "I have a couple of DVDs in my bag and I might need them," I explain. "Can I get to it during the flight?"

"Sure. No problem. The cargo hold is pressurized too, so you have access," Devin says.

"Great."

I spend half an hour examining the airplane, then begin looking at my watch as if I'm irritated at Nathan and his tardiness. "This kid's from the mountains," I explain to Devin as we sit in the cabin. "Doubt if he's ever been on a plane before. He's kinda rough around the edges."

"What kind of movie ya'll doing?" Devin asks.

"Documentary. The meth business in Appalachia."

Devin and I return to the terminal and continue waiting. I've forgotten something in my car, and I leave the building. Minutes later, I see Nathan's new pickup truck roll into the lot. He parks quickly, then hops out, eager. He's wearing cutoff denim shorts, a pair of white Nike running shoes, no socks, a flat-billed trucker's cap, and, best of all, a pink-and-orange floral-print Hawaiian shirt with at least the top two buttons unfastened. He grabs a stuffed Adidas gym bag from the back of his truck and bounds toward the terminal. I intercept him and we shake hands. I'm holding some papers.

"Sorry about the delay," I say, "but the airplane is here and ready to go."

"No problem." His eyes are watery and I catch a whiff of stale beer. Wonderful!

I lead him inside and to the front desk where Devin is flirting with the receptionist. I walk Nathan to the windows and point to the Challenger. "That's ours," I say proudly. "At least for this weekend." He gawks at the aircraft as Devin walks over. I quickly slip him Nathan's fake passport. He glances at the photo, then at Nathan, who at that moment turns from the window. I introduce him to Devin, who hands me the passport and says, "Welcome aboard."

"Are we ready to go?" I ask.

"Follow me," Devin says, and as we leave the terminal, I say, "Off to the beach."

On board, Devin takes the Adidas gym bag and stores it in cargo while Nathan falls into one of the leather chairs and admires his surroundings. I'm in the galley, preparing the first round of beers—the real thing for Nathan, one with no alcohol for me. When they're poured into ice-cold mugs, you can't tell the difference. I banter with Devin as he goes through the emergency procedures, nervous that he might mention our destination. He does not, and when he retires to the cockpit and straps himself in, I take a deep breath. He and Will give me the thumbs-up and start the engines.

"Cheers," I say to Nathan, and we tap glasses and take a gulp. I unfold a mahogany table between us.

As the jet begins to taxi, I say, "You like tequila?"

"Hell yeah," he replies, already the party animal.

I jump up, walk into the galley, fetch a fifth of Cuervo Gold and two shot glasses, and place them hard on the table. I pour two shots and we kill them, following them up with more beer. I have a buzz by the time we take off. When the seat belt sign is turned off, I pour another round of beer and we do more shots. Shots and beer, shots and beer. I fill in the conversation gaps with drivel about the film and how excited our financial partners are at the moment. This soon bores Nathan, so I tell him we have a late dinner lined up, and one of the young ladies there is a friend of a friend who could be the hottest chick on South Beach. She's seen a portion of our footage and wants to meet Nathan. "Did you bring any long pants?" I ask.

I assume the Adidas bag is filled with clothing about as tasteful as what I'm looking at.

"Oh yeah, got all kinds of stuff," he says, his tongue getting thicker by the moment.

When the Cuervo Gold is half gone, I look at the navigational map on display and say, "Only an hour to Miami. Drink up." We knock back another shot each, then I drain my glass of unleaded. I weigh at least thirty pounds more than Nathan, half my drinks have no alcohol, and my vision is blurred as we pass over Savannah at thirty-eight thousand feet. He's getting bombed.

I keep pouring, and he shows no signs of slacking off. As we pass high over my old stomping ground at Neptune Beach, I fix the final round. Into Nathan's beer mug, I drop two tablets of chloral hydrate, five hundred milligrams each.

"Let's kill these dead soldiers," I say, slamming them onto the table, and we turn bottoms up. I take it easy and Nathan wins the contest. Thirty minutes later, he's dead to the world.

I watch our progress on the screen next to the galley. We're now at forty thousand. Miami is in sight, but we are not descending. I pull Nathan out of his chair and drag him to the sofa, where I stretch him out and check his pulse. I pour a cup of coffee and watch Miami fade below us.

Before long, Cuba is behind us too, and Jamaica emerges at the bottom of the screen. The engines throttle back a notch, and we begin our long descent. I gulp coffee in a desperate effort to clear my head. The next twenty minutes will be crucial and chaotic. I have a plan, but so much of it is beyond my control.

Nathan is breathing heavily and slowly. I shake him, but he's unconscious. From the right pocket of his too-tight denim cut-offs, I remove his key ring. In addition to the one for his pickup, the collection includes six others of varying shapes and designs. I'm sure a couple fit the doors and dead bolts of his house. Perhaps a couple lock and unlock Bombay's. In the left pocket, I find a neat fold of cash—about $500—and a pack of gum. From the left rear pocket I remove his wallet, a cheap vinyl Velcro tri-fold that's sort of bulky. As I inventory it, I realize why. Our party boy had loaded up with eight Trojan condoms, stored at the ready on his left buttock. There are also ten crisp $100 bills, a valid Virginia driver's license, two membership cards to Bombay's, a business card for his parole officer, and one for a beer distributor. Nathan has no credit cards, probably because of his recent five-year stint in prison and his lack of a real job. I leave the cash in place, don't touch the Trojans, and remove everything else. I substitute the fake driver's license for the valid one and give Nathaniel Coley his wallet back. Then I gently place the fake passport in his right rear pocket. He doesn't move or twitch, doesn't feel a thing.

I go to the restroom and close and lock the door. I open the cargo hold, unzip my carry-on, and remove two nylon pouches with the words "First Aid" stamped in bold letters. I stuff these into the bottom of Nathan's gym bag, then re-zip everything. I walk to the cockpit, pull back the black curtain, and lean forward to catch Devin's attention. He quickly removes his headset and I say, "Look, this guy drank nonstop until he passed out. I can't seem to wake him up and there's not much of a pulse. We might need some medical attention as soon as we land." Will hears this even with his headset, and for a split second he and Devin stare at each other. If they were not descending, one of the two would probably step into the cabin and take a look at Nathan.

"Okay," Devin finally says, and I return to the cabin, where Nathan lies in near rigor mortis, but with a pulse. Five minutes later, I return to the cockpit and report that he is indeed breathing but I can't rouse him. "Idiot drank a fifth of tequila in less than two hours," I say, and they both shake their heads.

We land in Montego Bay and taxi past a row of commercial airliners at the gates of the main concourse. To the south, I see three other jets parked at the private terminal. There are emergency vehicles with red lights flashing, all waiting for Nathan. I'll need the chaos to aid in my disappearance. I'm far from sober, but the adrenaline has kicked in and I'm thinking clearly.

When the engines are turned off, Devin jumps up and opens the door. I have my briefcase and carry-on in my chair, ready for the opportunity, but I'm also hovering over Nathan. "Wait for Immigration," Devin says.

"Sure," I reply.

Two grim-faced Jamaican Immigration officers appear in the cabin and glare at me. "Passport please," one says, and I give him my passport. He looks it over and says, "Please leave the aircraft." I hustle down the stairs, where another officer tells me to wait. Two medics board the plane and I presume they're tending to Nathan. An ambulance backs up to the stairs, and a police car arrives with lights but no sirens. I take a step back, then another. There is a dispute about how to remove the patient from the airplane, and everyone—medics, Immigration officers, police— seems to have an opinion. They finally decide against using a stretcher, so Nathan is basically dragged out and handed down the stairs. He's limp and lifeless, and if he weighed more than 140 pounds, the entire rescue would have been botched. As he's loaded into the ambulance, his gym bag appears in the door and an Immigration officer quizzes Devin about it. Devin makes sure the authorities know that the Adidas bag belongs to the unconscious one, and it is finally placed in the ambulance with him.

"I need to go now," I say to the nearest officer, and he points to a door of the private terminal. I enter just as Nathan is being hauled away. My passport is stamped and my carry-on and briefcase are scanned. A Customs official tells me to wait in the front lobby, and as I do I see Devin and Will in a tense discussion with the Jamaican authorities. They probably have some tough questions for me, and I'd rather avoid them. A taxi swings through the gate and stops under the terrace outside the front door. A rear window comes down and I see my dear Vanessa, waving frantically for me to get in. When no one is near, I leave the terminal, jump into the cab, and we speed away.

She has a room in a cheap hotel five minutes away. From the third-floor balcony, we can see the airport and the jets come and go. Lying in bed, we can hear them. We are exhausted and running on fumes, but sleep is out of the question.

CHAPTER 34

Victor Westlake was attempting to sleep late on Saturday morning, but after the second call he got out of bed, made the coffee, and was contemplating a possible nap on the sofa when the third call jolted him and swept away any lingering drowsiness. It was from an assistant named Fox, who was currently keeping the Bannister/Baldwin file and waiting for something to monitor. There had not been a peep in over two weeks.

"It came from Customs," Fox was saying. "Baldwin left Roanoke yesterday afternoon on a private jet and flew to Jamaica."

"A private jet?" Westlake repeated, thinking about the $150,000 in reward money and wondering how long it might last if Baldwin was burning through it.

"Yes sir, a Challenger 604, chartered from a company in Raleigh."

Westlake thought for a moment. "I wonder what he's doing in Roanoke. Odd."

"Yes sir."

"Didn't he go to Jamaica a few weeks back? His first trip out of the country?"

"Yes sir. He flew out of Miami to Montego Bay, spent a few days there, then went to Antigua."

"I suppose he likes the islands," Westlake said as he reached for fresh coffee. "Is he alone?"

"No sir. He's traveling with a man named Nathaniel Coley, at least that's what's on his passport. However, it appears as though Coley is traveling with a fake passport."

Westlake sat the untouched coffee back onto the counter and began to pace around the kitchen. "This guy got by Customs with a fake passport?"

"Yes sir. But keep in mind it was a private aircraft and the passport was not actually examined by Customs. All they had was the copy sent in by the charter service, and they checked it against the No Fly List. It's pretty routine."

"Remind me to fix that routine."

"Yes sir."

"So the question, Fox, is what's Baldwin up to, right? Why is he chartering a private jet and why is he traveling with a man who's using a fake passport? Can you answer these questions for me, and soon?"

"If those are my orders, yes sir. But I'm sure I don't have to remind you how prickly the Jamaicans are."

"No, you don't." In the war on drugs, not all battles were fought between cops and traffickers. The Jamaicans, like many police agencies in the Caribbean, had long resented the bullying from U.S. officials.

"I'll get to work," Fox said. "But it's Saturday, here and there."

"Be in my office early Monday morning, with something, okay?"

"Yes sir."

———

Nathan Cooley awoke in a small, windowless room, dark except for the red glow of a digital monitor on a table near him. He was lying on what appeared to be a hospital bed—narrow with railings. He looked up and saw a bag of fluids, then followed the tube all the way down to the back of his left hand, where it disappeared under the white gauze. Okay, I'm in a hospital.

His mouth was as dry as salt and his head began to pound as he tried to think. He looked down and noticed the white Nike running shoes, still attached to his feet. They, whoever in hell they might be, had not bothered to cover him or dress him in a patient's gown. He closed his eyes again, and slowly the fog began to lift. He remembered the shots of tequila, the endless mugs of beer, the craziness of Reed Baldwin as the two of them got smashed. He remembered having a few at his bar on Friday afternoon as he waited for his trip to the airport, then on to Miami. He must have had ten beers and ten shots. What an idiot! Blacked out again and now hooked to an IV. He wanted to get up and move about, but his head was screaming and his eyes were bleeding. Don't move, he said to himself.

There was a sound at the door and a light came on. A tall, very dark nurse in a pristine white outfit entered the room in mid-sentence. "All right, Mr. Coley, time to go. Some gentlemen are here to take you." It was English, but with an odd accent.

Nathan was about to ask "Where am I?" when three uniformed officers marched in behind the nurse and looked as though they were ready to beat him. All three were black with very dark skin.

"What the hell?" Nathan managed to say as he sat up. The nurse removed the IV and disappeared, closing the door hard behind her. The older officer stepped forward and whipped out a badge. "Captain Fremont, Jamaican police," he said, just as they do on television.

"Where am I?" Nathan asked.

Fremont smiled, as did the two officers immediately behind him. "You don't know where you are?"

"Where am I?"

"You're in Jamaica. Montego Bay. In the hospital for now, but soon to be in the city jail."

"How'd I get to Jamaica?" Nathan asked.

"By private jet, and a nice one."

"But I'm supposed to be in Miami, at South Beach. There's some mistake here, you see? Is this a joke or something?"

"Do we look like the joking type, Mr. Coley?"

Nathan thought it was odd the way these people pronounced his last name.

"Why did you try to enter Jamaica with a fake passport, Mr. Coley?"

Nathan reached for his rear pocket and realized his wallet was missing. "Where's my wallet?" he asked.

"In our custody, along with everything else."

Nathan massaged his temples and fought the urge to vomit. "Jamaica? What the hell am I doing in Jamaica?"

"We have some of the same questions, Mr. Coley."

"Passport? What passport? I've never had a passport."

"I'll show it to you later. It's a violation of Jamaican law to attempt to enter our country with a bogus passport, Mr. Coley. Under the circumstances, though, you have far more serious problems."

"Where's Reed?"

"I'm sorry."

"Reed Baldwin. The guy who brought me. Find Reed and he can explain everything."

"I haven't met this Reed Baldwin."

"Well, you gotta find him, okay? He's a black guy, like you all, and Reed can explain everything. I mean, we left Roanoke yesterday around seven. I guess we had too much to drink. We were headed for Miami, to South Beach, where we were supposed to work on his documentary. It's about my brother, Gene, you know? Anyway, there's some big mistake here. We're supposed to be in Miami."

Fremont slowly turned and looked at his two colleagues. The

glances they exchanged left little doubt they were dealing with a confused and babbling moron.

"Jail? Did you say 'jail'?"

"Your next stop, my friend."

Nathan clutched his stomach and his jaws filled with vomit. Fremont quickly handed him a lined waste bin, then took a step back to stay clear. Nathan puked and heaved and gasped and cursed for five minutes as the three officers inspected their boots or admired the ceiling. When the episode was mercifully over, Nathan stood and placed the waste bin on the floor. He wiped his mouth with a tissue from the table and took a sip of water. "Please tell me what's going on," he said in a scratchy voice.

"You're under arrest, Mr. Coley," Fremont said. "Customs violations, the importation of controlled substances, and possession of a firearm. Why did you think you could enter Jamaica with four kilos of pure cocaine and a handgun?"

Nathan's jaw dropped. His mouth opened, but nothing escaped but warm air. He squinted, frowned, pleaded with his eyes, and tried again to speak. Nothing. Finally, he managed a feeble "What?"

"Don't play dumb, Mr. Coley. Where were you going? Off to one of our famous resorts for a week of drugs and sex? Was it all for personal consumption, or did you intend to sell some of it to other rich Americans?"

"This is a joke, right? Where's Reed? The fun's over. Ha-ha. Now get me outta here."

Fremont reached for his thick belt and removed a set of handcuffs. "Turn around, sir. Hands behind your back."

Nathan suddenly yelled, "Reed! I know you're out there! Stop laughing, asshole, and tell these clowns to knock it off!"

"Turn around, sir," Fremont said again, but Nathan did not comply. Instead, he yelled even louder, "Reed! I'll get you for this! Nice joke! I hear you laughing out there!"

The other two officers stepped forward and each took an arm.

Nathan wisely realized that resisting would not work. When the handcuffs were in place, they led him from the room and into the hallway. Nathan spun around wildly, looking for Reed or anyone else who might step forward and put an end to this. They walked past rooms with open doors, small rooms with two and three beds practically touching each other. They walked past comatose patients on gurneys parked against the walls, and nurses writing in charts, and orderlies watching television. Everyone is black, Nathan noticed. I really am in Jamaica. They shuffled down a set of stairs and through an exit door. When he stepped into the thick air and brilliant sun, Nathan knew he was on foreign soil and unfriendly territory.

A cab takes Vanessa back to the airport where she'll catch a 9:40 flight to Atlanta. She is scheduled to arrive in Roanoke this evening at 6:50. She will drive to Radford and check into a motel. I will not be joining her for a few days.

I take another cab to the downtown area of Montego Bay. Unlike Kingston, the capital, which is three hundred years old, Montego Bay is a new city that developed as resorts, hotels, condos, and shopping villages sprawled inward, away from the ocean, and finally met up with the neighborhoods. There is no main avenue, or central plaza, or stately courthouse in the center of town. Government buildings are scattered over a wide area, as are most of the professional buildings. My driver finds the law office of Mr. Rashford Watley. I pay the fare and hustle up a flight of stairs to a landing where a bunch of lawyers keep small, separate offices. Mr. Watley explained on the phone that he rarely works on Saturdays, but he'll make an exception for me. His ad in the Yellow Pages boasts of thirty years' experience in all criminal courts. When we shake hands, I can tell he's pleasantly surprised to see that I, too, am black. He probably assumed that as an American tourist I was like all the rest.

We take our seats in his modest office, and after a few pleasantries I get to the point. Sort of. He suggests that we dispense with the formalities and use first names only. So it's Reed and Rashford. I quickly go through the narrative about my background as a filmmaker, my current project involving one Nathan Coley, and so on, but before long I'm veering off course. I tell Rashford that Nathan and I came to Jamaica for a few days of fun. He got drunk and blacked out on the airplane, causing a medical emergency upon our arrival. I'm not sure, but I think he tried to smuggle in some drugs and was packing a gun. I managed to get away last night in the confusion. So I wish to retain Rashford for two purposes: first, and most important, to represent me and protect me from whatever hot water I might be in; second, to make some calls and pull some strings to find out about Nathan and the charges against him. I want Rashford to visit Nathan in jail and assure him I'm doing all I can to secure his release.

No problem, Rashford assures me. We agree on a fee and I pay him in cash. He immediately gets on the phone and checks with contacts in Customs and the police. I can't tell if he's hamming it up for me, but the guy knows a lot of people. After an hour, I excuse myself and walk down the street for a soft drink. When I return to his office, Rashford is still on the phone, scribbling away on a notepad.

I'm reading a magazine in the lobby, under a noisy ceiling fan, when Rashford appears and sits on his secretary's desk. Things are grim and he's shaking his head. "Your friend is in big trouble," he says. "First, he tried to enter with a bogus passport."

No kidding, Rash. I listen intently.

"Did you know this?" he asks.

"Of course not," I reply. I assume Rashford has never chartered a private jet and therefore does not know the routine.

"But much worse," he continues, "he tried to smuggle in a handgun and four kilos of cocaine."

"Four kilos of cocaine," I repeat, acting as shocked as possible.

"Found the powder in two nylon first-aid kits in his gym bag, along with a small pistol. What a fool."

I'm shaking my head in disbelief. "He mentioned buying drugs once he got here but said nothing about smuggling the stuff in."

"How well do you know this gentleman?" Rashford asks.

"I just met him a week ago. We're not exactly close friends. I know he has a history of drug violations in the States, but I had no idea he was an idiot."

"Well, he is. And he'll probably be spending the next twenty years in one of our fine prisons."

"Twenty?!"

"Five for the coke, fifteen for the gun."

"That's outrageous. You gotta do something, Rashford!"

"The options are limited, but allow me to go about my business."

"What about me? Am I okay down here? I mean, they checked my bags at Customs and everything was cool. I'm not an accomplice or guilty by association, right?"

"As of now, nothing. But I suggest you leave as soon as possible."

"I can't leave until I see Nathan. I mean, I gotta help this guy, you know?"

"There's not much you can do, Reed. They found the coke and the gun in his bag."

I start pacing around the small room, deep in thought, worried sick. Rashford watches me for a moment, then says, "They'll probably allow me to see Mr. Coley. I know the boys at the jail, see them all the time. You've hired the right lawyer, Reed, but, again, I'm not sure what can be done."

"How often do you see this—American tourists busted for drugs down here?"

He thinks about this, then says, "Happens all the time, but not like this. The Americans get caught on the way out, not bringing the stuff in. It's rather unusual, but the drug charges are not that crucial. We're soft on drugs but hard on guns. We have very tough laws, especially with handguns. What was this boy thinking?"

"I don't know."

"Allow me to go see him and make contact."

"I need to see him too, Rashford. You gotta work this out. Lean on your friends at the jail and talk them into it."

"It might take some cash."

"How much?"

He shrugs and says, "Not much. Twenty bucks U.S."

"I got that."

"Allow me to see what I can do."

CHAPTER 35

The pilots are calling my cell phone, but I refuse to answer. Devin leaves four frantic voice mails, all pretty much the same: the police have seized the airplane and the pilots have been told they cannot leave the island. They are staying at the Hilton, but not having any fun. Their office in Raleigh is screaming and everybody wants answers. The pilots are taking the heat for submitting a fake passport and will probably lose their jobs. The airplane's owner is threatening, and so on.

I don't have the time to worry about these people. I'm sure a man who owns a $30 million jet can figure out a way to get it back.

———

At 2:00 p.m., Rashford and I leave his office and he drives us ten minutes to the police department. The city jail is attached to it. He parks in a crowded lot and nods at a low-slung, flat-roofed building with narrow slits for windows and razor wire for decoration. We walk down a sidewalk and Rashford says a pleasant hello to the guards and orderlies.

He goes to a door and whispers with a guard he obviously knows. I watch without being obvious and no cash changes hands. At a desk, we sign a sheet on a clipboard. "I told them you're a lawyer working with me," he whispers as I scribble one of my names. "Just act like a lawyer."

If he only knew.

———

Rashford waits in a long narrow room the lawyers use for meetings if the police are not using it for anything else. There is no air-conditioning and the room feels like a sauna. After a few minutes, the door opens and Nathan Coley is shoved inside. He looks wild-eyed at Rashford, then turns to his guard, who leaves and closes the door. Nathan slowly sits down on a metal stool and gawks at Rashford. The lawyer thrusts a business card at him and says, "I'm Rashford Watley, attorney. Your friend Reed Baldwin has hired me to look into this situation."

Nathan takes the card and inches the stool closer. His left eye is partially closed and his left jaw is swollen. There is dried blood at the corner of his lips. "Where's Reed?" he asks.

"He's here. He is very concerned and wants to see you. Are you okay, Mr. Coley? Your jaw is swollen."

Nathan looks at the large, round black face and tries to absorb the words. It's English all right, but with a strange accent. He wants to correct this guy and explain that it's "Cooley" not "Coley," but then maybe the guy is trying to say "Cooley," but it just comes out differently in Jamaica.

"Are you all right, Mr. Coley?" the lawyer repeats.

"I've had two fights in the past two hours. Lost both of them. You gotta get me outta here, Mr. . . . ." He looks at the card but can't focus on the words.

"It's Watley. Mr. Watley."

"Fine, Mr. Watley. This is a big misunderstanding. I don't know what happened, what went wrong, but I ain't guilty of anything. I didn't use a fake passport and I damned sure didn't try to smuggle in drugs and a gun. Somebody planted that stuff in my bag, you got that? That's the truth and I'll swear on a stack of Bibles. I don't use drugs, don't sell 'em, and I damned sure don't smuggle them. I want to talk to Reed." He sort of spits his words through clenched teeth and rubs his jaw as he talks.

"Is your jaw broken?" Rashford asks.

"I ain't no doctor."

"I'll try to get one, and I'll try to get you moved to another cell."

"They're all the same—hot, overcrowded, and dirty. You gotta do something, Mr. Watley. And fast. I'll never survive in here."

"You've been in prison before, I think."

"I just spent a few years in a federal pen, but nothing like this. I just thought that was bad. This is pure hell. I got fifteen guys in my cell, all black but me, with two beds and a hole in the corner to piss in. No air-conditioning and no food. Please, Mr. Watley, do something."

"You're facing very serious charges, Mr. Coley. If convicted as charged, you could be sentenced to twenty years in prison."

Nathan drops his head and takes a deep breath. "I won't last a week."

"I'm confident I can get a reduction, but still you're facing a lot of time. And not in a city jail like this. They'll send you away to one of our regional prisons where the conditions are not always as pleasant."

"Then give me a plan. You've got to explain to the judge or whoever that this is all a mistake. I'm not guilty, okay? You gotta make somebody believe that."

"I'll try, Mr. Coley. But the system has to run its course, and unfortunately things move rather slowly here in Jamaica. The court will schedule your first appearance in a few days, then formal charges will be handed down."

"What about bail? Can I post a bond and get outta here?"

"I'm working on that now with a bail bondsman, but I'm

not optimistic. The court would consider you a flight risk. How much money is at your disposal?"

Nathan snorts and shakes his head. "I don't know. I had a thousand bucks in my wallet, wherever it happens to be now. I'm sure the money's gone. I had five hundred bucks in my pocket too, and it's gone. They've picked me clean. I got a few assets back home but nothing liquid. I'm not a rich man, Mr. Watley. I'm a thirty-year-old ex-con who was in prison about six months ago. My family has nothing."

"Well, the court will look at the amount of cocaine and the private jet and think otherwise."

"The cocaine is not mine. I never saw it, never touched it. It was planted, okay, Mr. Watley? So was the gun."

"I believe you, Mr. Coley, but the court will likely be more skeptical. The court hears such stories all the time."

Nathan opened his mouth slowly and picked at the dried blood at the corner of his lips. He was obviously in pain and shock.

Rashford stood and said, "Keep your seat. Reed's here. If anyone asks, tell them he's just one of your lawyers."

Nathan's battered face lights up somewhat when I enter. I sit on my stool, less than three feet from him. He wants to yell but he knows someone is listening. "What the hell is happening here, Reed? Talk to me!"

My act at this point is that of a frightened man who is not sure what will happen tomorrow. "I don't know, Nathan," I say nervously. "I'm not under arrest but I can't leave the island. I found Rashford Watley first thing this morning and we're trying to figure it all out. All I remember is that we got real drunk real fast. Stupid. Got that. You passed out on the sofa and I was barely awake. At some point, one of the pilots called me up to the cockpit and explained that air traffic around Miami was grounded because of weather. Tornado warnings, a tropical storm, really bad stuff. Miami International was closed. The system was moving north, so we circled to the south and were diverted over the Caribbean. We circled and circled and I really can't remember all of what happened. I tried to wake you but you were snoring."

"I don't remember blacking out," he says, tapping his sore jaw.

"Does a drunk ever remember passing out? No, he does not. You were bombed, okay? You had been drinking before we took off. Anyway, at some point we were getting low on fuel and had to land. According to the pilots, we were directed here, to Montego Bay, to refuel, then we were supposed to leave for Miami, where the weather had cleared. I'm drinking coffee by the gallon and so I remember most of what happened. When we land, the captain says just stay on the plane; we'll only be here for twenty minutes. Then he says that Immigration and Customs want to take a look. We're ordered off the plane, but you're in a coma and can't move. You barely have a pulse. They call an ambulance and everything starts going wrong."

"What's this shit about a fake passport?"

"My mistake. We fly into Miami International all the time, and they often want to see a passport, even for domestic flights, especially private ones. I think it goes back to the drug wars in the 1980s when a lot of private jets were used to haul drug lords and their entourages. Now, with the war on terror, they like to see a passport. It's not mandatory to have one, but it's very helpful. I got a guy in D.C. who can produce one overnight for a hundred bucks, and I asked him to crank one out for you, just in case we needed it. I had no idea it would become an issue."

Poor Nathan does not know what to believe. I have the benefit of months of preparation. He's getting hit fast and furious and is thoroughly bewildered.

"Believe me, Nathan, a fake passport is the least of your worries."

"Where'd the coke and the gun come from?" he asks.

"The police," I say casually but with certainty. "It wasn't you and it wasn't me, so that narrows the list of suspects. Rashford says this is not unheard of on the island. A private jet from America arrives with a couple of rich guys on board—rich, otherwise they wouldn't be buzzing around on such a fine airplane. One of the rich dudes is so drunk he can't hit his ass with both hands. Blacked-out drunk. They get the sober guy off the plane and get the pilots distracted with paperwork, and when the timing is perfect, they plant the drugs. Stuff it in a bag, just that simple. A few hours later, the jet is officially seized by the Jamaican government, and the trafficker is placed under arrest. It's all about money, cash."

Nathan is absorbing this as he stares at his bare feet. His pink-and-orange Hawaiian shirt has blood stains on it. There are scratches on his arms and hands. "Can you get me something to eat, Reed? I'm starving. They served lunch an hour ago, shit so nasty you can't imagine, and before I could take a bite one of my cellies decided he needed it more than me."

I say, "Sorry, Nathan. I'll see if Rashford can bribe one of the guards."

He mumbles, "Please."

"Do you want me to call someone back home?" I ask.

He shakes his head no. "Who? The only person I halfway trust is the guy who runs my bar, and I think he's stealing. I'm cut off from my family, and they wouldn't help anyway. How can they? They don't know where Jamaica is. Not sure I can find it on the map."

"Rashford thinks they might charge me as an accomplice, so I might be joining you back there."

He shakes his head. "You might survive because you're black and you're in good shape. A skinny white boy ain't got a chance. As soon as I walked into the cell, this big dude says he really likes my Nikes. Gone. Next guy wants to borrow some money, and since I don't have any money he wants me to promise to get some real soon. This leads to the first fight, which involved at least three of these thugs beating the shit out of me. I remember hearing a guard laughing, saying something about a white boy who can't fight too good. My spot on the concrete floor is right next to the toilet, which is nothing but an open hole, like an outhouse. The smell will make you gag and puke. If I move an inch or two, then I'm on somebody else's turf and there's a fight. There's no air-conditioning and it's like an oven. Fifteen men in a tight space, all sweating and hungry and thirsty and no one can sleep. I cannot imagine what tonight will be like. Please, Reed, get me outta here."

"I'll try, Nathan, but there's a good chance these guys might try to nail me too."

"Just do something. Please."

"Look, Nathan, this is all my fault, okay? That means nothing at this point, but I had no way of knowing we were flying into a storm. The stupid pilots should've told us about the weather before we took off, or they should've landed somewhere on U.S. soil, or they should've had more fuel on the airplane. We'll sue the bastards when we get home, okay?"

"Whatever."

"Nathan, I'll do anything I can to get you out of here, but my ass is still on the line too. It's gonna come down to money. This is nothing but a shakedown, a grab for money by a bunch of cops who know how to play the game. Hell, they wrote the rules. Rashford says they'll squeeze the owner of the jet and pocket a handsome bribe. They'll throw a bone our way and see how much cash we can scrape together. Now that they know we have a lawyer, he thinks they'll contact him pretty soon. They prefer to work their little bribery schemes before the case gets into court. After that, you got formal charges and judges watching everything. You understand all this, Nathan?"

"I guess. I just can't believe this, Reed. This time yesterday I was at my bar, having a beer with a cute girl, bragging about flying to Miami for the weekend. Now look at me—thrown into a filthy jail cell with a bunch of Jamaicans, and they're all lined up waiting to kick my ass. You're right, Reed, this is all your fault. You and your ridiculous movie. I should've never listened to you."

"I'm sorry, Nathan. Believe me, I'm so sorry."

"You should be. Just do something, Reed, and hurry. I can't last much longer back there."

CHAPTER 36

Rashford gives me a ride to my hotel and, at the last minute, graciously extends an invitation to dinner. He says his wife is an excellent cook and they would be delighted to have such an accomplished filmmaker in their home. Though I am tempted, primarily because I have nothing to do for the next eighteen hours, I beg off with the lame excuse of feeling bad and needing sleep. I'm living a lie, and the last thing I need is a long dinner conversation about my life, my work, and my past. I suspect there will be serious people following my trail, sniffing for clues, and a stray word here or there could come back to haunt me.

It's July, the tourist season is over, and the hotel is not busy. There's a small pool with a bar in the shade, and I spend the afternoon under an umbrella, reading a Walter Mosley and sipping Red Stripe beer.

Vanessa lands in Roanoke at 7:00 Saturday evening. She is exhausted but rest is not an option. In the past forty-eight hours, she has driven from Radford to D.C. to Roanoke, and flown from Roanoke to Jamaica and back by way of Charlotte, Atlanta, and Miami. Other than a fitful three-hour rest in bed in Montego Bay, and several catnaps on airplanes, she has had no sleep.

She leaves the terminal with her small carry-on bag and takes her time finding her car. As always, she notices everything and everyone around her. We doubt if she's being followed, but at this point in our project we take nothing for granted. She drives across the highway from the airport and gets a room at a Holiday Inn. She orders room service and eats dinner at the window as the sun goes down. At 10:00 p.m. she calls me and we speak briefly and in code. We're on our third or fourth prepaid cell phone and it's highly unlikely anyone is listening, but, again, we're taking no chances. I conclude with a simple "Proceed as planned."

She drives back to the airport, to the general aviation terminal, and parks next to Nathan's pickup truck. It's late on a Saturday night and there is no private air traffic, no movements in the empty parking lot. She puts on a pair of thin leather gloves and, using Nathan's keys, unlocks his door and drives away. It's Vanessa's first drive in such a vehicle and she takes it easy. Not far down the road, she pulls in to a fast-food parking lot and adjusts the seat and mirrors. For the past five years she's been driving a small Japanese model, and the upgrade is astounding and uncomfortable. The last thing we can afford is a fender bender or a set of flashing blue lights. Eventually, she makes it onto Interstate 81 and heads south, toward Radford, Virginia.

It's almost midnight when she leaves the state highway and turns onto the country lane to Nathan's house. She passes the double-wide trailer, home to Nathan's nearest neighbor, at fifteen miles per hour, making virtually no noise. In her own car, she's driven this road a dozen times and knows the terrain. The road winds past Nathan's and through some pastureland before passing another home, almost two miles farther into the country. Beyond that, the asphalt fades into gravel, then to dirt. There is no traffic because there is so little population. It seems odd that a thirty-year-old bachelor would choose such a secluded place to live.

She parks in his driveway and listens. Nathan's yellow Lab is in the backyard, in the distance, barking inside a large, fenced-in dog run with a cute little house to keep him dry. Other than the dog, though, there are no sounds. The darkness is broken slightly by a small yellow porch light. Vanessa has a 9-millimeter Glock stuck in a pocket, and she thinks she knows how to use it. She walks around the house, careful where she steps, listening to everything. The dog barks louder, but no one, other than Vanessa, can hear him. At the rear door, she starts using the keys. The first three fit neither the locked knob nor the dead bolt, but numbers four and five do the trick. She takes a breath as she pushes the door open. There are no sirens, no frantic beepings. She had walked through the same door just five days earlier during the first session of filming and noticed the dead bolts and the absence of an alarm system.

Once inside, Vanessa peels off the leather gloves and puts on a pair of disposable latex gloves. She is about to examine every inch of the house, and she cannot leave a single print. Walking quickly, she flips on lights, pulls down all the shades, and cranks up the air-conditioning. It's a cheap rental house being leased by an unmarried hillbilly who's spent the last five years in prison, so the decor and furnishings are sparse. There are a few sticks of furniture, the obligatory oversized television, and sheets on some of the windows. There are also dirty dishes stacked by the kitchen sink and dirty clothes on the bathroom floor. The guest bedroom is used to store junk. Two dead mice lay perfectly still in traps, their necks snapped in two.

She begins in Nathan's bedroom by going through a tall chest of drawers. Nothing. She looks under his bed and between the mattress and the box spring. She examines every inch of his cluttered closet. The house has a conventional, framed foundation, no concrete slab, and the hardwood flooring gives way slightly with each step. She taps the flooring, searching for a more hollow sound, for evidence of a hiding place.

I suspect Nathan has hidden his loot somewhere in the house, though probably not in one of the main rooms. Nonetheless, we have to look everywhere. If he's smart, which is a stretch, he has split it and is using more than one hiding place.

From his bedroom, Vanessa inspects the guest room, giving the dead mice plenty of space. At 12:30, she begins turning off lights, as if Nathan is winding down. Room by room she goes, checking every corner, every plank, every pocket. Nothing goes unturned or untested. It could be in the walls, the floors, the dry-wall above the ceilings, or it could be buried in the backyard or stashed in a safe at Bombay's.

The cramped basement has seven-foot ceilings, no air-conditioning, and unpainted cinder-block walls. After spending an hour there, Vanessa is soaking wet, and too tired to go on. At 2:00 a.m., she stretches out on the sofa in the den and falls asleep with her hand on the Glock's holster.

If Rashford was hesitant to work on Saturday, he was almost belligerent on Sunday, but I gave him little choice. I pleaded with him to accompany me to the jail and pull the same strings he'd pulled the day before. I gave him a $100 bill to facilitate matters.

We arrive at the jail just before 9:00 a.m., and fifteen minutes later I am alone with Nathan in the same room used yesterday. I am shocked at his appearance. His injuries are evident and substantial, and I wonder how long the guards will allow the abuse to continue. His face is a mess of gashes, open wounds, and dried blood. His upper lip is bloated and protrudes grotesquely from under his nose. His left eye is completely shut and his right one is red and puffy. He is missing one front tooth. Gone are the cutoffs and cute Hawaiian shirt, replaced by a dirt-stained white jump-suit covered with dried blood.

We both lean forward, our faces just inches apart. "Help me," he manages to say, almost in tears.

"Here's the latest, Nathan," I begin. "The crooks are demanding $1 million from the jet's owner, and he's agreed to pay it, so these scumbags will get their money. They're not going to charge me with anything, as of this morning. For you, they want a half a million bucks. I've explained, through Rashford, that neither of us has that kind of money. I've explained that we were just passengers on someone's jet, that we're not rich, and so on. The Jamaicans don't believe this. Anyway, that's where we are as of right now."

Nathan grimaces, as if it hurts to breathe. As bad as his face looks, I'd hate to see the rest of his body. I'm imagining the worst, so I don't ask what happened.

He grunts and says, "Can you get back to the U.S., Reed?" His voice is weak and scratchy; even it is wounded.

"I think so. Rashford thinks so. But I don't have a lot of cash, Nathan."

He frowns and grunts again and looks as though he may either faint or cry. "Reed, listen to me. I have some money, a lot of it."

I'm staring him straight in the eyes, or at least his right one because his left one is closed. This is the fateful moment upon which everything else has been created. Without this, the entire project would be a gargantuan disaster, one horrific and lousy gamble.

"How much?" I ask as he pauses. He does not want to go on, but he has no choice.

"Enough to get me out."

"A half a million dollars, Nathan?"

"That, and more. We need to be partners, Reed. Just me and you. I'll tell you where the money is, you go get it, you get me out of here, and we'll be partners. But you gotta give me your word, Reed. I have to trust you, okay?"

"Hang on, Nathan," I say, pulling back and throwing up both palms. "You expect me to leave here, go home, then come back with a sackful of money and bribe the Jamaican police? Are you serious?"

"Please, Reed. There's no one else. I can't call anyone at home. No one there understands what's happening here, only you. You gotta do it, Reed. Please. My life depends on it. I can't survive here. Look at me. Please, Reed. You do what I ask, get me out, and you'll be a rich man."

I back away some more as if he's contagious.

He's begging: "Come on, Reed, you got me into this mess, now get me out."

"It might be helpful if you explain how you made so much money."

"I didn't make it. I stole it."

No surprise there. "Drug money?" I ask, but I know the answer.

"No, no, no. Are we partners, Reed?"

"I don't know, Nathan. I'm not so sure I want to start bribing Jamaican police. What if I get busted? I could end up just like you."

"Then don't come back. Send the money to Rashford, get him to make the delivery. You can figure it out, Reed, hell you're a smart man."

I nod as if I like the way he's thinking. "Where's the money, Nathan?"

"Are we partners, Reed? Fifty-fifty, just me and you, man?"

"Okay, okay, but I'm not risking jail over this, you understand?"

"I got it."

There's a pause as we study each other. His breathing is labored and every word is painful. Slowly, he extends his right hand; it's puffy and scratched. "Partners, Reed?" he asks, pleading. Slowly, I shake his hand and he grimaces. It's probably broken.

"Where's the money?" I ask.

"It's at my house," he says slowly, reluctantly, as he gives away the most precious secret of his life. "You've been there. There's a storage shed in the backyard, full of junk. It has a wooden floor, and to the right, under an old Sears push mower that doesn't work, is a trapdoor. You can't see it until you move the mower and some of the junk around it. Watch out for snakes—there are a couple of king snakes that live there. Open the trapdoor, and you'll see a bronze casket." His breathing is labored and he is sweating profusely. The physical pain is obvious, but he's also tormented by the pain of such a momentous revelation.

"A casket?" I ask, incredulous.

"Yes, a child's casket. Closed and sealed, waterproof and airtight. There's a hidden latch at the narrow end, where the feet would go. When you lift it, the seals release and you can open the casket."

"What's inside?"

"A bunch of cigar boxes wrapped in duct tape. I think there are eighteen of them."

"You hid cash in cigar boxes?"

"It's not cash, Reed," he says as he leans closer. "It's gold."

I appear too dumbfounded to speak, so he continues, almost in a whisper. "Mini-bars, each weighing ten ounces, as pure as anything being mined in the world. They're about the size of a large domino. They're beautiful, Reed, just beautiful."

I stare at him for a long time in disbelief, then say, "Okay, as hard as it is, I'll resist asking a lot of obvious questions. I'm supposed to hustle home, go fetch the gold from a casket, fight off some snakes, somehow find a dealer who'll swap me gold for cash, and then figure out a way to smuggle a half a million bucks back here into Jamaica where I'll fork it over to some crooked Customs agents and police who'll then set you free. That pretty well sum it up, Nathan?"

"It does. And hurry, okay?"

"I think you're crazy."

"We shook hands. We're partners, Reed. You figure out a way to do it, and you'll be a rich man."

"How many dominoes are we talking about?"

"Between five and six hundred."

"What's gold worth these days?"

"Two days ago it was trading for fifteen hundred bucks an ounce."

I do the math and say, "That's between seven and a half and eight million bucks."

Nathan is nodding. He does the math every day of his life as he watches the price fluctuate.

There is a loud knock on the door behind me, and one of the jailers appears. "Time's up, mon," he says, then disappears.

"This is probably one of the stupidest things I'll ever do in my life," I say.

"Or maybe one of the smartest," Nathan replies. "But please hurry, Reed. I can't survive long."

We shake hands and say good-bye. My last visual of Nathan is a battered little man trying to stand, in pain. Rashford and I leave in a hurry. He drops me off at my hotel, where I run to my room and call Vanessa.

She's in the attic, where it's 120 degrees, picking through old cardboard boxes and broken furniture. "It's not there," I announce. "It's outside, in the storage shed."

"Hang on," she says as she climbs down the retractable ladder. "Has he told you?" she asks between breaths.

"Yes."

"Someone's here," she says, and through the phone I hear a loud doorbell chime. Vanessa ducks low in the hallway and reaches for the Glock. "I'll call you right back," she whispers into the phone and turns it off.

It's late Sunday morning. Nathan's truck is in his driveway. Assuming his friends would know he was away for the weekend, the presence of his truck would raise questions. The doorbell chimes again, and someone starts pounding on the front door. Then he yells, "Nathan, you in there? Open up."

Vanessa crouches but doesn't move. The banging continues, then someone else is knocking on the back door and yelling for Nathan. There are at least two of them, with voices of young men, no doubt friends of Nathan's who stopped by for some reason. They show no signs of leaving. One of them taps on his bedroom window, but he cannot see inside. Vanessa eases into the bathroom and wipes her face. Her breathing is heavy and she's shaking with fear.

They're pounding and yelling and will soon come to the conclusion that something is wrong with Nathan. They'll kick in a door. Instinctively, Vanessa strips down to her bikini panties, dries the sweat off her body, leaves the Glock near the bathroom sink, and steps to the front door. She opens it widely and the young man gets a most unexpected treat. Her brown breasts are large and firm; her body athletic and toned. His eyes drop from her chest to the panties, pinched together to reveal as much flesh as possible, then he catches himself. She's smiling and saying, "Maybe Nathan is busy right now."

"Wow," he says. "Sorry."

They're facing each other through a screen door, neither in a hurry to leave. Over his shoulder he says, "Hey, Tommy, over here." Tommy arrives at the front door in a rush and can't believe his eyes.

Vanessa says, "Come on, guys, give us some privacy here, okay? Nathan's in the shower and we're not finished with our business. Who shall I tell him stopped by?" She then realizes that in her haste she forgot to remove the latex gloves. Red panties, aquamarine gloves.

Neither can take his eyes off her breasts. One says, "Uh, Greg and Tommy, we, uh, were just sorta passing by." Both are entranced by her nakedness and baffled by the gloves. What on earth has this gal been doing with our buddy?

"I'll be happy to tell him," she says with a cute smile as she slowly closes the door. Through the window she watches as they back away, still slack-jawed and confused. They finally get to their truck, climb in, and start laughing as they leave the driveway.

After they're gone, Vanessa fixes a glass of ice water and sits at the kitchen table for a few moments. She's rattled and ready for a meltdown but cannot afford one. She's sick of the house and has serious doubts about the entire project. But she has to go on.

I'm in the back of a cab headed for the airport when I see the call. I've spent the last fifteen minutes imagining various scenes and conflicts inside Nathan's house, none of them with good endings. "Are you okay?" I ask.

"Yes, just a couple of rednecks looking for Nathan. I got rid of them."

"How?"

"I'll tell you later."

"Did they see you?"

"Oh yes. It's cool. We're fine. Where's the stuff?"

"Out back, in the storage shed. I'll stay on the phone."

"Okay." Vanessa checks the driveway once more to make sure there are no more visitors, then hurries out the back door and to the storage shed. The dog is growling and barking frantically, and I can hear him clearly in Jamaica.

I cannot make myself warn her about the snakes, so I silently pray that she does not encounter them. Digging through a grungy outbuilding is bad enough; throw in the snakes and she might freak out and disappear. When she steps into the shed, she describes the interior. She says it's like an oven. I relay Nathan's instructions, and we sign off. She'll need both hands.

She moves two empty paint thinner cans, kicks aside a burlap bag, pushes the Sears mower as far away as possible, lifts a sheet of plywood, and finds a rope handle. It's stuck, so she yanks it harder and harder until the door opens. There are no hinges, so the entire trapdoor bolts from the floor and falls against the wall. Under it, on the ground, as advertised, is a soiled bronze casket no more than four feet in length. Vanessa gawks at it in horror, as if she has stumbled upon a crime scene and found some poor child's body. But there is no time for fear or second-guessing, no time to ask, What in hell am I doing here?

She tries to lift the casket, but it is too heavy. She finds the latch, twists, and half of the top lid opens slowly. Mercifully, there is no dead baby inside. Far from it. Vanessa pauses to study the collection of small wooden cigar boxes all sealed with a band of silver duct tape and for the most part stacked in rows. Sweat is dripping from her eyebrows and she tries to swipe at it with a forearm. Carefully, she removes one of the boxes and steps outside under the shade of an oak. Glancing around, seeing no one, nothing but the dog, who's tired of barking and growling, Vanessa peels off the tape, opens the box, and slowly removes a layer of wadded newspaper.

Mini-bars. Little bricks. Dominoes. An entire casket full of them. Millions upon millions.

She removes one and examines it. A perfect rectangle, not quite a half inch thick, lined with a tiny border ridge that allows for precise stacking and storage. On the front side is stamped "10 ounces." And under that: "99.9%." And nothing else—no bank name, no indication of where it came from or who mined it. No registration number.

Using a prepaid credit card, I pay $300 for an Air Jamaica flight to San Juan, Puerto Rico. It leaves in an hour, so I find a bench near my gate and kill time, staring at my cell phone. Before long, it lights up and vibrates.

Vanessa says, "He's not lying."

"Talk to me."

"Love to, baby. We now own eighteen cigar boxes filled with these gorgeous little gold mini-bars, haven't counted them all yet, but there must be at least five hundred."

I take a deep breath and feel like crying. This project has been on the drawing board for over two years, and during most of that time the odds of a successful outcome were at least a thousand to one. A series of loosely connected events had to fall perfectly into place. We're not yet at the finish line, but we are in the home-stretch. I can smell the barn.

"Between five hundred and six hundred," I say, "according to our boy."

"He's earned the right to be trusted. Where are you?"

"At the airport. I bought a ticket, made it through Customs, and I'll board in an hour. So far, no problems. Where are you?"

"I'm leaving this dump. I've loaded up the good stuff and put everything back in its place. The house is locked."

"Don't worry about the house. He'll never see it again."

"I know. I gave his dog a whole sackful of food. Maybe someone will check on him."

"Get away from that place."

"I'm leaving now."

"Just follow the plan and I'll call when I can."

CHAPTER 37

It's almost eleven, Sunday morning, July 24, a hot clear day with little traffic around Radford. Vanessa wants to avoid another encounter with anyone who might see Nathan's pickup truck and get suspicious. She heads north on the interstate, past Roanoke, into the heart of the Shenandoah Valley, driving as cautiously as humanly possible with the needle stuck on seventy miles per hour and every lane change properly telegraphed with a turn signal. She watches the rearview mirror because it's now such a habit, and she watches every other vehicle to avoid any chance of a collision. On the passenger's floorboard, and on the seat next to her, there is literally a fortune in gold, a fortune in unmarked and untraceable ingots freshly stolen from a thief who stole them from a crook who took them from a gang of thugs. How could she explain such a collection of precious metal to a nosy state trooper? She could not, so she drives as perfectly as possible as the 18-wheelers roar by in the left lane.

She exits at a small town and drifts until she finds a cheap dollar store. The banner across the front windows advertises pre-back-to-school specials. She parks near the entrance and spreads a soiled blanket, taken from Nathan's, over the cigar boxes. She puts the Glock under a corner of the blanket, next to her, and analyzes the parking lot. It's virtually empty on a Sunday morning. Finally, she takes a deep breath, gets out, locks the truck, and hurries inside. In less than ten minutes, Vanessa buys ten kids' backpacks, all with a Desert Storm camouflage motif. She pays in cash and does not respond when the cashier quips, "Must have a lot of kids heading back to school."

She shoves her purchases into the cab of the truck and heads back to the interstate. An hour later, she finds a truck stop near Staunton, Virginia, and parks next to the rigs. When she's certain that no one is watching, she begins to quickly stuff the cigar boxes into the backpacks, two of which are not used.

She fills up the tank, eats lunch from a fast-food drive-through, and kills time roaming up and down Interstate 81, as far north as Maryland and as far south as Roanoke. The hours drag by. She cannot park and leave the jackpot. It has to be guarded at all times, so she flows with the traffic while she waits on darkness.

I'm pacing in a crowded and humid wing of the San Juan airport, waiting on a Delta flight to Atlanta. My ticket was purchased in the name of Malcolm Bannister, and his old passport worked just fine. It will expire in four months. The last time it was used, Dionne and I escaped on a cheap cruise to the Bahamas. Another lifetime.

I call Vanessa twice and we speak in code. Got the goods. Packages are fine. She's moving around, following the plan. If a spook somewhere is listening, then he's scratching his head.

At 3:30 we finally board, and then sit for an hour in the sweltering cabin as a howling storm pounds the airport and the pilots go mute. At least two babies are squalling behind me. As tempers rise, I close my eyes and try to nap, but I have deprived myself of sleep for so long I have forgotten how to doze off. Instead, I think of Nathan Cooley and his hopeless situation, though I have little sympathy. I think of Vanessa and smile at her toughness under pressure. We are so close to the finish line, but there are still so many ways to fail. We have the gold, but can we keep it?

I wake up as we lurch forward and begin rumbling down the runway. Two hours later we land in Atlanta. At Passport Control, I manage to avoid the counters manned by black Customs agents and instead pick a beefy young white boy who seems to be bored and indifferent. He takes my passport, glances at a nine-year-old photo of Malcolm Bannister, quickly compares it to the revised face of Max Reed Baldwin, and sees nothing unusual. We all look the same.

I am assuming Customs has by now notified the FBI that I left the country two days earlier, on a private jet bound for Jamaica. What I don't know is whether the FBI is still monitoring any possible movements by Malcolm Bannister. I'm betting they are not, and I want the FBI to think I'm still somewhere in the islands having a grand time. At any rate, I'm moving quickly. Since Malcolm no longer has a valid driver's license, Max rents a car at the Avis desk, and forty-five minutes after landing in Atlanta, I'm leaving the city in a hurry. Near Roswell, Georgia, I stop at a Walmart and pay cash for two more prepaid cell phones. As I leave the store, I drop two old ones into a trash can.

———

After dark, Vanessa parks the truck for good. She's been driving it for almost twelve hours and can't wait to get rid of it. For a moment she sits behind the wheel, in a space next to her Honda Accord, and watches a commuter airliner taxi to the Roanoke terminal. It's a little after 9:00 on a Sunday night, and there appears to be no traffic. The parking lot is almost empty. She takes another deep breath and gets out. Working quickly while watching everything around her, she transfers the backpacks from Nathan's front seat into the trunk of her car. Eight backpacks, each seemingly heavier than the one before it, but she does not mind at all.

She locks the truck, keeps the keys, and leaves the parking lot. If things go as planned, Nathan's truck will not be noticed for several days. When his friends realize he's missing, they will eventually notify the police, who will find the truck and start piecing together a story. There's no doubt Nathan boasted to someone that he was headed to Miami on a private jet, and this will cause the cops to chase their tails for a while.

I have no way of knowing if the authorities can link their missing man to Nathaniel Coley, the clown who recently left town with a fake passport, four kilos of coke, and a pistol, but I doubt it. He might not be located until someone down in Jamaica finally allows him to make a phone call. Whom he calls and what he tells that person is anyone's guess. He is more likely to count the hours and days until I return with a sackful of cash and start bribing people. After weeks, maybe a month, he'll realize his old pal Reed stiffed him, took the money and ran.

I almost feel sorry for him.

———

At 1:00 a.m., I approach Asheville, North Carolina, and see a sign for the motel at a busy interchange. Parked behind it, and out of view, is a little blue Honda Accord with my dear Vanessa sitting behind the wheel, the Glock at her side. I park next to her and we step inside our first-floor room. We kiss and embrace, but we are much too tense to get amorous. We quietly unload her trunk and toss the backpacks on one of the beds. I lock the door, chain it, and stick a chair under the doorknob. I pull the curtains tight, then hang towels from the rods to cover the slits and cracks and make certain no one can see inside our little vault.

While I do this, Vanessa takes a shower, and when she emerges from the bathroom, she is wearing nothing but a short terry-cloth bathrobe that reveals miles and miles of the prettiest legs I've ever seen. Don't even think about it, she says. She's exhausted. Maybe tomorrow.

We empty the backpacks, put on disposable latex gloves, and make a neat arrangement of eighteen cigar boxes, each secured with two precise bands of silver duct tape. We notice two have apparently been opened, with the tape cut along the top, and we set them aside. Using a small penknife, I cut the tape on the first canister and open the box. We remove the mini-bars, count them—thirty—then put them back inside and re-tape the lid. Vanessa scribbles down the quantity and we open the second one. It has thirty-two mini-bars, all shiny, perfectly sized, and seemingly untouched by human hands.

"Beautiful, just beautiful," she says over and over. "It will last for centuries."

"Forever," I say, rubbing a mini-bar. "Wouldn't you love to know what part of the world it came from?"

She laughs because we'll never know.

We open all sixteen of the sealed boxes, then inventory the mini-bars from the two that had previously been opened. They held about half the number as the others. Our total is 570. With gold fluctuating around $1,500 an ounce, our jackpot is worth somewhere in the neighborhood of $8.5 million.

We lie on the bed with the gold stacked between us, and it's impossible not to smile. We need a bottle of champagne, but at 2:00 on a Monday morning in a cheap motel in North Carolina, champagne does not exist. There is so much to take in here, at this moment, but one of the more glorious aspects of our project is that no one is looking for this treasure. Other than Nathan Cooley, no one knows it exists. We took it from a thief, one who left no trail.

Seeing, touching, and counting our fortune has energized us. I yank off her bathrobe and we crawl under the covers of the other bed. Try as we may, it's difficult to make love without keeping one eye on the gold. When we finish, we collapse with exhaustion and sleep like the dead.

CHAPTER 38

At 6:30 Monday morning, Agent Fox walked into the large office of Victor Westlake and said, "The Jamaicans are as slow as ever. Nothing much to add. Baldwin arrived late Friday night on a jet chartered from a company in Raleigh, a nice plane that is currently being seized by Jamaican Customs and can't come home. No sign of Baldwin. His friend Nathaniel Coley tried to enter with a fake passport and is now locked up just like the airplane."

"He's in jail?" Westlake asked, chewing on a thumbnail.

"Yes sir. That's all I can get as of now. Don't know when he might be getting out. I'm trying to get the police to check hotel records to find Baldwin, but they're hesitant to do so. He's not a fugitive; they don't like to piss off the hotels; it was the weekend; et cetera."

"Find Baldwin."

"Trying, sir."

"What's he up to?"

Fox shook his head. "It makes no sense. Why burn that much cash on a private jet? Why travel with someone using a fake passport? Who the hell is Nathaniel Coley? We've done a search in Virginia and West Virginia and found no possible hits. Maybe Coley is a good friend who can't get a passport, and they were trying to beat Customs so they can play in the sun for a few days."

"Maybe maybe."

"You got it, sir."

"Keep digging and report back by e-mail."

"Yes sir."

"I'm assuming he left his car behind at the Roanoke airport."

"He did, in the parking lot of the general aviation terminal. Same Florida license plates. We found it Saturday morning and have it under surveillance."

"Good. Just find him, okay?"

"And if we do?"

"Just follow him and figure out what he's doing."

Over coffee and gold, we plan our day, but we do not linger. At nine, Vanessa turns in the key at the front desk and checks out. We kiss good-bye and I follow her out of the parking lot, careful not to crowd the rear bumper of her Accord. On the other side of it, hidden deep in the trunk, is half the gold. The other half is in the trunk of my rented Impala. We separate at the interchange; she's going north and I'm going south. She waves in the rearview mirror, and I wonder when I'll see her again.

As I settle into the long drive, tall coffee in hand, I remind myself that the time must be spent wisely. No foolish daydreaming; no mental loafing; no fantasies about what to do with all the money. So many issues vie for priority. When will the police find Nathan's truck? When do I call Rashford Watley and instruct him to pass along the message to Nathan that things are proceeding as planned? How many of these cigar boxes will fit into the bank lockboxes I leased a month ago? How much of the gold should I try to sell at a discount to raise cash? How do I get the attention of Victor Westlake and Stanley Mumphrey, the U.S. Attorney in Roanoke? And, most important, how do we get the gold out of the country, and how long might it take?

Instead, my mind drifts to thoughts of my father, old Henry, who hasn't had contact with his younger son in over four months. I'm sure he's disgusted with me for getting busted out of Frostburg and shipped off to Fort Wayne. I'm sure he's puzzled by the absence of correspondence. He's probably calling my brother, Marcus, in D.C. and my sister, Ruby, in California to see if they've heard anything. I wonder if Henry's a great-grandfather yet, courtesy of Marcus's delinquent son and his fourteen-year-old girlfriend, or did she get the abortion?

On second thought, maybe I don't miss my family as much as I sometimes think. It would be nice, though, to see my father, though I suspect he will not approve of my altered looks. Truth is, there's a good chance I'll never see any of them again. Depending on the whims and machinations of the federal government, I could remain a free man or I could spend the rest of my life as a fugitive. Regardless, I'll have the gold.

As the miles pass and I cling to the speed limit while trying to avoid getting hit by the big rigs, I can't help but think of Bo. I've been out of prison for four months now, and every day I've fought the urge to dwell on my son. It's too painful to think I may never see him again, but as the weeks go by I have come to accept this reality. Reuniting with him, in some fashion, would be the first huge step down the road to normalcy, but my life from now on will be anything but normal. We could never again live together under the same roof, as father and son, and I see no benefit to Bo of knowing that I'm suddenly around and would like to have an ice cream twice a month. I'm sure he still remembers me, but the memories are certainly fading. Dionne is a smart, lovely woman, and I'm sure she and her second husband are providing a happy life for Bo. Why should I, a virtual stranger and a guy who certainly looks like one, pop into their world and upset things? Once I convinced Bo I was really his father, how would I rekindle a relationship that's been dead for over five years?

To stop this torment, I try to focus on the next few hours,

then the next few days. Crucial steps lie ahead, and a screwup could cost me a fortune and possibly send me back to prison.

I stop for gas and a vending-machine sandwich near Savannah, and two and a half hours later I'm in Neptune Beach, my old, temporary stomping ground. At an office supply store I purchase a heavy, thick briefcase, then drive to a public parking area for the beach. There are no security cameras and no foot traffic, and I quickly open the trunk, remove two of the cigar boxes and place them in the briefcase. It weighs about forty pounds, and as I walk around the car I realize it's too heavy. I remove one container and return it to the trunk.

Four blocks away, I park at First Coast Trust, and nonchalantly walk toward the front door. The digital thermometer on the bank's rotating billboard reads ninety-six degrees. The briefcase gets heavier with each step, and I struggle to act as though it contains nothing but some important papers. Twenty pounds is not a lot of weight, but it's far too much for a briefcase of any size. Every step is now being captured on video, and the last thing I want is the image of me lumbering into the bank with a heavy satchel. I worry about Vanessa and her efforts to access her lockboxes in Richmond with such a burden on her shoulder.

Heavy as it is, I can't help but smile at the astonishing weight of pure gold.

Inside I wait patiently for the vault clerk to finish with another customer. When it's my turn, I give her my Florida driver's license and sign my name. She checks my face and my handwriting, approves, and escorts me to the vault in the rear of the bank. She inserts the house key into my lockbox, and I insert my own. Noises click perfectly, the box is released, and I carry it to a narrow, private closet and close the door. The clerk waits outside, in the center of the vault.

The lockbox is six inches wide, six inches tall, and eighteen inches long, the largest available when I leased it a month ago for one year, at $300 per. I place the cigar box inside. Vanessa and I labeled each one with the exact number of mini-bars. This one has thirty-three, or 330 ounces, roughly $500,000. I close the box, admire it, kill a few minutes, then open the door and report to the clerk. Part of her job is to remain aloof with no suspicions whatsoever, and she does it well. I suppose she's seen it all.

Twenty minutes later, I'm in the vault at a branch of the Jacksonville Savings Bank. The vault is larger, the lockboxes smaller, the clerk more suspicious, but everything else is the same. Behind a locked door, I gently place another stash of mini-bars into the box. Thirty-two gorgeous little ingots worth another half a million bucks.

At my third and final bank, not a half mile from the first one, I make the last deposit of the day, then spend an hour looking for a motel where I can park just outside my room.

———

In a mall on the west end of Richmond, Vanessa wanders through a high-end department store until she finds the ladies' accessories. Though she acts calm, she is all nerves because her Accord is alone out there in the parking lot just waiting to be vandalized or stolen. She selects a chic red leather shoulder bag large enough to be called luggage. Its designer is well-known, and it will probably be noticed by the female clerks who run the banks. She pays cash for it and hustles back to her car.

Two weeks earlier, Max—she had always known him as Malcolm but she liked the new name better—had instructed her to rent three lockboxes. She had carefully selected the banks around Richmond, made the applications, passed the screenings, and paid the fees. Then, as instructed, she had visited each one twice to deposit useless paperwork and such. The vault clerks now recognized her, trusted her, and were not the least bit suspicious when Ms. Vanessa Young showed up with a killer new bag and needed access to the vault.

In less than ninety minutes, Vanessa safely stashes away almost $1.5 million in gold bullion.

She returns to her apartment for the first time in over a week and parks in a space she can see from her second-floor window. The complex is in a nice part of town, near the University of Richmond, and the neighborhood is generally safe. She has lived here for two years and cannot remember a stolen car or a burglary. Nevertheless, she is taking no chances. She inspects the doors and windows for signs of entry, and finds none. She showers, changes clothes, then leaves.

Four hours later, she returns, and in the darkness she slowly, methodically hauls the treasure into her apartment and hides it under her bed. She sleeps above it, the Glock on the night table, every door locked and latched and jammed with a chair.

She drifts in and out, and at dawn she's sipping coffee on the sofa in the den watching the weather on local cable. The clock seems to have stopped. She would love to sleep some more, but her mind will not allow her body to surrender. Her appetite is gone too, though she tries to choke down some cottage cheese. Every ten minutes or so, she walks to the window and checks the parking lot. The early morning commuters leave in shifts—7:30, 7:45, 8:00. The banks do not open until 9:00. She takes a long shower, dresses as if she's going to court, packs a bag and takes it to her car. Over the next twenty minutes, she removes three of the cigar boxes from under the bed and takes them to her car. These she will soon deposit in the same three lockboxes she visited the day before.

The great debate raging in her mind is whether the remaining three canisters will be safer in the trunk of her car or in her apartment under the bed. She decides to play it both ways, and leaves two at home while taking another one with her.

Vanessa calls with the news that she's made her third and final deposit of the morning, and is headed to Roanoke to see the lawyer. I'm ahead of her by a step or two. I visited my three banks a bit earlier, made the deposits, and am now driving to Miami. We have tucked away 380 of the 570 mini-bars. It's a good feeling, but the pressure is still on. The Feds can and will seize all assets under the right circumstances, and even the wrong ones, so we can take no chances. I have to get the gold out of the country.

I am assuming the Feds do not know Vanessa and I are working together. I am also assuming they have yet to link Nathan Cooley to me. I'm making lots of assumptions and have no way of knowing if they are correct.

CHAPTER 39

Stalled in construction traffic near Fort Lauderdale, I punch in the numbers to Mr. Rashford Watley's cell phone down in Montego Bay. He answers with a warm laugh as if we've been friends for decades. I explain I'm safely back home in the U.S. and life is swell. Forty-eight hours ago I was sneaking out of Jamaica after saying good-bye to both Nathan and Rashford, terrified I would be stopped by uniformed men before boarding the flight to Puerto Rico. I am stunned at how fast things are happening. I repeatedly remind myself to stay focused and think about the next move.

Rashford has not visited the jail since Sunday. I explain that Nathaniel has hatched a scheme to start bribing people down there and is having delusions about my returning with a box-load of cash. I've made a few calls, and it seems as if the boy has a long history with cocaine; still can't believe the idiot would attempt to smuggle in four kilos; can't begin to explain the gun. A moron.

Rashford agrees and says he chatted with the prosecutor yesterday, Monday. If Rashford can work his magic, our boy is looking at "about" twenty years in the Jamaican prison system. Frankly, Rashford advises, he doesn't think Nathaniel will survive long in the system. Based on the beatings he's received his first two nights in jail, he'll be lucky to live a full week.

We agree that Rashford will visit the jail this afternoon and check on Nathaniel. I ask him to pass along the message that I am hard at work securing his release, the visit to his home went as planned, and all things are proceeding as discussed. "As you wish," Rashford says. I paid his fee, so he's still working for me, technically.

I hope it's our last conversation.

———————

Vanessa once again makes the three-and-a-half-hour drive from Richmond to Roanoke and arrives promptly for a 2:00 p.m. meeting with Dusty Shiver, attorney for Quinn Rucker. When she called to schedule the appointment, she promised to have in her possession crucial evidence about Quinn's case. Dusty was intrigued and attempted to pry over the phone, but she insisted on a meeting, as soon as possible.

She is dressed fashionably in a skirt short enough to get attention, and she carries a smart leather attaché. Dusty jumps to his feet when she enters his office and offers a chair. A secretary brings in coffee and they manage some strained small talk until the door is closed for good.

"I'll get right to the point, Mr. Shiver," she says. "Quinn Rucker is my brother, and I can prove he's innocent."

Dusty absorbs this and allows it to rattle around the room. He knows Quinn has two brothers—Dee Ray and Tall Man—and a sister Lucinda. All have been active in the family business. He now remembers that there was another sister who has not been involved and has never been mentioned.

"Quinn is your brother," he repeats, almost mumbling.

"Yes. I left D.C. a few years ago and have kept my distance."

"Okay. I'm listening. Let's hear it."

Vanessa recrosses her legs and Dusty maintains eye contact. She begins, "A week or so after Quinn walked away from the camp at Frostburg, he almost overdosed on cocaine in D.C. We, the family, knew he would kill himself with the stuff—Quinn was always the heaviest user—and we intervened. My brother Dee Ray and I drove him to a rehab facility near Akron, Ohio, a tough place for serious addicts. There was no court order so they couldn't lock him down, but that's basically what happens at this facility. Quinn had been there for twenty-one days when the bodies of Judge Fawcett and his secretary were found on February 7." She lifts a file from her briefcase and places it on Dusty's desk. "The paperwork is all here. Because he had just escaped from prison, he was admitted under an assumed name—Mr. James Williams. We paid a deposit of $20,000 in cash, so the rehab facility was happy to go along. They didn't ask a lot of questions. They gave him a complete physical exam, complete blood work, so there's DNA proof that Quinn was there at the time of the murders."

"How long have you known this?"

"I cannot answer all of your questions, Mr. Shiver. There are many secrets in our family, and not many answers."

Dusty stares at her, and she coolly returns his look. He knows he will not learn everything, and at the moment it's not that important. He has just won a major victory over the government, and he is already laughing. "Why did he confess?"

"Why does anyone confess to a crime they didn't commit? I don't know. Quinn is severely bipolar and has other problems. The FBI hammered him for ten hours and used all the dirty tricks at their disposal. Knowing Quinn, he was playing games. He probably gave them what they wanted so they would leave him alone. Maybe he fabricated a tall tale so they would run around in circles trying to verify it. I don't know. Remember the Lindbergh baby kidnapping, the most famous kidnapping in history?"

"I've read about it, sure."

"Well, at least 150 people confessed to that crime. It makes no sense, but then Quinn can be crazy at times."

Dusty opens the file. There is a report of each day Quinn was in rehab, from January 17 through February 7, the Monday they found the bodies of Judge Fawcett and Naomi Clary. "It says here he left the facility on the afternoon of February 7," Dusty says, reading.

"That's right. He walked away, or escaped, and made his way to Roanoke."

"And why, might I ask, did he go to Roanoke?"

"Again, Mr. Shiver, I can't answer a lot of questions."

"So he shows up in Roanoke the day after the bodies are found, goes to a bar, gets drunk, gets in a fight, gets arrested, and he's got a pocketful of cash. There are a lot of gaps here, Miss . . ."

"Yes, there are, and with time the gaps will be filled in. Right now, though, it's not that important, is it? What's important is that you have clear proof of his innocence. Other than the bogus confession, the government has no evidence against my brother, right?"

"That's correct. There's no physical evidence, just a lot of suspicious behavior. Such as, why was he in Roanoke? How did he get there? Where did he get all that cash? Where did he buy the stolen guns? Lots of questions, Miss, but I suppose you don't have the answers, right?"

"Correct."

Dusty locks his hands behind his head and stares at the ceiling. After a long, silent gap he says, "I'll have to investigate this, you know. I'll have to go to the rehab center, interview the people there, take affidavits and such. The Feds are not about to roll over until our file is much thicker and we can hit them over the head with it. I'll need another $25,000."

Without hesitation, she says, "I'll discuss it with Dee Ray."

"The pretrial conference is in two weeks, so we need to move fast. I'd like to file a motion to dismiss the charges before the conference."

"You're the lawyer."

Another pause as Dusty leans forward on his elbows and looks at Vanessa. "I knew Judge Fawcett well. We weren't friends, but friendly acquaintances. If Quinn didn't kill him, any idea who did?"

She is already shaking her head. No.

The police found Nathan's truck at the general aviation area of the Roanoke Regional Airport late Tuesday morning. As expected, his employees at the bar became concerned Monday when he didn't show, and by late afternoon they were making calls. They finally contacted the police, who eventually scoured the airport. Nathan had boasted of flying to Miami on a private jet, so the search was not difficult, at least for his truck. Finding it did not automatically indicate foul play, and the police were in no hurry to start a manhunt. A quick background check on the name revealed the criminal record, and this did nothing to create sympathy. There was no family screaming for the lost loved one.

A computer search and a few phone calls revealed that Nathan had purchased the brand-new Chevy Silverado two months earlier from a dealer in Lexington, Virginia, an hour north of Roanoke on Interstate 81. The selling price was $41,000, and Nathan had paid in cash. Not the kind of cash often referred to when one writes a check, but hard cash. An impressive stack of $100 bills.

Unknown to the car dealer, or the police, or anyone else for that matter, Nathan had found himself a gold trader.

I finally find one myself.

After two trips into the vault of the Palmetto Trust in south-central Miami, I still have in my possession, in the trunk of my rented Impala, exactly forty-one of the precious little mini-bars, value of about $600,000. I need to convert some of them to cash, and to do so I am forced to enter the shady world of gold trading, where rules are pliant and adjusted on the fly and all characters have shifty eyes and speak in double-talk.

The first two dealers, lifted from the Yellow Pages, suspect I'm an agent of some variety and promptly hang up. The third one, a gentleman with an accent, which I'm quickly learning is not unusual in the trade, wants to know how I came to possess a ten-ounce bar of seemingly pure gold. "It's a long story," I say, then hang up. Number four is a small fry who pawns appliances out front and buys jewelry in the back. Number five shows some potential but, of course, will have to see what I've got. I explain that I do not want to walk into his store because I do not wish to be caught on video. He pauses and I suspect he's thinking about getting robbed of his cash at gunpoint. We eventually agree to meet at an ice cream shop two doors down from his store, in a shopping center, in a good part of town. He'll be wearing a black Marlins cap.

Thirty minutes later I'm sitting in front of a double pistachio gelato. Hassan, a large gray-bearded Syrian, is across from me and working on a triple chocolate fudge. Twenty feet away is another swarthy gentleman who's reading a newspaper, eating frozen yogurt, and probably ready to shoot me if I show the slightest sign of causing trouble.

After we try and fail at small talk, I slide over a crumpled envelope. Inside is a single gold bar. Hassan glances around, but the only customers are young moms and their five-year-olds, along with the other Syrian. He takes the mini-bar into his thick paw, squeezes it, smiles, taps it slightly on the corner of the table, and mumbles, "Wow." This he manages without the slightest hint of an accent.

I am amazed at how soothing that simple expression is. I have never thought about the gold being fake, but to have it legitimized by a pro is suddenly refreshing. "You like, huh?" I say stupidly, just trying to get something out.

"Very nice," he says, easing the bar into the envelope. I reach over and take it. He asks, "How many?"

"Let's say five bars, fifty ounces. Gold closed yesterday at $1,520 an ounce, so—"

"I know the price of gold," he interrupts.

"Of course you do. Do you want to buy five bars?"

A guy like this never says yes or no. Instead, he mumbles, talks in circles, hedges, and bluffs. He says, "It is possible, and it certainly depends on the price."

"What can you offer?" I ask, but not too eagerly. There are other gold dealers left in the Yellow Pages, though I'm running out of time and weary of the cold-calling.

"Well, that depends, Mr. Baldwin, on several things. One must assume in a situation like this that the gold is of, shall we say, the black-market variety. I don't know where you got it, and don't want to know, but there is a reasonable chance it was, shall we say, extracted from its previous owner."

"Does it really matter where—"

"Are you the registered owner of this gold, Mr. Baldwin?" he asks sharply.

I glance around. "No."

"Of course not. Therefore, the black-market discount is 20 percent." This guy doesn't need a calculator. "I'll pay $1,220 an ounce," he says softly but firmly as he leans forward. His beard partially covers his lips, but his accented words are clear.

"For five bars?" I ask. "Fifty ounces?"

"Assuming the other four are of the same quality."

"They are identical."

"And you have no registration, records, paperwork, nothing, correct, Mr. Baldwin?"

"That's right, and I want no records now. A simple deal, gold for cash, no receipts, no paperwork, no videos, nothing. I came and went and vanished in the night."

Hassan smiles and offers his right hand. We shake, the deal

is done, and we agree to meet at nine the following morning at a deli across the street, one with booths where we can do our counting in private. I leave the ice cream parlor as if I've committed a crime and repeat to myself what should be obvious; to wit, it is not against the law to buy and sell gold, at discounted prices or at inflated ones. This is not crack we're peddling on the street, nor is it inside information from a boardroom. It's a perfectly legitimate transaction, right?

Anyone watching Hassan and me would swear they were observing two crooks negotiating a crooked deal. Who could blame them? At this point, I am beyond caring.

———

I'm taking risks, but I have no choice. Hassan is a risk, but I need the cash. Getting the gold out of the country will require risks, but leaving it here could mean losing it.

I spend the next two hours shopping at discount stores. I buy random items such as backgammon sets, small toolboxes, hardback books, and three cheap laptop computers. I haul my goods into a ground-level motel room south of Coral Gables and spend the rest of the night tinkering, packing, and sipping cold beer.

From the laptops, I remove the hard drives and the batteries, and manage to replace them with three of my little bricks. Inside each hardback, I stuff one mini-bar wrapped in newspaper and aluminum foil, then bind it tightly with duct tape. In the toolboxes, I leave the hammer and screwdrivers, but remove everything else. Four mini-bars fit nicely into each one. The backgammon sets hold two bars without feeling suspicious. Using supplies from FedEx, UPS, and DHL, I carefully package my goods as the hours pass and I'm lost in another world.

I call Vanessa twice and we replay our days. She's back in Richmond, doing the same thing I'm doing. We're both exhausted, physically and mentally, but we encourage each other to keep going. Now is not the time to slow down or get careless.

At midnight, I finish and admire my handiwork. On the credenza there are a dozen overnight packages, all sealed and properly air billed, efficient-looking, not the least bit suspicious, and together holding thirty-two mini-bars worth roughly $500,000. For international shipments, the paperwork is tedious and I am forced to fudge on the contents. The sender is Mr. M. Reed Baldwin of Skelter Films in Miami, and the recipient is the same guy at Sugar Cove Villas, Number 26, Willoughby Bay, Antigua. My plans are to be there to receive them. If they arrive at their destination without incident, Vanessa and I will probably try similar shipments in the near future. If something goes wrong, we'll make new plans. Shipping like this is another risk; the packages might be searched and confiscated; the gold could be stolen somewhere along the way. However, I'm reasonably confident it will find its new home. I remind myself we're not shipping banned substances here.

I'm too wired to sleep, and at 2:00 a.m. I turn on the lights and my laptop and fiddle with the e-mail. It is to Mr. Stanley Mumphrey, U.S. Attorney, Southern District of Virginia, and Mr. Victor Westlake, FBI, Washington. The current draft reads:

Dear Mr. Mumphrey and Mr. Westlake:

I'm afraid I've made a grave mistake. Quinn Rucker did not kill Judge Raymond Fawcett and Ms. Naomi Clary. Now that I'm out of prison, it has taken me several months to realize this, and to identify the real killer. Quinn's confession is bogus, as you probably know by now, and you have zero physical evidence against him. His attorney, Dusty Shiver, now has in his possession clear proof of an airtight alibi that will clear Quinn, so prepare yourselves for the reality of dropping all charges against him. Sorry for any inconvenience.

It is imperative that we talk as soon as possible. I have a detailed
plan of how to proceed, and only your total cooperation will lead
to the apprehension and conviction of the killer. My plan begins
with the promise of complete immunity for myself and others,
and it ends with the precise result that you desire. Working
together, we can finally resolve this matter and bring about
justice.

I am out of the country and have no plans to return, ever.

Sincerely, Malcolm Bannister

CHAPTER 40

Typically, sleep is fleeting. In fact, it is so elusive and fitful I'm not sure I slept at all. There is so much to do that I find myself drinking bad coffee and staring at the television long before the sun rises. Finally, I shower, dress, load the overnight packages into my car, and hit the empty streets of Miami in search of breakfast. At nine, Hassan rumbles into the deli with a brown paper sack, as though he's been to the grocer for a few items. We huddle in a booth, order coffee, and while we dodge the waitress, we do the counting. His job is far easier than mine; he caresses the five mini-bars before dropping them into the inside pockets of his wrinkled blazer. I poke into the brown bag and struggle to count 61 stacks of $100 bills, ten per stack. "It's all there," he says, watching out for the waitress. "Sixty-one thousand dollars."

When I'm satisfied, I close the bag and try to enjoy the coffee. Twenty minutes after he arrives, he leaves. I wait awhile, then head for the door, nervously expecting a SWAT team to assault me as I hustle to my car. I keep $22,000 for the trip, and stuff $50,000 into two remaining backgammon sets. At a FedEx shipping office, I wait in line with five overnight packages and watch intently as the customers in front of me go about their business. When it's my turn, the clerk examines the air bills and nonchalantly asks, "What's inside?"

"Household items, some books, nothing of real value, nothing to insure," I respond, the words carefully rehearsed. "I have a place on Antigua. Just sprucing it up a bit." She nods as if she's really interested in my plans.

For standard business delivery, three days guaranteed, the bill comes to $310, and I pay with a prepaid credit card. As I leave the lobby, and leave the gold behind, I take a deep breath and hope for the best. Using the rental car's GPS, I locate a UPS office and go through the same procedure. I return to Palmetto Trust and it takes an hour to get into my lockbox. I leave behind the rest of the cash and the four remaining mini-bars.

It takes a while to find the DHL shipping desk in the sprawl of Miami International, but I eventually negotiate my way there and drop off more packages. I finally part with my Impala at an Avis station and take a cab to the general aviation section of the airport, far away from the main terminal. There are blocks of private aircraft hangars, and charter companies, and flight schools, and my driver gets lost as we search in vain for an outfit called Maritime Aviation. It needs a larger sign because the one currently in use can hardly be seen from the nearest street, and I'm tempted to bark this at the clerk when I walk in the door. I manage to bite my tongue and relax.

There is no scanner to examine me or my luggage, and I assume private aircraft terminals are not equipped with these machines. I expect to be scanned at some level upon my arrival in Antigua, so I'm playing it safe. I have about $30,000 in cash, with most of it hidden in my luggage, and if they dig through it and get excited, I'll play dumb and pay the fine. I was tempted to try to smuggle in a gold bar or two, to see if it can be done, but the risk is greater than the reward.

At 1:30, the pilots say it's time to board, and we crawl inside a Learjet 35, a small jet about half the size of the Challenger Nathan and I enjoyed briefly during our recent trip to Jamaica. The 35 can perhaps seat six people, but full-sized men would be shoulder to shoulder. Instead of a restroom, there is an emergency potty under a seat. It's cramped, to say the least, but who cares? It's far cheaper than a big plane, but just as fast. I'm the only passenger, and I'm in a hurry.

Max Baldwin on board here, with proper documentation. Malcolm Bannister has been retired, for the final time. I'm sure Customs will eventually notify some spook within the FBI, and after some puzzlement he'll report to his boss. They'll rub their chins and wonder what Baldwin is doing, what's his thing with private jets, why is he spending all his money? A lot of questions, but the big one is still, What the hell is he doing?

They will have no clue unless I tell them.

As we taxi away from the terminal, I quickly review the e-mail to Mumphrey and Westlake, then I press Send.

—————

It is July 28. Four months ago I left Frostburg, and two months ago I left Fort Carson with a new face and name. As I try to recall these past few weeks and put them into perspective, I begin to nod off. When we reach our altitude of forty thousand feet, I fall asleep.

Two hours later I am awakened by turbulence and look through the window. We are streaking over a summer thunderstorm and the small jet is getting bounced around. One of the pilots turns around and gives me a thumbs-up—everything's okay. If you say so, pal. Minutes later the sky is calm again, the storm is behind us, and I gaze down at the beautiful waters of the Caribbean. According to the NavScreen on the bulkhead in front of me, we are about to pass over St. Croix in the U.S. Virgin Islands.

There are so many beautiful islands down there, and so much variety. When I was in prison, I kept hidden in the library a *Fodor's Guide to the Caribbean*, a thick reference book with two dozen color photos, maps, lists of things to do, and brief histories of all the islands. I dreamed that I would one day be loose in the Caribbean, alone with Vanessa, just the two of us on a small sailboat, drifting from island to island in complete and unrestrained freedom. I do not know how to sail and I've never owned a boat, but that was Malcolm. Today, Max is starting a new life at forty-three, and if he wants to buy a skiff, learn to sail, and spend the rest of his life drifting from beach to beach, who can stop him?

The plane jolts slightly as the engines cut back a notch. I watch the captain ease down on the throttles as we begin a long descent. There's a small cooler by the door and I find a beer. We pass over Nevis and St. Kitts in the distance. Those two islands have attractive banking laws too, and I considered them briefly, back when I was at Frostburg and had plenty of time to dwell on my research. I considered the Cayman Islands but learned that they are now terribly overbuilt. The Bahamas are too close to Florida and filthy with U.S. agents. Puerto Rico is a territory, so it never made any of my lists. St. Bart's has traffic jams. The U.S. Virgins have too much crime. Jamaica is where Nathan now resides. I chose Antigua as my first base of operations because there are seventy-five thousand people, almost all black like me, not overcrowded but not sparsely populated either. It's a mountainous island with 365 beaches, one for each day, or so say the brochures and Web sites. I chose Antigua because its banks are notoriously flexible and known to look the other way. And, if for some reason the island displeases me, I'll be quick to move along. There are too many other places to see.

We slam onto the runway and screech to a halt. The captain turns around and mouths the words "Sorry about that." Pilots take great pride in their smooth landings, and this guy is probably embarrassed. As if I care. The only thing that matters right now is a safe exit from the plane and a smooth entry into the country. There are two other jets at the private terminal, and fortunately a large one has just landed. At least ten adult Americans in shorts and sandals are heading into the building to get processed. I stall long enough to fall in behind them. As the Immigration and Customs agents go through their routines, I realize there are no scanners for the private passengers and their bags. Excellent! I say good-bye to the pilots. Outside the small building, I watch the other Americans load into a waiting van and disappear. I sit on a bench until my cab appears.

The villa is on Willoughby Bay, twenty minutes from the airport. I ride in the back of the cab, windows down, warm salty air blowing in my face, as we twist around one side of a mountain and slowly descend the other. In the distance, there are dozens of small boats moored in a bay, resting on blue water that seems perfectly still.

It is a furnished two-bedroom condo in a cluster of the same, not directly facing the beach but close enough to hear the waves break. It's leased in my current name, and the three-month rental was covered by a Skelter Films check. I pay the cabdriver and walk through the front gate of Sugar Cove. A pleasant lady in the office gives me the key and a booklet on the ins and outs of the unit. I let myself in, turn on the fans and air-conditioning, and check out the rooms. Fifteen minutes later, I'm in the ocean.

At precisely 5:30 p.m., Stanley Mumphrey and two of his underlings gathered around a speaker in the center of a conference room table. Within seconds, the voice of Victor Westlake came on, and after quick hellos Westlake said, "So, Stan, what do you make of it?"

Stanley, who'd been thinking of nothing else since receiving the e-mail four hours earlier, replied, "Well, Vic, it seems to me that we first need to decide whether we're going to believe this guy again, don't you think? I mean, he admits he got it wrong the last time. He doesn't admit to lying to us, but instead says he just made a mistake. He's playing games."

"It will be hard to trust him again," Westlake said.

"Do you know where he is right now?" Mumphrey asked.

"He just flew from Miami to Antigua, on a private jet. Last Friday, he flew from Roanoke to Jamaica on a private jet, then reentered the country Sunday as Malcolm Bannister."

"Any idea what he's doing with all these weird movements?"

"Not a clue, Stan. We're baffled. He's proven himself quite adept at disappearing and at moving money around."

"Right. I have a scenario, Vic. Suppose he lied to us about Quinn Rucker. Maybe Rucker is part of the scheme and he played along so Bannister could get himself out of prison. Now they're trying to save Rucker's ass. Sounds like a conspiracy to me. Lying, conspiracy. What if we pop them with a sealed indictment, scoop up Bannister and throw him back in jail, then see how much he knows about the real killer. He might be more talkative from the other side of the bars."

"So you believe him now?" Westlake asked.

"Didn't say that, Vic, not at all. But if his e-mail is true, and if Dusty Shiver has an alibi, then we're screwed with this prosecution."

"Should we talk to Dusty?"

"We won't have to. If he's got the evidence, we'll see it soon enough. One thing I can't figure out, one of many, is why they sat on the evidence for so long."

"Same here," Westlake said. "One theory we're floating is that Bannister needed the time to find the killer, if, of course, we are to believe him. Frankly, I don't know what to believe at this point. What if Bannister knows the truth? We have nothing on our end. We don't have a shred of physical evidence. The confession is shaky. And if Dusty has a smoking gun, then we're all about to eat a bullet."

Mumphrey said, "Let's indict them and squeeze them. I'll call in the grand jury tomorrow, and we'll have an indictment within twenty-four hours. How much trouble will it be grabbing Bannister in Antigua?"

"A pain in the ass. He'll have to be extradited. Could take months. Plus, he might vanish again. This guy is good. Let me talk to the boss before you call in the grand jury."

"Okay. But if Bannister wants immunity, then it sounds as though he's committed a crime and wants a deal, right?"

Westlake paused a second, then said, "It's pretty rare for an innocent man to ask for immunity. It happens, but not very often. What crime are you thinking about?"

"Nothing definite, but we'll find one. Racketeering comes to mind. I'm sure we can bend RICO to fit these facts. Conspiracy to impede the judicial process. Lying to the court and the FBI. Come to think of it, the indictment is growing the longer we talk. I'm getting pissed, Vic. Bannister and Rucker were pals at Frostburg and cooked up this scheme. Rucker walked away in December. Judge Fawcett was killed in February. And now it looks like Bannister fed us a bunch of crap about Rucker and his motives. Don't know about you, Vic, but I'm beginning to feel as though we've been duped."

"Let's not overreact here. The first step is to determine if Bannister is telling the truth."

"Okay, and how do we go about doing that?"

"Let's wait on Dusty and see what he has. In the meantime, I'll talk to my boss. Let's chat again tomorrow."

"You got it."

CHAPTER 41

At a tobacco store in downtown St. John's, I see something that freezes me, then makes me smile. It's a box of Lavos, an obscure cigar hand wrapped in Honduras and costing twice as much in the States. The four-inch torpedo model sells for $5 in Antigua and $10 at the downtown Roanoke tobacco store called Vandy's Smokes. It was there that Judge Fawcett routinely purchased his favorite brand. On the bottom side of four of the fourteen Lavo boxes we now have stashed in banks, there are white square stickers advertising Vandy's, with phone number and street address.

I buy twenty of the Lavo torpedoes, and admire the box. It's made of wood, not cardboard, and the name appears to have been hand carved across the top. Judge Fawcett was known to drift around Lake Higgins in his canoe, puffing on Lavos while fishing and enjoying the solitude. Evidently, he saved the empty boxes.

The cruise ships have not arrived yet, so downtown is quiet. Merchants sit in the shade outside their shops, chatting and laughing in their seductive, lilting version of the King's English. I drift from shop to shop, oblivious to time. I have gone from the stultifying tedium of prison life, to the jolting madness of tracking a killer and his loot, to this—the languid pace of island living. I prefer the latter, for obvious reasons, but also because it is now, the present, and the future. Max is a new person with a new life, and the baggage is quickly falling by the wayside.

I buy some clothes, shorts and T-shirts, beach stuff, then wander into my bank, the Royal Bank of the East Caribbean, and flirt with the cute girl working the front desk. She directs me on down the line, and I eventually present myself to the vault clerk. She studies my passport, then leads me into the depths of the bank. During my first visit nine weeks ago, I rented two of the largest lockboxes available. Alone with them now, I leave some cash and worthless papers, and I wonder how long it will be before they are filled with little gold bars. I flirt on the way out and promise to be back soon.

I rent a convertible Beetle for a month, put the top down, fire up a Lavo, and begin a tour of the island. After a few minutes, I feel dizzy. I can't recall the last time I smoked a cigar and I'm not sure why I'm doing so now. The Lavo is short and black and even looks strong. I toss it out the window and keep driving.

FedEx wins the race. The first packages arrive Monday around noon, and because I have been anxiously roaming the grounds of Sugar Cove, I see the truck when it pulls up. Miss Robinson, the pleasant lady who runs the office, has by now heard the full version of the fiction. I am a writer/filmmaker, holed up in her villas for the next three months, working desperately to finish a novel and a screenplay based on said novel. My partners, meanwhile, are already filming preliminary scenes. Blah, blah, blah. Therefore, I am expecting approximately twenty overnight packages from Miami: manuscripts, research memos, videos, even some equipment. She is visibly impressed.

I'm really looking forward to the day when I can stop lying.

Inside my villa, I open the boxes. A backgammon set yields

two bars; a toolbox, four; a hardback novel, one; and another
backgammon set, two. A total of nine, all apparently untouched
during their journey from Miami to Antigua. I often wonder
about their history. Who mined the gold? From which continent?
Who minted it? How did it get into this country? And so on. But
I know these questions will never be answered.

I hustle into St. John's, to the Royal Bank of the East Caribbean, and put the precious ingots to rest.

———

My second e-mail to Messrs. Westlake and Mumphrey reads:

Hey Guys:
It's me again. Shame on you for not responding to my e-mail
of two days ago. If you want to find Judge Fawcett's killer, then
you need to work on your communication skills. I'm not going
away.

I'll bet your initial reaction is to trump up some bogus indictment
and come after me and Quinn Rucker. You can't help this
because you are, after all, the Feds, and it's just your nature.
What is it about our prosecutorial system that makes guys
like you want to put everyone in jail? It's pathetic, really. I met
dozens of good people in prison; men who wouldn't physically
harm anyone and men who would never screw up again, yet,
thanks to you, they're serving long sentences and their lives are
ruined.

But I digress. Forget another indictment. You can't make the
charges stick, not that that has ever slowed you down, but there
is simply no section of your vast Federal Code that you can
possibly use against me.

More important, you can't catch me. Do something stupid, and I'll disappear again. I'm not going back to prison, ever.

I have attached to this e-mail four color photographs. The first three are of the same cigar box, a dark brown wooden box handcrafted somewhere in Honduras. Into this box, a worker carefully placed twenty Lavos, a strong, black, rich, near-lethal cigar with a cone tip. The box was shipped to an importer in Miami, and from there sent to Vandy's Smokes in downtown Roanoke where it was purchased by the Honorable Raymond Fawcett. Evidently, Judge Fawcett smoked Lavos for many years and kept the empty boxes. Perhaps you found a few when you searched the cabin after the murders. I have a hunch that if you check with the owner of Vandy's he'll be well acquainted with Judge Fawcett and his rather rare taste in cigars.

The first photo is of the box as it would appear in a store. It's almost a perfect five-inch square, and five inches in height— unusual for a cigar box. The second photo is a side shot. The third is of the box's bottom, clearly showing the white sticker of Vandy's Smokes.

This box was taken from Judge Fawcett's safe shortly before he was executed. It is now in my possession. I would give it to you, but the killer's fingerprints are most certainly on it, and I'd hate to ruin the surprise.

The fourth photo is the reason we're all at the table. It is of three, ten-ounce, gold ingots, perfect little mini-bars without the slightest hint of registration or identification (more about this later). These little dudes were stacked thirty to a cigar box and tucked away in Judge Fawcett's safe.

So, one mystery is now solved. Why was he murdered?
Someone knew he had a pot of gold.

The big mystery, though, still haunts you. The killer is still out
there, and after six months of bumbling, stumbling, goose
chasing, puffing, posturing, and lying, you DO NOT HAVE A
CLUE!

Come on guys, give it up. Let's cut a deal and close this file.

Your friend, Malcolm

Victor Westlake canceled yet another dinner with his wife and
at 7:00 p.m., Friday, walked into the office of his boss, the Director of the FBI, Mr. George McTavey. Two of McTavey's assistants
stayed in the office to take notes and fetch files. They gathered
around a long conference table, all exhausted from another inter-
minable week.

McTavey had been fully briefed, so there was no need to cover
old territory. He began with his trademark "Is there anything that
I don't know?" This question could always be anticipated, and it
had damned well be answered truthfully.

"Yes," Westlake replied.

"Let's hear it."

"The spike in the price of gold has created a huge demand
for the stuff, so we're seeing all sorts of scams. Every pawnbro-
ker in the country is now a gold trader, so you can imagine the
crap that's being bought and sold. We ran an investigation last
year in New York City involving some rather established trad-
ers who were melting gold, diluting it, then passing it along as
basically pure. No indictments yet, but the case is not closed. In
the course of this, an informant who worked for a dealer got his
hands on a ten-ounce bar with no ID stamped on it. Ninety-nine

point nine percent pure, really fine stuff, and an unusual price. He dug around and found out that a man named Ray Fawcett came in from time to time and sold a few bars, at a slight discount, for cash of course. We have a video of Fawcett in the store on Forty-Seventh Street back in December, two months before he was murdered. Apparently, he drove to New York a couple times a year, did his trading, and drove back to Roanoke with a sackful of cash. The records appear to be incomplete, but based on what we have it looks as though he sold at least $600,000 worth of gold over the past four years in New York City. There is nothing illegal about this, assuming, of course, the gold was rightfully owned by Fawcett."

"Interesting, but?"

"I showed Bannister's photo of the gold to our informant. In his words, they are identical. Bannister has the gold. How much, we have no way of knowing. The cigar box checks out. The gold checks out. Assuming he got the gold from the killer, then he certainly knows the truth."

"And your theory is?"

"Malcolm Bannister and Quinn Rucker served together at Frostburg, and they were closer friends than we realized. One of them knew about Fawcett and his stash of gold, and they planned their racket. Rucker walks away from prison, goes into rehab for his alibi, and they wait for the killer to strike. He does, and their plan suddenly becomes operational. Bannister squeals on Rucker, who gives a bogus confession, which leads to an immediate indictment, and Bannister walks. Once he's out, he goes through witness protection, leaves it, somehow finds the killer and the gold."

"Wouldn't he have to kill the killer to get his gold?"

Westlake shrugged because he had no idea. "Maybe, but maybe not. Bannister wants immunity, and we're betting he'll also demand a Rule 35 release for Rucker. Quinn has five more years on his original sentence, plus a few extra for the escape. If you're Bannister, why not try to get your buddy out? If the killer is dead, then Rule 35 might not work for Quinn. I don't know. The lawyers are downstairs scratching their heads."

"That's always comforting," McTavey said. "What's the downside of dealing with Bannister?"

"We dealt with him last time and he lied to us."

"Okay, but what does he gain by lying now?"

"Nothing. He has the gold."

McTavey's tired and worried face suddenly became jovial. He chuckled, threw his hands into the air, and said, "Beautiful, brilliant, I love it! We gotta hire this guy because he's a lot smarter than we are. Talk about a set of balls. He gets his dear friend indicted for the capital murder of a federal judge and he knows the entire time he can get it unraveled and walk him out. Are you kidding me? We look like a bunch of fools."

Westlake couldn't help but join in the fun. He smiled and shook his head in disbelief.

McTavey said, "He's not lying, Vic, because he doesn't have to. Lies were important earlier, during the first phase of the project, but not now. Now it's time for the truth, and Bannister knows the truth."

Westlake nodded in agreement. "So what's our plan?"

"Where's the U.S. Attorney on this? What's his name?"

"Mumphrey. He's squawking about another indictment, but it's not going to happen."

"Does he know everything?"

"Of course not. He doesn't know that we know Fawcett was selling gold in New York."

"I'm having brunch with the AG in the morning. I'll explain what we're doing and he'll get Mumphrey in line. I suggest the two of you meet with Bannister as soon as possible and tie up the loose ends. I'm really tired of Judge Fawcett, Vic, know what I mean?"

"Yes sir."

CHAPTER 42

I wait for another delayed flight inside the sweltering terminal of V. C. Bird International Airport, but I'm not the least bit annoyed or anxious. By now, my fourth day on Antigua, my wristwatch is in a drawer and I'm on island time. The changes are subtle, but I am slowly purging my system of the frenetic habits of modern life. My movements are slower; my thoughts, uncluttered; my goals, nonexistent. I'm living for today and casting an occasional, lazy eye at tomorrow; other than that, don't bother me, mon.

Vanessa looks like a model when she bounces down the steps of the commuter flight from San Juan. A straw hat with a wide brim, designer shades, a summer dress that is delightfully short, and the easy grace of a woman who knows she's a knockout. Ten minutes later, we're in the Beetle and I have a hand on her thigh. She informs me she has been fired from her job because of excessive time off. And insubordination. We laugh. Who cares?

We go straight to lunch at the Great Reef Club, on a bluff overlooking the ocean, with a view that is hypnotic. The crowd is well-heeled and British. We are the only black diners, though all of the staff is of our kind. The food is just okay, and we vow to search out the local joints so we can eat with real people. I guess we're technically rich, but it seems impossible to think in those terms. We don't necessarily want the money as much as we want the freedom and security. I suppose we'll grow accustomed to a better life.

After a dip in the ocean, Vanessa wants to explore Antigua. We put the top down, find a reggae station on the radio, and fly along the narrow roads like two young lovers finally escaping. Rubbing her legs and watching her smile, I find it difficult to fathom that we have made it this far. I marvel at our luck.

————

The summit is at the Blue Waters Hotel, on the northwestern tip of the island. I walk into the colonial-style main house, into the breezy lobby, all alone. I spot a couple of agents in bad tourist clothing as they sip sodas and try to appear innocuous. A real tourist here has an easy, casual look, while a Fed posing as a tourist looks like a misfit. I wonder how many agents, assistant attorneys, deputy directors, et cetera, managed to wedge themselves into this quick little trip to the islands, spouses included of course, courtesy of Uncle Sam. I walk through archways, past gingerbread woodwork, along picket fences to a wing where business can be done.

We meet in a small suite on the second level, with a view of the beach. I am greeted by Victor Westlake, Stanley Mumphrey, and four other men whose names I don't even try to remember. Gone are the dark suits and drab ties, replaced by golf shirts and Bermuda shorts. Though it's early August, most of the pale legs in the room have not seen the sun. The mood is light; I've never seen so many smiles in such an important gathering. These men are elite crime fighters, accustomed to hard, humorless days, and this little diversion is a dream for them.

I have one final, nagging doubt that this could be a setup. I could be walking into a trap, with these boys ready to spring an indictment, a warrant, an extradition order, and whatever else it might take to drag me back to jail. In that event, Vanessa has a plan, one that assures the protection of our assets. She is two hundred yards away, waiting.

There are no surprises. We've talked enough on the phone to know the parameters, and we get down to business. On a speakerphone, Stanley places a call to Roanoke, to the office of Dusty Shiver, who now represents not only Quinn Rucker but his sister Vanessa and me. When Dusty is on the phone, he makes some lame crack about missing all the fun down in Antigua. The Feds roar with laughter.

We first review the immunity agreement, which basically says the government will not prosecute me, Quinn, Vanessa Young, or Denton Rucker (a.k.a. Dee Ray) for any possible wrongdoing in the murder investigation of Judge Raymond Fawcett and Naomi Clary. It takes fourteen pages to say this, but I'm satisfied with the language. Dusty has reviewed it too and wants a couple of minor changes from Mumphrey's office. Being lawyers, they are required to haggle for a bit, but eventually come to terms. The document is redrafted, in the room, then signed and e-mailed to a federal magistrate on call in Roanoke. Thirty minutes later, a copy is e-mailed back with the magistrate's approval and signature. In a legal sense, we are now Teflon.

Quinn's freedom is a little more complicated. First, there is an Order of Dismissal that clears him of all charges relating to the murders, and it contains some benign language inserted by Mumphrey and his boys that attempts to soften the blame for their misguided prosecution. Dusty and I object, and the language is eventually removed. The order is e-mailed to the magistrate in Roanoke, and he signs it immediately.

Next is a Rule 35 motion to commute his sentence and set him free. It has been filed in the D.C. federal court from which he was sentenced for cocaine distribution, but Quinn is still in jail in Roanoke. I repeat what I've said several times already: I will not complete my end of the deal until Quinn has been released.

Period. This has been agreed upon, but it takes the coordinated movements of several people, with instructions now coming from the speck of an island nation known as Antigua. Quinn's sentencing judge in D.C. is on board, but he's tied up in court. The U.S. Marshals Service feels the need to intrude and insists on moving Quinn when the time comes. At one point, five of the six lawyers in my meeting are on their cell phones, two while pecking away at laptops.

We take a break, and Vic Westlake asks me to join him for a cold drink. We find a table under a terrace beside a pool, away from the others, and order iced tea. He feigns frustration with the wasted time and so on. I am assuming he's wearing a wire of some variety, and he probably wants to talk about the gold. I'm all smiles, the laid-back Antiguan now, but my radar is on high alert.

"What if we need your testimony at trial?" he asks gravely. This has been discussed at length and I thought things were clear. "I know, I know, but what if we need some extra proof?"

Since he does not yet have the name of the killer, or the circumstances, this question is premature, and it's probably a warm-up to something else.

"My answer is no, okay? I've made that clear. I have no plans to ever return to the U.S. I'm seriously considering renouncing my citizenship and becoming a full-fledged Antiguan, and if I never set foot on U.S. soil again, I'll die a happy man."

"Somewhat of an overreaction, don't you think, Max?" he says in a tone I despise. "You now have full immunity."

"That might be easy for you to say, Vic, but then you've never spent time in prison for a crime you didn't commit. The Feds nailed me once and almost ruined my life; it's not going to happen again. I'm lucky in that I'm getting a second chance, and for some strange reason I'm a bit hesitant to subject myself to your jurisdiction again."

He sips his tea and wipes his mouth with a linen napkin. "A second chance. Sailing off into the sunset with a pot of gold."

I just stare at him. After a few seconds he says, a bit awkwardly, "We haven't discussed the gold, have we Max?"

"No."

"Let's give it a go, then. What gives you the right to keep it?"

I stare at a button on his shirt and say, clearly, "I don't know what you're talking about. I do not have any gold. Period."

"How about the three mini-bars in the photo you e-mailed last week?"

"That's evidence, and in due course I'll give them to you, along with the cigar box in the other photo. I suspect these little exhibits are covered with fingerprints, both Fawcett's and the killer's."

"Great, and the big question will be, Where's the rest of the gold?"

"I don't know."

"Okay. You must agree, Max, that it will be important to the prosecution of the killer to know what was in Judge Fawcett's safe. What got him killed? At some point, we'll have to know everything."

"Perhaps you won't know everything; you never will. There will be ample evidence to convict this killer. If the government botches the prosecution, it will not be my problem."

Another sip, a look of exasperation. Then, "You don't have the right to keep it, Max."

"Keep what?"

"The gold."

"I do not have the gold. But, speaking hypothetically, in a situation like this it seems to me the loot belongs to no one. It's certainly not the property of the government; it wasn't taken from the taxpayers. You never had possession of it, never had a claim. You've never seen it and you're not sure, at this point, if it even exists. It doesn't belong to the killer; he's a thief as well. He stole it from a public official who obtained it, we assume, through corruption. And if you could possibly identify the original source of the loot and tried to return it, those boys would either dive under a desk or run like hell. It's just out there, sort of in the clouds, like the Internet, owned by no one." I wave my hands at the sky as I finish this well-rehearsed response.

Westlake smiles because we both know the truth. There's a twinkle in his eye, as if he wants to laugh in surrender and say, "Helluva job." Of course, this doesn't happen.

We make our way back to the suite and are told that the judge in D.C. is still occupied with more important matters. I'm not about to lounge around the table with a bunch of federal boys, so I go for a walk on the beach. I call Vanessa, tell her things are proceeding slowly, and, no, I have not seen handcuffs or guns. So far, it's all aboveboard. Quinn should be released soon. She tells me Dee Ray is in Dusty's office waiting for their brother.

During his lunch break, the judge who had sentenced Quinn to seven years for trafficking reluctantly signed a Rule 35 order of commutation. The day before he had chatted with Stanley Mumphrey, Victor Westlake and his boss, George McTavey, and to underline the importance of what was before him, the Attorney General of the United States.

Quinn was immediately taken from the jail in Roanoke to the law offices of Dusty Shiver, where he hugged Dee Ray and changed into some jeans and a polo. One hundred and forty days after being arrested as a fugitive in Norfolk, Virginia, Quinn is a free man.

It's almost 2:30 by the time all the orders and documents are properly signed, examined, and verified, and at the last minute I step outside the room and call Dusty. He assures me we've "got 'em by the throat," all paperwork is in order, all rights are being protected, all promises are being fulfilled. "Start singing," he says with a laugh.

Six months after I arrived at the Louisville Federal Correctional Institution, I agreed to review the case of a drug dealer from Cincinnati. The court had badly miscalculated the term of his sentence, the mistake was obvious, and I filed a motion to get the guy released immediately with time already served. It was one of those rare occasions in which everything worked perfectly and quickly, and within two weeks the happy client went home. Not surprisingly, word spread through the prison and I was immediately hailed as a brilliant jailhouse lawyer capable of performing miracles. I was inundated with requests to review cases and do my magic, and it took a while for the buzz to die down.

Around this time, a guy we called Nattie entered my life and consumed more time than I wanted to give. He was a skinny white kid who'd been busted for meth distribution in West Virginia, and he was adamant that I review his case, snap my fingers, and get him out. I liked Nattie, so I looked at his papers and tried to convince him there was nothing I could do. He began talking about a payoff; at first there were vague references to a lot of money stashed somewhere, and some of it might be mine if I could only get Nattie out of prison. He refused to believe I could not help him. Instead of facing reality, he became more delusional, more convinced I could find a loophole, file a motion, and walk him out. At some point, he finally mentioned a quantity of gold bars, and I figured he had lost his mind. I rebuffed him, and to prove his point he told me the entire story. He swore me to secrecy and promised me half of the fortune if I would only help him.

As a child, Nattie was an accomplished petty thief, and in his teenage years drifted into the world of meth. He moved around a lot, dodging drug enforcement agents, bill collectors, deputies with warrants, fathers with pregnant daughters, and pissed-off rivals from other meth gangs. He tried several times to go straight but easily fell back into a life of crime. He was watching his cousins and friends ruin their lives with drugs, as addicts and convicted felons, and he really wanted something better. He had a job as a cashier in a country store, deep in the mountains around the small town of Ripplemead, when he was approached by a stranger who offered him $10 an hour for some manual labor. No one in the store had ever seen the stranger, nor would they ever again. Nattie was making $5 an hour, cash, off the books, and jumped at the chance to earn more. After work, Nattie met the stranger at a pre-arranged spot and followed him along a narrow dirt trail to an A-frame cabin wedged into the side of a steep hill, just above a small lake. The stranger introduced himself only as Ray, and Ray was driving a nice pickup truck with a wooden crate in the back. As it turned out, the crate contained a five-hundred-pound safe, too much for Ray to handle by himself. They rigged a pulley with a cable over a tree branch and managed to wrestle the safe out of the truck, onto the ground, and eventually into the basement of the cabin. It was tedious, backbreaking work, and it took almost three hours to get the safe inside. Ray paid him in cash, said thanks and good-bye.

Nattie told his brother, Gene, who was in the vicinity hiding from the sheriff two counties away. The brothers became curious about the safe and its contents, and decided to investigate. When they were certain Ray had left the cabin, they attempted to break in but were stopped by heavy oak doors, unbreakable glass, and thick dead bolts. So they simply removed an entire window in the basement. Inside, they could not locate the safe but did manage to identify Ray. Riffling through some papers at a worktable, they realized their neighbor was a big-shot federal judge over in Roanoke. There was even a newspaper article about an important trial involving uranium mining in Virginia, with the Honorable Raymond Fawcett presiding.

They drove to Roanoke, found the federal courthouse, and

watched two hours of testimony. Nattie wore glasses and a base-ball cap in case the judge might get bored and look around the courtroom. There were plenty of spectators and Ray never looked up. Convinced they were onto something, the brothers returned to the cabin, reentered through the basement window, and again searched for the safe. It had to be in the small basement because that was where Nattie and the judge had left it. One wall was lined with shelves and covered with thick law books, and the brothers became convinced there must be a hidden space behind the wall. They carefully removed each book, looked behind it, then replaced it. It took some time, but they eventually found a switch that opened a trapdoor. Once it swung open, the safe was just sitting there, at floor level, waiting to be opened. But that proved to be impossible because there was a digital keypad that, of course, required a coded entry. They toyed with it for a day or two, with no luck. They spent a lot of time in the cabin but were always careful about not leaving a trail. One Friday, Gene drove to Roanoke, about an hour away, went to the courtroom, checked on the judge, then hung around long enough for him to adjourn for the weekend, or until 9:00 a.m. Monday. Gene fol-lowed him to his apartment and watched him load his truck with what appeared to be a brown paper sack of groceries, a cooler, several bottles of wine, a gym bag, two bulky briefcases and a stack of books. Ray left his apartment, alone, and drove west. Gene called Nattie and said Ray was on his way. Nattie tidied up the cabin, replaced the basement window, swept away any boot prints in the dirt by the porch, and climbed a tree fifty yards away. Sure enough, an hour later Judge Fawcett arrived at the cabin, unloaded his truck, and promptly took a nap in a ham-mock on the porch as Nattie and Gene watched from the thick forest surrounding the A-frame. The following day, a Saturday, Judge Fawcett dragged his canoe to the water's edge, loaded two fishing rods and some bottled water, fired up a short, dark cigar, and shoved off across Lake Higgins. Nattie watched him with binoculars while Gene removed the window and hurried inside the cabin. The trapdoor was open, the safe was visible, but it was closed and locked. Out of luck again, Gene quickly left the basement, reinstalled the window, and retreated to the woods.

The boys were determined to find out what was in the safe, but they were also patient. Ray had no idea he was being watched, and if he was adding to his treasure each week, then there was no hurry. For the next two Fridays, Gene watched the exterior of the courthouse in Roanoke, but the judge worked late. A federal holiday was approaching, and they guessed the judge might get away for a long weekend. According to the newspaper articles, the bench trial was arduous and hotly contentious, with a lot of pressure on Judge Fawcett. They guessed correctly. At 2:00 p.m. Friday, the proceedings were adjourned until 9:00 a.m. the following Tuesday. Gene watched as Ray loaded up and headed for the lake, alone.

The cabin was too deep in the mountains for electricity or gas; thus, it had no air-conditioning or heating, except for a large fireplace. Food and beverages were kept on ice in the cooler Ray hauled back and forth. When he needed lights to read by at night, he cranked up a small gas generator outside the basement, and its low, muffled sound echoed through the valley. Usually, though, the judge was asleep by 9:00 p.m.

The basement was one room and one closet, a narrow space with small double doors. Inside the closet, Ray stored stuff that appeared to be forgotten—hunting clothes, boots, and a pile of old quilts and blankets. Gene cooked up the plan of hiding Nattie in there, for hours, with the idea that through the tiniest of cracks in one of the doors, he would be able to watch as the judge opened the safe and stashed away whatever it was he was hiding. Nattie, at five feet seven and 130 pounds, had a long history of hiding in cracks and crevices, though he was initially reluctant to spend the night in the closet. The plan was revised yet again.

On the Friday before Columbus Day, Judge Fawcett arrived at

his cabin around 6:00 p.m. and took his time unloading the truck. Nattie was curled up in the basement closet, virtually invisible amid the hunting clothes, blankets, and quilts. He had a pistol in his pocket in the event things went wrong. Gene was watching from the trees, also with a gun. They were nervous as hell, but also wildly excited. As Ray went about his business of settling in, he lit a cigar and the entire cabin soon smelled of rich tobacco smoke. He took his time, talked to himself, hummed the same song over and over, and eventually hauled a bulky briefcase to the basement. Nattie was hardly breathing as he watched the judge remove a law book from a shelf, flip the hidden switch, and pull the trapdoor open. He punched in the code on the keypad and opened the safe. It was filled with cigar boxes. He backed away and removed another cigar box from the briefcase. He paused for a second, lifted the lid, and took out a beautiful little gold ingot. He admired it, caressed it, then returned it to the box, which he then placed carefully in the safe. Another cigar box followed, then he quickly closed the safe, programmed the code, and closed the trapdoor.

Nattie's heart was pounding so violently he worried about shaking the entire closet, but he urged himself to stay calm. As he was leaving, the judge noticed the crack in the closet door and shoved it tight.

Around 7:00 p.m., he lit another cigar, poured a glass of white wine, and sat in a rocker on the porch to watch the sun fade over the mountains. After dark, he turned on the generator and puttered around the cabin until ten, when he turned it off and went to bed. As the cabin became still and quiet, Gene appeared from the woods and banged on the door. Who is it? Ray demanded angrily from inside. Gene said he was looking for his dog. Ray opened the door and they spoke through the screen. Gene explained he had a cabin about a mile away, on the other side of the lake, and his beloved dog, Yank, had disappeared. Ray was not the least bit friendly and said he had seen no dogs in the vicinity. Gene thanked him and left. When Nattie heard the banging and the conversation upstairs, he quietly sneaked out of the closet and left through a basement door. He was unable to relock the dead bolt, and the boys figured the judge would scratch his head and remain confused as to why the door wasn't properly locked. By then, they would be lost in the woods. The judge would search and search but would find no signs of entry, nothing missing, and would eventually forget about it.

Naturally, the brothers were stunned at what they had learned, and they began making plans to rob the safe. It would require an altercation with the judge, and probably violence, but they were determined to follow through. Two weekends passed and the judge stayed in Roanoke. Then three.

While watching the cabin, and the judge, Gene and Nattie had returned to their meth business because they were broke. Before they could get the gold, they were busted by DEA agents. Gene was killed, and Nattie went away to prison.

He waited five years before he strong-armed Judge Fawcett, tortured Naomi Clary, robbed the safe, and executed both of them.

"And who, exactly, is Nattie?" Westlake asks. All six of the men are staring at me.

"His name is Nathan Edward Cooley, and you'll find him in the city jail in Montego Bay, Jamaica. Take your time, he's not going anywhere."

"Might he also be known as Nathaniel Coley, your friend with the fake passport?"

"That's him. He's looking at twenty years in a Jamaican prison, so he might make this easy for you. My hunch is that Nattie will happily plead guilty to a life sentence in a U.S. prison, no parole of course, anything to get out of Jamaica. Offer him a deal, and you won't have to bother with a trial."

There is a long pause as they catch their collective breath. Finally, Vic asks, "Is there anything you have not thought of?"

"Sure. But I'd rather not share it with you."

CHAPTER 43

My storytelling talents hold them spellbound, and for an hour they pepper me with questions. I slog through the answers, and when I start to repeat myself, I get irritated. Give a bunch of lawyers the rich details of a mystery they've lost sleep over, and they can't help but ask the same question five different ways. My low opinion of Victor Westlake is raised somewhat when he says, "That's it. Meeting's over. I'm going to the bar."

I suggest the two of us have drinks alone, and we return to the same table by a pool. We order beers and gulp them when they arrive. "Something else?" he asks.

"Yes, as a matter of fact, there is something else. Something almost as big as the murder of a federal judge."

"Haven't you had enough for one day?"

"Oh yes, but I have one parting shot."

"I'm listening."

I take another swig and savor the taste. "If my time line is correct, Judge Fawcett was accepting and hiding pure gold in the middle of the uranium trial. The plaintiff was Armanna Mines, a consortium of companies with interests around the world. However, the majority partner is a Canadian company based in Calgary, and this company owns two of the five largest gold mines in North America. The uranium deposits in Virginia alone are worth an estimated $20 billion, but no one really knows for sure.

If a corrupt federal judge wants a few gold bars in return for a payoff of $20 billion, why not do it? The company gave Fawcett his jackpot; he gave them everything they wanted."

"How much gold?" Westlake asks softly, as though he doesn't want his own hidden mike to hear.

"We'll never know, but I suspect Fawcett received around $10 million in pure gold. He cashed in here and there. You have the informant in New York, but we'll never know if it went elsewhere and traded on the black market. Nor will we ever know how much cash was in the safe when Nathan finally got to it."

"Nathan might tell us."

"Indeed, but don't count on it. Anyway, the grand total is beside the point. It's a lot of money, or gold, and for it to travel from Armanna Mines into the somber chambers of the Honorable Raymond Fawcett, someone had to be the bagman. Someone arranged the deal and made the deliveries."

"One of the lawyers?"

"Probably. I'm sure Armanna had a dozen."

"Any clue?"

"None whatsoever. But I'm convinced a massive crime has occurred, with serious implications. The U.S. Supreme Court will hear the case this October, and given the pro-business leanings of the majority, it's likely Fawcett's gift to the uranium miners will stand. That would be a shame, wouldn't it, Vic? A corrupt opinion becomes a law. A huge mining company bribes its way past the statutory ban and is given carte blanche to wreck the environment of southern Virginia."

"Why do you care? You're not going back there, or so you say."

"My feelings are not important, but the FBI should care. If you launch an investigation, the case could be seriously derailed."

"So now you're telling the FBI how to run its business."

"Not at all. But don't expect me to remain quiet. Have you heard of an investigative reporter named Carson Bell?"

His shoulders sag as he looks away. "No."

"*New York Times*. He covered the uranium trial and has followed the appeals. I would make an incredible unnamed source."

"Don't do that, Max."

"You can't stop me. If you don't investigate, I'm sure Mr. Bell would love to. Front page and all that. FBI cover-up."

"Don't do it. Please. Give us some time."

"You have thirty days. If I hear nothing of an investigation, then I'll invite Mr. Bell down for a week on my little island." I drain my beer, smack the table with my glass, and get to my feet. "Thanks for the drink."

"You're just getting revenge, aren't you, Max? One last shot at the government."

"Who says it's my last?" I say over my shoulder.

I leave the hotel and hoof it down the long drive. At the end, Vanessa appears in the Beetle and we race away. Ten minutes later we park outside the private terminal, grab our light bags, and meet the Maritime Aviation crew in the lobby. Our passports are checked, and we hustle toward the same Learjet 35 that brought me to Antigua a week earlier. "Let's get out of here," I say to the captain as we climb on board.

Two and a half hours later, we land at Miami International as the sun dips below the horizon. The Lear taxis to a Customs office for reentry, then we wait half an hour for a cab. Inside the main terminal, Vanessa buys a one-way ticket to Richmond, through Atlanta, and we hug and kiss good-bye. I wish her good luck, and she does the same. I rent a car and find a motel.

At nine the next morning, I'm waiting outside Palmetto Trust when the doors are unlocked. My carry-on bag has wheels and I roll it into the vault. Within minutes, I extract $50,000 in cash and three Lavo cigar boxes containing eighty-one mini-bars. On my way out, I do not mention to the vault clerk that I will never return. The lease for the safe-deposit box will expire in a year, and the bank will simply re-key and rent it to the next guy. I fight the early traffic and eventually make it to Interstate 95, going north in a hurry but careful not to get stopped. Jacksonville is six hours away. The tank is full and I plan to drive without stopping.

North of Fort Lauderdale, Vanessa calls with the welcome news that her mission is accomplished. She has retrieved the bullion hidden in her apartment, emptied the three lockboxes in the Richmond banks, and is already headed for D.C. with a trunkful of gold.

I get stalled in construction traffic around Palm Beach, and this ruins my plans for the afternoon. The banks will be closed when I arrive at the Jacksonville beaches. I have no choice but to slow down and go with the flow. It's after six when I get to Neptune Beach, and for old time's sake I check into a motel I've used before. It accepts cash and I park near my room on the ground level. I roll the carry-on inside and fall asleep with it on the bed with me. Vanessa wakes me at ten. She is safely tucked away in Dee Ray's condo near Union Station. Quinn is there and they are having a delightful reunion. For this phase of the operation, Dee Ray has broken up with his live-in girlfriend and moved her out. In his opinion, she cannot be trusted. She is not family, and she's certainly not the first girl he has cast aside. I pass along my request to hold the champagne for twenty-four hours.

We—Vanessa, Dee Ray, and I—expressed strong misgivings about Quinn including his estranged wife in our plot. A divorce looks likely, and it's best if she knows nothing at this point.

Once again, I find myself killing a few minutes in the parking lot of a bank, First Coast Trust. When the doors open at 9:00 a.m., I wander in, as nonchalantly as possible, pulling an empty carry-on and flirting with the clerks. Just another sunny day in Florida. Alone in the vault, in a private stall, I remove two Lavos cigar boxes and place them gently into the carry-on. Minutes later, I'm driving a few blocks to a branch of Jacksonville Savings. When that lockbox is empty, I make my final stop at a Wells Fargo branch in Atlantic Beach. By ten I'm back on Interstate 95, headed to D.C. with 261 golden bricks in the trunk. Only the five I sold to Hassan for cash have disappeared.

It's almost midnight when I enter central D.C. I take a brief detour and drive along First Street, passing in front of the Supreme Court Building and wondering what will be the final outcome of the momentous case of *Armanna Mines v. the Commonwealth of Virginia*. One of the lawyers, or perhaps two or three of those involved in the case, once defiled the chambers of a federal judge with their filthy bribes. Said bribes are now in the trunk of my car. What a journey. I'm almost tempted to park at the curb, take out a mini-bar, and toss it through one of the massive windows.

However, better judgment prevails. I circle Union Station, follow the GPS to I Street, then to the corner of Fifth. By the time I park in front of the building, Mr. Quinn Rucker is bounding down the steps with the biggest smile I've ever seen. Our embrace is long and emotional. "What took so long?" he asks.

"Got here as fast as I could," I reply.

"I knew you would come, bro. I never doubted you."

"There were doubts, lots of them."

We're both stunned at the fact that we've pulled it off, and at that moment our success is overwhelming. We embrace again, and each of us admires how thin the other looks. I comment that I'm looking forward to eating again. Quinn says he's tired of playing the lunatic. "I'm sure it comes natural," I say. He grabs my shoulders, stares at my new face, and says, "You're almost cute now."

"I'll give you the doctor's name. You could use some work."

I've never had a closer friend than Quinn Rucker, and the hours we spent at Frostburg hatching our scheme now seem like an ancient dream. Back then, we believed in it because there was nothing else to hope for, but deep down we never seriously thought it would work. Arm in arm, we climb the steps and enter the condo. I hug and kiss Vanessa, then reintroduce myself to Dee Ray. I met him briefly years ago in the visitors' room at Frostburg when he came to see his brother, but I'm not sure I would recognize him walking down a street. It doesn't matter; we are now blood kin, our bonds solidified by trust and gold.

The first bottle of champagne is poured into four Waterford flutes—Dee Ray has expensive tastes—and we chug it. Dee Ray and Quinn stick guns in their pockets, and we quickly unload my car. The party that follows would seem implausible even in a fantasy film.

With champagne flowing, the gold bars are stacked ten deep in the center of the den floor, all 524 of them, and we sit on cushions around the treasure. It's impossible not to gawk and no one tries to suppress the laughter. Since I'm the lawyer and the unofficial leader, I commence the business portion of the meeting with some simple math. We have before us 524 little bricks; 5 were sold to a Syrian gold trader in Miami; and 41 are now resting safely in a bank vault on Antigua. The total taken from our dear pal Nathan is 570, worth roughly $8.5 million. Pursuant to our agreement, Dee Ray gets 57 of the glowing little ingots. His 10 percent was earned by fronting the cash Quinn was caught with; for paying Dusty's legal fees; for supplying the four kilos of Nathan's cocaine, along with the pistol and the chloral hydrate I used to knock him out. Dee Ray picked up Quinn when he walked away from Frostburg, and he monitored Nathan's release from prison so we would know exactly when to start the project. He also paid the $20,000 deposit to the rehab center near Akron for Quinn's phony cocaine problem.

Dee Ray is in charge of the yacht. As he's getting drunker, he hands over an itemized list of his expenses, including the yacht, and rounds it all off at an even $300,000. We're assuming a value of $1,500 an ounce, so we vote unanimously to award him another twenty bars. No one is in the mood to quibble, and when you're staring at such a fortune it's easy to be magnanimous.

At some unknown and unknowable point in the future, the remaining 488 bars will be equally divided among Quinn, Vanessa, and me. That's not important now—the urgency is in getting the stuff out of this country. It will take a long time to slowly convert the gold to cash, but we'll worry about that much later. For the moment, we are content to pass the hours drinking, laughing, and taking turns telling our version of the events. When Vanessa replays the moment in Nathan's house when she stripped naked and confronted his buddies at the front door, we laugh until it's painful. When Quinn recounts the meeting with Stanley Mumphrey in which he blurted out the fact that he knew Max Baldwin had left witness protection and left Florida, he imitates Mumphrey's wild-eyed reaction to this startling news. When I describe my second meeting with Hassan and trying to count 122 stacks of $100 bills in a busy coffee shop, they think I'm lying.

The stories continue until 3:00 a.m., when we're too drunk to go on. Dee Ray covers the gold with a quilt and I volunteer to sleep on the sofa.

CHAPTER 44

We slowly come to life hours later. The hangovers and fatigue are offset by the excitement of the task at hand. For a young man who has lived on the fringes of an operation adept at smuggling illegal substances into the country, the challenge of smuggling our gold out is light lifting for Dee Ray. He explains that we are now avid scuba divers, and he has purchased an astonishing collection of gear, all of it stored in heavy, official U.S. Divers brand nylon duffel bags, each with a solid zipper and a small padlock. We hustle around the condo removing masks, snorkels, fins, regulators, tanks, weight belts, buoyancy compensators, gauges, dry suits, even spearguns, none of which has ever been used. It will be on eBay within a month. The gear is replaced by an assortment of smaller U.S. Divers snorkel backpacks and dry bags, all filled with gold mini-bars. The weight of each bag is tested and retested by the men to see how much can be carried. The bags are bulky and heavy, but then they would be if filled with scuba gear. In addition, Dee Ray has accumulated a variety of luggage, the sturdiest cases he could, and all on rollers. We place the gold in shoes, shaving kits, makeup bags, even two small tackle boxes for deep-sea fishing. When we add a few items of clothing for the trip, our bags and gear seem heavy enough to sink a fine boat. The weight is important because we do not want to raise suspicion. Of much greater significance, though, is the fact that all 524 bars are now packed, under lock and key, and safe, or so we pray.

Before we leave, I take a look around the condo. It is littered with diving gear and packing debris. On the kitchen table, I see empty Lavo cigar boxes and have a twinge of nostalgia. They served us well.

At ten, a large van arrives and we load the scuba duffels and the luggage inside. There's barely enough room for the four of us. Vanessa sits in my lap. Fifteen minutes later we pull in to a parking lot at the Washington Marina. Its piers are lined with slips and hundreds of boats of all shapes rock gently on the water. The larger ones are at the far end. Dee Ray points in that direction and tells the driver where to go.

The yacht is a sleek, beautiful vessel, a hundred feet long, three decks high, brilliant white, and called *Rumrunner,* which seems vaguely appropriate. It sleeps eight comfortably and has a crew of ten. A month earlier, Dee Ray chartered it for a quick cruise to Bermuda, so he knows the captain and the crew. He calls them by name as we spill out and start grabbing bags. Two porters help with the scuba duffels and strain under the weight. But then, they've dealt with serious divers before. Passports are collected by the steward and taken to the bridge. Quinn's is fake, and we're holding our breath.

It takes an hour to inspect our quarters, get ourselves situated, and settle in for the ride. Dee Ray explains to the deckhands that we want the scuba gear in our cabins because we are fanatical about our equipment. They schlep it up from storage and haul it to our rooms. When the engines come to life, we change into shorts and congregate on the lower deck. The steward brings the first bottle of champagne and a tray of shrimp. We motor slowly through the harbor and into the Potomac. From passing boats, we get some looks. Perhaps it's unusual to see a yacht loaded with African-Americans. This is a white man's game, right?

The steward returns with all four passports and wants to chat.

I explain that I have just bought a place in Antigua, and we're going down for a party. He eventually asks what I do for a living (in other words, Where is this money coming from?), and I tell him I'm a filmmaker. When he's gone we toast my favorite actor—Nathan Cooley. Soon we're in the Atlantic and the coast fades away.

Our cabin is large by boat standards, which isn't very big at all. With four pieces of luggage and two scuba duffels we have trouble moving about. The bed, though, works fine. Vanessa and I have a quickie, then sleep for two hours.

Three days later we ease into Jolly Harbour, on the west end of Antigua. Sailing is serious business on the island and the bay is crowded with moored boats of all sizes. We ease past them, barely inching along, leaving almost no wake as we take in the views of the mountains on all sides. The big yachts are docked together at one of the piers, and our captain slowly maneuvers the *Rumrunner* into a slip between two other fine ships, one about our size and the other much larger. In this fleeting moment of living like the rich, we find it impossible not to compare the lengths of the yachts. We stare at the larger one and think, Who owns it? What does he do? Where is he from? And so on. Our crew scurries around to secure the boat, and after the engines die the captain collects passports again and steps onto the pier. He walks about a hundred feet to a small Customs building, goes inside, and does the paperwork.

A week earlier, when I was killing time and waiting on Vanessa to arrive on Antigua, I sniffed around the dock at Jolly Harbour until a yacht arrived. I watched the captain go to the Customs building, just as ours is doing now. And, more important, I noted that no one from Customs inspected the boat.

The captain returns; everything is in order. We have arrived on Antigua with the gold and with no suspicions. I explain to the steward that we want to move the scuba gear to my villa because it will be easier to use from there. And while we're at it, we'll take the luggage as well. We'll probably use the yacht to dive around the islands, and for a long dinner or two, but for the first day or so we'll stay at my place. The steward is fine with this, whatever we wish, and calls for taxis. While they are en route, we help the deckhands unload our bags and duffels onto the dock. It's quite a pile, and no one would suspect we're hiding $8 million in gold in luggage and scuba gear.

It takes three taxis to haul everything, and as we load up we wave good-bye to the steward and the captain. Twenty minutes later we arrive at the villa in Sugar Cove. When everything is inside, we exchange high fives and jump in the ocean.

AUTHOR'S NOTE

This is indeed a work of fiction, and more so than usual. Almost nothing in the previous 340-odd pages is based on reality. Research, hardly a priority, was rarely called upon. Accuracy was not deemed crucial. Long paragraphs of fiction were used to avoid looking up facts. There is no federal camp at Frostburg, no uranium lawsuit (yet), no dead judge to inspire me, and no acquaintance in prison scheming to get out, at least not to my knowledge.

Inevitably, though, even the laziest of writers need some foundation for their creations, and I was occasionally at a loss. As always, I relied on others. Thanks to Rick Middleton and Cal Jaffe of the Southern Environmental Law Center. In Montego Bay, I was assisted by the Honorable George C. Thomas and his staff of fine young lawyers.

Thanks also to David Zanca, John Zunka, Ben Aiken, Hayward Evans, Gaines Talbott, Gail Robinson, Ty Grisham, and Jack Gernert.

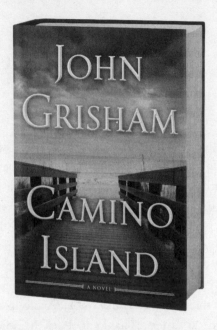